MISSISSIPPI RIVER MISCHIEF

Reviewers Love the Scotty Bradley Series

Royal Street Reveillon

"Herren's wit, ingenuity, and sharp social eye are a constant delight, and every time I read him I fall in love with New Orleans all over again. Scotty may have hung up his go-go boots, but I hope his adventures go on and on."—Alex Marwood, Edgar and Macavity Award–winning author of *The Wicked Girls* and *The Darkest Secret*

"A delicious, witty, deftly plotted mystery. Greg Herren offers up a compulsively readable tale."—Megan Abbott, Edgar-winning author of *Queenpin* and *Dare Me*

"What a treat to be able to read a brand-new book from Greg Herren featuring one of my favorite sleuths, Scotty Bradley...5 out of 5 for this favorite gay mystery series." —*Philip Bahr, Librarian, Fairfield Public Library*

"[A] witty, engrossing slice of New Orleans life (and death)...delicious bits of gossip and hints of hushed-up scandal...wry observations about old money in the new New Orleans...a plot full of lively characters and satisfying twists."—*Lia Matera, author of the Willa Jansson and Laura Di Palma series*

Baton Rouge Bingo

"I very much enjoyed this book. I love the way Mr. Herren writes, and the humor that he pops into the story from time to time...It is a pure and simple mystery, and I loved it...I recommend this book to anyone liking a good mystery with gay MCs."—*Love Bytes: Same Sex Book Reviews*

Lambda Literary Award Finalist *Vieux Carré Voodoo*

"Herren's packed plot, as always in this imaginative series... revels in odd twists and comic turns; for example, the third man of the ménage returns, revealed as a James Bond type. It all makes for a roller-coaster caper."—Richard Labonte, *Book Marks*

"This novel confirms that out of the many New Orleans mystery writers, Greg Herren is indeed one to watch." —*Reviewing the Evidence*

"[T]his was well worth waiting for. Herren has a knack for developing colorful primary and supporting characters the reader actually cares about, and involving them in realistic, though extreme, situations that make his books riveting to the mystery purist. Bravo, and five gumbo-stained stars out of five."—*Echo Magazine*

"Herren's work is drenched in the essence of the Big Easy, the city's geography even playing a large part in the solution of a riddle at whose end lies the aforementioned Eye of Kali. But unlike the city, it is not languid. Herren hits the ground running and only lets up for two extremely interesting dream sequences, the latter of which is truly chilling. Is this a breezy beach read? Maybe, but it has far more substance than many. You can spend a few sunny, sandy afternoons with this resting on your chest and still feel as if you've read a book. But even if you're not at the beach, Herren's work makes great backyard or rooftop reading, and this one is a terrific place to start."—*Out In Print*

Praise for Greg Herren

Sleeping Angel "will probably be put on the young adult (YA) shelf, but the fact is that it's a cracking good mystery that general readers will enjoy as well. It just happens to be about teens…A unique viewpoint, a solid mystery and good characterization all conspire to make *Sleeping Angel* a welcome addition to any shelf, no matter where the bookstores stock it."—Jerry Wheeler, *Out in Print*

"This fast-paced mystery is skillfully crafted. Red herrings abound and will keep readers on their toes until the very end. Before the accident, few readers would care about Eric, but his loss of memory gives him a chance to experience dramatic growth, and the end result is a sympathetic character embroiled in a dangerous quest for truth." —*VOYA*

"Herren, a loyal New Orleans resident, paints a brilliant portrait of the recovering city, including insights into its tight-knit gay community. This latest installment in a powerful series is sure to delight old fans and attract new ones."—*Publishers Weekly*

"Fast-moving and entertaining, evoking the Quarter and its gay scene in a sweet, funny, action-packed way."—*New Orleans Times-Picayune*

"Herren does a fine job of moving the story along, deftly juggling the murder investigation and the intricate relationships while maintaining several running subjects."—*Echo Magazine*

"An entertaining read."—*OutSmart Magazine*

"A pleasant addition to your beach bag."—*Bay Windows*

"Greg Herren gives readers a tantalizing glimpse of New Orleans." —*The Midwest Book Review*

"Herren's characters, dialogue and setting make the book seem absolutely real."—*The Houston Voice*

"So much fun it should be thrown from Mardi Gras floats!"—*New Orleans Times-Picayune*

"Greg Herren just keeps getting better."—*Lambda Book Report*

By the Author

The Scotty Bradley Adventures

Bourbon Street Blues

Jackson Square Jazz

Mardi Gras Mambo

Vieux Carré Voodoo

Who Dat Whodunnit

Baton Rouge Bingo

Garden District Gothic

Royal Street Reveillon

Mississippi River Mischief

The Chanse MacLeod Mysteries

Murder in the Rue Dauphine

Murder in the Rue St. Ann

Murder in the Rue Chartres

Murder in the Rue Ursulines

Murder in the Garden District

Murder in the Irish Channel

Murder in the Arts District

Young Adult

Sleeping Angel

Sara

Lake Thirteen

New Adult

Timothy

The Orion Mask

Dark Tide

Survivor's Guilt and Other Stories

Going Down for the Count
(Writing as Cage Thunder)

Wicked Frat Boy Ways
(Writing as Todd Gregory)

Edited with J.M. Redmann

Women of the Mean Streets: Lesbian Noir

Men of the Mean Streets: Gay Noir

Night Shadows: Queer Horror

Edited as Todd Gregory

Rough Trade

Sweat

Anything for a Dollar

Blood Sacraments

Visit us at www.boldstrokesbooks.com

MISSISSIPPI RIVER MISCHIEF

by

Greg Herren

2023

CREDITS
EDITOR: RUTH STERNGLANTZ
PRODUCTION DESIGN: STACIA SEAMAN
COVER DESIGN BY JEANINE HENNING

"Glass breaks so easily. No matter how careful you are."
Tennessee Williams, *The Glass Menagerie*

PROLOGUE

My name is Scotty Bradley.

My journey is just beginning, a present-day journey that I fear may open the doors of horror to me while linking my past to both my present and my future. A journey that will bring me to a strange and dark place, to the edge of a cypress swamp, to a house high above Bayou Maron. The house called Sunnymeade, in a community I've never really known, in a parish just upriver from Orleans, populated by family I have never known well and have not much desire to know better, relatives that are easy to forget and are usually only mere shadows in the back of my mind, shadows who will soon fill the days and nights of my today and my tomorrows, while reminding me that the family we find—more often than not—matters, loves, and cares more than the family into which we are born and to whom we are bound by blood.

Well, *that* rather sets a tone, doesn't it?

I do tend to gravitate toward the melodramatic when left to my own devices.

But just because something *seems* melodramatic doesn't mean it's not true. Sure, villains and heroes aren't as easy to spot in real life as they are in a melodrama. Life is filled with nuances and subtle shadings. But every so often you do come across a villain with no subtlety. I've met more than my fair share of those sociopaths. Sometimes I wonder if it's my fault, you know—I don't ever go looking for trouble, but that doesn't stop trouble from always finding me.

I've wondered if it's my *gift*. Yes, I've always been a little bit psychic. I can't tell you what games the Saints are going to win or the lottery numbers. It doesn't work like that. I don't really know how it works, to be honest. The best way I can explain it is to say that I have a connection with the Divine Feminine. The easiest way for me to channel the gift and use it is through reading tarot cards. My deck, a gift from another psychic, is old and worn now, but the cards somehow feel connected to me. I don't let anyone else handle them, unless I am doing a reading for them—something I try to do as rarely as possible because it doesn't always work—and whenever I pick them up, my fingers tingle a little bit.

That doesn't mean the answer I'm looking for always comes up in the cards. Sometimes the reading doesn't make sense. Sometimes it will later.

Also, sometimes I slip into a trance. While in the trance, I commune with the Goddess on another plane. She often speaks in riddles, which is frustrating. She first called me to join her on that plane when my life was in danger from a gang of neo-Nazi white supremacists. It doesn't happen very often, and like I said, something extreme has to be going on.

I can go years without visiting that plane in between dimensions, or wherever it is I go when She calls me.

What can I say? My life has always been a little on the melodramatic side.

And I truly appreciate the rare quiet moments around here.

Wild stuff happens to me all the time, you know? My life has been nothing but a long series of strange and unusual adventures that I'd have a hard time believing myself, had they not actually happened to me. *You're making that up* is how people usually respond to just one of my stories.

I appreciate the people who listen and don't believe me more than the ones who get that he's-not-in-his-right-mind look on their faces and melt away into the crowd.

What can I say? I just was never destined for the suburban nine-to-five, wife and two-point-three kids and a golden retriever and a white picket fence kind of life. Fortunately, that was the kind of life I was never interested in leading.

I've known I was gay for as long as I can remember. When pressed, I generally credit it to seeing Greg Louganis in a Speedo at the Los Angeles Olympics—that was the first time I can remember feeling the tug of desire and want for a man. It was a bit confusing. I knew somehow that being drawn to men wasn't right—every movie or television show I watched made that clear—so I kept it to myself, thinking it would change. But it wasn't a phase, something I grew out of in a few years. As I went through puberty and entered my teens, I was even more drawn to other guys. I started getting into the gay bars in the French Quarter when I was seventeen. For some reason, other gay men have always found me irresistible. I've never understood it. I mean, I guess I'm not hard on the eyes and I've always been in pretty good shape, but it's not like I stop traffic or something.

There are worse things, I guess. I never questioned it, just rolled with it.

And I still remember every one of Greg Louganis's dives. In vivid detail.

My name really isn't Scotty Bradley. Scott is my middle name. My first name is Milton. Yes, *Milton Bradley* is my name. My older brother Storm started calling me Scotty when I started school to spare me the merciless teasing of other kids. They teased me anyway, but not about my name. My parents are the embarrassments of their respective families. The Diderots—Mom's side—came over from France around 1720. They had a plantation up the river from New Orleans that made them wealthy but got into shipping after the Americans took over in 1803. Over the years the Diderots diversified and got richer and richer. Diderot blood is the bluest of the blue in New Orleans. Our family has provided the krewes of both Rex and Comus with kings and queens over the years. Papa and Maman Diderot live in an enormous house in the Garden District and sent Mom to all the right schools. She even was a maid of Rex and still carries the scars to this day.

The Bradleys are more recent arrivals, so the Diderots have always looked down their noses at them. They arrived after the Louisiana Purchase, and the original Bradley, Samuel by name, was a rags-to-riches story right out of a massive twentieth-century novel. The Bradleys aren't as rich or as socially prominent as the Diderots—Papa Bradley isn't in Comus, and Mom swears Papa Diderot blackballs him every time his name comes up—but make up for it by being even bigger snobs. They also sent Dad to all the right schools.

Mom and Dad found each other as teenagers—Maman Diderot claims they met at the Rex Ball, which Mom disputes—but they were kindred spirits.

I suppose the best word to describe Mom and Dad would

be *hippies*, but does that even mean anything these days? French Quarter Bohemians? Progressives? Socialists? Mom and Dad despise capitalism, racism, homophobia, sexism, you name it—if someone plans a protest against any injustice, my parents will be there in the front row with a bullhorn, leading chants. They don't trust the government, they don't trust the corporate media, and they always seem to be either planning or on their way to a protest.

I don't remember either of them ever having short hair. Mom coils hers into a massive braid, and Dad just holds his back with a rubber band. They flatly refused to go to the traditional universities their families attend—Diderot women usually attended the University of Virginia, and Bradley men went to Vanderbilt. They stayed in New Orleans and went to the University of New Orleans. They don't like the whole society thing, think it's based in white supremacy and not feminist at all, and don't participate. They consider themselves to be freethinkers and have never met a protest they wouldn't join. Some of my earliest memories are of protests—military bases, nuclear power plants, city hall, the state capital in Baton Rouge, oil companies and petrochemical plants—and Storm swears our first words were *I want to speak to a lawyer*.

Mom and Dad have been arrested so many times their rap sheet is as long as my arm.

And then there are our names.

They named my older brother Storm and my sister Rain. Both sets of grandparents were horrified Mom and Dad wouldn't give their children "normal" names. The story goes that the one time the Diderots and the Bradleys were able to come together was to keep my parents from naming me River, their original plan. They finally convinced Mom to give me a family name.

I can almost see the glint of glee in my mother's eyes when she gave in.

Milton was my maternal grandmother's maiden name, and Scott was my fraternal grandmother's family. So Milton Scott are family names.

But Milton Bradley was also a board game company back in the twentieth century.

I will forever be grateful to Storm—a hopeless tease but a great lawyer—for coming up with Scotty.

I've lived here in the French Quarter of New Orleans all my life. Well, except for two awful years away at college. Papa Bradley convinced me somehow that, unlike my siblings, I should follow the Bradley family tradition and go to Vanderbilt in Nashville. Neither set of grandparents were thrilled to have a gay grandchild, so I think going to Vanderbilt was kind of a *I may be gay but at least I'm going to Vandy* kind of thing. I hated it there. When your only experience in life is the French Quarter...yeah, I only lasted two years before flunking out and coming home. Both grandfathers tied up my trust funds until my thirtieth birthday in retaliation, but I didn't care. I was glad to be home.

Mom and Dad own a tobacco shop at the corner of Royal and Dauphine. They are also big stoners—they get the best weed, too—and rarely out of bed before noon. I grew up in the big apartment above the shop in the heart of the Quarter. My parents have never been your average, run-of-the-mill overprotective types, either. Their apartment is always filled with intellectuals and artists, smoking weed and drinking wine and debating social justice until the sun comes up and everyone goes home, intellectually stimulated and stoned out of their minds.

When I came out to them as a teenager, they were delighted. Since they are so countercultural, you can imagine their disappointment when their two eldest children were, in their view, squares. Storm became a lawyer, my sister Rain married a doctor, and both are deeply into the whole New Orleans society thing that my parents despised. My being gay made up for their deep disappointment in Storm and Rain. Mom was president of our local PFLAG chapter for several years, and they always march in the Pride parade. Mom loves shouting down the homophobic Christian protestors who show up every year for Southern Decadence and Carnival in her *I love my gay son!* pink T-shirt.

They're the best.

They also accepted both of my partners without question into the family.

Yes, *partners*. I told you my life isn't normal. Why have one partner when you can have two?

I'd believed for years that I would never have a serious relationship. I can be a lot to deal with, and when you add in all the other crazy shit that happens in my life? It's no wonder that I made it almost to thirty before meeting someone. I never really dated. I tricked and kept my distance. Most guys didn't want a happily-ever-after anyway. That rom-com stuff, where two opposites meet and are at odds and somehow magically fall in love? I didn't see that happening for me. I refused to buy into all that *someday my prince will come* nonsense. I just could never see myself settling down. I liked the freedom of not answering to anyone, doing what and who I wanted when I wanted.

And I didn't think I'd be a good parent. I can handle my nieces and nephews because I know I'll get to give them back to their parents at some point. But my own?

Yikes.

And given how not normal my life is…kids would only make it worse.

I've been kidnapped by criminals with evil plans for me so many times over the years I can't keep track of them all. The thieving scum at my health insurance provider are probably getting tired of paying for all the brain scans I need with far more regularity than your average human. I get hit in the head only slightly less frequently than an NFL linebacker.

And I have this incredibly bad habit of stumbling over dead bodies.

I've even been shot once or twice. Maybe three times? It's hard to keep track. I know I've been shot at more times than I care to count.

I met both of my guys on the same weekend. It was the Southern Decadence right after I turned twenty-nine and the last time I filled in for a dancer at the Pub. Yes, I used to be a go-go boy. When I flunked out of college and the grandparents cut off my trust funds to try to force me to go back, I got hired by a booking agency for male strippers called the Southern Knights. They sent me to dance at events and gay bars all over the country. It was a lot of fun. I had a lot of sex and did a lot of drugs and drank my fair share of liquor. When I left the Knights, I got certified as a personal trainer and was working at Riverview Fitness at Canal Place. I knew the managers at the Pub and sometimes filled in there when they were short a dancer. That Southern Decadence weekend, one of the porn stars they'd booked for that weekend OD'd on crystal, and they called me to fill in. I was behind on my rent, so I said sure.

I was always behind on my rent. My landladies, Millie and Velma, were old friends of my parents and they let me slide a lot.

That weekend was both the first time I was ever kidnapped *and* the first time I was ever knocked unconscious.

Good times.

But that was also the weekend when I met both Frank and Colin. Frank was still a Special Agent with the FBI in town working a case when our paths crossed. Colin was dancing at the Pub that weekend, too, but what I didn't know—didn't know until much later—was that he was also undercover working on a case. Colin, however, didn't work for the Feds—he worked for an international company called the Blackledge Agency. He once explained Blackledge as something that is necessary but shouldn't be. When corporations and governments need plausible deniability, they turn to Blackledge to handle their delicate situations. Originally a Mossad agent, Colin was recruited by Blackledge when he started questioning his role in those fraught situations.

Colin is very good at what he does. He rescued me once from some bad guys by scaling the side of JAX Brewery to the penthouse on top. I was drugged, and he carried me back down the side of the building like he did that sort of thing regularly. I still have nightmares about that descent. One thing led to another and somehow the three of us agreed to try to make it work and managed to form our own little family—a throuple, before anyone had ever heard of one. Colin is gone a lot for his work, and he can never really tell us anything about what he does.

Which sometimes means lying to us, which makes the trust thing kind of hard.

I should also probably mention that Frank is a professional wrestler. It's a long story, but it was something he'd dreamed of doing ever since he was a child. After Hurricane Katrina, we talked about it. I didn't have to work hard to convince him to chase that dream at long last. So what if he was in his forties? He was in great shape and looked amazing in the gear. He went to a training school for Gulf Coast Championship Wrestling in Bay City. When he climbed through the ring ropes the first time during a show, it was obvious to everyone he was going to be a star. You couldn't take your eyes off him—the thick yet lean muscled body didn't hurt, either. The audience responded to him, and he started climbing the ladder, eventually becoming one of their biggest stars. He was on the road a lot, putting on shows throughout the Gulf South to the cheers of crowds, and spending hours afterward signing autographs.

Did I mention how hot and sexy he looked in the tights and boots?

I loved watching him perform because the character he played in the ring loved to show off his body, flexing and preening to the whistles and cheers and catcalls.

Yet it always took me at least an hour and a beer to get him to take his shirt off on the dance floor in gay bars. Go figure.

We have his most popular poster framed and mounted in the living room. White boots, white kneepads, white trunks, white elbow pads, white tape around his wrists—and of course the big championship belt around his small waist. He's giving the camera a sly grin.

To me, it's the same look he gets on his face when he's horny.

That look has sold a lot of posters.

Women love him.

And of course, there's the dead body thing. Dead bodies keep showing up in my life, which is not something you ever get used to. I have a knack for catching criminals, it turns out—maybe it's part of the psychic thing, I don't know—but at least the police detectives whose cases I always somehow barge into, Venus Casanova and Blaine Tujague, don't find me as annoying as they used to in the beginning. Catch enough killers and even the cops will come around, you know?

What else…

Oh yes, we added Frank's nephew Taylor Wheeler to our family a few years ago. The only son of Frank's older sister Teresa, Taylor was disowned by his father when he came out to his parents after a semester in Paris. We'd stepped in immediately, inviting him to come live with us in New Orleans and getting him enrolled at Tulane to finish his education. He's a great kid, tall and smart and adorably young and cute, and what happened to him this past Christmas was so horrible for us. He was drugged by an older man and taken back to the man's hotel room. Taylor was unconscious, and when he was examined at the emergency room later, there were no signs of trauma or sexual assault. We got him on PEP—post-exposure prophylaxis—for HIV and got him regularly tested for STIs for the next three months.

I would have gladly killed that bastard, but someone else beat me to it. Apparently, he was killed before he could assault Taylor, who was passed out in the next room.

I told you—dead bodies turn up around me with alarming frequency.

Taylor's seeing a therapist now and seems to be doing okay. I worry about him—maybe too much—but never press. He knows I'm there for him whenever he needs, and that's the most important thing.

Frank has taken a break from wrestling. The story was he'd been injured in a car accident and was recovering. The belt was vacated and—well, long story short, the door was left open for him to go back whenever he was ready.

I feel like I'm forgetting something.

Oh yes! When I moved out of my parents' place in my early twenties, I rented an apartment on Decatur Street across from the Old Mint. The building was owned by a lesbian couple who were close friends of my parents, Millie Breen and Velma Simpson. The first floor used to be a mom-and-pop place run by Mrs. Duchesnay. She never came back after the building burned down that same Southern Decadence I met Colin and Frank. She was planning to, but after the building was finished, she lost her house in Mid-City when the levees failed after Katrina and moved away. It was a coffee shop for a while, until the proprietors skipped town owing months in rent and back wages to their staff. That space has been vacant ever since. Millie and Velma had the second-floor apartment, I lived with Frank and Colin on the third, and Taylor was up on the fourth. When Velma broke her hip, she decided to retire from her law practice and sell the building.

I bought it. Everyone had been telling me I need to invest, and I needed to buy a home ever since I turned thirty and gained access to my trust funds. Millie and Velma moved to their condo in Florida shortly after Christmas, and I've been trying to adapt to being a property owner ever since. We've been taking bids for work on the building—I want to turn all three apartments into a one-family residence, but I can't make up my mind what to do with the retail space on the first floor. It's very valuable, I know, but I don't need the money, and I am not entirely comfortable with that aspect of being a property owner.

One last thing—we'd not seen Colin since Christmas when Mother's Day rolled around. There was another dead body involved in that story, too.

But I don't want to give away too much...

CHAPTER ONE
THE HERMIT, REVERSED
A tendency to be a perpetual Peter Pan

"I think we should turn it into a home gym," I said into the gloom. "I mean, wouldn't it be great to just have to go downstairs to work out? And we can put in a sauna and a steam room. What do you think, guys?"

It was the Monday night after Mother's Day, and the termites were swarming.

That was why we were sitting around the living room in the dark. The only illumination in the entire building came from two blasphemy candles, flickering in the center of the coffee table. Modeled after Catholic prayer candles, one had a picture of Drew Brees in his Saints jersey with a halo and heavenly light shining on his head with the words *Pray to Breesus* around the base. The other was St. Chris Owens of Bourbon Street.

So, yeah—blasphemy candles. They're very popular here.

Yet even the scant pale light from the teardrop-shaped flames was enough to draw an occasional scout termite from the gloom. We wouldn't see it until it landed on the glass lip of one of the candles before dive-bombing into the flame. There would be a brief sizzling sound, and then the yellow flame flickered, turning briefly reddish as the termite immolated. Once it was consumed, the flame would be steady and yellow again.

The swarming rarely lasted more than an hour, but that hour seemed to last an eternity.

Termites have always been the bane of New Orleans's existence. The domestic kind were bad enough. Houses and buildings were tented to get rid of infestations, the bright yellow and red stripes announcing to the world that a termite Armageddon was happening inside. The city's original termite problem had grown exponentially worse since the particularly vicious Formosan variety had hitched a ride on a freighter to the fertile feeding grounds of our old, mostly wooden city shortly after World War II. The dampness of our climate must have made them feel like they'd arrived at termite Disney World. The little fuckers love wet wood, so the entire city was an all-you-can-eat buffet. They'd killed live oaks that had survived hurricanes, destroyed historic homes, and I'd heard that they could even chew through brick and mortar.

Maybe that was an urban legend, but it wasn't one I was interested in proving.

Formosan termites *swarmed*.

The first rule of surviving Formosan termite season was speed. Every source of light had to be turned off the moment you spotted the first scout. They're drawn to the light, like moths, but unlike moths, they're drawn to the light in the hundreds of thousands, turning your home into a scene from Cecil B. DeMille's ultimate cheesefest *The Ten Commandments*. The big streetlamps along Decatur Street outside drew the swarms, horrifying clouds of little monsters flying around, frantically trying to mate while shedding wings like revoltingly nasty snowflakes.

Every year they returned after Mother's Day like the swallows to Capistrano, and every year on Mother's Day morning I latched the shutters shut on the balcony windows and drew the heavy interior curtains closed. That helped reduce the swarming incidents inside the house some. Unfortunately, the nasty little vermin evolved a sixth sense that worked like a homing beacon, drawing them to any ray of light inside. And once the scout found it, he sent out word to the rest of the swarm. Within seconds the apartment would be filled with them, triggering nightmares for months. I only made the mistake of leaving the lights on once during swarming season. I'd forgotten once on my way out, coming home to piles of termite wings everywhere with their wingless little corpses scattered throughout the piles.

I was still finding wing debris months later.

But I'd learned a valuable lesson, one I'd never forget and would never repeat.

As awful as they were, there was no defeating the Formosan termites. You had to adapt to living with them for the few weeks of swarming season, while safeguarding your property as much as possible. The swarms had been much worse before Hurricane

Katrina, but not even Katrina's destructive winds and the flood caused by the levee failures could get rid of them once and for all.

I'd always hated them, but now that I'd bought the building on Decatur Street, termite season had become personal. I'd heard too many horror stories over the years about the damage termites inflicted.

"I hate termite season," Taylor said, like he'd read my mind. I love having him around. I'll never understand how parents can turn their backs on their children for being queer, let alone one as amazing as Taylor. Smart, kind, and polite, he'd handled himself well even after what happened to him back in December. He seemed to be doing okay, so I tried not to hover and worry about him.

Easier said than done.

I'll probably never stop worrying about him.

"They are pretty nasty," Frank replied, reaching in the gloom for the joint I'd just lit.

"You freaked that first time you experienced a swarm." I blew out smoke and placed it into his fingers. I'd fallen asleep that first spring Frank had lived here and forgot about the termites. I woke up to a crash and lots of swearing from the living room. I'd yelled for him to turn out the lights before rolling over and going back to sleep.

Frank had itched for days.

"We haven't been swarmed since." He took a hit and passed the joint over to Taylor.

"Hard to believe that was almost fifteen years ago," I replied, watching the cherry glow bright red as Taylor inhaled.

Frank had changed a lot in those fifteen years. If someone would have told him sixteen years ago that he'd be living in New Orleans one day and sharing a joint with his nephew, he would have called for the men in white coats. It hadn't been easy for him, shaking off twenty years of experience and training as an FBI agent, but he'd eventually adapted. Always the strong silent type, he'd never been overly comfortable expressing any feelings or emotions besides anger. He'd been raised with such a narrow view of what being a man meant, and twenty years as a Fed hadn't helped.

Toxic masculinity hurts everyone.

I still couldn't believe we'd been together for over fifteen years. We'd both changed so much since that Southern Decadence when we'd met.

The world has changed so much since then.

I took the joint from Taylor's outstretched hand, noticing in the candlelight how the veins bulged in his forearm now. Taylor had gotten a lot bigger in the five months since Christmas. Like Frank, Taylor was tall and lean. When he'd arrived in New Orleans, he couldn't have weighed more than a hundred and fifty pounds of muscle and bone and sinew. Trust me when I say it was his genetics and not a lack of appetite. Taylor has always eaten like a horse. Frank says he'd been the same way at that age. Years of eating properly and regular visits to the gym had turned Frank into the sexy older hunk-daddy I'd met. He could still pass for being in his forties, despite losing most of his hair in his late twenties. He was getting closer to sixty now than I wanted to think about.

I also hoped he was home to stay. I'd never ask him to give up his dream, of course—I want him to be happy, and if that means him being gone for substantial amounts of time, I can live with it. Of course, Gulf Coast wanted him back. He'd become one of their most popular stars, and still got hundreds of messages from fans missing him on his now mostly dormant social media accounts. Videos of his matches on YouTube have millions of hits. The promoter checked with him every few days in case he'd changed his mind. He hadn't, yet—but I believed he'd be back on the circuit once he was sure Taylor was okay and didn't need him.

But selfishly, I hoped he wouldn't go back on the tour. I liked having him around.

I felt pleasantly buzzed. If I had to spend an hour or so in the dark, the best way to do that was to be high.

Being high made everything better.

"So, what do you think? Our own gym on the first floor?" I asked as I blew out the smoke. Taylor reached for the joint as Frank waved it off.

Everyone kept telling me I was losing money by allowing the retail business space to sit empty and not renting out Millie and Velma's old place on the second floor. We'd pretty much settled on turning the building into a one-family residence. I wanted to have the stairs enclosed completely. Taylor's apartment on the fourth floor was what used to be called a bachelor apartment because the slope of the roof limited the space up there. It was one bedroom, a small bathroom, a kitchenette, an enormous closet, and a smaller living room—no balcony.

But we couldn't do anything until we decided what to do with the first floor.

I didn't like the idea of renting it out as a retail space. That would make me a landlord, too, and I still hadn't wrapped my mind around being a property owner. I didn't want anyone else having access to our back courtyard or to the back staircase.

I couldn't exactly explain it to anyone without explaining about the dead Russian spy I'd found Colin standing over when I got home that night last December.

"I really don't like the idea of letting another business move in on the first floor," Frank said. "I know it's a valuable space, but I do like the gym idea." I couldn't see his face in the dim light, but I sensed he was winking at me.

He didn't say *We don't need the money.* We didn't. We had trouble spending the quarterly distributions from my trust funds. I usually donated what was left from the last check to charity when the new one hit my checking account. Frank's pension from the FBI and whatever he made wrestling was his money to do with as he pleased.

We'd never told Taylor—or anyone—what Colin's job really was. All we said was that he was a troubleshooter for hire whose clients were international companies with internal security problems. It wasn't a complete lie and was close enough to what Frank and I believed he did to ring true.

Governments were a kind of international companies, weren't they?

We'd replaced the front gate with a steel door equipped with an intercom system and a security camera trained on it. There was razor wire mounted above that steel door. We'd done the same with the door in the shed that led into the parking lot behind the building. We'd embedded shards of broken glass on the roof of the shed to discourage break-ins that way.

I didn't like living in a fortress, but it was necessary.

We'd learned that the hard way during Christmas.

Taylor thought we'd beefed up the security because of what happened to him. He'd rolled his eyes and said he was fine and didn't need all these additional safety precautions.

We'd decided it was easier to let him think we were being overprotective rather than telling him the truth about Colin. Taylor was already on shaky emotional ground as it was.

I didn't like lying to him—in my experience, lies always tend to bite you in the ass when you're least expecting it—but we've kept him in the dark successfully so far.

"I'm going to call Cooper Construction tomorrow and tell them we want the first floor made into a home gym," I replied. My pleasantly buzzed mind took a little decorating trip. We'd need machines and weights, benches and barbells, mirrored walls, a ballet barre for stretching…sauna and steam room. Maybe a shower, too. "They can draw up the final plans for us to look over."

I wished I could see Taylor's face through the gloom. He seemed to be doing fine, and his therapy sessions with Dr. Rickoll, a handsome gay man I went to high school with, seemed to be working. He'd become obsessed with working out since Christmas, but Dr. Rickoll said that was normal. *Even though being able to defend himself, being stronger, wouldn't have protected him from being drugged, this is a coping mechanism and it's a healthy one. I'm working with him, of course, to help him understand it wasn't his fault, but that's a normal reaction— victims inevitably blame themselves for a while. It'll take some time, but he is making progress*, Dr. Rickoll had said. As a former trainer and someone who still worked out regularly, I'd suggested that I train him, but Dr. Rickoll advised against it. *He kind of should—needs to— do this on his own. He needs to feel some control over his life, and his body is something he can control.* He'd frowned. *We just have to keep an eye on him, so it doesn't develop into something unhealthy like body dysmorphia and an eating disorder.*

Given how much Taylor ate, I didn't see an eating disorder in his future.

We'd signed him up for a membership at the New Orleans Athletic Club rather than our gym, Riverview Fitness in Canal Place.

I'd given Taylor's trainer at the New Orleans Athletic Club my credit card number to keep on file.

Everyone from Dr. Rickoll to my mom kept recommending we give him the space he needed, and much as I wanted to wrap him up in a protective cocoon, I was doing my best.

But with a personal gym on the first floor, maybe I could suggest he get certified as a trainer. He seemed to like working out, and he'd bulked up some in those five months or so. He was drinking protein shakes and taking supplements, and he worked out every day except Sunday.

If Taylor didn't want to use the home gym, I wouldn't press

him on it. But with a place to work out so conveniently located on the first floor...

"I like my trainer," Taylor said just as my phone pinged on the table.

I flipped it over and saw a text message scrawled across the lock screen, which was a picture of Frank in white gear in the ring corner.

Hey, have you got a minute?

It was from my best friend, David Andrews. *Sure just sitting here in the dark*, I typed back.

David and I used to work out together back when we were both single. We'd met one night at the bathhouse in the Quarter and gone back to my room, where we realized we were sexually incompatible. We started talking and struck up a friendship. He was one of those people like Frank who finds it hard to put on weight, so we worked out together so I could train him. He'd done well at the gym—I was good at my old job—and put on about twenty pounds of muscle over the years. We'd continued working out together until he fell in love with Diego Sandoval during the last Carnival before Hurricane Katrina.

When my house had burned down during that long-ago Southern Decadence when I first met Frank and Colin, after a few weeks at Mom and Dad's I'd moved into the other side of the double shotgun David used to own over on Kerlerec Street. David had renovated the place himself and then bought one of the destroyed properties in the Lower Ninth after the floodwaters receded. He'd sold the double shotgun for way more than he'd paid, flipped that house in the Lower Ninth, and did the same for another house down on Spain Street. He was doing quite well for himself and gotten a teaching job at NOCCA—New Orleans Center for Creative Arts—after years of working at a Catholic elementary school. I didn't see David near as much as I used to, but I still met him and Diego at the Pub most Sundays for tea dance and to catch a pleasant buzz.

Lady Gaga and Beyoncé's "Telephone" started blaring out of my phone, and I could see David smiling and flipping me off in the little round circle above his name. I touched *accept*.

"Hey, whore," I said. David and I always greeted each other this way. I felt Frank and Taylor both rolling their eyes in the dark.

"I'm sorry to bother you, but I couldn't think of anyone else to talk to about this," he replied. He sounded different, not his usual happy-go-lucky self, so I bit back the teasing insult on the tip of my tongue.

Whatever this was, it was serious.

"You're not in the middle of anything?" he asked. Again, not like David. Since when did he care if he was interrupting me? That wasn't our relationship. Usually he loved interrupting me.

So it really *was* serious.

"Well, right now, we're just sitting in the dark waiting for the termites to stop swarming," I said in the same tone he'd used. "I think we're getting close to a decision on what to have done. I just hate having to move out during construction." Papa Diderot had offered us the use of the mother-in-law house behind his mansion in the Garden District.

Sure, it's lovely, but I've never had much desire to live in the Garden District.

He blew a raspberry. "You're such a princess. You get used to it. If I can live in a house under construction—"

"You were doing the work yourself," I reminded him. He'd always lived in the houses he was renovating. I'm not very handy, but I'd helped him gut that house in the Lower Ninth Ward after he bought it. "You didn't have workers in and out all day. And you never had to deal with the Vieux Carré Commission, either."

"True," he replied. "Are you doing something to the front of the building?" The Vieux Carré Commission was tasked with preserving the historical integrity of the French Quarter. They didn't care what you did to the inside, they didn't care what you did to your courtyard—but you needed their permission to do anything to the front of the building.

The part everyone can see.

"I really want to put a roof on my balcony," I replied, pinching the bridge of my nose. Sometimes you got lucky and the VCC was easy to deal with. Other times? Mom says it's like trying to convince the Gestapo to see reason. An obvious exaggeration, but that's Mom. "But if they won't let us, it's not the end of the world."

Fortunately, my sister Rain had a good friend who worked for the VCC. I was trying to hold that card for as long as possible without using it. So far, they hadn't said no to the balcony being roofed.

"So, what's up?" I asked, trying to keep my voice casual as the roar from a couple of motorcycles down on the street echoed off the buildings. "You didn't call me to find out about the renovations." *Please be something easy that I can handle, please.*

"No." He swallowed. "Look, there's a thing going on with one of my students. I don't know what to do, but someone has got to do something to help this kid…" His voice trailed off. "You know teenagers."

Well, I didn't used to, but I'd gotten a crash course from Taylor over the last two years.

"I'm not an expert," I replied. "Maybe Taylor's therapist—"

"Maybe I'm making too much of this—maybe it's nothing. But at the same time…" He sighed. "As a teacher I'm a mandatory reporter—" Okay, it really was serious. I wasn't liking the sound of this at all. "But at the same time, I don't feel right about potentially ruining someone's life. I guess that's why I wanted him to talk to you, see what you think."

Ruining someone's life? "David, what are you taking about? Should I be concerned?"

"No, no, I'm just high, sorry." He coughed and cleared his throat. "Okay, let me start over." I heard him taking another hit. "I mean, I know you're technically a private eye, and you have had a lot of experience with crime-solving…"

"So this is a professional call?" I couldn't see Frank's face in the gloom.

"Maybe? Kind of? I don't know what to do." David coughed again. "So, you know I'm the faculty advisor for the Gay Straight Alliance at NOCCA?" David also directed the school's musical productions. They were currently rehearsing *Chicago*—an interesting choice for a high school production, I thought, and I was curious to see David's take on the Fosse choreography.

"I'm still amazed that a high school in New Orleans even has such a thing," I replied, accepting the joint back from Frank. I took a hit and coughed out smoke. Times had changed a lot since I was in high school.

Of course, my high school had been run by Jesuits.

"Well, one of our most talented dance students is also a member of the GSA. Brody Shepherd. Anyway, he came to my office after school today to talk to me about a problem he's having, and I'll be damned if I know what to do." He coughed again. I could hear the *Rent* soundtrack in the background and smiled. David did love his Broadway musical scores.

"So, you thought you'd punt it to me?"

"It was you or the police."

That got my attention. "I'm going to put you on speaker, okay?" I said. "Taylor and Frank are here."

"That's fine," he replied as I switched to speaker function and put the phone back down on the coffee table. "Brody got a job at the food court at Lakeside Mall last summer—he has a single mom, it's just the two of them—and he met this man one day at the food court." He hesitated. "The man was our age, if not older. Definitely too old for Brody."

"He's a teenage boy," I said. "We're all hormones and bad choices at that age, you know that." And it's why you swore you'd never teach high school again, I refrained from reminding him.

"How old is Brody?" This was Frank. The cherry on the joint flared up again as he took another big hit.

"Brody is graduating next month, he just turned eighteen, so he was seventeen at the time they met."

"The age of consent in Louisiana for boys is seventeen," Taylor pointed out, and I hated that he knew that. He'd learned a lot about consent since Christmas.

"I'm getting ahead of myself," David replied. "Brody had only started coming out when he got the job, and he was working with another gay kid there. They became friends. This other kid, Paris, has always been out, I guess, and is from one of the river parishes. Anyway, Brody hadn't been working there long when he noticed that Paris had an older male friend who came to see him at the food court every weekend. He'd always have presents for Paris—underwear, that sort of thing."

"How old was Paris?" Frank asked in a neutral voice. I glanced at him but couldn't see his face.

"Paris had just graduated from high school, so eighteen, I guess." David went on, "After he'd been working there for about a month or two, Paris was killed by a hit-and-run driver outside the little town he's from. Verdun?"

Verdun. A chill went down my spine. Verdun was the parish seat of St. Jeanne d'Arc Parish, upriver from New Orleans.

Please let it not be that.

"After about a month, the older guy started coming back to the mall again, to the food court, and the two of them talked about missing Paris. Brody felt sorry for him because the older guy was clearly brokenhearted that Paris was gone. The older guy took Brody out for dinner, and then…"

The man was very complimentary about Brody's looks and his body, and showed a lot of interest in him.

"Brody was flattered, and he didn't see any harm in trading phone numbers with the guy."

After exchanging numbers, the man started texting with Brody—always polite, never inappropriate, just showing an interest in him. What initially began just as finding mutual comfort in their loss of Paris started becoming more than that.

"So, the man was grooming him?" Frank's voice dripped with disdain and contempt.

"They started going out to dinner every weekend, and soon he began buying Brody presents." First, it was cologne, or a nice pair of sneakers that Brody mentioned wanting but not being able to afford, or jeans. The man always wanted Brody to send pictures of him wearing the gifts.

But soon the gifts became a little more intimate.

"Expensive designer underwear, bikini bathing suits, thongs, jocks," David went on. "And Brody was soon sending the guy pictures of himself just wearing the gifts."

"Disgusting," Frank said from the gloom before I could say anything. The joint was now in Taylor's hands, and he stubbed out the roach in the ashtray.

"But not against the law," Taylor pointed out bitterly.

"Not against the law," David echoed. "It's not even considered child pornography—I know, I looked it up myself."

"But this all seems kind of innocent," I interjected. "This doesn't seem like something you'd need me or Frank to talk to the kid about."

"Brody's already got a full ride in dance at Tulane and has his entire future ahead of him, and I don't want to see it get fucked up because of something like this. That's why I am talking to you and not the school or the cops." David hesitated. "Brody wants this all to just kind of go away quietly."

"I guess I missed something, David," Frank replied. "I don't see what the problem is."

"I'm sorry, I'm telling this wrong," David said. "So, about a month ago, Brody broke things off with this guy."

"He was still involved with this guy up till a month ago?" This from Frank.

"Brody insists that nothing physical ever happened between them. But there's the pictures, and the videos…"

"Videos?" I replied.

"The guy got Brody to record himself with his phone," David said. "He now knows how stupid that was."

"I'm not following this," I said. "If he broke up with the guy, I don't see what the problem is. Yeah, it sucks he was stupid enough to send pictures and videos, but there's no crime there. I don't think nudes—even videos—would be enough to wreck his future. If he's going to dance?" I shook my head. "I follow a lot of dancers on Instagram, and believe me, some of the things they post…Yeah, tell him he's got nothing to worry about on that score."

David sighed. "There's more," he said glumly. There's always more, I thought as he continued. "The reason he came to talk to me today was because he got an anonymous text message…"

"And?"

"It was one of the underwear pictures he's sent this guy." David exhaled. "Which was freaky enough, but there was also a message. *Paris wasn't an accident.*"

"Paris wasn't an accident." Frank repeated the words. "So, he was murdered?"

"Didn't you say it was a hit-and-run?" I asked.

"Well, that was what the coroner ruled." David's voice sounded snarky. "But…"

"You don't think that was what happened?"

"I don't know. I'm not a private eye," David said. "But I looked online for reports about the accident, and it doesn't make sense to me." He exhaled. "Scotty, you know what these parishes are like, and especially St. Jeanne d'Arc Parish." He pronounced it the way we say it in Louisiana: *SENN-jendark.*

I inhaled.

"Do you mind talking to him?" David asked. "He's worried. He doesn't want any of this following him around for the rest of his life. He knows he was stupid—"

To say the least, I thought.

"But he wants you to see if you can poke around, find out what really happened to his pal Paris," David said. "He also wants you to speak to the guy, see if you can get the pictures and videos back for him. That's the most important thing—he still thinks his friend was killed in a hit-and-run."

"But you don't think so?" Frank asked sharply.

"Just from the way the body was placed in the road, Frank." David's voice shook. "He may have been hit by a car and killed, but his body had to have been staged."

"Why do you say that?"

"Look it up when you get a chance," David replied, "and see if you don't think the same thing as me. This whole thing is dirty, Scotty, and I'm worried for Brody. I think he's mixed up in something he may not be able to get out of."

"And just who was the older man?" Frank asked.

"The guy's name is JD Haver."

My entire body went cold.

Of course. I'd known it the moment David said St. Jeanne d'Arc Parish.

Jefferson Davis Haver IV.

Why did it have to be him?

Why wouldn't it be? a voice sneered inside my head.

"He's that parish president being sued about Isadora relief funds and insurance payouts. Brody has no idea what a total douchebag this guy is." David went on, not waiting for me to respond. "The dude is married and has kids. And you know he basically runs that parish. And if they are covering up the truth about how Paris died, who out there has that kind of clout to fake a criminal investigation?"

Jefferson Davis Haver IV.

I could hear my heart pounding in my ears.

Why did it have to be him, of everyone in this fucking state?

The Haver family has run St. Jeanne d'Arc Parish as a personal fiefdom since before the Civil War but after the German Coast revolt of the enslaved. Jefferson Davis Haver IV, JD to his friends, was the latest member of the family to ascend to power there. Considered one of the river parishes, it was just outside of New Orleans. About sixty percent of the parish is swamp or wetland, but they also have one of the few bridges across the river in the state—the Warren Sheehan Bridge, named after a longtime Louisiana politician.

If he was having sex with teenage boys, he'd make a perfect target for a blackmailer. Of course he was a family values politician—

praise the Lord and pass the ammunition, and can we bring back Jim Crow?

The kind of political power broker who *always* has dark and dirty secrets.

"Has he told Haver any of this?"

"He's afraid to," David replied. "He's afraid, period. So can I bring him over to talk to you tomorrow after school?"

"You can, but there's something about me he might want to know first."

"Oh?"

I closed my eyes. "*TL;DR.* Jeff Haver's grandmother is my great-aunt Charlotte, and that side of the family hasn't spoken to our side of the family in, oh, at least twenty years."

Family in Louisiana can be very complicated.

CHAPTER TWO
SIX OF CUPS
Happiness and enjoyment that come from the past

I couldn't fall asleep.

I sighed and rolled over. I opened my eyes and saw the digital clock on my nightstand. The numbers 02:40 glowed in red in the darkness.

Frank mumbled and shifted in his sleep next to me, rolling over so his back was to me. I stared at the ceiling in the darkness, debating. Should I get up and do something? Should I stay in bed and keep trying to fall asleep? The bed was comfortable, and the weight of the blankets felt comforting. There were dishes in the sink, and we'd left a mess in the living room. The blueprints were still spread out on the dining table. David wasn't bringing his student by until after school, so I had all day to clean up, but since I couldn't sleep...

Taylor had gone up to his apartment shortly after David called. The swarming was over for the night—Taylor checked through the slats on one of the shutters to make sure the cloud around the nearest streetlamp was gone. He had a test later in the week and wanted to study. He was so much more dedicated a student than I'd been, which was why he would graduate next year from one of the best schools in the South and I'd flunked out. Frank and I hadn't stayed up much later, catching a true crime documentary about the murders of some teenagers in a small Kansas town. Frank kept yawning all the way through, so I finally turned it off and we'd gone to bed. The moment Frank's head hit the pillow, he was asleep, breathing evenly within seconds and snoring shallowly through his nose.

I just couldn't turn my mind off, couldn't stop thinking.

Jefferson Davis Haver IV, of all people. Why did it have to be him?

Like I said, family can be complicated in Louisiana.

And considering what a homophobic piece of shit he'd always been, the irony that he was preying on teenagers was so perfect I was sorry his awful parents were dead because the scandal would have killed them both.

Maman Diderot's oldest sister, Charlotte, had married Jefferson Davis Haver III—Trey. I always thought they should call JD *Quad*. They'd never been close—there was a ten-year age difference between Aunt Charlotte and Maman. I usually only saw the Havers at family events—weddings and funerals, maybe the occasional special birthday or anniversary celebration—but Papa Diderot never made any bones about his intense dislike of the Havers. The last time I saw the Havers was at Aunt Charlotte's funeral, about two years before Hurricane Katrina. We'd all put on appropriately black clothing and driven out to St. Jeanne d'Arc Parish. The interment had been in the mausoleum in the family cemetery on the grounds of their estate, Sunnymeade. I'd wandered down to the boathouse, hoping to get some privacy so I could smoke the joint I'd brought with me. I was getting pleasantly high, dangling my legs off the dock, when JD's younger brother Beau showed up. JD was a few years older than me, but Beau was younger and a bit of a problem child for the Havers. He'd been involved in a drunk driving accident when in high school and some girl had died. He'd never been charged, and the whispers around the family were that the girl's family had been bought off. I'd never much liked Beau—when we were all kids he was the one who always started crying to get us all in trouble. He hadn't changed much since then, but they had shipped him away from St. Jeanne d'Arc Parish. He'd grown into a pasty-faced redhead with blotchy greenish freckles, a soft body, and an acne problem. His hair was already thinning, and he was sweating in the late June heat. He was married, but his wife hadn't come. I'd overheard Trey telling Dad that Beau and his wife were having problems.

I offered to share the joint with him, and he took it from me gratefully. I'd just taken it back when Storm came running down the sloping back lawn, calling my name. "Keep it," I said, handing it back to Beau and going back to meet Storm.

Apparently Trey had drunk too much, said something nasty to

Mom about my sexuality, and wound up with a face drenched in red wine. "We probably should go," Storm said, hustling me back up to the main house. Mom and Dad were already in their car in the driveway, waiting for me. As we headed down to the gate, I looked back at the hideous house, thinking, I'll never see this place again.

JD had been in the news as recently as two years ago, railing against some quote-unquote *queer books* carried in the parish library. Yes, Louisiana is a conservative state once you get outside the bigger urban areas. But gay-bashing? JD didn't need to gay-bash to win elections in the parish. Every Haver son succeeded his father as parish president, and they were all lawyers. The Haver law firm was wealthy and powerful, too.

And if you think the sheriff or the district attorney out there isn't owned by the Havers, think again. Beau killed a girl while driving drunk and never spent a minute behind bars.

That's pretty much it in a nutshell.

On the drive back to New Orleans after the funeral, Mom kept a running commentary going about what horrors the future held for JD and Beau.

"I told you when they were little they were the kind of boys you always see wandering around the frat house at three in the morning looking for passed-out girls," she said grimly through tight lips. "And nothing is ever their fault. Gina always let them get away with murder. Not her precious little angels." She snorted. "But they're Havers, and as long as they own St. Jeanne d'Arc Parish, they'll never be held accountable for anything." She shook her head. "And their daddy is no better than they are."

I'd heard the stories about Trey spending a lot of time on the wrong side of the tracks in the parish. Stories about brothels and strippers and illegal gambling and drugs, all the vice in the parish controlled by the Havers. Nothing happened in that parish without first being signed off by a Haver.

I smothered a laugh thinking about JD's wife's reaction when she found out her husband was, at the very least, bisexual.

I hadn't liked his wife Karen, either. I'd gone to that wedding— when had that been? Sometime when I was in my early twenties. I hadn't liked her, and the more I got to know her the less I liked her. She was the kind of Southern woman who proudly called herself a steel magnolia, but as Mom said, "That's just a genteel way of saying *raving bitch*."

I eased up out of bed, not wanting to disturb Frank, who just grunted and rolled over again. Like anything would wake him. I shook my head at myself and wandered down the hall in my underwear to the kitchen. I grabbed a bottle of Pellegrino and filled a glass. I sat down at the desk in the dining room and touched the space bar, waking up my computer. I opened a browser and typed *Jefferson Davis Haver IV* in the search bar.

The first article that came up was from *The Times-Picayune*, about the lawsuit being filed against JD and his law firm by Hurricane Isadora victims. I checked the date. The piece had run last Tuesday, which meant the lawsuit had been filed on Monday.

I sipped my fizzy water, remembering. Isadora had been an August hurricane last summer, the weekend before Southern Decadence. It came up quick, forming in the lower Caribbean Sea as a disturbance no one paid a lot of attention to, until it started moving northwest on Thursday afternoon. By Friday afternoon it was approaching Louisiana, barreling right toward New Orleans as a Category 3, with models showing it coming ashore as a Category 4.

We started getting ready that afternoon.

By Saturday morning it was heading directly for us. After Katrina, Papa Diderot had bought a ranch up near Shreveport so we'd always have a place to go should that disaster ever repeat itself. By Saturday afternoon most of the family was heading northwest to the ranch, but Mom and Dad had a natural gas line and a generator powerful enough to keep the juice on at their place, so we decided to stay and go over there if we lost power. If things got Katrina bad, we'd ride out the storm, hope the levees held, and head north afterward. Isadora jogged west as she got closer to the Louisiana coastline, so we didn't get the worst of it. We still lost power and a lot of trees came down, but New Orleans had dodged a bullet.

Unfortunately, the parishes west of New Orleans did not. The eyewall had passed over Houma and Grand Isle. The full force of a Category 3 hurricane crashed through St. Jeanne d'Arc Parish, leaving well over a billion dollars in damage in its wake. It had taken months for the power to be completely restored, and like always, insurance companies were dragging their feet about paying out claims. The Haver family law firm had stepped in, filing a class action suit and individual suits, forcing the insurance companies to settle and make good on the policies they'd written.

Last week, a group of JD's clients filed suit against him and the firm for never paying out the insurance settlements to the policyholders, who couldn't rebuild without that money.

I didn't hold out much hope for them winning if the case was heard in St. Jeanne d'Arc Parish. There was no justice there for anyone going against the Havers. An editorial had run that day in the paper, calling out all the corruption in St. Jeanne d'Arc Parish.

How bad did corruption have to be for a *New Orleans* newspaper to call it out?

I glanced down the screen. Most of the articles on this first page of results were about this recent lawsuit. I moved the cursor back up to the search bar, added *mysterious death Paris* to it, and hit enter again just as I heard something—a noise—from the back of the house.

From the staircase.

Goose bumps rose on my skin, and I felt my stomach twist.

I listened while the search results loaded on the computer screen.

It could have been my imagination.

Ever since finding the corpse of a Russian spy in the living room, I'd imagined all kinds of things.

It was probably nothing, just my paranoid subconscious acting up again as it had so many times over the past few months. The building was secure. No one could get in without a key unless they came over the roofs. And if someone came that way, they wouldn't use the back stairs.

I shook my head. That was just another problem with having a relationship with an international gun-for-hire—if someone wanting revenge on Colin managed to breach Blackledge's security, they'd find a trail that could lead right to our front door.

That was the story Colin had fed me at Christmas. A security breach had led the Russian assassin to our home.

And if they could hack Blackledge...

There was no telling how many people out there wanted Colin dead.

Or would be just as happy taking *us* out to make him suffer.

I still couldn't believe how naive I'd been to never have considered the possibility of something like that happening until it did. Goddess knows, since then it's all I've been able to think about, which was why we beefed up our home security as much as we could without drawing attention. Most people assumed we were either overreacting to Taylor's assault or the rising crime in the city.

We were more than happy to let them keep thinking that.

I yawned. The computer screen now read 3:17 a.m., and my bed was calling me. I loved having Frank home to share the bed with. I loved feeling his body shifting with every breath. His skin was warm and silky to the touch, the muscles beneath the skin hard and firm from years of work. I missed him when he was out on the road. I hated the reason he'd taken a break from his wrestling career, but I wasn't sorry he was home in our bed every night.

I listened again in the stillness.

Nothing.

Maybe I hadn't heard anything. Maybe I was just paranoid.

Who wouldn't be?

Wait—that was *something*, wasn't it? I didn't imagine that sound!

I slipped into the kitchen and unlocked the gun safe under the sink. I didn't like using guns, but I was a good shot and knew my way around a gun. I didn't like having guns in the house, but that ship had long since sailed. Frank had guns when he moved in, and of course there was an entire locked closet in the spare bedroom for Colin's armory. I also kept a nice aluminum baseball bat stashed by the front door to our apartment, just in case. Ironically, the bat had been a Christmas present from Frank. The look on Taylor's face when I'd unwrapped it had been priceless. He was clearly thinking *Why would you give Scotty a baseball bat?* as I hugged and kissed Frank.

I made sure the gun was loaded and crept down the hallway. I stood in the doorway to the bedroom and looked at my sleeping guy in the soft moonlight coming through the slats in the bedroom window shutters.

I loved him so much.

Frank fidgeted a bit before rolling onto his stomach. I covered his naked form with a light sheet and pulled on my own sweatpants.

I opened the back door and listened.

Cars passing on Decatur Street, the low murmur of Bourbon Street in the distance, the indistinct voices of people either at Café Envie down at the corner or walking by. No, nothing out of the ordinary. I closed the door and slid the dead bolt locked again.

I got the bottle of Pellegrino from the refrigerator before

walking into the living room to rescue the joint we'd smoked just before heading to bed. I sat down on the couch. I lit the joint, taking a long, measured drag, holding it until I coughed it back out. That pleasant buzz I'd had before going to bed slowly started creeping back into my brain, and I decided to enjoy it out on the balcony. The day had been way too hot and sunny to enjoy the balcony, but the temperature had dropped at least ten degrees since sundown. There was a lovely cool breeze coming from the river.

Frank was turning the balcony into a landscaped terrace. I'd never really made use of the space in all the years I'd lived here. The lack of a roof for shade made it too hot and bright out there for humans from late April till almost October. Since I can kill a cactus, I'd never bothered with plants. Frank had a surprising green thumb. He started using all this new free time he had now to convert the balcony into a lush garden. I liked all the ferns and plants. He'd mounted long boxes for geraniums on the outside of the railing, brought out cushions for the wicker chairs, and even had electric fans in the opposing corners to create a breeze.

Cooper Construction's plan for converting the building into a single residence included putting up a roof on this third-floor balcony, which would accommodate ceiling fans. Having a functional balcony all year round was something I'd never considered before, but now? I liked the idea.

A lot.

But we needed the Vieux Carré Commission's permission for that since it altered the appearance of the building.

It would be easier just to leave it as it was, but now that I'd had the idea, I couldn't let it go.

I slid my phone into my shorts pocket, then carried my glass and the still lit joint out onto the balcony. I looked down to the corner where Frenchmen Street branched off Decatur into the Marigny. The fire station was lit up, and I could hear the subdued roar of music and a crowd.

I took another hit and held it as long as I could.

I exhaled and almost coughed when I heard something from below.

It almost sounded...It *almost* sounded like the gate being closed gently so it wouldn't make a sound, didn't it?

You're just being paranoid, I told myself. It's the weed.

But it wouldn't hurt to be sure, would it?

Maybe it's Colin—no one else has a gate key.

Not likely. I'd given up on him coming back home.

I laughed ruefully. Since Christmas, Frank and I talked a big game whenever the subject of Colin came up. Despite all the tough talk, I knew we'd just be so glad he was alive and home safe and sound we'd forget all about the serious conversation we'd planned to have with him.

Tough talk was easy. Backing it up was something else entirely.

What if Taylor had come home first that night? Or had been with me?

I closed my eyes. That was what we both had to remember: Colin had lied to me about how Bestuzhev had gotten into the apartment.

There was also a pattern of him lying to us for what he claimed was our own good. Sure, he was involved in things he couldn't share with us—that was the nature of his job. When he'd first lied to us that last Carnival before Katrina, he'd disappeared for nearly three years, leaving us to believe the worst of him. When he came back, he'd been able to explain everything away. Had we been willing to believe anything he said because we loved him so much? Because we *wanted* to believe him, wanted him back in our lives, and it was easier to just believe him and not ask questions?

Just because he'd lied about how Bestuzhev wound up dead in our living room didn't mean another assassin or bad guy with an axe to grind with either Colin or Blackledge wouldn't turn up on our doorstep, armed to the teeth and out for blood.

And the next time it could be Taylor who came home first.

That was why we'd turned the house into as much of a fortress as we could with a building in the French Quarter. The door in the shed leading to the parking lot around the corner was now solid steel. We had cameras on both of those doors, another camera facing down into the courtyard from the roof, and there were cameras on both balconies on the Decatur Street side. Since the coffee shop had closed, the first floor's windows had been boarded up completely, and we'd had a metal gate placed in front of that door.

That door was padlocked.

Of course, someone could still break into one of the other buildings on the block and come over the roofs. It's happened before. There was no way to make the house completely secure. If we wanted that, we'd have to move.

I didn't like living like this, but I didn't want to move, either.

And breaking up with Colin wouldn't get us out of danger. It's not like we could email out a newsletter to some vast network of cutthroats, pirates, spies, and assassins on the dark web letting them know *Leave us alone—we've ended things with Colin.*

I laughed to myself.

Since that was the case, we might as well try to work things out with him, right?

I mean, the sex really was fantastic.

But we also had to take Taylor and his safety into consideration.

I sighed. All this worrying, all those conversations—all of it could be for nothing. For all we knew, Colin could be dead in a shallow, unmarked grave somewhere.

What was that?

It wasn't my imagination.

I'd definitely heard something that time, and the noise came from the back of the house.

The courtyard—or the stairs.

I *hadn't* been wrong about the front gate softly closing.

I stubbed out the joint in the ashtray and stepped back in through the window, leaving it open, not risking closing it in case it made noise. If someone had broken in, best to let them think the house slept in silence.

I left the lights off, feeling my way to the hallway. You'd think once you'd lived somewhere for over twenty years, you'd be able to navigate your way through it blindfolded, but I stubbed my toe on the sofa anyway. I swore, gritting my teeth. Why does that always hurt so much? I wondered, reaching my hands out to find the wall, and hoping there wasn't anything else on the floor that wasn't supposed to be there.

I was nervous. It should be incredibly difficult for anyone to break in.

Anyone who beat our security was dangerous.

My heart pounding in my ears, I opened the back door in the darkness and peered out into a clear May night. It was very dark back there. I shifted the gun in my hand. Should I turn on the flashlight app on my phone? Maybe it would be okay. The massive swarms were over for the night. There might be some stray termites out there, but why take the chance the light would attract one and he'd let his buddies know?

I'd be happy to go the rest of my life not cleaning up piles of termite wings again.

I took a deep breath and grabbed the railing. I steeled myself to look over the railing, but before I could I heard a thud from below. Someone muffled a curse in a voice I knew…

It can't be, can it?

I felt chills go through my body and my heart start racing as hope and adrenaline raced through my veins.

"Colin?" I cautiously called down the darkness of the stairwell, keeping my voice low. "Is that you?"

I hated that hopeful tone in my voice.

Well, better him than some assassin or spy.

"Scotty, can you *please* turn on a fucking light?" he replied. "I can't be held responsible for what happens if I trip again."

I gripped the railing so hard I thought it might break off in my bare hands. "It's termite season, dumbass," I replied as my hands started shaking. I opened the flashlight app and beamed the light over the railing.

He shielded his eyes as he looked up.

He was just as gorgeous as I remembered. The lower part of his face was covered in bluish stubble, and his thick curls had grown out quite a bit—the last time I saw him, his hair had been buzzed short. There was some more gray in the curls than I remembered, and he looked tired, but *He's alive* danced through my head, and I tightened my grip on the railing. I started gasping in breaths but stopped and inhaled deeply. I wanted to start dancing.

He's alive he's alive oh thank you Goddess he's alive.

I was relieved and happy, but…

For nearly six months, I'd been going back and forth on how I would react should Colin return to us. I swung between anger and worry and concern and back again.

Of course, every time he left there'd been the chance we'd never see him again.

It had always been rough, being involved romantically with— You know, I'm not even sure how to properly describe what he does. There was a part of me that was afraid to know. So Frank and I and everyone in the family got used to sometimes going months without hearing a word from Colin. He'd come to New Orleans to be with us between assignments. Those were marvelous times. Sometimes we'd travel to see Frank wrestle, sometimes we'd just be tourists in our own city, but every night the three of us would fall into bed together.

Have I mentioned how wonderful the sex is?

But the inevitable call would always come. He'd pack and be gone within a few hours every time, leaving us behind to worry.

I've never gotten used to it. I'd never get used to him not being able to tell us the truth about things.

And the last time I saw him, I helped him load a dead body into my car so he could dump it out in New Orleans East. There was a bayou out there that emptied into the Rigolets, the narrow watery passage connecting Lake Pontchartrain to Lake Borgne. When I tried to reach him later, his phone no longer worked. Trying to reach him through Blackledge was also fruitless because the only number I had was no longer in service. I'd gotten a text message right around Christmas from an unknown number that just said *Miss you coming home soon.*

I'd assumed that had been from him.

But as days, weeks, and finally months passed without another word from him, I'd begun to believe that the text had been a wrong number.

The story he told me that last night had also turned out to be all lies.

That body I helped him get rid of before Christmas? Colin had told me that he was part of the Russian mob and somehow Blackledge security had gotten breached, exposing Frank and me and our address, putting us in danger. He'd rushed back to New Orleans to make sure we were safe. Instead, he'd found Bestuzhev in our apartment, waiting with a gun. They fought and Bestuzhev was killed. Colin told me Bestuzhev had come to New Orleans to use Frank and me as leverage against Colin and Blackledge—but it wasn't true. The security camera on our front gate recorded the two of them arriving together.

He'd lied to me.

Again.

After things had settled down at Christmas, Frank and I had a frank conversation about what to do about Colin. With Taylor living with us now—what if that Russian killer had come home when Taylor was here? If Taylor had come home before I did? Were we putting Taylor at risk by allowing Colin to be a part of our life?

Of course, the night Colin killed the Russian was also the same night Taylor was drugged and maybe assaulted. I couldn't be happy that Taylor hadn't come home instead of going to the Brass Rail after that party at the Royal Aquitaine Hotel.

We'd gone back and forth for hours. We had finally decided that what was best for Taylor and for us was to break things off with Colin if he should ever return.

But now he was coming up the stairs safe and in one piece, and all I could think was how happy and relieved I was that he was alive, that he'd made it home to us again, and—

He swept me up into a massive bear hug, lifting me up off my feet into the air, which isn't easy, since he's a little shorter than I am. He also outweighs me by about forty pounds of solid thick hard muscle. Just feeling his massive chest pressing against mine, I could feel myself starting to get turned on...

But damn, I was glad he was alive! I was glad to see him!

I couldn't help myself. I choked up a little bit and put my head down on his shoulder so he wouldn't see my tears.

"Hey, hey, what's this?" he whispered. "No crying."

I wiped at my eyes with my hand as my feet came back to rest on the wooden landing. "I—"

"Is Frank home?" He took my hand in his and pulled me to the apartment door.

"I—"

But I was too late to stop him, he was already bouncing on his toes down the hallway calling Frank's name.

Oh no, I thought as I hurried after him in the darkness. Frank had been furious when I told him about what I'd walked in to that night. Frank was the one who made me think about what might have happened had Taylor come home first. Frank had taken even longer to forgive Colin for the *last* time he'd lied to us about anything.

Although to be fair, Frank *had* been kidnapped by operatives working with Colin—he just hadn't known it was meant to keep him safe from another murderous gang of Russians.

People don't take kindly to being kidnapped and held against their will, even if it's for their own good. Trust me, I know from personal experience.

But when I reached the bedroom, Colin was in Frank's arms,

and they were holding on to each other for dear life. I cleared my throat, and they made room for me in a big group hug.

"I'm so glad to be home," Colin said, nuzzling my ear while Frank started kissing my throat. "You boys have no idea how much I've missed you."

"Well, you could always show us," Frank replied with a lusty leer. "We've wasted enough time already."

Colin swept Frank up into his arms and kissed me on the cheek again. "And we're still wasting time, aren't we?" he whispered. "So come on, already."

I followed him as he carried Frank back to the bed.

CHAPTER THREE
ACE OF SWORDS, REVERSED
Beware of using too much power to achieve an end

Tree frogs were croaking and cicadas humming. The moon was behind a cloud, so everything around was bathed in an eerie bluish-silver light. The air was thick and heavy with wetness. Somewhere nearby there was a splash—either a fish jumping or something falling into the water. As my eyes grew accustomed to the strange darkness, I began making out shapes—trees with Spanish moss dripping from the branches, things floating in the eerie black water, logs or alligators. I was sweating, my nostrils clenched from the stench of damp and wet rot. I was sitting in the front of a pirogue, gliding silently through the still water. I didn't know where I was, even after the clouds moved and the bright glare of the full moon was exposed. I could see better now that the silvery light had brightened, and I could see I was passing through a swamp. For a moment I panicked, remembering that every time I'd ever been in a swamp I'd been in danger. But the panic died down as quickly as it had arisen when I realized I'd never been in this place before; nothing was familiar to my eyes. I tried to turn back to see who was poling the pirogue down this bayou through the swamp but found that I couldn't.

"There is no need to see behind," an ethereal female voice breathed into my ears. "Always look forward, for there is nothing to be gained by looking back."

We passed beneath a canopy of massive live oak limbs covered with green moss and with the curls of gray Spanish moss dangling just above us. I waved my arms at a cloud of gnats as we entered an enormous open space, a lake in the middle of the swamp ringed with live oaks and cypress trees, towering high above into the night sky. And on the other side of the clearing—the words Blind Lake *inserted themselves somehow into my brain—I could see a large paddle wheel steamboat, listing to one side*

*and shoved up against a shallow embankment on the far side. On the side
I could read the words* River Princess. *It was blindingly white, almost
glowing in the moonlight, but as the pirogue glided across the glass-like
surface of the hidden lake and the River Princess grew larger as we came
closer, I could see the damage to the boat. The silver-blue moonlight that
made the white paint glow also covered up a multitude of things needing
repair. The railings along the decks were battered and missing in places. I
could smell wood rotting, the horrific stench of death and decay. The boat
was dead. One of its smokestacks was bent and leaning at an impossible
angle.*

*As we continued to drift, the steamboat began to glow brightly, first
white, then yellow, and then red, as though the ship were aflame. I could
hear the crackle of fire and smell the smoke, but I could also smell...
bacon...*

Bacon?

Everything began fading into a swirling black and gray fog.

I pushed myself through the fog and opened my eyes, blinking
at the ceiling for a moment as I recognized it had been a dream—
real as it had seemed—and I let go of the tension the dream had left
as knots in my back and shoulders. I closed my eyes and breathed
deeply, in and out, centering myself.

Feeling better, I sat up in the bed and opened my eyes again.
The blinds were open, letting in some incredibly bright and warm
daylight. I was alone in the bed. Scooter, curled up on Frank's pillow,
opened an eye before shutting it again. He moaned and groaned,
stretched out a bit, then curled up again.

I yawned and stretched. I took another deep inhale of the smell
of frying bacon, and my stomach growled.

Colin came home last night, I remembered, a grin tugging at
the corners of my mouth.

All these years later, and the sex was still amazing.

Amazing.

I slid out of the bed and stripped the blankets, then tossed them
into a pile in the corner. I started to strip the sheets but hesitated,
not wanting to disturb Scooter. I can do the sheets later, I decided,
pulling on a pair of sweatpants. Grabbing a tank top out of a dresser
drawer, I walked into the bathroom and brushed my teeth. As I
washed my face, an image of Colin the last time I'd seen him flashed
through my mind.

It had been cold and damp that night as I'd hurried home from the party at the Royal Aquitaine Hotel. I had an umbrella, but the rain had stopped. A cold gray mist had hung in the air that night. I remembered thinking as I walked quickly through the lower Quarter that it was the kind of night that made it easy to believe in ghosts. I'd come up the back stairs, burst into our apartment, a little surprised we'd left the lights on—

And then I walked down the hall to the living room to find him standing there, panting. His shirt was torn, torso bloodied, face bruised and swelling in places.

He was standing over a dead body, a pool of blood spreading across my hardwood floors.

And he'd lied to me. Maybe it was for my own good, but he still lied to me again.

I sighed. We'd both been so swept up in the excitement of seeing Colin safe and in one piece that we hadn't talked. About anything.

And now that he was home, all those questions and doubts seemed unnecessary.

But…we couldn't just let this go.

He'd still killed someone in our *home*, making me an accessory to murder—and if that wasn't bad enough, he'd lied to me about what had happened and how and why.

I could hear my brother Storm the lawyer saying *There's no statute of limitations on murder.*

So, yes, I was happy Colin was alive and back home safe and sound, but I still felt like we needed to have a serious talk about the future.

He disappeared without a word other than a cryptic text message on Christmas—which said he was on his way home.

He hadn't said it would take almost six months. He must have made a wrong turn at Albuquerque.

He couldn't have found a spare second in all that time to call, text, email?

Every day that passed since getting that text, I had to wonder if he couldn't come home because he was in an unmarked grave somewhere.

That first month or so after Christmas had been rough. Taylor was still withdrawn from everything he'd been through, and every time someone rang our buzzer I got a jolt of adrenaline-driven terror that it was the cops.

Frank reassured me numerous times that the case had no doubt gone cold and wasn't a priority for the NOPD anymore. "Besides, it's not like the cops don't have plenty on their plates already," he'd gone on to say, "and you did sell the car."

And that made me feel even guiltier. Not only an accessory after the fact, but an argument could be made that I was a coconspirator. There could have been evidence in the trunk tying Bestuzhev to us. So, I'd hindered a police investigation *and* destroyed evidence.

But I couldn't drive that car again, knowing it had been used to move a dead body. I'd traded it in when we bought the new one.

Whoever wound up buying it from the dealership had no idea the car was used in the commission of a crime.

I did feel guilty about that, too.

I rubbed my eyes. *You were never meant to have a normal life like everyone else, remember? Just keep rolling with it. Life doesn't give you anything you can't handle—it's how you handle it that matters.*

My phone vibrated on the nightstand. I touched the screen to bring it to life.

There was a new text from David. *Still cool to come by with Brody at four?* I looked at the time on the screen. 10:17.

I sent a thumbs-up emoji and put my phone back down.

I'd forgotten about Brody in the excitement about Colin coming home.

My good old cousin, Jefferson Davis Haver the fucking Fourth.

Of all the teenagers in the state of Louisiana for older men to perv on, my stupid cousin the asshole had to pick one of my friends' students.

Family in Louisiana can be extremely complicated.

I think it's a Southern thing, really.

Just who did they think they were? A Diderot not good enough to marry a Bradley?

Neither Papa nor Maman Diderot had ever liked Deuce much. I didn't remember Deuce—he'd died years before Charlotte—but Mom loathed him because he'd allowed a petrochemical plant to be built on the west bank of the river in St. Jeanne d'Arc Parish.

"Like we needed another major polluter in Cancer Alley," she still groused, all these years later. Cancer Alley was what people called the stretch of river between New Orleans and Baton Rouge. It was lined with petrochemical plants, one after another, and Louisiana wasn't really known for its commitment to protecting the environment. The plants were always built near poor communities—usually Black—and the overall health of those communities has been deteriorating ever since. Every so often someone trying to make a name for themselves will try to bring attention to the growing instances of cancer in those communities. People grumble, there are protests, and then nothing happens.

Nobody with political power in Louisiana cares about those poor Black communities. Our politicians have always only cared about money and power. The EPA might as well not exist for all the good it did Louisiana. The coastline was eroding away at the rate of a football field per hour, and nothing was being done.

Mom said nothing would be done until the Gulf was lapping at the city limits.

I thought that was a pretty optimistic outlook.

"How much money do you make off that plant?" I remembered hearing Mom sneer at JD's father, Trey, once at a family gathering when I was young. "Was selling your soul worth it?"

Yeah, Mom and Dad hated the Havers and everything they stood for.

The fact they'd turned *Jefferson Davis* into a family name for their eldest sons for four generations running was bad enough. At least JD ended that tradition.

I'll take progress where we can get it, you know?

The thing that bothered Mom and Dad the most about our Haver relatives was they didn't stand for anything other than their own power. They were also willing to do whatever was necessary to keep and maintain that power. The parish had been staunchly Democratic after the Civil War until the Civil Rights Act turned it a ruby red area. JD was all about family values, putting prayer back into school, and demonizing queer and Black people. You know the act—we've seen it a million times before.

And like so many others like him, dear old JD was apparently a closet case who liked young boys.

If I had a dollar for every homophobic right-winger who turned out to be light in his loafers, I wouldn't need my trust funds anymore.

As far as I was concerned, JD could and should be exposed for his hypocrisy and ruined. There's nothing I hate more than a hypocrite.

But there was the kid to consider.

He hadn't done anything wrong. Even if he'd encouraged JD, the kid—Brody—was the victim here. Exposing JD might mean exposing the kid, and was that fair?

How far were the Havers—JD—willing to go to hold on to their power?

I knew of at least one death they'd covered up, that girl who'd died when Beau was driving drunk. How many more were there I didn't know about?

JD wouldn't go down easily.

We had to be careful.

It hadn't been easy keeping Taylor's name out of the murder investigation last December. Taylor hadn't seen or heard anything—he'd been drugged and unconscious in the bedroom of the hotel suite when the murder had happened. I know Papa Diderot pulled a lot of strings to keep Taylor's name out of the media. The killer had confessed, after all, so there wasn't a trial. Our primary concern had been journalists trying to get a story.

Brody Shepherd was even younger than Taylor. He was a kid. He didn't need this kind of thing following him around for the rest of his life.

I shook my head. Why do people keep nude photos on their phones?

I mean, I get why you take them. Frank and I were always taking sexy pictures of each other. We sometimes yielded to the loneliness when he was out of town and did the whole video thing with each other. But I always downloaded all that to a backup hard drive on our main home computer system, the files password-protected in case Tyler found them, then wiped it off my phone. Colin had all kinds of sophisticated software loaded into our systems to keep them safe from hackers, but why take chances by leaving that stuff on your phone or in your cloud or whatever virtual storage you used?

How many celebrity nudes need to get hacked from people's phones before people learn not to leave that kind of shit on their portable devices?

The last time I'd seen JD had been his grandmother's funeral, so he'd been, what, in his late twenties, early thirties? He was good-looking enough, with thick reddish-blond hair and that pale porcelainlike white skin. He'd played football for his local Catholic school—St. Thomas Aquinas—and he'd looked then like he'd kept himself in shape since high school. His wife Karen had been attached to him like a barnacle the entire time. She was pretty—she'd been a sorority queen at LSU, and I think maybe had done pageants? I'd found her cold and a little dull, always deferring to JD on everything. She was the kind of woman Mom despised. "Doesn't she have a brain of her own?" Mom had said as we drove back to New Orleans afterward.

I'd never gotten any ping of gaydar from JD, but gaydar wasn't an exact science. He'd never said anything homophobic to me, but his parents had always kept me at arm's length once they knew. Maybe he'd buried his desire for men so deeply because of his parents that it didn't trip my gaydar?

I shuddered at the thought of having JD's parents.

We wouldn't have a relationship, I thought as I walked down the hallway toward the kitchen and the marvelous bacon smell.

Colin was in the kitchen, making breakfast. All he was wearing was an apron tied around his waist. Frank was sitting at the desk in the living room, wearing his reading glasses and frowning at the computer screen. All he wore was a pair of gray sweatpants cut off very high on the thigh.

I swatted Colin's bare bottom as I moved past him to the Keurig, yawning as I put another K-Cup into it. I hit the brew button and slid a mug into place. "Taylor could walk in at any moment, you know, and there you are, at the stove bare-assed." It was, as I was happy to note again, a very *nice* bare ass. Firm, round, and hard to the touch.

"Taylor already left for school, so I knew the coast was clear." Colin smiled at me, using tongs to flip the bacon. "You were dead to the world when he went down the steps." Toast popped up. He grabbed it and started buttering the browned slices.

I added creamer and sweetener to my coffee and took a sip. It was perfect. I nodded at Frank. "What's Hot Daddy doing?"

"Checking email," Colin replied, sprinkling shredded cheese onto the eggs he was scrambling in my cast-iron skillet. He gave them another stir before setting the wooden spoon down and putting his arms around me, pulling me in tight. I lightly kissed his forehead as he rested the side of his face against my chest. "It's so good to be back home," he whispered. "I've missed you both so much."

His arms were so strong, and I felt myself melting into the embrace. He smelled slightly musky from the night's activities. "We need to talk," I said into his warm, firm neck. I felt guilty. I gently extricated myself from the hug. "All three of us."

He nodded. "I know." He started spooning food onto plates. "I owe you both an explanation, and I am so sorry it took me so long to get back here after I texted at Christmas, but first, I have some news I wanted to share with you both. Bring Frank his plate and we can talk while we eat."

As soon as we had all sat down at the dining room table, Colin cleared his throat. "Okay, well, first, I need to tell you that I've left Blackledge. This last case I did for them was my last. Angela knows, she understands, and we've got that all worked out. I'm officially retired now." He shrugged his muscular shoulders, smiling at us both. "I loved my work, but I'm also getting older, starting to slow down a bit—and when your reflexes aren't quite as lightning-like as they used to be, well, that's how you end up dead." He shook his head, and once again, I noticed gray strands in the short blue-black curls. "Not to mention how much I miss you both when I'm gone. I hate being away from you guys, and I don't want to do that anymore." He shook his head. "I should have quit long ago."

"You should have quit the first time you had to lie to us." Frank didn't look up from his plate.

Colin looked back and forth between our faces. His eyebrows came together as his smile faded slowly. "I—I thought this would be good news. You both...you're not as happy about this as I thought—*hoped*—you would be." His voice cracked on the last few words.

"Of course we're happy," I answered before Frank could say anything. I didn't trust his temper. I reached over and put my hand on top of Colin's. "Colin, you have no idea how happy we both are to hear that." I looked over at Frank, who was still focused on eating. "But...you lied to us." The *again* was implied by my tone.

Colin nodded. "I lied to you about Bestuzhev last winter. He wasn't already inside the house when I got here." He took a deep breath. "I'm sorry I lied to you both, but it was easier to lie than to try to explain when I had to get rid of the body and get back out of the country before he was found." He went on, "Bestuzhev—I didn't lie about Blackledge security being breached. I can't reveal a lot, or even what the case was about, but he worked for a Russian oligarch with strong ties to the Russian government, and we were working to block something the Russians were trying to do." He gave us a feeble smile. "We succeeded, but only temporarily. You'll know what they were up to because—well, because it'll eventually be in the news."

"So why—"

"We'd intercepted a message from Bestuzhev's controller to him. They knew Blackledge was working to stop them, and they knew I was controlling the operation. They'd hacked into Blackledge's server—that issue has been corrected, I might add—and so my own cover here in New Orleans was blown. Bestuzhev was coming here to kill you all, including Taylor." He covered his face with his hands. "We managed to get a tail on him almost immediately, and I took Blackledge's private jet here so I could get to New Orleans first. I tailed him from the airport and caught him by surprise outside on the street. He was on his way here. I held my gun on him and brought him inside." He took another deep breath. "And yes, I interrogated him first, to try to get as much information out of him as I could. But he managed to get loose somehow, we struggled, and I had no choice but to shoot him." He bowed his head. "And then you came home, Scotty. I was terrified the entire time I was here with Bestuzhev that you might come home, which was kind of why I was so sloppy—and how he got loose—and I had to get back to Europe with the intel I'd gotten from him before killing him. I'm sorry I lied, but I didn't have a choice. If I'd only had more time, but"—he glanced back up at me, over to Frank, and back again—"this whole situation is why I decided I had to get out. I can't stand the thought of the two of you in danger—"

"We're not in danger anymore?" Finally, Frank said something. I shot him a dirty look he pretended not to see.

"We think we were able to scrub everything out of their system about my life here in New Orleans," he replied grimly. "We have someone on the inside—the Russians, I mean. They were able to redact things in my physical file and deleted all mention of me from their electronic records, but yes, there's always a chance." He sighed. "I don't blame you if you want me to go—I know I shouldn't have lied, I know it's not the first time I wasn't completely honest with you both, but I swear it's the last time."

"It's the danger, Colin," I said. "It was different when it was just me and Frank at risk. But with Taylor living here now—"

"Angela has promised to continue monitoring them for us," Colin said.

"The damage is already done," Frank said before I had a chance to say anything. "If there's a risk, it doesn't matter anymore whether you're still involved with us or not. If your enemies, or Blackledge's, can find out about us, it won't matter to them, will it, if we break up with you?"

"It's unlikely. The Ninjas are also keeping their ears open." The Ninja Lesbians were Rhoda and Lindy, Mossad agents Colin had trained when he worked for the Israeli government. We'd worked with them any number of times over the years and considered them friends. "And I'd feel better, anyway, knowing I'm here to protect the two of you—and Taylor—from any threat." He looked back and forth between our faces. "I just want to be Colin Cioni from now on and live out my life with you both. But if that's not what you want—"

"Colin…" I gestured feebly. "We love you, you know that. You know we both have always wanted you here with us full-time rather than just between jobs or when you can take some time off. But you've lied to us before. How can we believe what you're telling us now?"

"Fair." He licked his lips. "But can I at least have a chance to regain your trust?"

Frank and I looked at each other. Frank nodded slightly, the big softie.

He always *talks* tough.

But he has a gooey caramel center.

"Of course," I replied, expelling my breath, hoping we wouldn't live to regret it. "I bet Taylor was happy to see you."

"He looks great," Colin replied. "He's been working out?"

"All things considered, he's doing okay," Frank added. He cleared his throat. "Some things have happened since we saw you last." Frank told him the story of our remake of *It Happened One Christmas*—the movie you won't be seeing on the Hallmark Channel when the season rolls around again.

I watched Colin's face cycle through shock, horror, outrage, and anger. He looked at me. "And this all happened the same night I killed Bestuzhev?" His voice sounded husky and strange.

I nodded. "Taylor texted me in the morning." *Three or four hours after you left with the body.*

He wiped at his eyes. "I...I don't know what to say. He's okay now?"

"He's processing everything still. He seems okay, but he has bad times now and then," I replied. "The working out is part of it, we think. We think he'll feel safer if he's stronger. But he seems to be doing okay."

"I'm so sorry I wasn't here." Colin's voice broke. "I've missed so much over the years."

"Yes, well," I said, scratching my head. Were we just rationalizing because we loved him and wanted him here with us?

No, a voice said in my head, *you love him and when you love someone, you trust them. You love him, so you trust him. You trust him that when he says he had to lie to you for your own good, you have to believe him.*

"No more lies?" I asked, looking over at Frank.

"No more lies," Colin replied, smiling at us both.

"Then the subject is closed." Frank clapped his hands together. I felt a knot of tension between my shoulder blades relax.

Well, that went better than I thought it would.

I changed the subject. "Did Frank tell you about David's student?"

He looked over at Frank, frowning. "No?"

I filled him in on what was going on with David's student Brody.

Colin frowned when I finished. "I'm not sure I'm following what David wants us to do. Look into the hit-and-run? But if they closed the case..."

"That doesn't mean anything in St. Jeanne d'Arc Parish," I replied. "You know all those old movies about rural Southern places with corrupt sheriffs and governments, where they make their own laws? That's St. Jeanne d'Arc Parish. I don't know that there's anything we can do," I replied. "But he's going to bring Brody over this afternoon so we can talk to him, get a better idea of what's going on." I added some sweetener to my coffee. "I mean, maybe someone hacked his phone, but I don't know. I can't see anyone hacking into a dance student at NOCCA's phone. The parish president's phone? One who is being sued by hurricane victims for stealing their insurance settlements?" I scoffed. "I'm sure if we start digging, we'll find that JD is up to his elbows in all kinds of crimes and corruption." I slapped my hands together twice and stood up.

"Christ." Colin rubbed his eyes. He pushed his chair back and stood, stretching. His apron came untied, and he grabbed for the strings as the apron swung out, flashing me. "I've really missed a lot being gone all the time. Poor Taylor."

"You're not the only one," Frank replied, his eyes drinking in Colin's thick muscles. "How do you think *I* felt? I'm his uncle."

"Stop it, both of you." I held up both hands. "It's okay, Colin— Frank and I have already been through the whole gauntlet from blame to denial to, well, you name it. If we've learned anything from our years together"—I grinned at him—"it's that we can't control the universe any more than we can control the weather. Should I have gone with them to the Brass Rail that night? Should I have asked him to walk home with me instead? Even with my gift, such as it is, I can't see the future any more than anyone else can."

"Well"—he folded his arms, and the veins in his shoulders bulged—"that may be, but I'm going to be around a lot more now." He looked from me to Frank. "Hearing all this makes me even more sure I made the right choice about retiring." He rested his forearms on the back of his chair.

"How did Angela take it?"

"She wasn't thrilled to lose me, but she understands. It was just a matter of time." He scratched his head. "Like I said, I'm not getting any younger, and I'm...I'm not as quick on the draw as I used to be. I hate admitting that—"

"We're all getting older, Colin," Frank pointed out.

"Yeah, yeah, but in my line of work even slowing up a second can make the difference between life and death." His voice was grim. "This last mission? There were a couple of times where I got lucky—and if I hadn't, I wouldn't be here right now." He sighed. "I miss you guys. I miss being in your lives. I don't want to be someone just using this place as a home base and gone for months at a time. I want to have a life."

I tried not to let my delight show on my face. No more worrying and wondering when we'd hear from him again? Maybe no more fears about Russian spies breaking in? And even better, no need to ask him to choose between us and Blackledge? That long conversation Frank and I had been planning and dreading to have was no longer necessary.

Frank got up and pulled Colin into a big hug, and I joined them.

And yes, we wound up back in the bedroom.

Have I ever mentioned how great the sex is?

We spent the rest of the morning and well into the afternoon in bed, until I realized it was getting late. David would be bringing Brody by soon. Colin went upstairs to shower, while Frank and I took turns downstairs.

"We're really going to have to move him downstairs," I said, rubbing a towel over my head while Frank pulled on a pair of shorts. "Taylor should have his own place, and if Colin isn't going to be gone anymore..." I sighed. My heart sank at the idea of having to have the plans redrawn another time. "We're going to have to ask them to redraw the renovation plans. Maybe...maybe we could turn the two bedrooms on the second floor into one big suite? And then Taylor can have this floor. And we can just use his old place for storage or something."

"I'll call Cooper Construction tomorrow," Frank said, reaching over to massage my shoulders as the doorbell chimed. "And we want a gym on the first floor."

"I'll buzz them in." I pulled on my sweatpants. "Finish getting dressed."

CHAPTER FOUR
PAGE OF CUPS
A handsome young man with dark hair and light eyes

I don't know what I was expecting, but the seventeen-year-old David escorted up our back staircase that afternoon wasn't it.

I was pulling on a T-shirt and hoping I didn't smell too much like I'd been having the most amazing sex all afternoon as I opened the door and stepped out onto the back landing. It was a warm day, about eighty degrees or so, and the sky was pure blue without even the slightest hint of a cloud anywhere. I heard the front gate slam shut with a clang, and a few moments later I heard footsteps coming up the staircase.

Cooper Construction had recommended finishing closing in the stairs. I liked the idea. The stairs themselves were already enclosed by a wall. The landings were open to the elements on the outside. But with the landings open to the air like that, the resultant lack of climate control on the stairs had always been a pet peeve of mine. I'd sweat to death in the summer going down to the second floor to do the laundry. I had to put on layers in the winter when it was cold. The wall could be insulated and then covered with drywall to hide it. Instead of putting up more walls to enclose the landings, we were going with plates of unbreakable glass tinted to lock out harmful UV light. We would need another HVAC system for the stairs alone. I liked the idea of the glass—the other companies had wanted to wall the landings in, with smaller windows—because I loved the views.

I mean, I can see the spires of the cathedral from my landing.

I didn't want to lose that view.

I was lost in thought and leaning against the newel post when David and Brody reached the midfloor landing.

I got my first glimpse of Brody Shepherd about ten seconds

later when he looped around the newel post and put a foot up on the bottom step.

My jaw dropped.

I've never been good at guessing ages.

Everyone under thirty looked like a fresh-faced twink right out of high school to me now.

Taylor turned twenty-one just after Thanksgiving. Despite his towering over me—he says he's six feet four, but I think he's taller, he tends to slouch to make himself seem shorter—to me, he always looks like a kid just starting high school. He's gawky and gangly and all limbs and elbows and bone. Taylor's also a bit shy. Raised evangelical, he'd had a lot of nonsense about sexuality and sin engraved into his head. He's still adjusting to knowing that he isn't damned for all eternity for being gay. I mean, the church he was raised in thinks the Southern Baptists are too liberal, so what chance did he have, growing up in a small town in rural Alabama, surrounded by people who thought homosexuality was worse than murder?

There had always been something hesitant and tentative about Taylor. It had gotten worse since Christmas.

Who could blame him? What happened to him would wreck older, more put together people. So that was what I'd been thinking in terms of Brody—another wide-eyed, fresh-faced, gangly kid who looked barely old enough to shave, let alone be targeted by a predatory older man.

But Brody Shepherd was nothing like Taylor.

Good-looking wasn't enough of a description when it came to Brody. It wasn't enough. Brody was almost breathtakingly beautiful. He moved with fluid elegance, with the casual self-assurance of someone aware that most people stopped to take a better look at him. As I watched him coming up the last set of stairs, I couldn't help but wonder if this was how Zeus had felt when he first laid eyes on Ganymede.

Brody walked on the balls of his feet, with his right hand gracefully placed on the railing as he climbed the stairs. His skin was gorgeous, dewy and soft looking yet still masculine, a rich olive color that had turned dark golden brown where exposed to the sun. Framed with a messy mop of wild, thick, bluish-black curls, his face was angular: a strong chin with a dimple in the center, high cheekbones with hollows beneath, and a wide mouth with thick sensual red lips. There were creases in his cheeks from smiling. His eyes were the deep blue of the Gulf of Mexico where it's deep, a vibrant rich sapphire with gold flecks that sparkled and danced as our eyes met. His eyes were framed by long, curling lashes. He was about my height of five eight, maybe a little taller. He was wearing a tight white V-neck Calvin Klein T-shirt that looked painted onto his muscular, defined torso—the abs so defined I could see the bumps through the ribbed cotton. The sleeves tightly hugged his strong defined biceps, and the arms were road-mapped with thick bulging blue veins. His hands and fingers were long and graceful, like they were meant to pose and be carved in marble. He was wearing a pair of dark blue stretch jeans that clung to the beautifully shaped muscles of his legs like a second skin. His teeth were absurdly white, and he glided up onto the landing next to me.

And he had a magnetic charisma that drew your attention and made it hard to look away.

This kid was going to be a star someday.

He was standing close enough to me that I could smell his deodorant and feel the heat off his skin. "I'm Brody," he said in a deep, husky voice with an almost flirtatious lilt that caught me off guard. His breath smelled minty and fresh, like he'd just brushed his teeth.

I shook myself out of the trance. "Scotty." I held out my hand and he took it. His hand was warm and dry and calloused. He held my hand for maybe a second too long as his eyes met mine again.

He smiled, the dimples deepening into his cheeks. His eyes flicked up and down my body. I was wearing a black Saints T-shirt and a pair of sweatpants, and I could almost hear his thoughts as he appraised me.

Not bad for an old guy—bet he was superhot when he was young.

I felt about a thousand years old.

David came up behind him. "Hey boo," he said, giving me a hug. He was still wearing his teacher drag: button-down white and blue striped shirt, blue slacks, dark socks, and white and blue oxfords. David was a fraction shorter than me. His frame was smaller than mine, and his body had the high metabolism of a teenager—getting him to put on weight had been a challenge. In the years since, he'd maintained the muscle I'd helped him put on.

David was a handsome man, with thick white hair and pale skin that burned easily. His red hair had turned white before we'd met, back when he was still in his twenties. His blue-gray eyes twinkled like he was always up to mischief of some sort. He'd started growing a lengthy white beard for some reason. I thought it made him look like a Confederate general.

"How's Diego?" I asked, pressing my cheek to his gently and returning his hug.

"He's good, wants you boys to come over for dinner sometime soon." David squeezed me back, whispering in my ear at the same time, "Thank you for doing this."

"I have a surprise of my own," I whispered back. "Colin came home last night."

David did a double take. "What?"

"I'll call you later," I said, walking back over to the door. "Come on inside, guys, do you need anything? Water? Tea?" I stopped myself before saying *weed*.

Not in front of one of David's students!

I held the door open for them. I followed Brody down the hallway, marveling at how that stretch denim emphasized how perfectly shaped and rock hard his ass was from years of dance. He wasn't wearing a belt, so the waist of the jeans was riding down. The exposed skin of his lower back was smooth, tanned, and hairless. His waist was almost absurdly, unrealistically small. His shoulders were broad, and I could see the cords of muscle in the back of his neck.

Ballet will do that to a body.

He gracefully sat down into one of the wingback chairs and crossed his legs a little primly at the ankles, his toes overextended into a deep point, the feet arched, his calves flexed and hardened inside their sheath of denim.

Frank was sitting at the desk, beads of water glittering on his head. He smelled like soap, making me more aware of how musky I must smell.

"Nice to meet you," Frank said, not looking up from the screen. "I'm Frank Sobieski, and our other partner, Colin, will be down soon, he's taking a shower." He frowned at the computer screen.

Brody's body shifted in such an unmistakable *I so don't want to be here and I'm just humoring Mr. Andrews* way that it almost made me laugh out loud. Ah, teenage ennui, how I remember you! He clicked off his phone and slid it into the pocket of his jeans before turning his attention back to me. He let out a long-suffering sigh and folded his arms, his biceps peaking and the thick blue veins bulging larger. "I don't know, maybe coming here was a mistake." His handsome face twisted into a scowl. His thick black eyebrows met over the bridge of his nose. He shrugged, the muscles in his shoulders rippling. "I shouldn't have said anything to Mr. Andrews in the first place."

I recognized that look on his face and smothered a bit of a grin. Boy, did I recognize that mentality! He reminded me a lot of me at that age, but I don't think I was ever as ripped and defined as him even at my peak dancing-on-a-speaker-at-the-White-Party-in-Palm-Springs shape. Dance was an art that builds that kind of body—and ballet was the most difficult and most demanding of all the different disciplines. Ballerinos and ballerinas spent hours in rehearsal and practice, stretching and twisting their bodies into almost impossible shapes, defying gravity by leaping through the air at full extension and getting more height than a professional basketball player going in for a fast-break dunk.

Brody knew the kind of reaction his handsome face and god-of-the-dance body provoked. He was already so used to it he probably never noticed the way people went out of their way to please him. He was so used to getting what he wanted when he wanted it because he was so exquisitely beautiful that he took it for granted.

Pretty privilege. This kid will always have people serving him first, giving him better service, buying his drinks, and paying for his meals. He'll land a rich older man someday.

He already has, I reminded myself, *which is why he's here.*

He was still a kid, no matter how gorgeous he was.

You were picking up men at gay bars when you were his age, I reminded myself. *But I was different.*

Were you? A little voice whispered in the back of my head. *How exactly was it different for you? Did you really know what you were doing? Those men you picked up—or you let pick you up—had no idea you weren't legal. Hardly fair to them, was it?*

I pushed that thought out of my head.

"Now, Brody, I didn't make you do anything. You *asked* me for help," David said, taking a seat in the other wingback chair. "Has something changed since you came to my office yesterday?"

"No, but you didn't tell me there'd be so many people." Brody sniffed, a touch of teenage whine in his voice. He looked from me to Frank and back again.

"I can go upstairs if you'd prefer," Frank said, shooting a glance at me that I couldn't read.

"That would be *awesome*, would you mind?" Brody switched from sulky to excited in the blink of an eye. His smile grew bigger and wider, the wattage in his smile and eyes going up higher than I'd have thought possible.

Yes, he was someone used to getting his way.

"Sure," Frank replied, giving me another look, "I'll take these blueprints up and see if Colin has any thoughts." He slipped his phone in his pocket, picked up the tubes, and planted them under his arm.

Brody didn't speak again until the door shut behind Frank. He turned to me and said, "I hope you don't mind, but Mr. Andrews"—he hesitated, glanced at David, and then back at his hands again—"said you went through something similar when you were my age?"

"Your wrestling coach?" David prompted.

I froze.

What the actual fuck?

I hadn't thought about Coach Phelps in years.

And I couldn't believe *David* had told this kid about *Coach Phelps*.

I could feel my cheeks getting hot. David gave me an apologetic look.

David wouldn't share that without a good reason, I thought, but I still didn't like it.

"And like, even now, I don't care about what happens to JD," Brody went on, either not noticing my discomfort or just not caring. "I mean, I'm not stupid. I know it was stupid of me to send him those pictures and all, but…" He flushed beneath the tan, but the added color only made his skin look even more golden brown than before. "I still don't think that was wrong. Maybe not smart, but, you know, I'm a dancer." He gave me that brilliant smile again. "I'm going to dance onstage wearing a lot less than any bathing suit or underwear, so it's not a big deal." He frowned, his thick lower lip jutting out. "Buying me some nice things? Wanting me to take pictures wearing what he bought me?" A muscle twitched in his jaw. "And you know how people are. I don't care. It's my business and nobody else's." He gracefully waved a hand in the air to indicate how little he cared. "But I don't want to go *viral* for something like this."

I understood that. We'd worked our asses off making sure Taylor hadn't gone viral last Christmas.

"This would follow me for the rest of my fucking life, and no one would even pay attention to what a great dancer I am, all they would ever say is *Isn't he the one who got involved with that politician and ruined his life?* And it would always just be a goddamn Google search away from anyone who wanted to find out something about me, you know? What ballet company is going to hire someone that notorious?" His face twisted. "No thanks. The internet is forever, and I am not going to be known as that teenage fuckboy." His voice shook.

I glanced at David, who shook his head slightly. "David mentioned your friend," I said softly. "The one killed in the hit-and-run?"

Brody's lower lip trembled and his eyes got watery. "I can't believe JD had something to do with it," he said quietly. "He wouldn't do that."

You'd be surprised at what the Havers are capable of, Brody.

"Why don't you start at the beginning?" I heard myself asking. *Coach Phelps.*

I took a deep breath and pushed all that negative energy out of my brain. This wasn't about *my* past, but helping this kid.

Brody made a face, his thick lips pouting. "None of this would have happened if my mom hadn't made me get a job last summer."

It had been a punishment. He'd overspent on the credit card his mother had given him for dance supplies, and she'd blown her top. "My dad isn't in the picture and never has been—it's always just been me and my mom," he explained in an aside. "Mom decided I needed to get a job and pay the bill myself. You know, teach me a lesson." He'd wound up getting a job through a friend's sister at the food court at Lakeside Mall in Metairie on the weekends. "That was where I met Paris Soniat. He trained me." Brody had always known he was gay, but Paris was the first openly gay teenager he'd met. "I came out to him after a couple of weeks," Brody said shyly, looking down at his beautiful hands. "He was great, you know? He was out there, didn't care what anyone thought about him, and he was from a river parish." Brody rolled his eyes. "And I thought, you know, if he could be out and proud out there in the country, I certainly could be in New Orleans. So I started coming out to people." He beamed. "It was *amazing*. No one really cared—no one thought it was a big deal except some asshole boys at school." He rolled his eyes dramatically. "But I'm the best dancer at NOCCA, so who cares what those losers think?" He pulled out his phone and fiddled with it for a moment before passing it to me. "That's me and Paris."

I recognized the background of the food court at Lakeside Mall. I'm not much of a mall person, but that mall was the only place in the New Orleans area with an Apple Store. Two young men beamed happily at the camera, wearing the brown polyester blouse and slacks of one of the smaller fast-food chains. Brody looked gorgeous, even in that uniform beanie. His curls were too thick to be contained by the hat. Some errant locks were escaping out. The boy he was standing next to was slightly shorter, his hair bleached platinum blond with a bright blue streak on the left side, and his nose was pierced. He was making the duck lips face celebrities think makes them look sexy in selfies. His gray eyes sparkled, and his pale forehead was dotted with pimples.

"Cute," I said noncommittally as I passed him back the phone.

He slipped it back into his pants pocket. "I know, right?" He shook his head. "Paris was"—he looked up at the ceiling, trying to find the word—"special. There was no one else like Paris." He wiped at his eyes. "Sorry, I still miss him."

After he'd worked there about a month, an older man—"in his forties, at least"—stopped in at the mall. He'd specifically waited for Paris's register to come open, letting other people go in front of him when other cashiers freed up. "I noticed that, you know, because most people are dicks about waiting in line. And then later, when Paris had a chance, he went out and talked to the guy, and you know how you can tell when it's not just, you know, a casual talk?"

I nodded. I knew exactly what he meant.

"So, I asked him about it and he told me the guy was this lawyer back where he's from, Verdun. A big-time important rich lawyer, and he'd been seeing Paris for a couple of months behind his wife's back." He smiled. "I thought, you know, of course Paris is going out with a rich older man who buys him presents and treats him nice. Paris told me I needed to find someone like that."

I glanced over at David, whose lips were compressed into a tight line and whose face had reddened.

"Then, right after the Fourth of July, when I got to work my manager was really upset, called us all into the office." His voice broke again. "That's when we found out Paris had been killed." He took a deep breath, and I could tell he was barely holding it all together. "And then, a couple of weeks later, Paris's older guy came in…looking for me. He asked me if he could take me out to dinner after my shift, you know, so we could talk about Paris. He didn't have anyone he could mourn with, what with the wife and all."

And that was how it started.

Brody's voice shook. "And so, he started coming in every weekend, only now to see me. And he started buying me presents, wanting me to take pictures wearing the stuff, same as Paris. But he never touched me—I want to be clear about that."

I raised my eyebrows.

"I mean, I knew he wanted to get into my pants," Brody said in a matter-of-fact tone that let us know it wasn't the first time someone wanted in his pants, nor would it be the last. He sounded more resigned to it as his fate than arrogant. "But at least he was nice about it, you know? He was interested in me, not just…you know. He was respectful, you know?" He looked down as he blushed harder.

What you aren't saying, Brody, is that you liked the old man, too.

"And you didn't know who JD Haver was?" I asked. "You never looked him up online?" I thought everyone looked up everyone online nowadays, especially kids.

"I didn't know who he was, and I didn't care," Brody went on, shaking his head so the curls bounced, "He was just this, you know, older guy who was nice and took an interest in me. He never said anything weird, or creepy, or anything. I never felt unsafe or uncomfortable, and he let me know up front he respected me and wasn't going to take, you know, advantage of me." He smirked. "Like he could if I didn't want him to, you know?"

Ah, youth.

"So, he finally invited me out to dinner when I got off work one night, and I said sure, so we went to the Chili's just up Vets." He sighed. "And that's when he gave me the first underwear gift."

It was a bag from Macy's, with over a dozen pair of designer briefs in a variety of styles and colors.

I looked at David, who grimaced in an *Oh, it gets better* kind of way. "And you didn't think that was off in any way?"

He rolled his eyes. "Well, *obviously* he wanted to fuck me, Scotty, but I know what I'm doing. And why *not* send him selfies of me modeling the stuff he bought me?" He smiled again. "I look good in my underwear."

I'm sure you do.

This continued for the rest of the summer. JD would come have lunch at the food court, talk to him, meet him later for coffee or dinner, and give him another bag of presents. Always underwear of some type, but always expensive.

"Once school started, I was able to quit, and that kind of cooled things off for me and JD," Brody went on. "Sure, we still texted back and forth, and sometimes I'd send him a selfie, but it wasn't anything, you know? I'm too young to be tied down to anyone yet, you know? But I had it under control, and everything was fine. About a month ago I told him…I told him he shouldn't text me anymore."

"Brody—" David interrupted.

"All right, my mom made me stop seeing him." His face blushed even harder. "She looked at my phone." He sounded incredulous, like he still couldn't believe this egregious invasion of his privacy. "She threatened to take my phone away, and she grounded me anyway." He pouted against the injustice of it all. "But it was fine, you know. I was getting busy, and I'm going up to New York to audition for Juilliard in a couple of weeks, so it was, you know, *whatever.* She still shouldn't have looked at my phone, though."

I chose not to pursue that indignity. "How did JD take it?"

"He was disappointed, but he understood. He's not a monster." His curls bounced as he jerked his head in David's direction. "And I thought that was the last of it." He sighed again. "But then Monday morning someone sent me this." He pulled his phone out and pressed his thumb on the screen, bringing it all back to life. His fingers flew over the screen, and then he held it up.

It was a text message with an image attached, and the image was Brody in a pair of black Versace underwear, winking at the camera.

He really looked amazing.

I tore my eyes away from the picture and read the message. *Your friend Paris was murdered and they covered it all up.*

Brody used his index finger to scroll. "The number is blocked, somehow, or I can't see it." His eyebrows came together again over this nose. "I don't know what to do." For the first time since he arrived, he sounded like a kid.

A kid who's about to get in trouble for doing something he was warned not to do.

"Give me your phone." I held out my hand for it.

He hesitated for a moment, then passed it over to me. Colin's laptop sat on the dining room table. One of the good things about having a partner who worked for a company that did Special Ops was the technology access. Colin had showed me once how to clone a phone with his laptop with the SIM card. I sat down at the table, used a safety pin to extract the SIM card, and slid it into a slot in the side of the laptop. A program opened automatically. *Clone?* a pop-up box asked, and I clicked *yes*. It asked me to name the new folder, and I typed out BRODY'S PHONE. A progress bar popped up, and within a few moments the green bar went all the way across, and the screen flashed *Finished, would you like to make another copy?*

Instead, I pressed the little button next to the slot for the SIM card and it popped out. I slid it back into the phone and handed it back to Brody. "If there's any way to trace that phone, we'll be able to do it. I can't promise anything—"

"I hate to think what happened to Paris wasn't an accident." Brody shivered.

"We can look into that, too," I replied. "I'm sure it's just someone trying to get under your skin, but it's worrying that they have access to the pictures you sent JD. You're sure no one else could access them?"

"No, I don't think so." His face relaxed into a smile, and he somehow became even handsomer. "I mean, I don't know how I'm going to pay you—Mr. Andrews said maybe we could work something out?" One of his eyebrows went up. "I mean..." His tongue flicked over his lips briefly.

"Don't worry about payment, son," I replied, trying to channel Frank's sternest FBI Special Agent voice, emphasizing *son*. "We're just glad to be able to help out."

Brody looked disappointed. "Well, if you change your mind, I sometimes dance at the Brass Rail on Friday nights." He fluidly rose to his feet in one graceful, languid movement.

"Are you old enough—" I started.

"I have a fake ID." Brody rose to his full height and raised his chin, daring me to challenge him for having one.

"I had one when I was your age," I replied. "Come on, I'll walk you out."

David whispered, "Thank you," into my ear as I hugged him good-bye.

I watched them go down the stairs, and once I heard the gate clang shut, I texted Colin and Frank to come back down.

"Wow, I'm so glad Taylor didn't turn out like that kid." Frank shook his head as he walked back into the living room. "I kind of got the sense he would have been more than happy to—"

"Don't even say it out loud." I held up my hand. "He seems kind of mature for his age, I will give him that. I mean, I was sleeping with older men at his age, too—and I had a fake ID—but he just seems so young..." As I heard the words coming out of my mouth, I felt as old as Methuselah.

Frank gave me an odd look. "It doesn't matter how young or old he looks, Scotty. He's a minor." He ran his hand over his scalp. "I honestly don't know how I feel about this, to tell you the truth. I get what he's saying—who wants that to be the first thing that comes up when you're googled—but at the same time, I kind of don't like the idea that we're basically helping cover up for a pedophile." His frown got deeper. "And an antigay politician on top of that. If ever anyone needed to be exposed...If only there was some way we could do it without bringing Brody into it."

"I feel pretty confident that the three of us can figure out a way to do just that," Colin said as he walked back into the living room. He exhaled. "But that kid—he's going to have a lot of trouble in his life if he isn't careful. He's a good-looker, for sure."

"He's almost Taylor's age," Frank pointed out, that vein in his forehead popping out like it always does when he's starting to lose his temper. "It would be like having sex with Taylor."

I could tell by the look on Colin's face that thought horrified him as much as it did me.

Taylor was a kid—but this kid was even younger than Taylor.

Putting it into that context made my stomach turn.

I cleared my throat and changed the subject. "Do you think you'll be able to trace where those text messages came from?"

Colin smiled and started tapping keys on his laptop again.

"And I think tomorrow I'm going to drive out to St. Jeanne d'Arc Parish and have a chat with good ole cousin JD," I said grimly.

CHAPTER FIVE

SIX OF SWORDS

Journey over water

It was bright and sunny the next morning as Frank and I headed west on I-10.

We'd decided to split up. All three of us didn't need to head out to St. Jeanne d'Arc Parish, after all. Colin was better at the internet stuff than both Frank and me, so he was going to stay home and try to find out whatever he could about the number that sent Brody the text message. He was also going to dig into Paris Soniat's death.

Which meant he probably would be hacking into the parish government, but what we didn't know wouldn't hurt us.

Right?

We rode in silence, other than the Donna Summer playlist streaming through the car stereo. I was lost in my own thoughts, remembering past visits to Sunnymeade. It had been a long time. I'd googled JD myself before leaving the house. The most recent photograph of him had been in the parish paper a few weeks earlier. He'd given a press conference about the status of the parish's gambling boat. It had been damaged during Hurricane Isadora. The casino boat usually docked on the west bank of the river, not far from the petrochemical plant. But with the storm coming, the decision had been made to move the boat off the river and into the more protected waters of Bayou Maron. But Isadora's path had shifted, and she'd blown in right through St. Jeanne d'Arc Parish. The boat, docked in a hidden lake within the swamp, had been damaged in the storm and hadn't been moved since. The press conference was to announce that a new corporation had been formed and had bought out the previous corporation, and renovations would soon be underway again.

JD was smiling in the picture, but he wasn't aging well. He'd put on weight, his face was flushed the florid red color that comes with years of alcohol abuse, and his red hair was thinning on top. He combed it over, trying to hide it.

But the thing I couldn't get over was the boat's name was the *River Princess*, and the hidden lake? They called it Blind Lake, because you didn't know it was there until you were right on it.

Just like in the dream I'd woken up from yesterday.

Which meant the dream was likely a message from the Goddess.

And that meant they were both important.

Donna was wailing about dimming all the lights as we sped past the Loyola exit. "I kind of love that New Orleans is basically an island," Frank said as the highway started to rise as we reached the end of dry land. "You can't leave the city without crossing a bridge."

Just ahead of us the highway kept rising, up on pylons as the road started crossing through the swampland on the edge of the lake.

"I like that we're cut off from the rest of the country." He went on, glancing over at me with a slight smile. "It'll come in real handy during the zombie apocalypse."

"You can take the River Road north without crossing water," I replied with a slight laugh, resting my head against the passenger window and closing my eyes. My stomach was in knots. It always was whenever I was in a car on a highway. I've never much liked cars, and I really hate driving. It's probably all the accidents I've been in. My car insurance bill is off the charts—the company shareholders probably have a private island in the Caribbean named after me. "But not when the spillway is open." The Army Corps of Engineers had built the Bonnet Carré Spillway as part of their flood protection system for the city. When the river gets too high for comfort, they can open the spillway, diverting the rising water into Lake Pontchartrain and relieving pressure on the levee system. It always causes a battle between environmentalists, shrimpers, and politicians. The river is dirty, polluted, and freshwater, while Lake Pontchartrain, which is really a tidal bay, is brackish. The river water kills off shrimp, fish, and oysters and isn't good for the lake's ecosystem.

The city always won those battles.

The old River Road followed the river's twists and turns inside the river levee system. Before the highways were built, it was pretty much the only road into New Orleans. No one used it as much anymore. Because it followed the river instead of running in a more straight line from New Orleans to Baton Rouge like I-10 did, the old road was used now primarily by tourists looking for plantation tours, and local traffic.

Frank laughed. "It's shameful, really, that I've lived here for fifteen years and never done any of the tourist stuff."

I shook my head. "I've lived here almost my entire life and I haven't either, except for field trips in high school. Maybe we can plan an excursion, now that Colin's home for good. And it could be educational for Taylor. We can be tourists so long as we don't act like tourists." I pulled out my phone and made a reminder note. "You're okay with Colin being back with us now, aren't you?"

"It would be hypocritical to not be, wouldn't it?" He raised his shoulders in a slight shrug. "Maybe we didn't know the whole story when we first met him, but by the time we decided to try this relationship, we knew what we were getting into," he said, flipping the signal on and pulling into the right lane as we approached the off-ramp to I-310. "And yeah, sure, he could be lying to us *now*. But I do think he loves us both, and…" His voice trailed off. "We've got to trust him, don't we? It's easier to have doubt when he's not here."

Frank followed the exit off the highway, and we started climbing. The lake shimmered to my right in the late morning sun. As we came around the big sweeping turn of the exit, off to the side of the elevated highway I could see the wetlands below us. Maybe ten feet below the concrete, what little visible water I could see was covered in a yellowish-green slime. Most of the water was hidden by swamp grasses grown tall from beneath the water's surface. Had I not known better, I'd have thought it was solid ground. Cypresses and live oaks in their infancy poked up out of the water and grass. Some were bent into odd angles, probably courtesy of the winds from Hurricane Isadora last year. We still had another three miles in Jefferson Parish before we'd cross over into St. Jeanne d'Arc.

I wasn't convinced dropping in on JD at his office in the parish building was the best idea. But Frank was right that making an appointment might have put him on guard. I hadn't seen him in years, after all, so what reason could I have for wanting to see him now? If we couldn't catch him at his office, we'd drive out to Sunnymeade. The house was a short drive from Verdun.

I pulled up my web browser and typed *Havers St. Jeanne d'Arc*

Parish into the search bar. The first thing that came up was that same article from earlier in *The Times-Picayune* about the restoration of the *River Princess.*

"*Getting the* River Princess *back up and running is a priority for all of us here in the parish office,*" JD was quoted as saying. "*It's one of the largest employers in the parish, so of course it's a priority.*"

I raised an eyebrow. If his firm was being sued over insurance settlements from Isadora claims, there had to be some shady shit going on with the casino boat. I laughed at myself. It was Louisiana. Of course there was some shady shit going on!

Curious, I typed *River Princess hurricane insurance settlement* into the search bar. All that came up was an old article from the days after the storm had passed, with JD stating for the record that he hoped the insurance companies wouldn't delay the payments needed to get the parish back on its feet again.

Typical politician double-talk. Whenever a Louisiana politician was talking about money, you could be sure some—if not all—of it was going to end up in his pocket.

The Havers undoubtedly had made some major enemies during their generations of political dominance of the parish, especially since they considered themselves to be above the law.

I typed *Beau Haver drunk driving* and the very first hit was exactly what I was looking for.

I'd remembered right.

JD's younger brother Beau, who'd liked to cut up frogs and pull wings off flies when he was small, had been involved in a drunk driving incident. He'd been nineteen and one person had been killed. Three couples had gone out for the evening in Beau's oversized pickup truck. At shortly after midnight, he'd run the truck off a bridge over the Bayou Maron. One of the girls, McKayla Bissonnette, had been thrown out of the truck. It had taken just over a week to find her body where the current had carried it into the swamp. Beau had been charged with vehicular manslaughter and drunk driving, but there had been no Breathalyzer administered at the crash site. In fact, he hadn't been given one until almost four hours later at the hospital. He'd still blown positive, but he'd also had four hours for the alcohol he'd consumed to get out of his system.

So how drunk *had* he been?

He'd pleaded guilty to a lesser offense—reckless endangerment—and had gotten a slap on the wrist: a ten thousand dollar fine and probation for three years.

He also never spent one night in jail.

I felt sure the Bissonette family weren't big fans of the Havers.

I wanted to catch JD at his office and not have to head out to Sunnymeade. I had never liked JD's wife Karen very much. She was one of those women peculiar to the South to whom family, legacy, and history were everything—I think she may have even been chapter president of the Daughters of the Confederacy. She'd been a Golden Girl at LSU—she brought it up in every conversation—and had been third runner-up Miss Louisiana.

She was the kind of woman who could unironically say things like *It's not hate to celebrate our heritage.*

Sure, Karen, but the heritage *actually* is hate, dear.

Mom called her Lady Macbeth.

I didn't want to be the one who had to tell Karen Reardon Haver her husband was trolling for teenage boys in malls.

"I still think we should go to the house first," Frank said. "And we should have called before leaving the house. Why don't you call him now?"

"Element of surprise," I replied, shaking my head. "And you've never had the pleasure of meeting his wife—trust me, JD is the one we want to talk to. Karen would sense danger and shut down, lie, not tell us anything." I looked back at the wetlands we were driving past. "You don't understand how powerful JD and the Havers are out here, Frank. No one gets elected or holds office in St. Jeanne d'Arc without being anointed by JD. We also can't just march into his office and ask him if he killed Paris Soniat." I tapped my head against the window a couple of times. "But we can tell him that someone has access to pictures he wouldn't want made public. He'll listen to that." I tapped my chin with my index finger. "And we can poke around about Paris. Someone could just be fucking with Brody—someone who knows about him and JD, knows what trouble it could cause."

"I just hope I don't punch your cousin out," Frank said through gritted teeth. His face was reddening, and that vein that always pulses in his forehead when he's upset was throbbing. "I fucking hate men like that."

"Like what?" I shrugged. "Family values politicians are all the same, really. They try to legislate against their own desires because they hate themselves so much. It's a cliché at this point, really."

"That's not what I mean," Frank barked out a harsh laugh. "Men like your cousin, men like Eric Brewer—they're predators and I hate predators. They say they can't help who they're attracted to, but it's about power and control. It always is. And grooming—"

I stared at him. "Grooming?" I laughed. "You met Brody. You think that kid needed to be groomed?"

Frank gave me a side glance, eyebrows up. "Scotty, it doesn't *matter*." He placed his hand on my leg and squeezed. "A teenager isn't mature enough to make those kinds of decisions—you know that as well as I do—and the ones who think they are, absolutely are not." He shook his head. "That's why the consent laws exist. Someone underage can't consent because they don't know what they're consenting to. And teenage boys—all they think about is being horny and getting off. For a skilled groomer who knows what he's doing, those kids are sitting ducks. It's sickening."

I felt my stomach starting to sour a bit. "Do you think *I* was groomed?" I blurted out. "Because I wasn't. I knew what I was doing, Frank."

"Did you?" His voice was gentle and kind. "Or were you manipulated by an authority figure?"

I opened my mouth, but nothing came out.

Coach Phelps.

Oh, sweet Goddess.

First David, now Frank.

I've always been a little on the small side. I'm barely five nine now and weigh one seventy-five, give or take. I'd been a very small kid, skinny and short, destined to be a ninety-eight-pound weakling getting sand kicked in my face at the beach. The other boys somehow sensed there was something different about me, even before I knew what it was myself. I was eight the first time someone called me a fairy.

I thought they were saying *ferry*, which was confusing. I just ignored the assholes and did my own thing.

But things changed in junior high, and not for the better.

When I hit puberty, with hair growing in places it never had before and my voice always cracking at the worst possible time, I realized that those rotten kids had been right. I *was* different. They were noticing the girls and talking about pussy and tits and getting laid.

Me? I was noticing the boys, stealing glances in the showers and the locker room, hoping against hope no one ever caught me, knowing my life would be over if someone did.

I had crushes on some of the other boys, never daring to talk to them. I'd dream about kissing them when I was alone in my room at night, replaying the images I'd memorized while playing with myself. One day in the seventh grade I caught the ire of one of the football meatheads, and my school days became a living hell. The football players were the highest caste at school. Everybody wanted to be them, like them, be liked by them. If I was a target for the football team, no one in my class was going to stand up for me.

Fag, fairy, homo, femme. They shouted it at me in the hallways, outside after school, whenever and wherever they saw me. It didn't have to be in school, either.

And they laughed. Oh, how they laughed.

It was horrible. The teachers had to be aware of it—how could they miss the laughs and nasty comments in class? How I hated the teachers for pretending it wasn't happening, for turning a blind eye while the gay kid got tortured. I was so ashamed. There was something different about me, something wrong.

I didn't want to tell Mom and Dad because I was afraid. I was afraid they'd be ashamed of me, would turn on me like the kids at school, even the ones I'd thought were friends. I wanted to die. Every morning before school I felt sick to my stomach. Every day I prayed to the Goddess to destroy the school, to do something, anything, to make it all stop somehow.

Storm picked me up one day after school, They were shouting after me as I ran to the car, opened the door. *Fag! Femme! Fai—* I slammed the car door shut, out of breath.

He looked at me as I fastened my seat belt, my face burning. Had he heard? He gestured with his thumb at the gang of idiots, laughing and joking about twenty yards from the car. "This happen all the time?" he asked in a low voice.

Ashamed, all I could do was nod, blinking back the tears.

He looked back over to where they were standing. "If I turn the wheel just right and shove my foot to the floor, they wouldn't have time to get out of the way." His eyes gleamed. "Not all of them, anyway. I bet I could take out at least four of them."

I've never wanted anything more in my life.

"They're not worth ruining my life over," he said, shifting the car back into drive and checking his mirrors before pulling away from the curb, "but we can't just let this go." He drummed his fingers on the steering wheel. "They pick on you because they think you're smaller and weaker," he went on. Storm was big where I was small and would eventually reach six three. "You need to go out for the wrestling team."

"The wrestling team?"

"The wrestling team." He grinned at me when he stopped at a light. "A wrestler—even one who's not very good—can always take down and control someone who doesn't know how. You need to learn how to defend yourself. You become a wrestler, and they'll leave you alone. And if they don't…" He drew his index finger across his throat.

I was willing to try anything, so I went out for the junior high wrestling team.

And found out that I *loved* wrestling. I loved everything about it. I loved getting faster, learning to trust my training, learning how to use my opponent's weight against them. And I was good at it, a natural. I only had to be shown a move once before I mastered it.

I could take down anyone who fucked with me.

And once I had them down, I could immobilize them and cause a little pain.

I liked that idea.

It was also a socially acceptable way for me to have body contact with other boys.

And I was good at it. I was MVP of the team in eighth grade.

Coach Phelps was my high school wrestling coach.

Like me, he was small. He couldn't have been much taller than five five, at most, but weighed about a hundred and fifty pounds of solid muscle. He was severely bowlegged. He always wore a singlet under his shorts to wrestling practice, showing off the thick black hair on his chest and arms. He'd wrestled in college and was devoted to the sport. He was a great coach—in only a couple of years he'd turned our program from a loser to one of the strongest in the state. He was in his late twenties, had a wife and a baby daughter. He also taught Driver's Ed, Health, and PE but wasn't one of those horrible gym teachers who picked on kids or made them feel awkward and uncoordinated. Like, when we were playing basketball, some of the boys didn't know how to dribble and shoot. He set the kids who did know to play up with a pickup game of shirts and skins, then took the other kids aside and taught them the fundamentals. That was his philosophy of teaching—kids can learn how to do anything if someone will just show them how, and no teacher should ever make a student feel bad about themselves.

Is it any wonder he'd been voted Favorite Teacher every year since he was hired?

He had a great sense of humor and loved being around kids. The first time I saw him on the mats in a singlet at practice I forgot about every boy I'd ever had a crush on. I stopped fantasizing about the Soloflex guy and Marky Mark. Coach Phelps liked me too—he liked my work ethic, my willingness to give a hundred percent for the entire practice, how well I handled criticism and coaching, my total dedication to the sport, my ability to focus. Whenever he would praise me in front of the rest of the team, I felt bad—thinking if he only knew how much I got off on wrestling with these boys, feeling their muscles and struggling against them, trying to come out on top. If he knew how sexual it all was for me, he would kick me off the team.

I dreamed about Coach Phelps at night.

It was the summer before my junior year when it happened. Coach Phelps asked me to help him at a wrestling clinic for kids out in Plaquemines Parish at a YMCA. It was the kind of thing Mom and Dad definitely approved of—helping out underprivileged kids, trying to keep them off drugs and out of gangs by focusing on a sport. It was a weekend thing, so we wound up staying at a Holiday Inn that Saturday night.

It all began innocently. I was wearing a pair of cutoff sweatpants, sitting on my bed watching some random television show. Coach Phelps was lying on his bed in sweatpants. He wasn't wearing a shirt, and I kept stealing glances over at his bare chest, his thickly defined muscular arms and shoulders. I loved the way his chest and abs were covered with hair. I'd never really seen him shirtless before, so I was trying to take pictures with my mind camera for masturbatory purposes later.

I was just wondering what he looked like in his underwear when he said, "You know, Scotty, I was thinking you haven't gotten that single leg ride down yet."

"Huh?" I didn't know what he was talking about. I was pretty good at single leg rides.

He stood up and walked over to my bed. "Here, let me show you how you're doing it."

Before I knew it, he was on top of me, his legs wrapped around mine, but it was pretty easy for me to counter it. I wound up on top of him, controlling his legs with mine while I tried to get a grip on his arms. To my horror, I felt my dick getting hard. My crotch was up against his butt—which was round and hard as a rock—and I pulled back from him, letting go.

He rolled over onto his back and grinned at me. "See how easy it was for you to reverse me out of that?"

I put my hands down in front of my crotch so he couldn't see I was turned on.

I wanted to die, be anywhere else but there.

He winked at me. "It's okay, Scotty. Physical contact can lead to arousal. See?"

He pointed down at his crotch. He was aroused.

"When I was your age, I always jacked off before practice and matches so it wouldn't happen." He went on as though he wasn't aware I was dying from embarrassment.

I couldn't take my eyes off his tented sweatpants.

"Maybe we should just go ahead and take care of this"—he stroked himself—"so we can get to work."

It continued all through my junior year—every chance we had to be together, we were.

Sometimes I would stay late after practice, and we would go into his office and lock the door. Sometimes I would meet him at a motel out on Airline Drive in Kenner. I was horny constantly—what teenager isn't? Part of the appeal was the danger. I knew we would both be in trouble if anyone caught us. But I was all caught up in it. I knew he was married. I knew he had a couple of kids. But at night, in my bed, I got swept away by fantasies of being with him, living with him, of going to sleep with his arms around me every night.

I loved Coach Phelps.

I never called him by his first name. I always called him Coach.

And he loved me.

I won the State Championship my junior year. The tournament was held up in Baton Rouge, and after getting my trophy, Coach and I drove back to New Orleans. He took me out to dinner at Ruth's Chris Steakhouse, the one on Veteran's Boulevard in Metairie. When we got back into the car, he said, "You mind stopping at my house? My wife is off at her parents' in Biloxi."

I never said no to a chance to be with Coach.

We were in bed, just lying there with our arms around each other in the afterglow, talking about what college scholarship offer I should take, when his wife walked in.

The rest of the night was a blur to me, as I scrambled to get my clothes on, as they screamed at each other. I felt sick to my stomach, my wonderful steak dinner churning and turning to acid. I fled from the house, terrified, running down the street with my backpack slung over my shoulder, until I finally was able to find a gas station with a pay phone so I could call a cab.

I never saw Coach again. He never returned to school—rumors swirled around campus. A substitute came in and finished teaching his classes for the rest of the semester. I tried calling his home a couple of times, only no one ever answered. About a week later I called and got that horrible message that the phone was no longer in service. Somehow, I knew his life had been destroyed, ruined, wrecked forever by what we had done together.

All for love.

I never wrestled again.

"I guess I never thought about it that way," I said quietly as we drove past the *St. Jeanne d'Arc Parish* sign. "But...I can see what you're saying. But Frank, I already knew I was gay before I met Coach. *I* had a crush on *him*."

"You were a teenager, he was your coach, at least ten years older than you and an authority figure—kids always get crushes on authority figures," Frank went on. "You think you had any say in any of it, really? Did you ever think you could say no?"

"I never wanted to say no."

"You were a horny kid. He was an adult. If he wanted to have sex with a guy"—he took his hand off my leg and waved it—"there are how many gay bars in the Quarter? No matter what his damage— you said he had a wife and kids, didn't he?—he should have been looking for men his own age. Not hooking up with kids he was supposed to be *protecting*."

I swallowed. I'd never thought about it that way.

I'd never thought about it much at all.

It was just part of my past that I didn't think about.

"I don't know."

"Scotty, if Taylor was four years younger, what would you have thought about Eric Brewer..." His voice trailed off. "You think your coach being only twelve years older is somehow better than Brewer being thirty years older than Taylor?"

I turned to look out the window. My head was reeling.

I hadn't been a victim!

Had I?

And Frank was fifteen years older than me.

I shook my head. No, I hadn't been groomed. I'd always liked older men, that was all.

We crossed the river on the Warren Sheehan Bridge and soon reached the end of the highway. Frank turned left and followed the *Verdun* sign.

"I still think we should have made an appointment," Frank groused. "If he's not in, or won't see us—"

"If he won't see us at the office, we'll go to Sunnymeade," I replied. I felt weird, unsure of myself, my mind racing. Why had Frank never said anything about Coach to me before, if that was how he felt? "I'd rather not deal with his wife. She's a piece of work, trust me."

We passed through fields of sugar cane and corn, past trailers parked on blocks and small and tidy houses tucked behind wide green lawns, barns filled with hay, and the occasional pasture with lowing cows and horses.

Verdun was a small town like so many other small towns, bisected by a railroad line that crossed a bayou. The municipal building was ugly, probably built in the 1950s like its ugly counterparts in New Orleans that looked like they'd escaped from communist Eastern Europe. Frank pulled into the parking lot, and we walked in the front doors. There were no metal detectors in the lobby, which I marveled at, and a big wide circular desk with a woman of about fifty or so seated behind Plexiglas. Against one wall was an enormous model of a steamboat, the kind Mark Twain used to write about. It was inside a glass case, and above it on the wall was a sign reading *Model of* River Princess *Casino Boat Renovation Plans.*

It was the steamboat from my dream.

I approached the woman's desk. "May I help you?" she asked. She was still a handsome woman, but her looks were starting to fade a bit with time. She tried to repair some of the damage with makeup, but not successfully. Her voice was quivering a bit, and her eyes were reddened, like she'd been crying.

"Hi, my name is Scott Bradley." I gave her my biggest smile. "I'm a cousin of JD Haver's from New Orleans and thought, since I was over here, I'd stop in and say hi."

Her lower lip began to quiver. "I—oh my, I—" She took a deep breath. "I'm sorry to be the one to have to tell you this, but JD—Mr. Haver—I'm sorry to say he's dead." A tear slipped out of one eye, dragging mascara behind it as it traveled down the side of her face. She managed to hold it together just long enough to say, "Someone shot and killed him."

CHAPTER SIX
THE WHEEL OF FORTUNE, REVERSED
Luck has deserted the seeker for the time being

I couldn't have heard that right. Frank and I looked at each other. He looked as puzzled as I felt. I turned back to her.

"Dead?" I echoed. "But...how? When?"

"I'm sorry," she said, gulping and grabbing another tissue to dab at her swollen eyes. She blew her nose and continued, her voice quivering, "It's just awful—I mean, yesterday he was here and happy as a clam without a care in the world and now..." Her voice broke, and she reached for another tissue. "I can't believe I won't see him again." Her voice welled and broke on the last word, and she blinked furiously, dabbing at her eyes again.

"You poor thing, this must be such a shock. I'm so sorry for your loss," Frank said, his voice deep and professionally concerned. It's amazing how quickly he can still switch over into Special Agent mode, even after sixteen years of retirement. "Do you need some water?" He looked around. "Is there anyone who can cover for you? Maybe you should take the rest of the day off."

She shook her head violently. "No, there's no one else," she said sadly. She took a deep breath and held it for a moment. "Besides, JD would want—need—I have to hold down the fort." She wadded up the tissue and tossed it into a trash can. "All I would do if I went home is just cry, so I might as well be...useful." Her voice shook again on her last word. I watched her visibly pull herself together, the professional mask she usually wore behind the desk dropping down over her face. She looked at me. "Did you say you were JD's cousin? This must be such a shock for you, too."

I opened my mouth but shut it again. She was the receptionist at the parish office. She probably knew where all the bodies were buried around here. "Yes." I've never been a good actor, but she wasn't in her right state of mind anyway. She'd be more receptive talking to a grieving, shocked cousin. "I can't believe it," I said, hoping I didn't sound as phony to her as I did to myself. "I haven't seen him in such a long time, and since we were around…" I covered my eyes with my hands but could see Frank trying not to grin. "Wow. Mom and Dad—wow."

She reached over and grabbed my hand. Hers was smaller than mine, hot and damp and soft. Her fingernails looked gnawed, the cuticles ragged and torn. There was a bandage around her pinkie, and a very plain gold wedding band on her left hand. "Are you going to be okay?"

"I just can't believe it."

Frank asked, "When was the last time you saw him?" He'd switched his tone subtly, making his voice sound more empathetic. "What time did he leave yesterday? Did he work the full day?"

She blew her nose again, with a loud honk. "He always leaves around five," she replied. "I stay until six, just finishing up things and gathering stuff to take to the post office to drop off—it's on my way home, and it's more efficient and—oh, poor Mrs. Huber! And the children will have to come back from school." She shook her head again. "Oh, it's terrible, an absolute tragedy." She wiped at her eyes again. "Oh, what are we going to do without JD?" Then, with a visible effort, she managed to pull herself together and smiled weakly at us both. "I'm sorry, I didn't catch your name."

"Bradley, Scotty Bradley. JD's grandmother was my great-aunt. This is my partner, Frank Sobieski. Thank you," I replied, gesturing to Frank, who inclined his head to her slightly.

"Miss Charlotte?" she smiled weakly. "Miss Charlotte was a firecracker."

To say the least.

She held out her slender hand. "My manners! You must think I was raised by wolves. I'm Vicky Schultz, and I've worked reception here at the municipal building since…well, a long time. I'm so sorry about your cousin." She stumbled over the last words, her voice breaking on *cousin*. After I shook her limp hand, she offered it to Frank. "It's nice to meet you both. I just wish—I just wish the circumstances weren't…well." She stopped, a pained look on her face.

I'm not Daniel Day-Lewis, but what the hell? I swayed a bit and leaned against Frank, covering my face with my hands. I wouldn't be able to summon tears, but I hoped I guessed right about Vicky.

Frank put his arm around my shoulders and patted my head. "Do you want to sit?" he asked kindly. "Do you need some water? You've had a shock."

"How—how did he die?" I asked. "I can't believe it," I said, keeping my voice hushed and placing a hand to my forehead. "I haven't seen him in so long and I was—I was looking—"

Vicky had struck me as the kind of woman who slipped into High Function Mode in a crisis, and I'd been right. My distress drove any and all thoughts of her murdered boss out of her head, and she switched into caregiver mode. She efficiently directed Frank to take me into a lounge that opened off the reception area. Before I even had time to sit down on the uncomfortable sofa, she'd brought me a small cup of water from the dispenser near her desk. I smiled at her as I took the cup and downed it. "But—but what happened, Mrs. Schultz?" I asked.

She shook her head. "He never made it home last night. This morning, when Mrs. Haver realized he hadn't been home, she alerted Sheriff Perkins, and just a few hours ago they found his car parked along Bayou Road, and he was"—she closed her eyes and steeled herself to continue—"facedown in the bayou. Someone shot him." She started crying again, excusing herself and heading back out into the lobby.

"I guess we don't need to worry too much about the potential blackmail," Frank said, lowering his voice so she couldn't hear.

"It has to be tied together somehow," I whispered back. "It can't be a coincidence."

"Usually it's the blackmailer who ends up dead, not the target," Frank replied. "I've got a bad feeling about this…Hang on, here she comes."

Mrs. Schultz was dabbing at her eyes and the hand that offered me another Dixie cup of cold water was shaking slightly.

"You said someone *shot* JD? I can't imagine—" I looked over at Frank, who picked up the ball.

"Did JD have many enemies, Mrs. Schultz? Can you think of anyone who'd want him dead?"

She glanced at the door nervously. "*Well*," she whispered, "I don't want to get anyone in trouble, but you know all those awful people are suing him?" She pursed her lips in disgust. "And after everything the Haver family has done for this parish, too. If they just hadn't gotten lawyers involved, they would have gotten their money. It takes time! No insurance company is going to write a check until they absolutely have to. The disloyalty! Like JD wasn't looking out for their best interests." Her lips compressed tightly. "You know he didn't take a retainer? He wasn't going to even charge them. He felt it was a service he owed the community."

People tend to only get lawyers when they think there's no other option, I thought, remembering Storm opine on that very subject more times than I'd care to remember. My brother was a very good lawyer, and he resented the bad reputation his profession carried.

"And there's the Bissonnettes," she said darkly. "They've had it in for the entire Haver family ever since their daughter was killed all those years ago. It wasn't JD's fault. That was *Beau*. But everyone blames JD for his brother's crimes, and it's so unfair." Her voice rose.

"Beau?" I asked. The kid who cut up frogs and pulled wings off insects? Fried ants with a magnifying glass? "Beau doesn't still live out at Sunnymeade?"

She snorted. "You haven't talked to your kin much, have you? No, Beau is in Houston and— No, I shouldn't gossip." She pressed her lips tightly together.

"How did JD seem yesterday?"

"You ask a lot of questions," she replied.

Frank pulled out his private eye badge. "We're actually private detectives, ma'am."

"I wasn't honest with you," I said. "JD is my cousin—his grandmother was my grandfather's sister—but we didn't just happen to be in the neighborhood. We came out here specifically to speak to JD. About a case."

She looked back and forth between us, calculating. We must have passed muster. "It was a normal day, no different really than any other," she mused. "JD was in a good mood—that wasn't usual, at least not lately, not since the lawsuit was filed. He's been in a mood ever since then. But he was acting like all his problems were over."

"Problems?"

She rolled her eyes. "So many problems. But the biggest headache has been the renovation of the *River Princess*."

"The casino boat? The one from the model in the lobby?"

"Yes," she nodded, "there have been a lot of struggles with the insurance company. They don't want to pay out because they claim moving the *River Princess* off the river and into Bayou Maron was what resulted in the damage. And if they didn't pay out, we wouldn't be able to get the boat going again. So the casino people weren't happy, either. But he left the office yesterday afternoon to meet with them out at the boat—" She noticed our blank looks and laughed. "I'm sorry, of course you wouldn't know anything about that!" Her laugh had a hint of hysteria in it. "JD has been working his butt off to get the *River Princess* repaired and back on the river doing business again." She sniffed. "*Some* people think they know better than JD, but he's been president of this parish for fifteen years and it's not his fault Hurricane Isadora wrecked the boat. Why can't those stupid insurance people understand that?" Her lips tightened into a thin line. "That man was working himself into the grave—"

"You said he left yesterday afternoon to meet with the casino people?" Frank interrupted her gently.

She nodded. "He left here around four but never made it back to Sunnymeade." She tittered, holding a shaking hand up to her mouth. "Karen—that's Mrs. Haver, you know—called me around nine last night, wondering where he was. I told her I hadn't seen him since he left." She frowned. "I got the impression she didn't believe me for some reason, I can't imagine why."

I didn't believe that. I was sure Vicky Schultz had *plenty* of theories about where JD was and what he could have been up to— and I was equally sure she'd lied to Karen Haver any number of times covering for him.

If anyone was keeping all of JD's secrets, my money was on Vicky.

"I finally got her off the phone, but this morning when I got here, he still hadn't turned up. Karen called me to see if he was here. I tried his cell phone, but it went to voice mail, so I texted and emailed a couple of times, and then when Sheriff Joe—that's Joe Perkins, he's been parish sheriff for going on thirty years—got here, I told him we might have a situation."

"Where was he found?"

"Excuse me—Sheriff!" she shouted, jumping up to her feet and rushing out of the room. Frank and I didn't have a chance to say anything before she returned with whom I had to assume, based on the uniform, badge, and gun, was the parish sheriff. "Sheriff, this is JD's cousin"—she turned to me—"Scott Bradford and Frank Zelinski?" She gave me a rueful, apologetic smile.

"Scott Brad*ley*." I stood up and shook his rough, calloused hand with a smile. He smelled slightly of dried sweat and cigarette smoke. "And this is Frank *Sobieski*." Maybe Sheriff Joe Perkins was more progressive minded than he looked, but the river parishes weren't exactly known for their embrace of difference.

And sheriffs in sparsely populated parishes like this one hold a lot of power.

Law and order have always been weaponized in the South to protect the status quo—no matter how evil the status quo might be. In St. Jeanne d'Arc Parish, the status quo was the Haver family.

JD's death created a power vacuum in the parish. How old were his kids again? Who was going to take over? I had no idea how the succession in parish government worked.

"Nice to meet y'all," Joe Perkins drawled pleasantly. He could have been any age between forty and seventy, but standing beside Frank while they shook hands, he looked old enough to be Frank's father. His face was browned and wrinkled into folds from years of exposure to sun and wind. He was slightly over six feet tall, give or take, and he had the unfortunate build of many older country men—the spindly thin legs, the massive belly and waist, his pants belted below the swell of stomach—making him look like an egg mounted on pencils. The polyester brown pants enveloped the thin legs, while the buttons on the shirt were straining not to pop off. Gray hairs stuck out above the collar of the white T-shirt he had on underneath. His teeth were nicotine-yellowed and crooked, but the iron gray hair was immaculately trimmed and carefully slicked into place. He took off his mirrored sunglasses, and the previous effect—the stereotypical arrogant rural sheriff from countless Burt Reynolds movies—was gone once his twinkling brown eyes were exposed. He smiled, the folds and creases in his face slipping into place.

His hand was dry, rough, calloused, and strong as he shook my hand. "Sorry to meet you under such circumstances," he drawled with a hint of a Cajun accent. "My condolences on your loss." He ran a hand through his hair. "Why don't you join me in my office and get you out of Vicky's hair." He winked at her. "And remember, I don't want to talk to no reporters, okay?"

"Got it, Sheriff."

We followed him across the reception area and up a flight of stairs to the second floor. The upstairs was carpeted, the walls paneled in a fine dark faux wood that screamed *masculine*. Framed photographs were mounted at regular intervals on the walls—mostly sports teams, from Little League up to high school level, with engraved gold name plates on the bottoms of the frames. He opened a door marked *Parish Sheriff* and led us into a waiting room, comfortably furnished in what my mom calls Late Twentieth Century Fragile Masculinity. Leather wingback chairs, more dark paneling, and the mounted light fixtures along the walls had green enamel covers directing the light down. A modest desk was situated at the opposite end of the hallway door, and a young woman who looked like she was fresh out of college was seated behind it, typing and frowning at the computer screen. The nameplate on her desk read *Celeste Pitre*. She wasn't in uniform, but rather was wearing a smart tan pantsuit over a bright red silk shirt. Her shoulder-length brown hair was parted firmly in the middle, and she had a heart-shaped face that was all sharp angles. Her cheekbones looked like they could slice paper, and so did her chin. She was wearing too much makeup—or needed to find a different makeup idol outside the cast of *RuPaul's Drag Race*. There was a slender gold watch on her left wrist, and a small diamond winked from her left ring finger in its gold band.

"No interruptions, Celeste," Sheriff Perkins said as he walked past her desk and opened the door in the wall behind her, gesturing us in.

His inner office was a shrine to LSU sports.

One entire paneled wall was covered with framed front pages of the Baton Rouge *Advocate* celebrating the football national titles in 2003 and 2007, and several of the baseball championships. Behind his massive desk were mounted framed *Times-Picayune* covers for the NFC and Super Bowl title wins back in 2010. There was also a framed signed Drew Brees jersey. His desk lamp had been made from an LSU football helmet.

"Did you go to LSU?" I asked, sinking down into one of the chairs in front of the desk.

He nodded, his eyes moving to the framed newspaper front pages. "Yeah, but we weren't very good when I was there," he said with a grin. He leaned back in his chair and looked at first me, then Frank. "So, you boys just happened to head on out here today looking for JD?" His voice was casual, friendly—way too friendly for a rural Louisiana sheriff.

It's easy to dismiss stories about corruption in the smaller, rural parishes as relics of the past—but this wasn't New Orleans. Parish sheriffs had a lot of power, and who in this parish did he answer to now? If the Havers ruled St. Jeanne d'Arc Parish like a medieval fiefdom for over a hundred years, they were propped up by people like Sheriff Perkins.

A parish sheriff without a boss had a lot of power indeed.

We would need to be very careful.

"As I told Ms. Schultz"—no sense in seeming overly familiar with her, typical Southern good ole boys didn't like that much in my experience—"I am JD's second cousin—my mom and his dad were first cousins, and we were in the area—"

"Where you boys from?" he interrupted me pleasantly. I could see Frank wasn't responding well to the *boys*—his face was starting to redden and I could see the vein in his forehead.

"New Orleans," I replied quickly before Frank could say anything.

"And y'all just happened to be in the area today?" A smile twitched at the corner of his mouth. "The day we found your cousin's body. That's a mighty big coincidence, boys. Where were y'all last night?"

"At home in New Orleans." I didn't look at Frank. "To be honest with you, Sheriff, Frank and I came out here specifically to see JD—we didn't have an appointment."

"And what was your business with JD?" He was still smiling, but his eyes were as cold as a snake's.

"Sheriff..." Frank leaned forward and removed his wallet, pulling out his private eye badge and license and placing it on the desk.

After we'd first met, Frank and I had both taken a course, apprenticed, and become licensed private eyes. We'd even had an actual office briefly, but most of what we did was background checks and research for Storm's firm. We kept our licenses current, but we'd closed the little office we rented on Frenchmen Street after Hurricane Katrina. I still did some work for Storm now and then, mostly to keep the license rather than any great desire to be an investigator. I'd read Tammy Wynette had kept her beautician's license current until the day she died, just in case.

I'd done the work and wanted to keep it.

"You got one, too?" This was directed at me. The Sheriff puckered his lips like he was sucking something sour as he examined the badge with his eyebrows raised.

"I didn't bring it with me."

"I gotta tell you boys, I don't much like outsiders coming into my parish and messing around with my cases like some kind of hotshots." His eyes narrowed. "We may not have the resources y'all have in Orleans Parish"—he spat the last two words out—"but we also don't have the amount of crime y'all have, either."

Crime in New Orleans was a dog whistle to the rest of the state. Sure, there's a lot of crime in New Orleans—there always has been. It's been a major port city since its founding. We had a legal red-light district for decades. Our cops are bribable, and the elections joke is *Vote early and often.*

When New Orleanians talk about crime, it's with kind of a *What can you do?* air. No politician seems to know how to fix the problem, so it's just one more thing we locals talk about—like potholes, corruption, unreliable public transportation, and the constant catering to tourism. Crime was something else for us to endure, like the termite swarms and hurricane season.

But when people from outside New Orleans bring up the city's crime problem, it's usually the white-flight racists in the suburbs who didn't want their kids to go to public school with Black kids after integration. Since fleeing to the suburbs, they've created this bizarre fantasy about the good old days when New Orleans was just like Mayberry.

Narrator voice: *It never was.*

"We're not interested in your murder case, Sheriff," I said. "The best people to handle a murder are the cops, of course. We came out to see JD about another case, something we can't really discuss with you." *Privilege only covers private eyes when they are working for a lawyer,* I heard Storm's voice in my head saying. I knew Storm would cover for me if it came down to it, but I'd rather not put him into a position to get in trouble with the Louisiana Bar. "Pertaining to a client."

He leaned back in his chair and steepled his fingers on his chest.

"Sounds like this might be something I need to look into." His smile wasn't friendly. "I got me a dead parish president—murdered, shot in the back, at that—and who knows what the hell else is going to shake loose around here now." He shook his head, adding, "And private eyes don't have privilege like lawyers do."

"We're actually working for a lawyer." I lied easily. Storm would back us up. "You can check with him if you like." I hoped he wouldn't. I hated having Storm lie for me—once we were out of here, I should give him a heads-up.

"That's interesting." The sheriff picked up a pen and started playing with it, rolling it between his fingers dexterously. "And JD had something to do with your client's case?" There was a slight mocking note in his voice, almost like he was making air quotes around *your client's case*.

"Well," Frank said smoothly, "I *am* retired from the FBI—did twenty years with the Bureau. Scotty and I have been licensed private eyes for almost fourteen years now. You remember when Mike the Tiger was kidnapped a while back?" He jerked a thumb in my direction. "Scotty is who found him, and we solved the case. We've cracked a lot of cases over the years, Sheriff. We'd be happy to share information with you, but we need to check with our client and his attorney first." He leaned forward and whispered, "Our client is a *minor*, Sheriff, so I am sure you understand the need for discretion?"

Playing the Mike the Tiger card was genius. I could almost see the wheels turning as the sheriff followed what Frank said to its logical conclusion—although I would have bet a million dollars he thought the minor was *female*. "Yes, that does make a difference." He looked at me. "You were the one that found Mike?" He cracked a smile. "I seem to recall that the Coast Guard had to rescue you."

"Yes." I forced a smile on my face. I try not to think about the past and bad things that have happened. "They set me, Frank's nephew, and Mike adrift on a boat without power in the Gulf."

"Sounds like you did the entire state a service, son." He stretched, yawned, and put his elbows on the desk. "I'll be honest with you boys. Most murders we have here are easy—drugs, domestic disturbances, an argument gets heated and someone pulls a gun—that sort of thing. This…" He shook his head. "JD Haver was a lot of things, but the voters in this parish loved him, and they're going to want to see justice done, and soon. I don't have the kind of men with the right kind of training to do this kind of work. I could hire you both as consultants, would that be something you might be interested in doing? You gotta know that I can't share everything with you, though—some things I'll have to keep quiet, you understand—but maybe that way you could see clear to sharing some information with me." He held up his hands. "I don't need to know who your client is or anything. But why did they hire you, and why did you come to see JD?"

"I think consulting is a good idea," Frank said smoothly before I could say no. "And you have to understand our client's privacy is of the utmost importance to us."

"Understood."

Frank looked at me, and I resisted rolling my eyes. "A friend of ours who teaches high school brought one of his students to see us. The student knew JD, met him while working at the food court at Lakeside Mall in Metairie." It was going to be tricky not using pronouns for Brody. "JD became interested in our client, began exchanging text messages, bringing gifts, seeing our client outside the mall." I closed my eyes. "JD would buy our client gifts, and then want, um, photographs of our client modeling the clothes. It was always underwear or bathing suits…but our client finally asked JD to leave them alone." Not using pronouns was harder than you'd think.

I don't think Sheriff Perkins was ready for that reveal yet.

"And he didn't?"

"It's a little more complicated than that," Frank went on. "That should have been the end of it, no harm no foul—there was no physical contact, or so our client claims, but the texts, well, they got raunchy. Monday, our client started getting messages from an unknown number—screenshots of text conversations between our client and JD, as well as some of the pictures. Our client is concerned that someone has access to those conversations and photos and felt obligated to let JD know that they'd fallen into the hands of a third party."

"Blackmail?" Sheriff Perkins breathed.

"Our client wanted us to see if JD was also getting the messages, since he had more to lose, or if he knew anything about what was happening. At the very least, let him know it might all be coming out sometime soon."

Sheriff Perkins looked ill. "I really was hoping it wasn't kids."

"Like I said, our client claims nothing physical happened," I replied, leaving *There's probably more than just our one client* implied. "Just the flirting and the texting. Our client doesn't want to be associated with any scandal, for obvious reasons." I heard Brody saying *I don't want people to hear my name and think oh that's the kid who messed around with that politician.* "So we'd like to leave them out of this as much as possible."

"Well, we haven't found JD's phone yet," Sheriff Perkins said. "But with the cloud and things nowadays, getting hold of his phone's contents shouldn't be too hard." I could see him writing on his notepad *Find out who JD's phone provider was and get a subpoena from Judge Hawley.*

"Do you have a timeline for his movements yet?"

Sheriff Perkins whistled. "He left the office yesterday at three to meet"—he frowned and flipped back through his notepad—"with the new casino people—"

"New casino people?" Vicky hadn't mentioned this.

He nodded. "After the hurricane, with all the insurance issues, the old casino group decided to sell their interest to a new group. JD was meeting with the new group out there, to show them the damage and what needs to be done renovating and refloating the *River Princess.* They met with him out at Blind Lake, where the boat is now, and he left them shortly after five. He didn't tell them where he was going—and we haven't been able to find anyone who saw him between then and when his body was found this morning." Perkins's voice was grim. "Facedown in a drainage canal alongside the River Road, actually—not close to Sunnymeade, nearer to Belle Riviere." Frank looked confused, but I knew what he meant. Belle Riviere was another old plantation where Black people were formerly enslaved, renovated into a museum/bed-and-breakfast/special event rental. "Leave the casino people to me. We've already talked to everyone at Sunnymeade—but you being kin"—he nodded at me—"they might tell you more than they'd tell me."

I could have sworn Vicky said he'd been found in Bayou Maron, but it was an easy mistake. There were so many creeks and bayous and drainage canals in the river parishes it was easy to get them wrong.

We both stood. "All right, then, we'll head on out to Sunny-meade."

He handed us a business card and took our numbers. He saluted as we left his office. "Look forward to hearing from y'all."

"Think we'll ever hear from him?" I asked as we walked back to the car.

"No." Frank grinned. "But at least he didn't tell us not to get involved."

"Consultants." I shook my head. "I mean, it's great that he's open to our help, but I don't quite trust the man."

"Why?"

I grinned. "You're not from here." I slid into the passenger seat. "The Havers own this parish, which means they own Sheriff Perkins. And if you don't think he'll do whatever he needs to do to protect the Haver family, well, think again. The sheriff's department is their enforcement arm."

"You make it sound like the Mafia."

"Well," I said as he backed out of the spot, "they *are* a crime family—and I bet there are a lot of people in this parish who aren't sorry he's dead."

CHAPTER SEVEN
EIGHT OF PENTACLES, REVERSED
Intrigue and sharp dealing

"Should we have asked him about Paris Soniat?" I asked. Frank was waiting for an opening so he could turn right out of the parking lot onto Bayou Road.

"He'd just give us the official story," Frank replied, not taking his eyes off the line of cars whizzing by. "And that consultants thing? He just wants to keep an eye on us, know what we're doing. Thanks for letting me take the lead on that, by the way."

Before I could reply, my phone started ringing. I pulled it out of my pants pocket. The screen displayed Colin's smiling face and bare chest. His name appeared across the top. I touched the answer button and clicked it over to speaker. "Colin, before you say anything, we've got some news for you." I took a deep breath. "JD Haver was found shot to death this morning in a drainage ditch out in the country."

"Holy shit." Colin whistled. "You don't think—you don't think Brody had anything to do with it?"

It hadn't crossed my mind, but Frank, still watching the traffic, replied, "I don't think so. He was last seen last night around seven, and he was found this morning. Sure, Brody could have made it out here, but…"

"There's no motive," I pointed out. "Brody had no reason to kill JD, but JD had all kinds of motive for killing Brody." As I heard the words coming out of my mouth, I could have smacked myself stupid. Why hadn't that occurred to me before?

Like he was reading my mind, Colin said, "No, JD had no reason to think he had anything to fear from Brody. And even if he did, Brody's primary concern was protecting JD, right? He asked for help because he didn't know how to warn JD—"

"And JD couldn't have known someone had accessed those pictures and had texted Brody." That made me feel better. If anything had happened to Brody because we hadn't thought he'd be in danger… "And JD, as far as we know, had no idea anyone thought he had something to do with Paris Soniat's death."

"Did you find out anything about that?" Frank asked.

"The news reports—what there were—were pretty basic. He was found on Bayou Road, outside the city limits, about a mile or so," Colin went on. "He was close to a bridge, and they found him lying in the road, which just doesn't seem right to me. If he was hit by a car…" His voice trailed off. "I'm going to see if I can access the parish sheriff's server—oh, never mind, you didn't hear that. But I'd like to see the coroner's report. I did get some information about his family—there was a mother and a sister, apparently no father in the picture. I'll text that information to you."

"Hit-and-run seems pretty cut and dried," Frank replied, drumming his fingers on the steering wheel. "Why would someone try to make out like that was a murder? I suppose he could have been run down."

"According to the story in the paper there, he'd run out of gas and was walking back into town." I could hear his frown. "No one seemed to know what he was doing out there. He'd just talked to his sister right before he was killed, and everything seemed fine. He didn't tell her what he was doing or where he was going, just that he'd be home later…and of course, he never did make it home."

Poor kid, I thought. How hard must it have been to be openly gay out here in the middle of Conservative America?

"And did you learn anything from the sheriff?"

"Not really," I replied. "He's not opposed to us checking around, but that was more about the power vacuum out here, I think."

"What do you mean?"

I sighed. "Look, the Havers have owned this parish for generations. One after another, passing the parish presidency and senior partnership in their law firm from father to son like they were kings or something. Now, JD's dead. Beau lives in Houston and never joined the family firm. JD's sons are both in college, they aren't old enough. So until Jefferson Davis Haver the Fifth is old enough to pass the bar, there's a leadership vacuum. Sheriff Perkins is one of the players out here, and maybe he's going to try to take over." I laughed. "Not that Karen Haver will allow that for a second. I think the sheriff is going to find out what Karen is made of."

"We're going to head out there," Frank said, moving his neck. "I cannot believe this traffic." I glanced over at him. Whenever Frank's angry or upset, a muscle in his jaw twitches and a vein shows up on the side of his forehead. No sign of twitching muscles or pounding veins, so he was fine.

So far.

"I don't know how far we want to pursue this, to be honest," Frank added. "Like Scotty said, the sheriff was fine with us if we don't interfere with his investigation, and we share everything we find with him. But I don't really care who killed JD. That's not our job, and he kind of had it coming. So…I don't know."

What?

I didn't like JD, but I don't know that anyone deserves to be murdered.

"Well, we should make sure that nothing's going to lead back to Brody, at least," I said. I exhaled. "If he didn't want to be known as *that kid who messed around with the pervert politician* I doubt he wants to be *that kid who messed around with the pervert politician who was murdered*." I shrugged. "I know I wouldn't. And if the murder has nothing to do with Brody, why drag him into it?"

Frank's head whipped around. He gave me an odd look, one I couldn't read. He opened his mouth to say something but turned his attention to the seemingly endless stream of traffic.

What the hell was that look for?

"Did you have any luck tracing the text message?" I asked, slightly frowning. Something was going on with Frank. Was he upset about Colin coming back?

Nah, that couldn't be it. He'd been just as excited as I was to see Colin Monday night.

I'd wait till we were off the call before asking.

"Yes, and it didn't take long," Colin replied. "The message came, as we figured, from a burner phone, a cheap disposable you can buy almost anywhere—mini-marts, truck stops, gas stations, Dollar General. I traced the phone number back to a lot from the manufacturer that was delivered to a convenience store out there in Verdun, a Grab 'n' Go on Bayou Road—I'll text you the address when I hang up." He hesitated. "You do know how burner phones work?"

I rolled my eyes. "I'm not just a pretty face," I teased. "They're basically pay-as-you-go phones, aren't they? Mostly used by criminals and poor people who can't afford regular cell service or have bad credit? The phones are basically cheap and disposable. You buy cards with minutes, and there's a code on the back that the user has to enter to get access to their time. They're extortionate—I think they charge like ninety-nine cents or so per call, so you're basically spending another dollar every time you make a call, which is—"

"A lot more than pay phones used to be," Frank said. An opening in the traffic was coming. "Hang on," he said as he floored it. He whipped the wheel hard to the right, throwing me against the passenger door. "Sorry," he mouthed at me once we were heading down Bayou Road.

"I was also, um, I managed to trace the minutes being used to the same convenience store, but they were purchased with cash. The store's inventory system doesn't seem to record anything identifying the individual phones being purchased, unfortunately. And since they paid cash—"

"There's no way to trace the phone or the minutes," I finished for him. "Well, I suppose hoping the blackmailer was stupid enough to use their own phone was a reach in the first place." I tapped my fingers on my leg. "JD was meeting with the casino people about the *River Princess*, but Sheriff Perkins didn't go into more detail than that. Apparently, JD made the meeting, they talked for a few hours, and he left shortly after seven. He didn't tell them where he was going, but they assumed he was heading back to Sunnymeade." Something nagged at me. There was that dream I'd had. I hadn't mentioned it to either Frank or Colin. It might not have been a message from the Goddess. It could have been just a dream. I couldn't help but think the *River Princess* was important. "Can you find out what's going on with the *River Princess*? And what casino people JD is dealing with? Vicky, the receptionist at the parish office, said that there was a new investor group that had bought out the old one after the storm. I know the boat was damaged in Hurricane Isadora—anything you can find on the casino boat would be helpful, I think."

"Can do." I heard his fingers clicking on his keyboard. "I'll also text you guys the dates and times the phones and minute cards were sold. Maybe if they have surveillance cameras…?" Colin sighed. "But given how primitive their inventory system is, I doubt if the store would keep their footage for long. It *may* back up to the cloud, but my guess is they went with the cheap option—it's just on an overwriting loop every couple of days. I'm trying to see what I can find out about the store and its systems…"

"If you're hacking, it goes without saying don't get caught," Frank snapped as we drove along Bayou Road. It was also a state highway, lined with houses and the occasional business—beauty salons, interior designers, dry cleaners and boutiques, toy shops— pretty much everything you could think of was along Bayou Road. The branches of enormous swamp oaks dripping Spanish moss formed a canopy over the road. Every fast-food place you can imagine, Walgreens and CVS and a Winn-Dixie, car repairs, and the occasional bridge over a murky looking bayou.

Colin laughed. "The great thing about Blackledge technology is it leaves no trace," he said smugly. "You wouldn't believe the systems I've hacked into."

"I don't think we want to know," I replied.

Frank gave me another look as we stopped at a red light at an intersection. One corner was the Grab 'n' Go, one was a Starbucks, and the other two were Shell and Texaco gas stations. I could smell grease from the fast food places, and my stomach grumbled a little bit. The light changed. After we crossed through the intersection, Frank pulled into the Grab 'n' Go parking lot. He pulled into a spot near the front door, next to a filthy Ford pickup truck. The tires were enormous, and the cab was raised so far off the ground I didn't see how anyone could climb into it without springs on their shoes. Frank turned off the engine.

"We're actually at the Grab 'n' Go," I said, "if the address is"—I squinted at the numbers over the double doors—"1423 Bayou?"

"That's the place. Hang on." I could hear his fingers hitting the keys. "The inventory system doesn't specify which phone was sold at what time, just that a phone was sold. Three were sold last Monday—one around eight in the morning, another around one, and a final one at seven thirty p.m., give or take a minute or two, if they have surveillance footage." His tone indicated that he didn't think that would be true. "All three were sold with minute cards, too, but only one of the phones and one of the minute cards have been activated. I don't know which phone was sold when, but I do know that our phone was activated that same night, around ten. It was that night that Brody got the first text message."

"Logically, we can assume that the last phone sold was the phone we're looking for," Frank said. "That's odd about the other phones. Why buy a phone and minutes, if you aren't going to use it?"

"Maybe it was the same person, buying them at different times, so they could switch it up in case Brody tried tracing the messages?" I asked. "This person was able to access either Brody's phone or JD's, right?" JD wouldn't have shared them with someone voluntarily. "So, whoever we're looking for has technical expertise—"

"Or has access to it," Colin corrected me.

"Or has access to it, so why wouldn't they just use a VPN to change the router signal?" I wasn't sure if I'd asked that correctly—I am horrible with technology and often resort to getting Taylor to help me with my computer and my phone. Taylor's help always comes with a lecture about learning how to do everything for myself. It's a fair point, but I don't see any point. When I got my first iPhone, I learned how to use it. Then they started upgrading and changing how the operating system works.

It was easier just to get Taylor to help.

"Burner phones are harder to trace," Colin replied simply. "I'm not even sure the police have the access to this kind of technology yet."

I saw Frank make another face. "Okay, well, find out about the *River Princess* and the casino people, and if you can run some financials on JD—"

"Consider it done. See you tonight." He hung up.

"Okay, what?" I asked Frank, making sure the call was disconnected.

He frowned. "What?"

"You keep making faces," I said. "You're really not hard to read, Frank—"

"Doesn't it bother you that he still has access to Blackledge technology?" Frank raised an eyebrow, and his face flushed a little bit. No twitch in his cheek or vein on his forehead, though. "I know Angela Blackledge and Colin were tight, but do you really think if he left her employ, she'd let him keep his Blackledge laptop with all those hacking programs and access to databases?" he scoffed. "At the very least, it's proprietary property he shouldn't have access to anymore."

I hadn't thought about that, but he was right. "You think he's still working for them?"

Frank threw up his hands. "I don't know, Scotty. I don't know what to think anymore." He scowled. "Colin has lied to us any number of times, and always because he *has* to for our own safety. What if he's just on another case for them, and he's using our place as a safe house? It wouldn't be the first time." He shrugged. "I mean, if the only person who knew about us was Bestuzhev...and he's dead, no one knows about us. If Colin is telling the truth."

"We have to believe him, Frank, otherwise what are we doing here?" I sighed. Frank was right—no matter how much I wanted him to be wrong. Colin had lied to us because of his job several times, and we always forgave him. It was a pattern we'd repeated, over and over, and might continue repeating for the rest of our lives. We loved him. That was the problem. How many times had he saved me over the years, or Frank, or my parents, or someone we cared about?

Once a liar, always a liar.

But he wasn't lying when he said he loved us. I'd never believe that he just used us for whatever reason he might have.

I'd stake my life on that.

Because he always came back, didn't he?

But there had always been a *reason* he'd come back, hadn't there? A case of some sort, whether it was finding Kali's Eye or the Napoleon Death Mask or...

I slumped down into my seat. "I'll stay here while you go inside and ask about the security cameras." I could see one, mounted on the far end of the building from where we were parked. I could see from the car that there was also one mounted on the ceiling. The windows were covered with beer and lottery and cigarette ads. Where there was open glass, it was dirty. "One might do better than two."

"Okay." Frank got out. I watched him walk to the front door in his tight jeans. I smiled a bit. Damn, he was fine. The broad shoulders, the thick veins in his muscular arms, the small waist, the firm hard ass, the long muscular legs—I was damned lucky to have him.

And Colin, too, a voice added in my head.

"And Colin, too," I said aloud as another car pulled into the lot and up to one of the gas pumps. It was a muscle car, a black Chevrolet Camaro with flames painted on the hood and as far along the side as I could see. The back end was raised higher than the front, and it was louder than it should have been. It was what Mom always called an I'm-sorry-about-your-dick car. "Guys who have to have loud engines and lots of horsepower under the hood," she'd say with a sly wink, "usually aren't much good in the sack, if you know what I mean."

I watched as a young man with long greasy hair climbed out from behind the steering wheel. His brown hair was pulled back into a ponytail, and he was wearing a sleeveless black Metallica T-shirt. His jeans were ripped and dirty. He sauntered with a rolling gait to the front door of the little store. Frank almost bumped into him on his way out, and it looked like the guy might have taken some offense to Frank. They exchanged a few sentences before the guy went inside and Frank got back into the car.

"What was that about?"

Frank fastened his seat belt and started the car. "Just some punk-ass bitch who thinks he's tougher than he really is." He shifted the car into reverse and looked back over his shoulder. "Colin was right, they just have a hard drive—a DVD—that records over itself every two days." He sighed. "We can't find who bought the phone that way. The girl working there—honestly, the state of public education in this state is a disgrace—couldn't remember selling any of the phones, even though she was there for the afternoon and evening sales. She seemed offended that I thought she should."

He backed out of the spot, able to pull back on Bayou Street when the light held up traffic for him. "You still want to run out to Sunnymeade?"

"What do you think?" I rubbed my eyes. "Karen has always been a stone-cold bitch, but she's got to be shaken up, don't you think? Besides, both Vicky and Sheriff Perkins know we're here, know JD was my cousin—it'll look weird if we don't stop by, you know?"

"Well, we're already out here, so we might as well try," Frank said as we drove past more fast-food places and stores and gas stations. We drove alongside a murky looking bayou for a while, and I spotted a motionless alligator floating in it. Sunnymeade was about a mile past the city limits, and once we passed the *You are now leaving Verdun! We hope you come back soon!* billboard, it wasn't long before a long, low brick fence appeared on the left side of the road. It was high enough so you couldn't see anything past it, but low enough to jump over. We followed the fence for about another mile or so before we reached the front gates, which were open.

Frank turned left and drove through the gates.

The driveway was straight and lined with massive ancient live oaks in a slightly less impressive replica of the driveway at the more famous Oak Alley plantation farther upriver. But while *that* drive ended at a classic antebellum style Southern plantation mansion with gorgeous columns, Sunnymeade was something else entirely. When the French originally owned Louisiana and the property belonged to a French family, it was called Belle Marais, because the far edge of the property ended in swampland. The original house—only one drawing still existed of that house, which had been a typical Caribbean-style house—had burned during the German Coast uprising of 1811, when the enslaved people of the river parishes rose up to fight for their own freedom, burning houses and killing their captors as they marched toward New Orleans. The revolt failed, and the house that was built to replace the original was more along the lines of Oak Alley, Houmas House, and the others: columns, perfectly square house, galleries on upper and lower floors. When the heiress to Belle Marais had married the original Haver, Thomas, he'd changed the name of the place to Sunnymeade. The second house had burned to the ground in the 1880s, and the first Jefferson Davis Haver had built an absurd-looking Victorian house, with balconies and towers and cupolas and a widow's walk up on the roof. It sprawled out haphazardly in both directions. The story was he didn't want to live in a house called *swamp*, even if the French word for it was pretty.

Mom always said if the Havers ever went broke, the house was too ugly for tourists to want to visit.

The house had always looked alive to me, like a nasty sprawling parasite swallowing up visitors whole. The last time I had been here had been for Great-Aunt Charlotte's funeral.

I'd never cared much for my cousin JD, so the feud that kept our sides of the family away from each other had been kind of a blessing. He'd been a few years older than me, but spoiled and selfish and perverted even as a kid. JD was the first person to show me nude pictures of women, salivating over the airbrushed breasts in *Playboy* and *Penthouse*. He was the worst kind of kid—the kind who was always pinching and punching, all in the name of fun, but if I returned the favor, he'd tell on me to get me in trouble. He'd met Karen when they'd both been at LSU—she'd been a Golden Girl with the marching band, a Chi Omega, and the Dream Girl of Beta Kappa, JD's fraternity. She was phony and snobbish, from the white Protestant northern part of the state, near Monroe, with oil money on both sides. She was pretty if you liked that pageant look so many Southern women with money tend to go for—curvy breasts and hips, tiny waist, and lots and lots of hair and makeup. She was pretty, and she and JD looked good together up there at the altar in front of the minister. She drank too much at their wedding reception and threw up on her father during the father of the bride dance.

At Charlotte's funeral, JD and Karen didn't seem very happily married. Of course, she was pregnant and already had one toddler. They bickered and sniped at each other. There was a tightness to her lips that made her look perpetually pissed off, and she had frown lines rather than laugh lines. It wouldn't have surprised me had anyone told me JD was fooling around on her—they seemed to have one of those marriages. The surprise had been his interest in teenage boys.

Frank pulled into the little parking area just off to the side of the main house, and we got out of the car. "Let me do the talking at first," I said, remembering with a wince how JD had said something homophobic to me at Storm's wedding—clearly projection—as I went up the steps and rang the bell. I heard footsteps coming, and then the door opened.

And I found myself staring into the eyes of my old high school wrestling coach.

CHAPTER EIGHT
TEN OF CUPS, REVERSED
Chance of betrayal

I was drifting downward through a grayish swirling cloud.

I could hear water lapping against something, smell damp in the air, still descending slowly. The cloud seemed to press against me, hugging me, caressing my body and wrapping it into an almost protective cocoon around me. I felt safe, warm, secure. As I continued my descent, the cloud became less thick, and I could see dark shapes and forms. Trees? Buildings? I wasn't sure, but as the cloud continued to thin, I started hearing things besides the lapping water—cicadas, tree frogs, the sounds of the swamp. I felt at peace the way I always did when I came to this place between dimensions or realities or universes or whatever this place where I went when the Goddess called to me.

And the fog cleared, and I was sitting in the prow of a pirogue, gliding quietly over the bayou water. The lapping sound was the bayou water brushing up against the levee. We were heading for a bridge that I recognized. It was the bridge over Bayou Maron, the place where my cousin Beau had his drunk driving accident. Where that girl died.

But before I could even finish thinking about it—trying to remember her name—we were under and past the bridge. We were heading now into the swamp, with its high grasses and cypress trees and live oaks. This was the same path we'd taken in my dream, and I recognized landmarks as we went by them—the cypress tree that had been split by lightning, the old abandoned rusting out houseboat tied to a dock that had collapsed, the silent drifting alligators.

And then we came into the clearing at Blind Lake.

The River Princess *was exactly where it had been in my dream, on the far side of the small lake, resting against a bank of the lake, listing badly to one side. I hadn't noticed in my dream that one of the smokestacks was gone, swept away by Hurricane Isadora. As we floated across the still surface of the lake, the battered steamboat began to glow again.*

"Why are you showing me this?" I whispered. "Is the casino boat important?"

There was no answer from behind me, which is where I assumed the Goddess was seated. The boat kept gliding silently toward the boat. I could see that the listing was probably due to damage to the hull on this side, because the lower deck was barely above the surface of the water. I wondered if it hadn't sunk more because it was already resting on the bottom of the lake. But would they have moved it here to a shallow place? Wouldn't that be more dangerous?

"Why are you bringing me here?" I asked, looking back over my shoulder.

Her face was always blurry to me. I assumed it was because no human being could look on the face of the divine without being driven mad. She was wearing the robes of a Grecian goddess, the flowing tunic with folds, all in white and glowing in the moonlight. She held on to the side of the pirogue with her hands, but the boat was moving. "Pray for a brave heart," She said. She's said that to me before, when I was in danger.

"If I am in danger, can't you tell me from whom?"

"The answers you seek lie in the past." She went on like I hadn't spoken. "The past always has an impact on the present and the future, but you must look to the past."

"Any particular time?" My voice came out a lot more snarky than I'd intended, and I winced. It didn't take much to offend her.

"You'll know when the time comes," She replied. "Remember the Gordian knot, and the truth will make itself clear to you."

I opened my eyes.

Frank was smiling down at me. As I struggled to sit up, I oriented myself. The front gallery at Sunnymeade. I was lying on the porch, just past the stairs. The front door to the house was wide open and cold air was streaming out. "You okay?" he asked with a wink.

I nodded. I felt a bit woozy, but other than that I was fine. "Used to freak you out when I went into a trance."

"I've gotten used to it over the years." He glanced over at the door. "The guy who answered the door? Not so much. I thought *he* was going to pass out, so I sent him to get some water."

The guy who answered the door.

Coach Phelps.

That had to be my imagination, right?

And then he was coming out the front door, carrying a sweating bottle of water. He looked ashen, but it was definitely him.

After all these years.

All I could do was blink.

I opened my mouth to say something, but nothing came out. I could hear my heart beating in my ears, and everything on the periphery of my vision went gray. Memories flooded through my brain like a wild montage, going past so quickly I couldn't recognize them all. My first time seeing him, in his gray cotton singlet that fit him like a glove. The way his eyes sparkled with he smiled, genuinely amused. The feel of his hot calloused hands on my arms, my shoulders, my back, and my butt. The way he smelled vaguely of Drakkar Noir and Irish Spring over the musky smell of dried sweat and masculinity. How flat and ridged his stomach was, the light dusting of black hair between his pecs and the trail of hairs leading down to his groin. I remembered that very first time, when he rolled me over onto my back and guided me inside, the way he moaned slightly and his eyes half-closed.

I remembered his wife walking in on us in their bed.

"Are you okay?" I heard his voice asking again, and I pulled myself together. Deep, soothing breaths. Focus on the heartbeat and slowing it down to normal.

"I'm sorry, just had a dizzy spell. Probably just low blood sugar. Is that for me?" I gestured at the water, which he handed to me. I twisted off the top and downed half the bottle.

I felt Frank's hand rubbing my lower back. I glanced up at him. His face was worried, the brows knit together above his nose, and he was also a little confused.

I got to my feet with Frank's help—was still a bit wobbly—and smiled at my former wrestling coach. "I'm so sorry, you must have— thank you for the water. I'm okay now."

"Are you sure?" This from Frank.

If you only knew, honey.

"I'm sorry, this really isn't a good time," Coach Phelps said, looking from me to Frank and back again. He gave me that look— you know, the one that says *You look familiar but I can't remember from where*—before he smiled faintly, furrowing his brow and tilting his head to one side as he looked at me. "Do I know you?"

I felt a hysterical laugh brewing up and fought it back down.

He didn't recognize me.

Okay, yeah, sure, it had been almost thirty years, but I'd recognized *him*, hadn't I?

I heard Frank saying *He groomed you* again in my head.

I bit my lower lip. He'd recognize the name, surely?

And the years had been kind to my old wrestling coach. He still had that thick dark brown hair with just a hint of auburn in it, but there were a few noticeable gray hairs mixed into it now. He still parted it on the side the way he did thirty years ago. There were more lines on his face than I remembered, and the skin under his chin was starting to sag a bit, but those were the brown eyes with golden flecks I remembered. His three-piece navy-blue suit fit perfectly, and I could see he was still muscular and fit. The shoulders were still broad and his waist just as narrow as I remembered. He was wearing navy-blue oxfords. There was a very expensive looking watch on his left wrist—but I didn't see a wedding band on either hand.

Here we go, I thought, managing to smile and say, "Is Karen in? We'd like to see her."

He frowned. "I'm afraid this is a bad time—"

I held up my hand. "We know about JD," I said softly. "I'm actually a cousin of his from New Orleans." No sense in pretending here. "We came out to talk to him and stopped by his office first. Once we heard"—I made a gesture with my hands—"I wanted to see if there was anything I—we—could do."

He kept looking at me. "I—I can see if she wants to see you," he said hesitantly. "I didn't catch your name?"

I took a deep breath. "I'm Scott Bradley and this is my partner, Frank Sobieski."

The name didn't register. He didn't react, not even a blink. "I'll check with her, just give me a moment, okay?" The door closed again.

He didn't even recognize my name.

"You think she'll see us?" Frank asked. His voice sounded a thousand miles away.

I walked over to one of the metal chairs on the gallery and sat down. "I don't know," I replied. I shook my head. *Get it together*, I chided myself.

He didn't remember me. He didn't recognize either my face or my name.

How do you forget the kid you were in bed with when your wife came home? That blew up your life? That cost you your marriage, career, and family?

The answer was simple.

Frank had been right.

Coach Phelps had never loved me. He was just another pedophile.

I felt nauseous.

"Are you sure you're okay?" Frank's eyebrows were raised, and he looked concerned. "You look kind of green."

"I guess I'm having a delayed reaction to JD's death, maybe," I heard myself saying, lying. Why?

Frank would kill him, that's why.

The front door opened, and Coach Phelps stood there, beckoning us to come in. I pushed myself to my feet and followed Frank.

"Come in." He stepped aside so we could enter, and we walked into the foyer of Sunnymeade. Coach Phelps may not have recognized me, but Sunnymeade looked exactly as it had the last time I'd been here. The hardwood floor polished to within an inch of its life. The pristine, glittering chandelier hanging from the ceiling, yards above our heads. The hanging staircase, with the railing that had been carved from a single piece of wood—it was one of the most prized and famous parts of the old mansion. There was a side table with an enormous antique case standing on it, a mirror just above it. I could see down the hall. The heavily framed paintings of Haver ancestors still haughtily judged everyone who came into their sight line.

"I'm Dan Phelps, pleased to meet you. I am"—he swallowed and shook his head—"*was* JD's chief of staff." He put a hand to his forehead and rubbed it. "I'm sorry, it's all still such a shock to me. I still can't believe he's dead, you know, I just saw him yesterday." He shook his head. "I'm sorry, I'm really not at my best today."

"It's understandable, Dan," Frank said kindly. He held out his hand for Dan to shake.

I braced myself again for no reason. He had no idea who I was. I shook his hand—softer and less calloused than I remembered, but still strong. Did I look *that* different than I did in high school? Sure, I wasn't a dewy innocent sixteen-year-old anymore, but had I changed so much from that kid as to be unrecognizable?

"Bring them into the drawing room, Dan," a female voice called from inside the door to the left of the foyer.

Before he could say anything, a woman appeared in the big double-doored entry to the drawing room.

"Scotty Bradley," Karen said, her heels clacking on the floor as she walked over and threw her arms around me. "It's been too long." She kissed my cheek. She smelled of roses and lilacs. She took me by the hand and led me into the drawing room, Frank and Coach Phelps at our heels.

Like Coach Phelps, Karen had aged well. She'd been strikingly beautiful when she'd been a bride. I'd often wondered, all through their engagement and the wedding, why she'd settled for JD. Even at his best, JD had never been a handsome man. Pudgy and prone to extra weight, he also had been very pale and sunburned easily. His mother—who'd insisted we call her Aunt Barbara—had hovered over both her sons protectively, spoiling them and convincing them they were special. I'd figured JD and Beau would change when they finally got out from under her thumb at college.

Karen probably couldn't still fit into her old Golden Girl costume from her days at LSU, but she was still properly proportioned. She'd stayed relatively slim, despite having two children of her own. She was wearing a pair of black slacks and a salmon silk blouse, a rope of pearls around her neck and her still thick chestnut-brown hair pulled back into a tight ponytail—what my mother used to call an Uptown facelift. There were new lines on her face, but she was still quite beautiful. Her eyes were slightly reddened and swollen. Her makeup was shabby and disheveled, but I imagined her makeup was the least of her concerns for the moment.

She blinked at me. "What brings you out to Sunnymeade today of all days? I couldn't believe it when Sheriff Perkins called."

I glanced at Frank. "Karen, I'm so sorry to drop in like this unannounced and today of all days. Are you okay?"

She gave me a shaky smile. "I've had better days, but…" She exhaled. "I'm holding it together." Her face started to crumple, but she gathered herself.

"This is my partner, Frank. We're both private eyes—"

"Private eyes?" Coach—*stop that*—Dan replied, his eyebrows heading upward.

"A case brought us out this way today," I went on smoothly, ignoring the interruption. "And I thought, you know, why not stop by JD's office since we're out here, and say hello? You can imagine our shock and surprise to find out—"

"Sit, sit." She waved her left hand tiredly. Her voice sounded a bit raw. Her lengthy nails were painted flame red. "Yes, not the best timing, but how could you have known?" she said, her voice tired and small. "This is a time for family and forgetting about the stupid feuds from the past." She stepped back and rubbed her nose with the back of her hand. "The kids are on their way back down from school, and Beau—" She shook her head. "I've been trying to reach him all morning, but some things never change." Her voice became ice cold.

The front drawing room had always offended my sensibilities. The last time I was here, this room had been done in Straight White Man Toxic Masculinity Chic: mounted animal heads and shellacked fish everywhere, the walls painted a bewildering seafoam color, all the furniture big and heavy and dark. But this remodel was much worse. The room had been completely redone in a stark black and white modern minimalist style. The tables were all chrome and glass. The animal heads and fish were gone, and the seafoam had been covered with an off-white to reflect the uncomfortable looking furniture. The only thing that was the same was the painting of the Civil War Haver, Andrew Jackson Haver—the Havers had a long and proud history of naming their children after racist politicians—in its heavy gilded frame. The painting had been restored since I'd last seen it. I remembered it as dark and gloomy, but the restoration had cleared off decades of dirt and grime so that I could now tell he'd posed for the painting in an office of some sort—none of that had been visible before.

Andrew Jackson Haver had not been blessed with the kind of looks that should have been preserved for eternity in oil.

No matter how beautiful the women they married were, the Haver genes insisted on making the men ugly.

She wobbled a little as she walked over to the wet bar. She was barefoot, and the bottoms of her feet were dirty, like she'd been walking outside without her shoes. She picked up a small glass, placed two ice cubes into it, and splashed whiskey over them— Johnnie Walker Black Label. "Sit, sit, sit." She waved her hand, holding on to the wet bar with the other when she lost her balance slightly. She'd been drinking for quite some time, I realized, but who could blame her?

Frank and I sat down on the black couch, which managed to be even more uncomfortable than it looked. Dan walked over to where she was standing and gently took the glass from her fingers. "I think you've had enough," he said in a low voice we still could hear. "You don't want to pass out before the kids get home, do you?"

She raised a hand delicately to her eyes and rubbed her forehead. She looked over at us. "You want a drink?"

We both demurred, and Dan led her delicately back to a chaise lounge and gently helped her sit and recline.

"I'm so sorry—" I started but she cut me off abruptly.

"Dan, would you mind leaving me alone with them?" She turned a brittle smile to him, and I saw lipstick was smudged on one of her upper teeth. She wasn't doing well. The Karen I remembered would have held it together no matter the cost. This was the most real I'd ever seen her.

"Karen—"

"Now." Her voice cracked like a whip, and Dan left the room without another word, pulling the double doors closed behind him. She carried her glass over to a stiff-looking stuffed chair and sat down across a coffee table from us. "I apologize for not being at my best, but I've had a bit of a day." Her voice sounded softer, more lilting, and more heavily accented. "You said you were both private eyes? Well, how much do you charge? I want y'all to find out who killed JD."

Frank and I exchanged a look. "Karen—"

She snorted. "If you think I trust Sheriff Perkins to figure out the difference between his ass and a hole in the ground, you'd be thinking wrong. Perkins is a fool, a corrupt pig feeding at the Haver trough here in St Jeanne d'Arc Parish for decades. A useful fool, JD used to call him, but he doesn't have the brains God gave a—oh, I don't know, a duck, I suppose."

"Why did you ask Mr. Phelps to leave?" Frank replied, pulling out his phone and pulling up the Notes app.

"Dan Phelps was JD's chief of staff, not mine." She smiled, baring her teeth. "Personally, I can't stand the man—there's something about him that raises my hackles. Don't know what it is, or why, but…" She shrugged and leaned forward. She glanced back at the closed doors for a moment. "If I leave it to Perkins, the murderer will never be caught," she whispered. "And he's too stupid to find anything. But…there are some things JD was doing I'd prefer we kept quiet. And if you're doing the investigating…"

"You can control what goes public and what doesn't," Frank finished for her. "Or at least be able to get ahead of the story."

She tilted her head and winked at him. "It's all about optics nowadays."

"So, what was JD doing that you don't want people to know about?" I asked, thinking about Brody and the pictures.

"JD has never been one to keep it in his pants"—she hiccupped, excused herself, and went on—"so there are any number of people we've had to pay off over the years. And then there's all the shit with the casino boat." She rolled her eyes. "I swear to God, I want to burn that thing to the waterline."

"We've been told JD was working on the restoration of the *River Princess* with a new group of investors?"

"Well, JD and I originally only owned a piece of the boat," she replied. "The original investment group cut bait when Isadora wrecked the boat. Once they got their insurance money, they weren't interested in getting the ship back afloat and the slot machines running." She snapped her fingers. "They couldn't get out of Louisiana fast enough. So that left me and JD owning a white elephant slowly sinking in Bayou Maron. So we've been looking for new investors ever since—we were able to buy the other investors out cheaply once they got their insurance payout, the fucks. I don't suppose either one of you wants to buy a fixer-upper casino boat? No? I didn't think so. So, how much do you charge?"

I suspected when she sobered up, she'd regret hiring us. But if we could get her to keep talking now…

"Do you honestly think someone murdered JD over the casino boat?"

"There's no telling what all he was into," she replied grimly. "I don't know everything, and what I do know made me not want to know any more."

"That's the second time you've alluded to JD being involved with dangerous things, or people," Frank observed.

"Are you hired or what?"

Frank glanced at me, and I gave a slight nod. He quoted her a daily rate and an amount for the retainer, neither of which made her bat an eye. "When the retainer runs out, we can discuss whether or not you want us to continue," Frank said. "I don't have a formal contract with me—"

"Let me get my checkbook."

I didn't think she was capable of standing, let alone walking very far, but when she pushed herself up to her feet, she walked quickly and nimbly out through the double doors. "Do you think this is a good idea?" I hissed at Frank as soon as I was sure she was out of earshot.

He shrugged. "I don't see the problem. This way we can be sure we keep Brody out of everything, you know?"

"That's really important to you, isn't it?" I replied.

He sighed. "I know you think he's mature for his age, but he's still a kid no matter what, Scotty. And now with JD murdered... well, now he wouldn't just be the kid who was messing around with the politician, he'd be involved in a murder investigation. And you know how that works. Nobody would ever bother finding out he wasn't the killer or wasn't involved, they'd just remember that he *was* involved in some way." He rubbed his eyes. "And how do you know Dan Phelps?"

That came out of nowhere. "Who says I know him?"

Frank laughed at me. "Milton Scott Bradley"—he placed a hand on my leg—"we have been together now for almost fifteen years. If you think I don't recognize the look on your face when you run into someone you've slept with before, think again." He smirked. "And it happens enough for me to know the look."

Given how he felt about Coach Phelps, I didn't think telling him now was the best idea.

It would probably be better to never let him know Dan was really Coach Phelps.

Maybe he wasn't as wrong about the grooming as you want to believe.

"I'll tell you later," I said, hoping he'd forget, knowing he wouldn't. "Not here."

"He didn't seem to recognize you," Frank teased.

And thank the Goddess for that.

"I guess I didn't make an impression," I replied weakly.

It was strange. Yes, it had been almost thirty years, but had I really changed that much? Sure, my face and skin no longer had that soft glow young men have, and my eyelashes had thinned out some. There were lines radiating out from my eyes and mouth that didn't used to be there. I'd filled out physically more than when I'd been in the 138-pound weight class. My muscles were significantly bigger than they were then, and my waist was three sizes bigger than when I was a kid. I thought I'd been doing a pretty good job of aging well.

Yet he didn't recognize me.

Which meant I'd been *nothing* to him.

But maybe he'd blocked out the memory of what I looked like. He couldn't have pleasant memories associated with me, after all. The last time I'd seen him was that horrible day his wife walked in on us.

How many years had I felt guilty about that? About ruining his life?

I'm friends with people on social media that I went to high school with. It always mystified me when I'd get a friend request or a follow from someone from my horrible days at Jesuit. I hadn't had a lot of friends—the bullying in junior high made me kind of toxic for most of the boys, and even on the wrestling team I hadn't made any real friends—but it was interesting to me how forgetful nostalgia made people. It crossed my mind more than once to send them a message—*Remember when you called me a fag in Louisiana History? Good times!*—but never bothered. If they wanted to remember high school as the best times of our lives or whatever platitude they wanted to throw up on my feed along with a scanned picture from the yearbook on #throwbackthursday instead of what horrible miserable little people they'd been, good for them. Mom told me once that the worst thing about people's cruelties is that most of the time it was carelessness—they didn't think enough of you to care that they might hurt your feelings. They just thought they were being funny, and two minutes later it left their mind. Then they see me years later on social media and remember me from something or another from their youth at Jesuit and impulsively send a friend request.

Picking on you and calling you names was just a bit of fun, nothing terribly deep—hope you weren't scarred! Such good times, right?

I thought Coach Phelps had been in love with me. I'd been in love with him. I'd believed that for all these years...

He was grooming you, Scotty. That's how they work.

I bit my lower lip as Karen strode back into the room, checkbook in hand. She wrote a check to *Sobieski and Bradley* for the amount Frank suggested, tore it off aggressively, and held it out to him. Frank took it, thanked her, and placed it inside his wallet.

"Bring the contract by tomorrow and I'll sign it." She poured herself another glass of whiskey. She looked at me. "I'm glad you came by, Scotty." She took a sip of the whiskey, grimacing as it went down. "I've always thought that families shouldn't feud with each other. JD could never even tell me what it was about in the first place."

"I think everyone's forgotten everything except that they are supposed to be mad," I lied. No sense in bringing up how the Haver family had helped Beau get away with manslaughter when he was a teenager when she was this drunk. Who knew what other crimes the Havers had gotten away with in the years since?

"South Louisianans love to hold a grudge," she observed. "What do you need from me to get started?"

Frank started asking questions, and I made notes on my phone.

Karen had last seen JD yesterday morning. He was already on his way out by the time she came down for breakfast, and he told her he wouldn't be home until late. The Havers had separate bedrooms with a connecting door—no explanation was offered—so after watching television last night, she went to bed early. No, she hadn't communicated with JD during the day, and that wasn't uncommon. As she talked about their marriage, she didn't come out and say it, but I got the sense that their marriage…wasn't a marriage anymore. Separate bedrooms, separate lives—I couldn't help but wonder what she was getting up to on her own. It sounded like she kept herself busy. She was currently planning a gala for the Daughters of the Confederacy in Baton Rouge—I'm sure my feelings about *that* were written plainly on my face—and she had various other clubs and activities. She was president of her alumnae group for her sorority, Chi Delta. "I left the connecting door open when I went to bed last night, but I never heard him come in. When I woke up this morning, I saw he hadn't come home, but didn't think too much about it. JD sometimes works late into the night and sleeps on the sofa in his office. I was having breakfast this morning when Sheriff Perkins called." Her voice wavered on those last words, and she wiped at her eyes. She was upset, just not willing to show it in front of people she didn't know.

I rose. "We'll come by tomorrow with the contract for you to sign, Karen, and we'll have some more questions."

She waved her hand wearily. "I'll be here. Do you mind closing the door behind you?"

Once the door was closed, I heard her start crying.

CHAPTER NINE
SIX OF CUPS, REVERSED
Living in the past instead of the present

"Well, at least we know Karen can pay us," I observed as we pulled out of a Shell station back out onto Bayou Road. Stomach growling, I'd gone inside to buy a protein bar and get us each a bottle of water. I ripped the package open and gulped down the protein bar in about three bites.

"I'm hungry, too," Frank commiserated as we turned right onto the state highway that would take us back over the river and to I-10. "Why don't you text Colin and have him order pizza for dinner."

"Good idea," I said as we drove toward the river on the raised state highway. I pulled my phone out of my pocket and fired off a quick text to Colin. He put a thumbs-up on the text. Ah, technology. What did we used to do before cell phones?

The dance playlist Frank queued up on his phone finished, and without taking his eyes off the road, he switched it over to a Fleetwood Mac playlist. We were both singing along to the *Rumours* album as we crossed the Sheehan Bridge over the river and started driving over the marsh. The low sun of the early evening was bright, and traffic was heavier than I'd expected. Hopefully our timing would be right, and we'd miss the rush hour nightmare of I-10.

I glanced over at Frank, drumming along to the music on the steering wheel. He had a slight smile on his face because he was enjoying the music. The smile made the edges of the angry red scar on his right cheek crinkle up a bit.

"I think the casino boat is a lot more important than we've been thinking," I said slowly. "That's where I was. During the trance. I was in a pirogue with the Goddess, paddling through the swamp, and we came out in the hidden lake where they docked the boat before the hurricane. I don't know why She showed me that, but I also had the same dream a couple of nights ago—me in a pirogue in the swamp, seeing the *River Princess*. I didn't mention the dream because it was, well, it could have just been a dream and meant nothing. But the Goddess took me there, to the same place. So it has to be important, right?"

"I don't see how the boat has anything to do with Brody and Paris." Frank frowned.

"Brody just wanted us to talk to JD and let him know about the texts he was getting," I pointed out. "JD's dead, so it doesn't matter anymore."

"Unless those texts are related to his murder."

"We can't rule out that they may not be," I said. "JD has a lot of enemies—more than we'll probably ever know. But having Karen hire us puts us into a better position to find out things." I barked out a laugh. "For sure Sheriff Perkins was yanking our chain, but if we're working for Karen? He'll tell us anything we need."

"What did you think of that Phelps guy, JD's assistant? He seemed kind of slimy to me."

I glanced over at Frank. His tone was innocent, and so was the look on his face. His eyes were on the road, his right hand still tapping out the bass line of "Go Your Own Way" on the steering wheel. There wasn't anything more to his question. He suspected nothing.

I didn't want to tell Frank that Dan Phelps was the same Coach Phelps from my past.

How do you bring that up in casual conversation? *I think I want pepperoni and mushroom pizza for dinner, and oh, by the way, JD's assistant is the same person you think groomed me in high school.*

Yeah, maybe not the smoothest approach.

Maybe it could wait until I digested it some more.

I was still processing the knowledge Frank thought I'd been groomed.

It was a sobering thought.

I *had* been vulnerable as a teenager. I hadn't had many friends at Jesuit High. Storm had been right—being on the wrestling team ended the bullying. It had also helped me with my self-confidence. Mom and Dad were always great parents. Once I came out they couldn't have been more supportive. They learned about gay culture, history, and politics. It wasn't their fault that society and culture weren't designed to make gay kids feel good about themselves. Being a wrestler changed me. It was just me out there on the mat. Winning and losing were entirely up to me. As I got better and weight training made me stronger, my confidence grew. Coach Phelps had helped with that.

Yes, I had a crush on him. I remembered that clearly. I used to watch him at practice, in his sweaty tank top and gray sweatpants. I fantasized about him at night, alone in my bedroom. There were other guys at Jesuit High I was attracted to, but I forgot about all the rest once Coach was in my sights.

I'd wanted him so badly that when he made a move on me, I just figured he'd noticed me watching him.

Was it possible he'd picked me as the weakest member of the herd?

I finished the protein bar. My mouth was so dry I could barely chew, so I took a swig of water and looked out the car window. My eyes were getting a bit wet, and I didn't want Frank to see. He'd ask and I wasn't ready for that conversation yet.

Had it been *different* than I remembered?

I rested my forehead against the glass, feeling the vibration of the tires through the window. Frank was older than me. Colin was also older than me. I'd always liked older guys. When I was sneaking into the gay bars with a fake ID, everyone I picked up was older than me. I didn't know any gay guys my own age.

Had the experience with Coach changed my wiring?

Was that why I'd always been into daddies?

It had never occurred to me I would ever run into Coach again, anywhere.

I'd been broken-hearted when he disappeared. It was after that I started haunting the gay bars in the Quarter. I wasn't even seventeen. But as I lost myself in exploring my sexuality with strangers I met in the bars, I forgot about Coach. The ache went away, and when I did think about him, it didn't hurt. I felt guilty about him for a while, but that also eventually faded away. I hadn't seduced him, after all.

I wasn't the one with a wife and two small kids.

I wasn't sure how to feel about him not recognizing me, either. How could he have forgotten the student he was with when his wife caught him at last? I'd have thought my face would be burned into his memory banks.

I peered at my face in the side-view mirror. Did I look *that* different from when I was a teenager? Those were still my same eyes, chin, nose. I hadn't turned into a troll.

But just because Coach hadn't recognized me at first sight didn't mean he *wouldn't* at some time. With my luck, it would be at an inopportune time.

So I had to tell Frank and Colin both.

And…I realized part of my reluctance was shame.

I was ashamed.

I wasn't used to that feeling.

"You know," Frank said, interrupting my thoughts. A blistering Lindsey Buckingham guitar solo was coming through the speakers, "Now that we're working for Karen Haver, Sheriff Perkins will have to cooperate with us. I don't think he'll tell us anything that will incriminate him, of course, but he's not going to want to piss off JD's widow—especially not while she's grieving."

"Not if he wants to remain sheriff," I replied. I blinked the wetness out of my eyes and looked back at him.

"You don't think JD's murder had anything to do with Brody, do you?"

"We can't rule it out," I replied as we started climbing the ramp to I-10, which was already bumper-to-bumper traffic. "Maybe. I don't think Brody did it, if that's what you're asking."

My stomach growled again. That protein bar wasn't going to be enough.

"It just doesn't make sense to me," Frank went on. "Why send the screenshots to Brody? He's a kid, he doesn't have any money—"

"Unless that's part of the game the blackmailer was playing," I pointed out. "Send the pictures to Brody, expecting he'll freak out and get in touch with JD. It's more sadistic that way—he finds out from Brody, and then every time he gets a message on his phone—"

"He has to wonder if it's from the blackmailer," Frank finished for me. "So that would mean it's *personal.* Someone criminal would go straight to JD, use the leverage to get money or whatever they wanted from him. This person—whoever it is—wants JD to suffer, too."

"Well, that doesn't narrow it down at all." I couldn't help but laugh. "There's no telling how many people in or around the parish have a reason to hate or resent the Haver family. Maybe we should check in with the local paper?" The *Valmont Times* wasn't much of a paper. It was a weekly, and while it did focus on parish news, they also weren't about to ruffle any political feathers. I tried to remember if *The Times-Picayune* had a river parishes edition. I made a note on my phone to look it up. I knew Avignon, over in Redemption Parish, had a daily newspaper, and since it was in a different parish, might not mind stepping on Haver toes.

"Maybe Paige could help?" Our friend Paige Tourneur was the editor of *Crescent City* magazine. She'd worked at the *Times-Picayune* before jumping ship after Hurricane Katrina. I'd met her at a party in the Garden District a while ago, and we'd become friendly. She'd also helped keep Taylor out of the coverage from last Christmas's murder.

"Maybe." It wasn't a bad idea. Paige was pretty cool.

Frank snorted. "Promise her an exclusive on JD's murder and she'll do whatever we want her to."

I only had one bar out here, so I texted her: *Hey in a spotty service area but might need to call you later on or tomorrow if you prefer?*

Three dots appeared, and then: *either is fine.*

"Okay, that's set," I said, slipping my phone into my pocket. My stomach protested again.

"That car is following us again," Frank said, glancing at the rearview mirror. We were on the downward slope of the on-ramp, but traffic was barely moving.

You can always count on rush hour traffic in New Orleans to be a nightmare.

I looked back over my shoulder.

"Three cars back, you can't see him now because of the small-dick truck."

I could see the enormous pickup truck he was talking about, but nothing behind it. "All the way out of the parish?"

"I didn't notice him until we were on the ramp," Frank replied. "I don't know if that's a deputy or not, Scotty. Would a deputy follow us out of the parish?"

"I wouldn't think so since he has no jurisdiction out here," I said slowly, "but like I said, St. Jeanne d'Arc—the Havers *own* the parish. So if Sheriff Perkins thought he was helping the Havers out, there's no telling what he'd order his men to do."

I felt a chill run down my spine.

Parish sheriffs could make people just disappear.

I made another note on my phone: *Make sure Perkins knows Karen hired us.*

She could hold his damned leash.

Stuck in barely moving traffic on I-10 with someone who might not wish us well following us was probably not the best time for me to break the news about Coach. Frank was an excellent driver. If we needed to ditch our tail, the only person I'd rather have behind the wheel besides Frank was Colin.

Unfortunately, Frank was also one of the few good drivers in Louisiana, so driving made him tense. Sometimes he'd burst out with a *you fucking asshole* or *I hope you die slowly and painfully* or a *yeah fuck you trash*. Whenever I'd comment on these periodic road rage episodes, he'd always calmly reply, "Hey, they're the ones putting our lives at risk with their carelessness. It's not like I hunt them down or anything."

Which was a fair point.

But because he was so tense while behind the wheel, I tried not to talk about things that might make him angry. I was still processing seeing Coach again after all this time. I didn't like the idea that I'd been groomed—I'd never seen myself as a victim in that situation, but now?

Had there been so many teenage boys he couldn't remember us all?

I also couldn't trust Frank to not punch out Coach the next time he saw him, either.

Frank takes protecting the people he loves seriously.

"Yeah, I don't think we can trust Sheriff Perkins," Frank said over Stevie Nicks digging her own grave with a silver spoon. "And Karen seemed to be taking her husband's murder very well, didn't you think?"

"Yeah, I noticed that, too," I replied, reaching down to turn the music down a bit. "But people grieve differently. Maybe she was focusing on dealing with things to take her mind off it, I don't know. She did hire us to find out who killed him."

"Well, if anything happened to me, I don't think I'd like it much if that was how you reacted. I'd like to think you'd be a bit more upset than she was," he said, taking his eyes off the parking lot full of cars in front of us long enough to smile and give me a wink. "You don't think she might have had something to do with it?"

"The cops always say the first person they look at is immediate family—the spouse most of all," I replied, rubbing my nose. "But if you think Sheriff Perkins isn't going to tiptoe around her and handle her with kid gloves, well, that's not how things work in the parishes. Perkins owes his job to JD—no one gets elected in St. Jeanne D'Arc Parish that JD doesn't want to see elected, you know? The Haver machine controls the entire parish, and no one is going to piss off Karen—especially with JD gone." I closed my eyes. "Their oldest son isn't old enough to take over—JD the Fifth and the other one are at LSU, I think. So it'll probably be Karen until JD the Fifth graduates from law school."

"How do you know he's going to law school?"

"The Haver heir always goes to law school. Their law firm is the basis of their power in the parish." I made another note—*more details about the lawsuit against the firm re: Isadora settlements.*

"The King is dead, long live the Queen?"

"Something like that." I shook my head. "I always figured she was the brains of the outfit anyway. JD…" I sighed. "I always had the feeling that he wasn't really all that smart—if he hadn't been born a Haver with all that comes with it, he'd be living in a trailer and selling meth." I rubbed my eyes again. "We're going to have to tell her about Brody at some point. I just didn't think today was the right time."

"You didn't know JD very well?"

"Well, Mom and Dad couldn't stand the Havers, and we'd only come out here for family things when Papa Diderot made us." I shrugged. "And even Papa Diderot couldn't handle it after Beau killed that girl." I made another note: *Check out who else involved in Beau car crash and trace girl's family.* "At big events, like funerals and weddings, we all show up, of course—and everyone is very cold and distant and polite. When we were kids, JD was…" I scrunched up my face, remembering. "He was spoiled and always wanted his own way. His younger brother Beau was even worse—he was his mother's favorite. He did whatever he wanted—he ordered us around a lot. Rain went off on him one time about how he treated us. JD was Storm's age, Beau was about the same age as Rain. They were all older than me." Which meant JD and Beau used to pick on me whenever Storm and Rain weren't around.

I'd forgotten that.

"And Beau's in Houston now?"

"If Vicky is to be trusted." I inhaled sharply. "Damn." I pulled my phone and called Mom. It went to voice mail—Mom was terrible about her phone, always had the sound turned off and could never find it—so I left a brief message about JD and asked her to let everyone in the family know. I hung up.

"Shouldn't you call Papa Diderot and let him know?"

"Better to let Mom handle it. She's better at that sort of thing than I am." I moaned. "Oh God, the *funeral*. We'll have to go to the funeral—well, *I* do, you and Colin don't have to." I laughed. "I don't know how homophobic JD and Karen personally were, but you and Colin and Taylor don't have to go to the funeral."

He grimaced. We were now creeping under Clearview Parkway. My stomach growled again. *That'll teach you to skip lunch—you know better than that.* Frank maneuvered into the left lane to take the 610 bypass and skip a lot of traffic. The 610 bypass was the faster way for us to get home, anyway. "This traffic," he muttered. "We should have stayed later out there, maybe got something to eat before we headed back." I heard his stomach growl. "Something to keep in mind for the next time we head back out here. Should we come back tomorrow? It's a hell of a commute."

"I'll ask Karen if we can stay at Sunnymeade." I hated the thought. But he was right. It was at best an hour's drive out to the parish, and depending on traffic, it could take even longer to get home. "I mean, we could email her the contract, but if we're going to actually try to catch his killer, it doesn't make sense for us to commute from the city." I couldn't remember ever staying over at Sunnymeade. It was always a day trip for us, no question about staying. "But what about Taylor?"

"I don't want him left with Colin," Frank snapped, his face reddening.

"Frank—"

"Look, I know we agreed not to talk about this without him present, but the more I think about it, the less I like it." He gripped the steering wheel so tightly his knuckles whitened. "We talked about this all before, Scotty. And just because he's back now doesn't mean, you know, we're in the clear." He cleared his throat. "You said yourself you didn't like living in a fortress. And what if someone from his past comes after him?"

"But that was always the case," I pointed out. "We just never thought about it because we figured Blackledge was secure." *As far as we know, they could still be secure.*

I hated that little voice.

"I want to believe him," I went on, my voice sounding a little hollow. "And I want to trust him."

"I love him, too, Scotty," Frank replied. "But sometimes love isn't enough."

The traffic started moving faster. We were almost to the bypass. My stomach growled again, and I was just thinking about ordering from Mona's, a Mediterranean place a block away from the house on Frenchmen Street, when my phone started ringing again—the ringtone was Lady Gaga's "Bad Romance"—and Colin's face smiled at me from the screen. I clicked to answer. "Hey, boo, I'm putting you on speaker so Frank can hear."

"Where are you guys?"

"Just about to get on the 610," I replied. "We should be home soon. Can you order pizza for dinner? I was just about to call."

"Sure. How did the rest of the day go out there?"

I filled him in on the latest developments as we exited the highway onto the bypass, and as expected, there wasn't nearly as much traffic. "What did you find?" I asked once I finished the update. "Anything?"

"Well"—he sighed—"I'm not having a lot of luck tracing the original parent company for the casino boat. The boat itself now belongs to one of JD's holding companies—River Princess Entertainment—but the casino license was issued to another holding company, which is a subsidiary of another company, and so it goes—a massive rabbit hole that's clearly meant to disguise or hide who really owns the business."

"I got the impression from Karen that JD owned the business," I replied with a frown.

"It's possible. The holding company with the license—Mississippi River Gaming Company—this all could be a tax dodge, or it could be something shadier." He exhaled. "Usually when I've run into this kind of thing, it's because the mob is usually involved somehow, so they try to bury their ownership so deep only the IRS or a forensic accountant can unravel the mess and get to the truth. I should think, though, that the state wouldn't want to issue a gaming license without doing due diligence and—"

I laughed. "You've not spent nearly enough time in Louisiana if you think that's the case, boo." I shook my head. "JD basically ran that parish, and so politicians owe him favors—that's how things work down here, you know, all the *scratch my back I'll scratch yours* kind of thing." In Louisiana it wasn't a surprise to find out a politician was corrupt—it was a shock if they weren't. I think Louisiana may hold the record for felony convictions by elected officials. "You think this might have something to do with the casino boat? That JD might have pissed off the wrong person and got killed for his trouble?"

"It's a theory," he replied. "I'll keep digging. I've not found anything to indicate that Brody wasn't a one-off, though."

"He wasn't a one-off," Frank said, putting on his signal as we approached the Elysian Fields exit. "I can tell you with certainty as an ex-Fed. Remember, Brody wasn't who JD was seeing first. JD only got involved with Brody after Paris was killed in that hit-and-run. So there's two, right there." Frank slowed as we went down the off-ramp at Elysian Fields. The light at the bottom was red. "There's a pattern of behavior, always. If we go back far enough and ask the right questions of the right people, we'll find Paris and Brody weren't the first, probably not even among the first *ten* JD did this with." His tone made his disgust clear.

Yeah, he was not going to take the news well about Coach Phelps.

Maybe I could break it to him over dinner?

"I don't know how we would go about finding his past, um, victims," I replied. "It's not like we can put an ad on craigslist or something."

"You said his wife hired us—well, you two—to help with the investigation?" Colin said. "And the sheriff was fine with it? That's odd, isn't it?"

"The Havers *are* St. Jeanne d'Arc Parish," I replied. "They don't have the capability to do an actual investigation themselves without getting the state police involved, and I don't think anyone in St. Jeanne wants the state police poking around—no telling what you'll find there if you turn enough rocks over."

"Well, see if we can get access to his electronics—phone, laptop, so forth," Colin said.

"We'll be home soon," I replied as Frank turned right onto Elysian Fields. I disconnected the call.

We rode along in silence until we pulled into our parking garage on Barracks Street. Once we were in our spot and the automatic door had come back down, Frank turned off the car, and I said, as

I unlocked the door from the garage that opened into the shed in our courtyard, "I have something to tell you, but I didn't want to say anything in the car."

Frank laughed as he pulled the cord on the overhead light. The shed had been a disaster area when Millie and Velma owned the building. As soon as I'd bought it, the first thing Frank had done was clean out and organize the shed. Now it was neat and tidy, everything in its place and everything properly labeled—the way it should be. I wasn't quite the neat fanatic that Frank was—I liked things neat and clean, but if there were dishes in the sink it didn't keep me up at night. "You and your weird thing about driving," he said, opening the door into the courtyard. The fountain was on, splashing water coming out of the mouths of the dancing dolphins and cupids, stained green with moss and mildew. "No matter how mad or upset I get, it doesn't affect my driving."

"*You* haven't been in as many car accidents as I have, either," I retorted.

"I also haven't been kidnapped as often as you have, either."

I grinned at him. Colin and Frank may have had to rescue me a few times, but Frank had been kidnapped by the bad guys himself more than once. "Yeah, but this is a big one." I hesitated in front of the fountain. "Come on, let's get upstairs so I can tell you and Colin both at the same time." I couldn't remember if Colin knew the story about Coach Phelps. Had I ever told him? I remembered exactly when I told Frank. It was right after he'd moved down here and Colin was out of the country on a job for Blackledge. We'd started talking, for some reason, about our first times. Frank's had been in college with his big brother at his fraternity—it was hard for me to imagine Frank in a fraternity, let alone in college and virginal—and I'd told him about Coach Phelps.

I'd been high at the time, but I didn't remember him reacting negatively.

The apartment smelled like pizza and my stomach growled as I walked in. Frank pushed past me and went into the kitchen, divvying up the food. Colin was still at the desk, typing away at his keyboard. "Come on, get your food, I have something to tell you both and it's not going to be easy."

They joined me in the living room. "So, you remember, Colin, I told you about meeting JD's chief of staff? Dan Phelps?" Colin nodded, and Frank's eyebrows came together in the center of his nose. I took a deep breath. "Dan Phelps is Coach Phelps, my high school wrestling coach."

Frank closed his eyes, taking several deep slow breaths as his face reddened. The nerve in his jaw began twitching. The vein rose in his forehead.

"The guy who molested you when you were in high school?" Colin frowned.

So, I had told him. "If you can call it molesting when I was willing," I replied, more sharply than I'd intended.

"It doesn't matter if you wanted it or not," Colin said, almost word for word what Frank had said. "You were a kid, you couldn't consent, and he was the adult. He should have known better." He winked at me. "Granted, having seen pictures of you in your singlet from high school I can understand why he wanted you, but no—look but don't touch. You were a kid. A horny gay kid at an all boys school who was bullied and picked on and made to feel terribly unwelcome there." He snapped his fingers. "You were just a ripe apple waiting to be plucked, and he should have known better. He deserved to lose his job and his wife. He was lucky he didn't wind up in jail."

I glanced from him to Frank and back again. "Have you two talked about this?"

They both nodded, both looking a little ashamed.

"It can't be a coincidence," Frank said, putting down his slice of pizza and wiping tomato sauce from the corners of his mouth. "He just happens to work for your cousin, who also had a history of fucking teenagers." He got up and walked over to one of the windows. The shutters were still closed from the termite menace, and it was starting to get dark outside. Soon we'd have to turn off all the lights. "And your cousin—after we find out what he's been doing with poor Brody—gets murdered."

Colin whistled. "That is a lot of coincidence."

"So, we're no longer considering the casino as a potential motive?"

Frank smiled. "We're not ruling anything out—it's too early in the case to do that. But if we're looking for people with a motive for killing JD Haver? If he knew and associated with other pedophiles—"

"They'd all have a reason to want him dead," I finished.

This just kept getting better and better.

CHAPTER TEN
THE TOWER
Conflict, change, unforeseen catastrophe

Before anyone could say anything else, my phone started playing "Telephone." I pulled it out of my pocket. David's face stared at me from the screen. I held up a finger and pressed accept. "Hey, whore, what's up?" I said in my usual teasing voice.

"Scotty, Brody's missing." David's voice sounded strained, stressed. "Oh God, I don't know what to do!"

"Missing?" I held up my hand to shush both Frank and Colin. They both gave me puzzled looks. "Are you sure?" I mouthed *David* at them, and their faces turned grim. "Calm down, take a few breaths, and tell me everything from the beginning."

I could hear him breathing in and out, and finally he exhaled. "Brody is in my second period Voice class. He didn't show up, which was odd. I checked with the office, and his mom hadn't called in to let us know he'd be out. I called his mother to make sure he was okay." David sighed. "She freaked out. According to her, he left the house last night sometime after seven. She said he had a study date, and he didn't come home before she left for work. She usually gets home after he's left for school, so this was the first she was hearing of it. Maybe I shouldn't have had him talk to you? I don't know. I just feel so guilty."

"Don't, David, that's—it's not your fault. For one thing, who even knew he'd talked to us?" I replied. "We don't know for sure something happened to him—"

David interrupted me. "Well, I went ahead and talked to all the kids at rehearsal to see if they knew anything, and they didn't. I talked to some of his friends, the kids he usually hangs out with, and they didn't know. The kid he was supposed to have a study date with knew nothing about it," David went on. "So, he lied to her to get out of the house and—"

"Wait—Colin and Frank are here, I'm going to put you on speaker," I interrupted him. I put the phone down on the table and clicked it over to speaker. "Guys, Brody is missing. No one has seen him since last night." I filled them in quickly on what David had already shared. "David, did he say anything to you when you took him home last night?"

David took a deep breath. "After we left your place, I dropped Brody off at home because it was on my way. I waited for him to get inside before leaving. That was the last time I saw Brody."

"What did you talk about in the car?" This from Frank, who met my eyes. He looked worried.

"He thanked me for introducing him to you. He seemed better than he had on the way there. He'd been fidgety and nervous on the way over but was a lot more relaxed on the way home. We talked about the show, his upcoming audition with Juilliard. He didn't say anything to me about a study date. I don't remember what exactly he said, but I got the impression he was planning on staying in last night."

"But he told his mother he had a study date." This was Colin, looking up from the notepad where he was scribbling notes.

"She works the graveyard shift at Touro—she's an ICU nurse and a single mother," David replied. "She doesn't usually leave home until around nine, but they're very close."

Not close enough for him to tell her about the older men he was involved with, I thought.

David was still speaking. "She and Brody have an understanding that he always had to let her know where he is, and he's usually very good about it. I called her after second period and got her voice mail. I tried Brody's phone, but it went straight to voice mail. She called me back after she woke up, right before rehearsal this afternoon, and Brody didn't show for that, either." He laughed grimly. "Brody loves to perform, and he loves rehearsal. The joke is Brody will get out of his deathbed to perform."

"And this isn't like him?" Frank asked.

"No, Brody has—*had*—perfect attendance."

"Why didn't the office call his mother?"

He sighed. "They send emails nowadays, Scotty. And Ms. Shepherd sleeps during the day while Brody's in class. She's a single mom, his dad's not in the picture. I got to know her when Brody was in *A Chorus Line* last fall." David sometimes volunteered to direct the school's musicals. I'd taken Taylor with me to see *A Chorus Line*. It was pretty good for a high school production. "So, when a kid's marked absent, the office sends an email. Usually the parent will reply—they're always sorry they didn't call or email, blah blah blah. When the office told me he never showed up and she hadn't answered their email…well, I decided I should call her."

You're taking a big interest in this kid, I thought, immediately pushing it out of my head. David wasn't into boys, never had been. Diego was younger and smaller than David—hadn't he always liked them to be younger and smaller?

Stop that right now.

This is Colin and Frank's fault—they've put grooming into my head. I'd have never thought about that before.

"And what did she say?" This was Colin, still taking notes.

"She told me that he'd left shortly before eight, saying he had a study date. He didn't say with who but that wasn't unusual—he usually meets study dates at a nearby coffee shop, Café Egalite? She prefers him to be home when she leaves for work, but…it was a study date. Since he's usually gone by the time she gets home from work, she didn't think anything of it when she got home this morning. She didn't think anything was wrong until she got my message."

"So, no one has seen him since last night just before eight?" I glanced at my watch. It wasn't quite seven yet. "And she doesn't know who his study date was with?"

"She didn't ask. She did call the police but—well, it hadn't been twenty-four hours yet, and they didn't take her seriously. Told her not to worry, he'd turn up sooner or later, and it was too early to file a report. Now she doesn't want to. Says the cops don't care about her son, so why bother them anymore?"

I could already see where this was going. "She should still file a missing persons report with the police," I said, "so there's at least a record of it being reported."

"She'd rather talk to you," David said. "I told her that you… well, that he'd heard something recently about Paris Soniat's death maybe not being an accident, so I introduced him to you guys, and you'd promised to look into it. She wants to talk to you."

"David." This was Frank. That muscle was twitching in his cheek. "Does she know about JD?"

The Final Jeopardy question.

"I didn't tell her," David finally replied. "Do you have to tell her? I promised Brody—"

"Who is missing now," Frank finished. "And you may want to check the news. Sometime last night, sometime *after* the last time anyone we know saw Brody, someone shot and killed JD Haver."

"JD is *dead*?" David's voice cracked on the last word. "Oh my God."

"May not have anything to do with Brody being missing, but that would be quite the coincidence. I don't like coincidences." Frank made a face and met my eyes. *Is he talking about Coach?* I wondered as he continued. "It just seems weird to me, and I am sure it would to the NOPD, that one went missing around the same time the other was shot, don't you think? Does Brody have a car?"

"I don't think so," David replied.

"He had to get to work at the mall somehow," Colin pointed out, making another note. "If he has a car, we can get the plate number from his mother." He looked at me. "So his mother doesn't know anything about him and JD?"

"Not from me," David replied.

Didn't he say his mother made him break off with JD? That she'd looked at his phone? I didn't bring it up. Instead, I said, "I don't see how we can keep the JD thing from her *or* from the police, David." It sucked for Brody, but he wasn't missing when we'd promised to try to keep everything on the down-low for him.

Then it hit me like a sucker punch.

Maybe they're both dead.

If JD's murder had anything to do with Brody, that is. It was possible that JD's murder had nothing to do with Brody. The Havers had a long, colorful history of abusing the law and corruption in St. Jeanne d'Arc Parish. Brody could be off somewhere doing something that had nothing to do with JD.

JD's murder and Brody's disappearance didn't have to be related, of course.

"You think Brody might be dead, too, don't you, Scotty?" It was like David read my mind.

"I didn't say that!"

"No good deed," David replied darkly. "But he said he wanted help!"

"You need to stop blaming yourself," I replied. "What about his phone? Can't his mom track his phone?"

"His phone isn't on—that was the first thing she checked, since her calls were going to voice mail and he's not answering her texts." The three of us exchanged glances. A teenager whose phone wasn't on? That was cause for alarm. "That's not good," I said finally.

"Well, the police didn't think it was a big deal," he snapped. "A kid whose phone isn't on is a red alert to me. But what do I know? I'm just a *teacher.*"

"Why don't I meet you at her place?" I reached for a notepad. "Give me the address, and I can meet you there in about twenty minutes."

He gave me a Bywater address on Louisa Street. "I'll let her know we're on our way." He hung up.

I took the last bite of my slice of pizza and wiped sauce from my chin. I washed it down with the last of my water. While I was swallowing, Colin said, raising an eyebrow, "So JD is dead and now Brody's missing." He shook his head. "This is getting weird—and I haven't even told y'all about the casino boat stuff yet, not to mention some of the other shady shit the Havers have been getting up to out there."

"Nothing would surprise me at this point," I replied, getting up.

"I bet his mother is sorry she didn't ask more questions," Frank said. "Kids, you know. I don't think I could ever be a parent. It's rough enough with Taylor, and he's in college."

"It never ends when you're a parent," Colin replied. "Scotty's parents worry about him all the time."

"Scotty's parents have good reason to worry."

"And fuck you, too, Frank." I stood up, balling up the garbage and shoving it all into the garbage can. "Kids always lie to their parents. He lied to her to get out of the house—I bet Brody does it all the time, it's just never been an issue before."

Frank shook his head. "Teenagers never change—I used to lie to mine all the time. There must be a connection to JD's murder. It's too much of a coincidence. And why send those texts to Brody? What to gain there?"

"Maybe the killer hoped Brody would reach out to JD, which would panic him for sure, don't you think?" Colin replied. "It's the only thing that makes sense. Think about it. You hate JD and you've got some information that could damage him, if not ruin him. It's sadistic, but maybe…maybe they wanted him to suffer a bit."

"Then why kill him?" Frank replied. "Ending the game before it started?"

"Why kill them both?" I reached for the keys. Something was nagging at me—a memory or something just on the outer edges of my brain, just out of reach. The more I tried to grasp it, the farther it slipped out of reach. "Colin, why don't you drive me? Frank, while we're talking to Brody's mother, I want you to do a web search for—oh, anything involving teenage boys, pedophiles, St. Jeanne d'Arc Parish, etc." Paris and Brody established a pattern for JD. There had to be more young men in his past. It was just a matter of finding them.

Frank nodded, a little puzzled, probably wondering why I wanted Colin to come with me instead of him. Colin was better at the web stuff than either of us, and he could access—a very nice way to say hacking—almost anything online. But this didn't need the kind of deep dive/dark web things Colin could do so well, and I wanted to talk to him alone.

Once Colin was backing the Jaguar out of our parking garage onto Barracks Street, he said, with a raised eyebrow and a slight half smile, "So what did you want to talk to me about privately?"

"Was I that obvious?" One drawback to being involved with a former FBI agent and a—I've never known what to call what Colin was. A soldier of fortune? International agent for hire? Hired assassin? They were both skilled interrogators trained to observe body language, looking for tells and other signs of lying. I'm not a big fan of lying in the first place—no matter how good you are at it, you'll always get tripped up in the end—and so I try not to, unless it's for their own good. Even then, I feel so guilty I'm surprised they don't figure it out immediately. "Colin, I know you lied to us about Bestuzhev. Again."

He turned right at Chartres and headed downtown. He didn't say anything until he was turning onto Esplanade. "What do you mean?" His voice was quiet and soft.

A tell with Colin, that meant *I'm not admitting anything until I know how much you know.*

I sometimes wished I loved him even just a little bit less.

I swallowed and closed my eyes. "Colin, you confessed to

Frank and me that your original story about Bestuzhev waiting for you, gun drawn, in the living room was a lie, that you actually tracked him to the house and brought him inside at gunpoint." I looked out the window. A parade of bicycles with glittering lights decorating the spokes of their wheels was passing by on the other side of the avenue. "But we have a security camera on the front gate. And when I reviewed the footage from that night, I saw you and Bestuzhev arrive *together*." I took another deep breath. "You both looked like you were having a good time—you had your arm around his shoulders! That means you lied to us. *Again.*" I could hear my voice shaking. *Get a grip, Scotty.* I closed my eyes again. "I don't care about me. I don't care if you can't tell me what really happened that night. I love you, and if you feel you need to lie to me, I trust that there's a good reason. It's just the Taylor thing. He's a kid with his whole life in front of him, and—"

"I wondered about the beefed-up security." He turned off Elysian Fields onto Royal Street. "It's because—"

"We've let Taylor and everyone think we turned the house into a fortress because of what happened to him."

"Does Frank know?"

"I didn't tell Frank about the security footage—don't worry, I erased it." My voice shook. "Which means I've been lying to Frank, too. I don't like lying, no matter how good the reason. I don't want to keep lying, either." I put my hand down on his thigh. "But that's up to you. But—we're going to have to spend the rest of our lives worrying about whether some enemy from your Blackledge days will show up wanting revenge. Was that even true? Did we even have to worry about that, Colin?"

"Scotty, I can't tell you who Bestuzhev was, or why killing him was necessary." His voice was calm, soft, soothing. "But no, there was never a security breach at Blackledge." He gripped the steering wheel hard. "I told you that to explain why he was there. I didn't think you'd understand."

"So how did he wind up in New Orleans?"

"We had been keeping an eye on him for a while. I had already established contact with him once before on another case, so he knew me, not as a Blackledge operative. I followed him to New Orleans—"

"To kill him." I closed my eyes. "What if we'd been home?"

"I knew you weren't." He held up a hand. "I would have never

brought him there if I thought I was putting any of you in danger."
He swallowed. "I knew Frank was on the road. I knew Millie and
Velma were in Florida. And I knew you and Taylor had plans."

"I don't want to know how you knew all of this, do I?"

"I keep tabs on all of you." His voice was so quiet I could barely
hear him over the tires bouncing over potholes. "And we had agents
in place, staking out the apartment—"

"But you didn't know I was coming home!" His silence was
deafening. "Oh my God, *you knew I was coming home.*"

"If you two don't want me to stay—" His voice was low, quiet,
sad.

"That's not what I'm saying. Frank and I—we both love you,
you know that." The relief I was feeling that we didn't have to
worry about enemies seeking vengeance from his Blackledge days
was great, but I didn't know how to feel about this revelation. He'd
brought a killer home to our place with the intent of killing him,
turning my living room into a killing floor.

The smart thing to do was to tell him to go.

I don't think I've ever done the smart thing in my life.

"I did lie." His voice was low as he swung around the corner
onto Louisa. He pulled up in front of the house we were looking for
and turned to me as he shut the engine off. "He didn't follow me
here—I followed *him*. The Ninjas heard chatter about Bestuzhev
coming to New Orleans—I can't tell you why." He looked at me
in the light from the streetlight. "I tracked him to a guest house on
Ursulines. I waited for him to come out, and—" He sighed. "I put
my arm around him and held a gun against him, escorted him over
here. I couldn't take care of him in the street, of course, and the best
option was to just bring him here. I knew Frank was wrestling out
of town, and I thought I could kill him and clean up the mess and
no one would ever know." He gave me a faint smile. "But of course
he tried to jump me and we struggled…and you came home." He
turned and stared out the windshield. "I never wanted to hurt you
and Frank, ever. I know I've had to lie to you before because of the
job, but that's why I decided to leave Blackledge and, you know, have
a life here with the men I love." He reached over and grabbed my
hands with his big strong ones. "It kills me knowing that I put all of
you at risk. Do you want me to tell Frank?"

I exhaled and unlocked my door. "I think you should—but it

can wait until we get all this"—I fumbled for the right word and gave up—"whatever this is cleared up, but we all need to sit down and talk about it. And come up with a plan for moving forward." Impulsively I leaned over and kissed his cheek, the stubble scratching my lips a bit. "I do love you. I'm happy for you to be home permanently. You and Frank both." The great irony of me being in a three-way relationship—Taylor called it a throuple, but I didn't like that word—was that somehow, I managed to spend a great deal of time at home alone. Colin had always been off somewhere on assignment for Blackledge while Frank toured around the Gulf Coast with wrestling promotion. "I'm going to have to get used to the two of you being around more."

I got out of the car and opened the gate. The house was a double camelback shotgun but had been converted into a single-family home at some point in its past. The house was painted bright blue with yellow shutters. The front windows were ablaze with light, and the front porch lights were also on. This part of the neighborhood had flooded after Katrina, but the water hadn't risen high enough to get inside the houses. The massive destruction was on the other side of St. Claude Avenue and the Lower Ninth, on the other side of the Industrial Canal.

I bounded up the stairs and knocked.

A woman in her mid to late forties opened the door just as Colin joined me on the porch. "Ms. Shepherd?"

She was a tall, thin woman, and it was easy to see where Brody got his coloring from. Her skin was olive, like his, fine strands of gray entwined in her thick black hair, and she was slender and long-limbed. She was pretty, letting herself age naturally. Brody had also gotten her big round dark eyes. She was wearing a Saints T-shirt and a pair of black sweatpants that had seen better days. "You two must be Mr. Andrews's—er, David's, friends?"

We introduced ourselves quickly and she ushered us inside. When the house had been renovated into a single family dwelling, the wall dividing the living rooms from each other had been removed, opening up a large space with a shiny hardwood floor, a chandelier, and the walls painted sea blue with coral trim. An enormous framed black-and-white poster hung between the windows on the far wall—it was Brody, I realized looking closer, doing a grand jeté, his head thrown back, his legs in a perfect split, the toes hyperextended so the feet bent in ways feet shouldn't bend. He was shirtless and wearing white tights that clung to every muscle fiber in his legs like another layer of skin. "Beautiful image," I commented.

"Call me Wendy," she said, offering us a seat and something to drink, which we declined. Colin pulled out his notebook. "Mr. Andrews—*David*—wouldn't tell me what Brody talked to you two about," she said softly, her voice shaking. Her eyes were red-rimmed and I could see she was trembling slightly. "I did file a police report finally, once it was twenty-four hours." She made a face. "New Orleans cops, though. What are they going to do?" Her voice dripped contempt. "Not a damned thing, that's what."

"Ma'am—"

"*Wendy.*" She raised her voice and then smiled a little in surprise at how loud she'd been. "Please, call me Wendy."

"Wendy." Colin's voice was kind and soft. "Why don't you tell us what you told the police?"

"It was a normal night," she said, wiping at her eyes. "At seven he told me he was going over to Café Egalite to meet with some friends to study for a test. I was getting ready for work so wasn't really paying as much attention as I probably should have. It wasn't a big deal. I'm a single mom, and Brody's dad has been out of the picture since he was a baby. I trust Brody, he knows that. He's earned it, you know? He's a good kid. He studies hard, he works hard at his dancing, and I think he has what it takes to make it. He's never given me a reason to doubt him. So, when I got home and he wasn't here—hadn't slept here, either—"

"Does he always make his bed?" I asked.

She nodded. "He does. At first when I looked in, I thought maybe he had an early rehearsal or wanted more time at the barre—ballet, not a place to drink, the cops thought I meant drinking, like an eighteen-year-old would go drinking on a school morning—but he usually leaves a note. But he doesn't always. That was when I remembered that I'd changed his sheets yesterday after he left for school, and *I* had made the bed." Her voice shook a little bit. "And I am the one who always puts his teddy bear in the center of the bed. He doesn't do that." She took a few shaky breaths. "It was just a little thing, you know, that made me happy. And he hadn't been there. And he wasn't at school." Tears began slipping out of her eyes again, and she angrily wiped them away. "So why did Brody want to talk to you?"

Colin and I looked at each other. *No, there's no need to bring JD into this yet*, he seemed to be saying with his eyes. "He got a text message the other day about a friend of his who'd been killed in a hit-and-run last summer." I swallowed, hoping I was doing the right thing. It wasn't untrue. "This upset Brody."

"Paris." She nodded. "Such a sweet boy, too. Brody was crushed when he died. What did the text say?"

"It alluded to his death being murder," I said, licking my lips. "Paris was involved with a much older, married man—"

"Look, I know Brody was sexually active." She smiled at the look on our faces. "Brody didn't keep things from me. And a mother knows. He came out to me when he was fourteen. I also know that if he was going to keep something from me, it would probably be about his love life. I get the sense he told you some things you're worried he didn't share with me, and you don't want to betray his confidence." She started wringing her hands. "If you're thinking he's out with a boyfriend, and you're worried that might upset me… the most important thing is making sure he's okay. So, if you think he might be with a boyfriend—"

I glanced over at Colin, who gave me a slight nod. "Did you know he was being…" I fumbled for a word. *Harassed* was what I wanted to say, but was it harassment? He accepted the gifts, he flirted with JD. "Harassed by an older man?"

Her eyes widened. "Harassed? What do you mean?"

Haltingly, I explained what Brody had told us, ending with us finding out that the man—I didn't name him—had been found shot to death just this morning.

She went pale. "You don't think Brody—"

"We don't think anything just yet, Wendy," Colin said in his most professional voice. "Did the police take his devices?"

"Well, no, they told me I didn't need to worry, and he'd probably turn up, can you believe that?" She shook her head. "I can't find his phone, so he must have it with him."

"Does he have a laptop?"

She nodded. "But he must have taken it with him. But his iPad is still here." She motioned for us to follow. She led us down a hallway back to his room. It was neat and tidy. The walls were covered with images of dancers, thumbtacked to the wall. There was an enormous poster of Baryshnikov in flight in pale blue tights on one wall. She walked over to his desk and picked up an iPad, stashed between the desk and the wall, and unplugged the charger. "They didn't take it." She handed it to me.

I touched the screen, and this time the lock screen appeared. The wallpaper was another shot of Brody, this time up on a toe with a leg bent and raised like he was about to spin. His head was thrown back and his face was lit up with a smile of joy. "Do you mind if we take this?" I asked. "If the police want it, we'll of course turn it over to them, but in the meantime…"

"His PIN code is my birthday, 0-4-2-8." She reached onto a shelf in the bookcase and pulled out a high school yearbook from the year before.

I typed the numbers in. The screen changed, showing thumbnails of all his apps. The background picture was of Brody in a leap, everything pointed, his arms, legs, and body making beautiful lines.

I touched the mail icon and smiled as his inbox opened before me.

He was signed into everything, so no hacking was required.

CHAPTER ELEVEN
THE MOON
Unforeseen perils

"I don't like this," Colin said as I shut the passenger door and put on my seat belt. "You don't think he ran away, do you?"

I sighed as Colin started the car. "I don't know, Colin," I replied, opening the iPad case I was holding. It had already gone back to sleep. "I'm more worried that someone took him, to be honest. I know coincidences do occur, but there are way too many here for there not to be something behind everything." I shook my head. "Brody didn't strike me as the type who'd go out looking for trouble, but I also don't know him very well." I never went looking for trouble, either—it just somehow always managed to find me.

I've always been hopeless when it comes to technology. I'd been a late adopter to the computer and internet age. I didn't even have a computer when I first met the guys. They were expensive, and I didn't think I needed one. Whenever I did need to use one, I used to just walk over to David's, when he still lived in the Marigny, and use his. Frank was the one who convinced me I needed to get my own. Before he moved down here, we used to chat on the computer until late in the night. Fortunately, Frank and Colin are whizzes, and Taylor can do things with his phone I'll never be able to learn. I'm lucky I know how to use the remote for the television—and sometimes I need help with that.

I have a kind of mental block when it comes to tech. But I also don't need much from a computer, just access to the internet and a couple of other programs, like Word and Excel. I use a program to manage my bank accounts that must have been designed for five-year-old since I was able to learn it so easily. I'd resisted getting a cell phone for as long as I could—no one *needs* to get ahold of me *right now*—and was still using a flip phone years after everyone else started switching to smartphones. I don't care about playing computer games, and I'm not a big fan of watching television or movies on a smaller screen.

Brody's iPad wasn't the most recent model, but I recognized this one. I'd had this version myself before upgrading all of ours last fall. I touched the home button and the screen lit up. I typed in the passcode, then touched the mail icon on the bottom row of the screen, which had a red bubble with the number *36* inside. I scrolled down the list of emails. Brody got a lot of junk email. The first five real emails were from Wendy, all with the subject line WHERE ARE YOU PLEASE CALL ME NOW. Below hers were a few from David, essentially the same subject line. I didn't recognize some of the names in his inbox, and I wasn't sure I felt comfortable reading his private emails. I heard Taylor's voice in my head, scoffing, *People my age don't email each other. That's what texts and Snapchat are for.*

If Brody and his friends used Snapchat, that's all gone for good. The primary appeal of the app was that the messages disappeared after a short period of time. There was probably a way to get them back, but that was way above my expertise and pay grade.

I reached the bottom of the inbox without seeing JD Haver's name.

I tapped my fingers on the armrest.

Where are you, Brody? What happened to you?

He didn't have a car, but he'd left home around seven. Interesting that was the also the last time anyone had seen JD before he was murdered, but that *had* to be a coincidence.

Brody had no reason to kill JD—unless he'd found out something more about Paris's death?

Stop speculating, I said to myself and clicked on the Messages icon. The little red balloon over the app said *38*. But when the app opened, I could see that most of the new messages were from either Wendy or David. Others were from names I didn't recognize, probably classmates. Almost everything sent today was asking where he was, if he was okay, to get in touch as soon as he could. There was a flirty exchange with someone named Elvis that dated back several weeks…and yes, there were pictures. My face heating, I went back to the list and kept scrolling.

There it was. *Unknown.*

I touched it, and the picture popped up in the preview panel.

Yes, that was definitely Brody, making duck lips for the camera and tightening all the muscles in his upper body. What he was wearing didn't count as underwear or a swimsuit, there wasn't enough material. It was basically strings running around his body and a triangular patch of black cloth with red trim. It didn't hide anything. *Like your wrestling singlet in high school did?* That was a fair point. The singlets revealed everything. We just pretended erections weren't happening.

And the message: *Be careful with JD Haver. Your buddy Paris wasn't an accident.*

Brody had replied, *Who is this? How did you get my picture?*

Unknown never replied.

And just down the list, past a few more names, I saw JD.

I took a deep breath and touched the name.

The conversation had been going on for a long time. I kept scrolling by, flicking my finger to get through the entire thing back to the beginning, but pictures kept flashing by. They were all of Brody. Jocks, underwear, thongs, bikinis—you name it, Brody had posed in it. His muscular development was impressive, but that was ballet for you. There wasn't any body fat on him, anywhere. His entire body looked hard. You could see muscle striations under his skin. I kept scrolling and stopped at one where he was standing en pointe, the other leg raised high in front of him with the toe hyperextended. He was wearing red underwear and a big goofy smile, and he'd crossed his eyes.

JD had replied, *Your body is so amazing! I can't believe what you can do with it!*

I felt my stomach tighten a bit at that one.

I scrolled down a little more slowly, and the next picture I came across was him wearing a gold lamé jockstrap. He was turned sideways to the camera, his left side to the lens. His left foot was in front, the right in back, and he twisted at the waist, dipping his left shoulder slightly. His buttocks were clenched, their muscularity and shape emphasized by the tight gold straps cupping his backside and running along his lower back.

JD: *Your ass looks amazing in that jock!*

I felt a wave of nausea and glanced over at Colin.

I heard Frank saying again, *He groomed you, Scotty. He was an authority figure and he used that to get you to do what he wanted.*

I rested my head against the window. Reading the text

conversation between Brody and JD, it sounded *exactly* the way Coach and I used to talk to each other. He'd never had me pose for pictures—you still had to take them in to be developed in those days—but he'd liked having me dress up for him. He liked me in singlets, jocks, underwear, Speedos…

And sometimes wrestling was our foreplay.

No wonder seeing Frank in his ring attire always turned me on so much.

I felt nauseous.

"You feelin' okay over there?" Colin glanced over at me as he drove down Louisa Street. "You look kind of green."

"I don't know," I replied honestly. "It's…well…running into Coach Phelps again. I don't know, Colin. I mean, I…" It felt stupid to say it. I gritted my teeth and closed my eyes. "I always *believed* he loved me, you know, that I was special. I felt guilty that I ruined his life. But now, I don't know what to think."

"It's a lot." He reached over and put his big hand on my leg, and I felt that electrical charge I always did whenever we touched. "I never gave it much thought. It was just a part of your past, and it didn't seem to be having any negative effects on you as an adult. You're…well, not the most *normal* person I've ever known, Scotty, but who says what's normal?"

"I was just reading the texts between JD and Brody," I admitted slowly. "It reminded me so much of the way Coach used to be with me…"

I flashed back to the last time I'd been with Coach before the state championships. We'd gone up to Alexandria for a regional meet. I'd won, of course, qualifying for the state tournament. We were staying at a cheap motel on the edge of town. We'd only gotten one room. That night he'd had me pose for him while he played with himself on the other bed. Jocks, underwear, the sweaty singlets I'd worn in the tournament. I can still feel the wet Lycra of my Jesuit High singlet, drenched and soaked with my sweat, against my skin as he climbed up next to where I was standing on the bed and slowly started peeling it off my body, kissing his way down my torso as he unwrapped it.

I shuddered.

But it doesn't change you or your life. So what if Coach never loved you and was just a lech with a thing for teenage boys? Like your cousin JD?

"It's rough, I know. But it was a long time ago, and you've always seemed fine to me." He stopped, squeezed my leg, and turned left onto Royal Street.

"I don't think I want to talk about it anymore," I replied as the car bounced over a pothole.

"Anything jump out at you on his iPad?"

"Probably better to wait until we get home to take a good look at it." I closed the case again. "It's paired with his phone, and as best I can tell, he's still signed into everything." Taylor was always lecturing me about this very thing. *What if someone picks up your phone! Sign out of everything!* It also drove him nuts that I always stored my passwords in my browser. *You're literally begging someone to rob you blind, Scotty—that's exactly the kind of thing crooks are looking for. If they can figure out your sign-in to unlock it, they can do anything they want with your stuff—they can access your credit cards and bank accounts and steal your identity.* He'd convinced me not to have the apps for my bank or credit cards on either my phone or my iPad. He was right, I didn't need the ability to access balances or make payments on my devices. "And it's probably better if you and Frank were the ones to examine it. As y'all are always reminding me, I'm a Luddite." I hesitated. "But can you copy all the data on this? If the NOPD ever decide to take Brody's disappearance seriously, we'll have to turn this over."

But it was ours until then.

Taylor had once tried to explain to me why it was so important to have all the technology from the same company, but as he got farther into it, my eyes crossed. Something about sharing documents and files? He might as well have been talking in Latin for all the sense it made to me. Long story short, we lived in an iHouse. All the computers, all the tablets, all the phones—we even had an Apple TV. The one thing I *did* remember from Taylor's lengthy explanation, which I'd assumed was a roundabout way to talk me into getting him a new laptop and the Apple TV—and I'd been right—was that his phone and his iPad mirrored each other. He could even use the iPad *as* a phone.

My iPad didn't. Come to think of it, I wasn't even sure where mine was. I never really used it. I'd already decided not to replace it when it got old—I had a phone and a computer, what else did I need?

But the bottom line was Brody's iPad was the next best thing to having his phone.

I hoped he was okay. I closed my eyes and leaned my head against the headrest, saying a quick prayer to the Goddess to watch out for the kid.

"Jeez, dude, get off my ass," Colin muttered, breaking into my reverie.

I opened my eyes. The entire cab of the Jaguar was flooded with light. I turned in my seat and looked back over my shoulder. All I could see were the blinding headlights of an enormous pickup truck. I couldn't tell the make or model or color. But he was following way too close. If we had to suddenly stop, he'd slam right into us.

"Pull over and let him pass if he's in such a fucking hurry," I said, resisting the urge to flip him off. The way he was driving, he clearly wasn't right in the head, and Louisianans were very fond of their guns. I wasn't in the mood for getting shot.

I turned back around. We were almost to the train tracks that used to serve as the unofficial borderline between the Marigny and Bywater neighborhoods. I smiled. These neighborhoods had always been considered a bit sketchy back in the days before Katrina. The gentrifiers had come in with a vengeance. St. Claude, which used to be a tired old avenue of run-down businesses, boarded-up buildings, and liquor stores, was being revitalized, too. The car bounced over the tracks with the truck still less than half a car length behind us. I looked back again as we went through an intersection. There was plenty of parking on the right side of the street on this block. Without using his signal, Colin expertly whipped the wheel to the right and out of center of the road, braking and slowing as we cruised along the sidewalk before stopping. The truck shot past us, slammed on the brakes with a loud screech, and almost went up on two wheels as it took the next corner and accelerated again with the scream of tires and the stench of burnt rubber.

"I guess he was in a hurry," I said. My heart was racing. I've always hated riding in cars. I've been in so many car accidents I can't even keep track of them all anymore. It seemed like at least fifty percent of the time whenever I got into a car, we'd get into an accident.

"Asshole," Colin said, checking to make sure it was clear before pulling away from the curb. He laughed. "I don't think I'll ever get used to the way people drive here."

"We do have the worst drivers," I replied. Even if I hadn't been in all of those accidents—none of which were my fault, for the record—our car insurance rates would have still been exorbitant. Supposedly New Orleans had some of the highest rates in the country. The explanation—we had so many uninsured motorists.

Maybe that was true. But to me, it was more about how many shitty drivers there were.

We waited for a white Toyota to go by before Colin pulled away from the curb.

"What do you think, Colin?" I asked in the silence as we made the weird jog to the right when we crossed Franklin Avenue. Franklin Avenue is where the streets in the Ninth Ward turned sharply again to follow another bend in the river, so the streets didn't exactly align. "It can't be a coincidence that Brody disappeared the same night JD was murdered."

"Are you wondering if Brody somehow got a car and drove out to St. Jeanne to kill JD?" Colin turned his head to wink at me. "Did he strike you as a killer?"

"Well, no, not actually," I replied. "I don't—*oh my God look out!*"

The last words were shouted as my hands went to the dashboard and I braced myself for the coming impact. The massive pickup truck—or maybe it was a different one—had pulled up at the intersection at Spain Street, heading toward the river, and stopped, blocking the road. Colin slammed on the brakes and the car slid sideways a bit as it slowed, the tires screeching in protest. The Jaguar stopped maybe two or three feet from the side of the truck. I jerked forward, straining against the seat belt, before jerking back into the seat from the momentum.

"Holy shit," I gasped out. I was breathing too hard. My heart pounding and my mouth dry, I saw the front and back doors of the truck open.

Two men get out.

Both were carrying guns.

They assumed a shooter's stance and aimed the guns at us.

Without even thinking I slid down as far in the seat as I could. What the hell?

"Hang on," Colin shouted and slammed the car into reverse, pushing down on the gas pedal. The tires squealed again—in my peripheral vision, a curtain moved in one of the windows of the houses lining the street but dropped back into place. Colin looked back over his shoulder and backed up much faster than I was comfortable with. I thought I heard gunshots. The windshield spider-webbed, and something hot buzzed past my ear, and sparks flew from the hood. When we reached the end of the block, Colin slammed on the brakes and turned the wheel hard to the left. The car spun smoothly around the corner as Colin shifted the car back into drive before it came to a stop again, and he floored it and flew down St. Roch toward St. Claude. I could smell burning rubber and something else as he slowed the car down. I closed my eyes as we shot across St. Claude Avenue to the honking of horns and the screaming of other brakes. He didn't slow, and we went up on two wheels as he passed through the neutral ground and slammed back down onto all four, the carriage bouncing a bit as Colin kept his foot down on the pedal. He zoomed around cars like they were standing still, and still crouched down in the seat, my breath coming too fast and my heart about to leap through my ribs, I couldn't watch what was happening, what he was doing. Colin was a fantastic driver—he'd been trained in evasive techniques—and I couldn't have hoped for a better person to be behind the wheel, helping us escape whoever that was.

Streetlights and houses and the neon signs from businesses on St. Claude blurred as Colin sped toward the intersection at Elysian Fields. The light at St. Claude was red, and there was no oncoming traffic, so Colin turned left onto Marigny Street, behind the little shopping plaza with the Robert's and the new Starbucks, just across the street from the Phoenix. Marigny was a street in desperate need of repair, so Colin drove slower than I would have preferred. I slid back up in my seat, keeping an eye out for the big truck, but didn't see it anywhere. Colin turned right back onto Royal and turned onto Elysian Fields. By the time he pressed the garage door opener and pulled into our spot, my heart was back to normal and my breathing was under control.

I didn't feel relieved, though, until the big steel garage door had descended and closed.

"Are you okay?" Colin asked me, turning on the overhead light and looking me up and down, presumably for bullet holes.

"I am now." I turned and pointed at the back seat. "That's where the bullet that went past me wound up. It was a little too close, if you want my opinion."

"We'll need to get the windshield replaced," he said idly.

I punched his shoulder. "Who were those guys?"

"Ouch and stop." He pulled away from me, giving me an odd, confused look. "Why would I know who that was?"

I made a face. "Two gunmen just basically appear out of nowhere and start shooting at us, and you wonder why I'm asking you?" I stared at him. "Come on, dude." I opened the car door and winced as I stood up. My muscles had all tightened up from stress— I'd need to do some yoga stretching before I went to bed. "I don't think it's too much of a stretch to assume they were after you. I mean, when strange killers show up out of nowhere, it usually has something to do with you and your job."

He looked hurt for a moment but then nodded, a little sadly. "I can't even get angry or be hurt because it's true." His voice sounded small. He wiped at his eyes. "I know you can't trust me completely, and I know it's my fault. I'm sorry about Christmas, Scotty—you'll never know how sorry I am about that." His voice wavered. "Every time I think about what might have happened…it was a risk." He swallowed. "And I wasn't thinking like a partner, I was thinking like an operative. That's why I left Blackledge." He half laughed. "Well, part of the reason. I can't stand the thought of putting any of you in danger again. I can't stand the thought of having to lie to you again. I don't want to even think like an operative anymore. It's such a lonely life…"

I wanted to put my arms around and kiss the tears away, hold him and reassure him that we loved him, that I loved him, and we'd figure it all out the way we always did.

But I wasn't so sure this time.

"Okay, if those men weren't after you, then who the fuck were they?" I asked after a few moments of an incredibly awkward silence.

"I would tell you if I knew, I swear."

Would you?

I caught myself before the words came out of my mouth. The adrenaline was wearing off, and I was starting to feel exhausted. "I'm sorry," I said. "I was worked up from the excitement." *Were you?* a snarky little voice whispered in my head. "And scared." I started shaking. While I tried to get it under control, Colin came around to my side. He pulled me into his arms, putting his hand on my head and cradling it against my chest. His strong, powerful arms felt amazing around me. I could feel his chest rise and fall with every breath, the beating of his heart. He smelled a little musky, slightly sweaty beneath his cologne. It felt so nice, sitting there with him holding me tight.

He kissed the top of my head. "It's okay for you not to trust me," he whispered, hugging me tighter. "I know I blew it, and I know I have to earn everyone's trust back. I'll spend the rest of my life doing that if I have to. I love you, Scotty. I love Frank. I love your family and Taylor, and you're all the family I've not had since I was a kid."

I took a deep breath, disentangling myself from him, and kissed his cheek. "It'll all work out, I know," I said.

But if those men weren't after Colin, why had they come after us? Who would be after us? Whoever killed JD wouldn't even know Karen hired us, let alone how to find us.

It didn't make sense.

Who could they be?

I wanted to believe him, more than anything.

I'm just not destined to have a quiet life like everyone else.

CHAPTER TWELVE
QUEEN OF WANDS
An energetic, vivacious, and strong woman

Still shaking a bit from the excitement, I followed Colin up the back stairs. When we got to the landing outside our apartment, I looked out and saw a cloud of termites swarming around a streetlamp on Barracks Street. Great, I thought, home just in time for the termites.

Colin opened the back door, and Scooter yowled at me, rubbing up against my calves and meowing. I picked him up and held him up over my head. "You're such a demanding little diva," I said in my only-use-it-for-talking-to-the-cat voice. I brought him back down and cradled him in my right arm and started scratching his belly with my left hand as I stepped inside and kicked the door closed behind me. In response he touched my nose with his paw like the adorable little snuggle bunny he was.

I could hear voices from the living room down at the end of the hallway. The apartment reeked of marijuana. All the lights were out, but I could see a flickering glow in the living room. There was a feminine laugh—more of a cackle, really—and I felt a grin spread across my face. I knew that laugh.

Paige!

I took a deep breath to shake off what just happened and walked down the hallway.

I'd met Paige Tourneur-Tujague at a housewarming party in the Garden District last year, and we'd hit it off almost immediately. Paige was cool. She had her own unique style. She favored flowing garments in bright cheerful colors. Her blond-streaked red hair was usually tied up with a colorful scarf. She was on the short side, maybe about five feet tall in stocking feet. She often wore heeled shoes to give her a little more height. She was slim but curvy. Her most striking feature was her mismatched eyes—one brown, one blue. I wasn't sure how old she was, but she had to be around my age, give or take a few years. She also had a wicked, snarky sense of humor and was almost as fond of weed as we were. She was now editor-in-chief of *Crescent City* magazine, a local glossy monthly magazine focusing on New Orleans culture. She had worked for the *Times-Picayune* on the crime beat before she left to take the editorial job. She had connections and sources everywhere. She'd turned *Crescent City* into a must-read in her years at the helm. We'd gone to her wedding in late April to Ryan Tujague, a lawyer and a member of an old New Orleans society family. Ryan's younger brother Blaine was a police detective we'd worked with several times. New Orleans may have changed a lot in the years since Katrina, but it was still a very small town. Paige had been a huge help in keeping Taylor's name out of the news about Eric Brewer's murder at Christmas, and we'd come to think of her as part of our extended family.

She was always up for a good time.

"Hey there," I said as I walked into the living room. Three blasphemy candles flickered on the coffee table. Paige was exhaling a huge cloud of smoke, followed by a coughing spasm as she locked her eyes on me. She held up a finger.

"There you are!" she exclaimed as she finished coughing. She wiped tears out of her eyes and leapt up from one of the wingback chairs. She swayed a bit as she walked toward me. She went up on tiptoe to give me a kiss on the cheek as I wrapped her up in a big hug. A good day. "I was in the neighborhood when Frank called me—and oh my God is that *Colin!*" She disentangled from me and launched herself at Colin. He grinned and caught her. He threw his arms around her and spun her around off her feet a few times.

I sank down next to Frank on the couch. Gratefully, I took the lit joint he offered me. My heart was still racing. I took a big hit and passed it to Colin, who still had an arm around Paige. I took it back from him and took another big hit. I could feel the calm spreading through my body as my muscles relaxed. Yes, this is better, I thought happily as I leaned against Frank.

"Are you okay?" Frank whispered.

"We were followed," Colin said grimly. "A big truck, raised on those obnoxious tires. It was a dark vehicle, looked like a newer model. I noticed them following us on the way over there, but...

they didn't try anything until we were coming back here." Tersely, he gave them a quick overview of what had happened.

Frank put his hand on my leg when Colin started talking. As Colin kept talking, Frank's hand curled into a fist. I couldn't really see in the gloom, but I'm sure his jaw was twitching.

"Damn," Paige replied, sitting back down in her chair. "You guys sure you're all right?"

"My heart rate is finally coming down now, so I guess we're okay." I smiled at her. "You know, I was just thinking this afternoon— we should pick your brain about this case. So glad to see you. How was the honeymoon?"

They'd gone to Europe for three weeks. "Gorgeous." Paige exhaled and stubbed the roach out in an ashtray. "And the food, my word." She sighed again. "You guys have to go to Europe."

I hid a smile. Paige didn't know what Colin's job was, either. Colin probably knew Europe better than a tour guide.

"Where's Taylor?" I asked Frank.

"Said he was meeting friends for a drink at the Lantern," he replied with a slight shrug. The Golden Lantern was an old neighborhood gay bar only a few blocks from the apartment. "I didn't see any reason to tell him to stay home."

"And you called Paige?"

"And then he called Paige," she said. She got up and walked over to a window, peering through the slats. "It looks like the coast is clear—the streetlights on Decatur are clear."

Colin flipped on the chandelier, using the dimmer to make the light lower.

I pulled another joint out of the cigar box and lit it, holding it out to Paige. She took it from me with a wide grin. "Ironically, I was thinking about calling you guys anyway because I was in the neighborhood. When Frank called, I was just finishing having dinner with a friend over at Snug Harbor"—Snug Harbor was a few blocks away down Frenchmen Street, known for their burgers and live music in the late evenings—"and I said, why don't I just stop by? It's been a minute since the wedding, and I missed you guys. Having Colin here is just lagniappe." She plopped back down in her chair. "You can imagine how hard I laughed when he asked me if I knew anything about the Havers of St. Jeanne d'Arc Parish!" She laughed again, delighted. "One of my first stories at *The Times-Picayune* was covering your cousin's drunk driving accident." She leaned back in the chair, crossing her legs at the ankles and grinned at us before shaking her head, her red and gold ringlets bouncing. "Terrible thing, really. That poor girl. And I felt so bad for her boyfriend."

Colin sat down on my other side and pressed his leg against mine. "Why don't you tell us what happened, Paige? Scotty told us some, and I'm sure I read some of your pieces in the paper, should have checked the byline"—he gave her a big wink—"but I'm sure there was stuff you couldn't run because you couldn't verify it."

"I can tell you what didn't happen." She picked up a glass of white wine and took a sip. "That poor girl didn't get justice, and Beau Haver got away with vehicular manslaughter, at the very least." She took another sip of wine and ruefully sighed. "You like to believe—*want* to believe—things have changed since the bad old days in the parishes, when a ruling elite could hold power for generations. That case?" She shook her head. "I couldn't believe what I found was going on out there. The Havers"—she nodded at me—"whom I can't believe you're related to, I might add as a sidebar, Scotty, are absolute monarchs out there. And that sheriff? Joe Perkins? Just a consigliere who enforces their edicts."

"We don't really claim them," I replied. "My great-aunt Charlotte Diderot married Beau and JD's grandfather, so they're cousins. Until today I hadn't been out there since Aunt Charlotte's funeral."

"Second cousins, or first cousins once removed?" Paige frowned. "I can never keep the degrees of kinship straight. I'm so sorry you're related to the Louisiana version of the Borgias. Anyway, the worst thing about it was there really wasn't anything that could be done. St. Jeanne d'Arc is a home rule parish."

"Ah." Seeing the blank look on Frank's and Colin's faces, I added, "Louisiana has *home rule* parishes. All it really means is that's the opposite of how government really works. It means the parish has the power to make its own decisions about everything that's not strictly prohibited by the state or federal constitution. It gets tricky legally."

Paige nodded. "The state tends to not meddle in parish business if they have home rule." She rolled her eyes. "It was *so* frustrating. And then last year they did the same thing with that hit-and-run." She made air quotes around the last three words.

I raised my eyebrows and Frank's hand on my leg squeezed. I

put my hand down on top of his and shook my head slightly. Paige was a great reporter. Once you started reading one of her pieces, you couldn't stop until you finished. But in real life, Paige was very scattered, and when she was stoned, it was worse. She said her mind was just always moving on ahead. You had to let her tell the story the way it came to her. She was always thorough, but she always meandered a bit.

"There was a lot of stuff I couldn't report—people refusing to go on the record, even as an unnamed source—so I couldn't verify anything." She frowned at me. "People who were willing to go on the record couldn't because I couldn't verify their information. And I couldn't get anything out of the sheriff's office." She made a face. "Big shock."

"But this is the twenty-first century," Colin said. "If someone was killed and the driver was drunk—"

She shook her head. "Corruption never dies, Colin. I'm sorry to talk shit about your family, Scotty…"

"No need. We're all aware of who and what the Havers are." I waved a hand. I was feeling a little mellow, and the stress and anxiety of what had just happened began to lift. I wondered how much Frank had told her about what we were doing. Best to pretend like he'd said nothing to her about JD or Brody.

"It was Beau's senior year, and he and his girlfriend and two couples they always hung out with decided to go to a party out on Bayou Maron," she replied. "Beau's girlfriend was a girl named Kylie Schultz. His two best friends were Tommy DuPré and Merlin Hess, their girls were McKayla Bissonnette and Britney Laborde." She made a face. "Beau, Tommy, Merlin, Kylie, McKayla, and Britney, Lord help us. Anyway, the party was at a boy named Jeremy Schlechter's family's place—the Schlechters are like a second-tier version of the Havers in the parish. His parents were in New York, so he decided to have a party.

"The party would eventually be broken up around one in the morning when neighbors called the sheriff about the noise, but the three couples were already long gone. Beau decided he was bored at the party around eleven o'clock, and the kids were used to doing what Beau wanted. They were all tipsy already, but Beau was the kind of drinker who never stopped until he got completely stumbling, falling down, drooling drunk—that's a direct quote from his best friend Merlin, I might add." So, he liberated an unopened bottle of

Jack Daniel's, and they all left in his pickup truck—he had one of those massive ones—and they went out driving around, drinking."

Alcohol affected Beau in a negative way. Sure, Beau was arrogant—he was a Haver, so a crown prince of the parish with all the privilege that went with that—but he wasn't so bad when he wasn't drinking. But his friends all knew that when he got really drunk, he turned into a different person—a violent, cruel, insulting asshole that they'd all nicknamed Jack, trying to turn something serious into something they could joke about, laugh off. As they drove around the backroads of the parish that night, passing the bottle around, Beau began to show signs of turning into Jack. Jack loved to drive fast, drive into fields, and do doughnuts in the truck. He thought it was funny when his friends acted scared or got worried. As the truck hurtled around in the dark and Beau's behavior and driving became more and more erratic, Merlin tried to get Beau to let him drive. The kids were getting more and more afraid as Jack drove them faster and faster, going up on two wheels making turns, ignoring their screams and cries—until Jack crashed the pickup into one of the bridges across Bayou Maron. The airbags deployed, but the momentum of the accident shifted the truck to the right, and the passenger side back door opened, rumbling the back seat passengers out and down into the murky waters of the bayou.

It only took a few seconds more before the truck followed them into the water.

They didn't find McKayla Bissonnette for almost a week. Her body had somehow floated down the bayou and into the swamp. Her body was found by some kids out fishing. She'd been dead when she hit the water, the coroner's report found. Her neck had snapped, probably from the impact of the truck hitting the bridge.

Both Jeff Davis II and III had shown up at the Valmont Hospital, talking to the kids as their lawyers and trying to convince them not to talk to the cops, or at least not to say who was driving the truck when it wrecked. Beau wasn't given a Breathalyzer—none of them were—until just before they were discharged from the hospital some four hours after the accident.

"One wasn't administered on the spot?" Frank's voice was disbelieving.

"The sheriff's department in St. Jeanne d'Arc Parish wasn't

about to do anything to a Haver," Paige said, her voice dripping scorn. "That good-for-nothing Sheriff Perkins—"

"Perkins was the sheriff back then, too?" I asked.

"No, the current sheriff Perkins is the son of the previous Sheriff Perkins," Paige rolled her eyes. "You know how these parishes work, Scotty. The Havers control the government and the courts and the sheriff. The sheriff protects the Havers." She smirked. "It's even in Merlin's police statement—he came right out and told them *You won't do anything because he's a Haver.*"

"But what about the girl's family?" Colin asked.

"Merlin testified that Beau was driving. Beau testified that Merlin was driving. Tommy couldn't remember, and both surviving girls also swore they couldn't remember. So the inquest closed with no charges being filed, it was Merlin's word against Beau's, and his friends wouldn't back either of them. So..."

"Beau got away with killing her," Frank finished. "What happened to the other kids? And the girl's family?"

Paige shrugged. "No one would talk, really, once the coroner's inquest was finished. Her death was ruled an unfortunate accident. There were rumors that the Havers paid off the Bissonnette family—paid off all their families."

"Even Merlin's?" I asked. Merlin had a motive for killing Beau, but not for JD. But did he still? The accident had been nearly thirty years ago. Why wait until now, and why go after the brother rather than the driver?

"That was the story. But Merlin had nothing to do with it, I can promise you that." She went on, "He was angry, very angry, about how it all went down and how Beau killed his girlfriend and got away with it. The Havers got a restraining order against him at one point—I do remember that. I felt so bad for Merlin. He loved that girl—she was in his arms when the accident literally ripped her out of them and killed her. I can't imagine how you live with something like that." She shuddered. "I kept all my research on the Havers, all my notes. I'd be happy to email it all over to you guys. I thought about writing a book about the Havers—everyone in the parish alluded to them getting away with this sort of thing all the time—but no one would ever give me specifics because they were afraid of the Havers. I couldn't write a book that was all hearsay and rumors. Because they would have sued me."

"You mentioned a hit-and-run?" I asked.

"After McKayla never got justice, I kind of kept an eye on the Haver family." She winked at me. "I was pretty sure at some point they'd fuck up, and you bet your ass I was going to cover the story. So, when I heard about the hit-and-run, and saw the crime scene photos..."

"You saw the crime scene photos?" Colin glanced at me.

She nodded. "I have a connection in the Louisiana Highway Patrol. You see, the kid's body—Paris Soniat—was found on a state highway, outside of town. So when someone driving by saw the body, they called it in. Louisiana Highway Patrol came out, was working the scene, when Sheriff Perkins and his men showed up, claimed jurisdiction, and tried to confiscate everything they'd collected. I'll send you the photos." Her eyes hardened. "There's no way that kid was hit by a car. The way the body was placed, the way it looked—you'll see when I send them to you. And they called it a hit-and-run and that was the end of it. I have Paris's mom's contact info—I'll email that to you, too. The mother didn't believe it for a minute. And there were rumors, all unconfirmed, of course, nothing I could run, but his mother believed Paris was seeing someone. He wouldn't tell her anything about it."

The three of us exchanged glances.

She glanced at her watch. "Oh, I'd best get going." She pulled out her phone and fiddled with it. "Ah, my Lyft will be here in five minutes." She bounded out of her chair and hugged me, did the same with Frank and Colin.

"I'll walk you down," Colin said, standing up.

"Remember I shared." Paige grinned, pointing her index finger at each of us. "So I expect all the exclusives on the Haver murder."

I heard the door shut behind them and filled Frank in on what we'd found at Brody's, producing his iPad with a flourish. His delighted smile faded as he asked me about the men with guns who tried to ambush us.

"He swears it's nothing to do with him, but I don't know," I said miserably. I reached under the couch for the cigar box that held my deck of tarot cards. I slid down to the floor as I shuffled. "What did you find out about the casino?"

"The *River Princess* originally belonged to the Havers, did you know that?" He scooted down the couch so he was sitting behind me, with a leg on either side of me. "They owned several steamships back in the day. When they sold off the others, they kept that one and kept it parked on the bayou behind their house for decades. JD's father was the one who had the bright idea of turning it into a casino boat, docking it on the river just below the Sheehan Bridge, and taking it out onto the river long enough for it to be considered a moving vehicle rather than stationary. It went bankrupt twice in the late 1990s, which was when the original investment group sold out to Princess Casino LLC, a new investment group that took over. I haven't had much luck finding out who was behind Princess Casino, but Princess Casino decided to take the insurance payout after Isadora and cash out." Frank dug his fingers into my shoulder muscles and started massaging.

He gives the best massages.

I spread out the cards and started reading.

Danger from across water

Pray for a brave heart

A double-dealing man who cannot be trusted

A woman who is greedy and manipulative

Disaster

Well, that wasn't much help.

I swept the cards back up into a pile, wrapped them in their blue silk, replaced them inside their box, and swept it back under the couch.

I rubbed my eyes. "I know it can't be a coincidence that Brody disappeared the same night JD was murdered," I said.

Frank picked up Brody's iPad case from the table and flipped it open. I told him the passcode, and he unlocked the screen. "Interesting that the Messages app has no number on it," he said, holding it out for me to look at. I reached out and tapped the app.

It opened.

There were no messages.

"That's weird." I opened the Settings app. "They were just there. I looked at them in the car on the way here." I started scrolling.

So where had they gone?

"Someone deleted all his messages from his phone." Frank's voice was grim. "Which means—"

"Which means someone took Brody," I finished for him as the front door opened and shut again. Scooter climbed into my lap, headbutted me a couple of times, then curled up and went to sleep in my lap.

"He may have done it himself," Frank replied as Colin walked back into the living room. "He may have realized keeping those messages from JD—as well as the mystery messager—was dangerous in the long run."

"He was in danger the moment he started messing around with JD." Colin plopped down on the couch next to Frank. "And if the Havers are anything like Paige said—"

"They're worse than she said," I interrupted. I could feel a headache starting to form behind my eyes. "Much, much worse."

"Then Brody was a threat to them," Colin said. "Beau was responsible for that girl's death. They pulled strings and bought off people to keep him out of jail. What would they do to protect JD and his reputation? What would happen to JD in St. Jeanne if it got out that he was messing around with teenage boys?"

"Probably nothing," I said bitterly. "Moral purity is only an issue for progressive politicians, as we all know now. The conservatives can do whatever the fuck they want, and their base will keep voting for them."

"Paige made it sound like there's already rumblings in the parish about toppling the status quo," Colin said. "We need to talk to Paris's mother. I want to hear what she thinks."

"You think it has something to do with JD's murder?" I said skeptically. "I don't think we need to bother with the car accident. That was a long time ago. Had Beau been the one who was murdered, I'd think the accident was relevant. But it was the older Havers who covered up Beau's crime, not his brother. And if anyone was going to be killed over McKayla Bissonnette's death, it would have been Beau, don't you think? And all this time later? It doesn't make sense."

"People hold grudges for a long time," Colin insisted. "You talk about that all the time—how long grudges get held in Louisiana. Maybe something triggered one of the other victims, and they decided the Havers needed to pay."

"Maybe." I rubbed my forehead, stubbing out the joint after taking a last hit from it. "I think someone said he was living in Houston…" My head was all foggy, and I couldn't think clearly. I looked over my shoulder at Colin. "And those gunmen…"

"I told you I don't know anything about that," Colin said.

"And I believe you," I replied, thinking *Well, I'm working on it.* "But maybe it has something to do with the casino?"

"You're thinking organized crime?" Frank said. "But what about Brody?"

"I don't know." I stood up and stretched, yawning, and put the iPad back on the coffee table. "I'm tired. Why don't we go to bed and get a fresh start in the morning?" I put a hand on each of their chests. "Want to join me?"

The sex was, as always, fantastic.

Chapter Thirteen
Page of Wands Reversed
A gullible and foolish young man

I couldn't sleep.

I was in the middle. Colin was asleep with his back to me, but my body was pressed up against his warm, strangely soft skin. Frank was to my right, snoring slightly, his left leg draped over my right. Their breathing had synced in their sleep. The rhythmic pull of the rise and fall of their chests usually lulled me into sleep. Scooter was curled up on the other side of Frank, occasionally groaning a bit, dead to the world. It was warm and cozy and comfortable there in the bed with the boys…yet I was wide awake.

I opened my eyes. I slid up in the bed carefully and looked over Frank to the nightstand. The red numbers on the alarm read 2:11.

Why couldn't I sleep? We'd had some marvelous and athletic sex after going to bed. I'd certainly smoked enough to knock me out for the night. But it *had* been a wild couple of days, hadn't it?

I didn't feel like a victim. I'd never thought of myself as one. I'd been hot for Coach Phelps.

You also assumed he was so in love with you he was willing to risk his wife and family and career for you—but was he?

I hated not being sure.

I'd always figured I was the anomaly in his life.

Yes, Scotty, because you are just so irresistible no man, gay or straight, can help themselves when you're around.

Arrogant much?

I shivered.

Might as well get up.

Carefully, trying not to disturb anyone else, I slid down beneath the covers until I reached the foot of the bed, then slipped down off the end of the bed. The bed squeaked slightly as it shifted. Scooter sighed, readjusted himself, and went back to sleep. I pulled on my sweatpants and walked down the hall to the kitchen. I grabbed a bottle of water from the refrigerator and carried it into the living room. I flipped on the living room chandelier and sat down on the couch.

Brody's iPad was still sitting on the coffee table, plugged in to an extension cord. I uncapped the water, took a slug, and picked up the iPad.

There was half a joint perched on the edge of the big ceramic muffuletta-shaped ashtray, and I sparked it back to life. A couple of hits and I stubbed it back out, leaning back into the couch with a relaxed sigh of relief as I flipped open the iPad cover.

"Where are you, Brody?" I asked under my breath as I typed in the passcode with my index finger. The screen cleared, and all the app icons showed up over the image of Brody in flight, his legs extended in a perfect split, feet and toes hyperextended, head thrown back in joyous exaltation. There were little red numbers on his social media apps. I touched the Messages app to see if we'd been wrong earlier or the iPad had glitched, but there weren't any. Every single message, deleted.

"Should've screen-capped everything," I mused. Taylor always was reminding us to screenshot things in case they were deleted. *Always keep the receipts*, he'd say.

I should have listened.

But we'd cloned his phone. Surely the messages were still there?

Colin's laptop was on the dining room table. I considered looking up the messages there but...the technology thing. Colin's laptop always made me nervous. There was so much spyware and software and things I didn't understand on that thing. I was afraid I'd trigger something or accidentally delete something crucial.

Or fire a nuclear weapon or something. I felt the same way about driving his Jaguar.

I touched the Facebook app icon and the familiar screen opened in front of me. I was a bit surprised he had a Facebook page under *Brody Shepherd*—Taylor had told me most teens had two pages, one that their family could see and another under a variation of their name for their friends. He'd shown me how to toggle between the accounts—making sure I didn't see the name on his friends account—but there was nothing here. If Brody did have another account, they weren't linked.

All notifications were from the main feed, likes and comments and tags, none from Messenger. I pressed the notifications icon, and a drop-down of the new notices appeared. I scrolled down but didn't see anything of interest. They were all likes or shares he was tagged in, and none of them meant anything. I went through his pictures folder. Most of his pictures were of him dancing. No candids or shots of him hanging out with friends, which was strange, but this page was G-rated and Mom approved.

So there had to be another account.

If I was a teenager trying to hide a Facebook page from my mother, where would I hide it?

I opened the browser. There were three tabs open. One was the New Orleans Ballet Company website, another was open to Juilliard's website, and the third was a dance supply company, open to results for a search for dancer belts.

I opened his Twitter account. He only had thirty-seven followers but was following well over a thousand accounts. I looked through his followers but nothing jumped out at me. He was following lots of ballerinas, ballerinos, and dance companies. I checked his feed. After scrolling down a bit, some revealing shots of young men with incredible bodies popped into the timeline. They'd been shared by various, similar-type accounts—Hot Male Models, Male-licious, Body by Boyz. The original tweets included links to a pay-for-play website, Just4Fans. I'd never been to the site, but I knew what it was: a service where for a monthly fee you could subscribe to certain people's content—and the content wasn't restricted. Anything went on Just4Fans, and you could find anything you were into on there as well.

Too bad this wasn't around when I was in my twenties and broke all the time, I thought as I clicked on one link.

It took me to their website, which had a generic landing page—white background, blue boxes with white text. *Join or sign in to support your favorite content creators!*

Porn for the twenty-first century.

I closed the link and looked at his Twitter feed again. He

had no new DMs, and his mentions were just likes on things he'd tweeted several days earlier—photos of dancers in motion. I opened his direct messages, but there weren't any.

Unusual, but not impossible.

His Instagram feed was more of the same. No direct messages from anyone, just notices that people he followed had posted stories or liked something he'd posted. I scrolled through his feed. Again, he followed mostly ballet dancers from all over the world and some of his classmates from NOCCA. I touched his name to go to his own images and started scrolling through his posts. Lots of pictures of him in his tights or shorts, doing stretches or leaps or spins, his hair slick with sweat, the T-shirt damp and clinging to his torso, his face determined and concentrating. But in his bio, there was another link—it wasn't a hyperlink, but a YouTube address. I grabbed a pad of paper and wrote it down—one day I'd learn how to cut and paste on a mobile device, but today wasn't that day—and opened his YouTube app.

I closed the screen asking me if I wanted to join YouTube's streaming service and found myself on Brody's YouTube channel: NOLA Dancer Boy.

Most of his entries were short videos. They looked like they'd been shot with someone's phone, but the visual and sound clarity was amazing. The videos were of him dancing, stretching, spinning, and leaping, sometimes alone, sometimes paired with other dancers, sometimes with a girl he'd lift elegantly and toss like she weighed only a feather.

It was the YouTube history, though, that bore real fruit for me.

Most of his viewed videos were of other dancers. I recognized Nureyev, Baryshnikov, and a beautiful Italian ballerino named Roberto Bolle. There were videos recorded from live performances. There were also some Taylor Swift videos—her versions of "Red," "You Belong With Me," "Love Story," and "Blank Space"—and some ABBA, and just as I was about to close the app and head back to his socials, I noticed a video at the bottom of the list. I hadn't scrolled down far enough to see the thumbnail, and only the top sentence of the video's title was mentioned—it looked like it said *ripped dancer flexing*—and scrolled down more.

The whole title was *ripped dancer flexing (link in bio)*.

The thumbnail was Brody, shirtless, both arms up and flexed

so the biceps peaked, veins popping and muscle striations visible beneath the skin. Brody's face wore a big smile for the camera. He also looked about twelve years old. The date on the video was from a few weeks ago. He looked older in person.

I recognized the posters on the wall behind him—it was his bedroom.

I made the video full-screen, then tapped play.

The video was seven minutes of Brody flexing for the camera. Every so often he would step toward the computer, like he was reading what was on the screen. Then he would step back, smile, and change poses. He flexed his arms, his triceps, his shoulders, his back, and then tilted the camera down so it could broadcast his amazing legs. He was wearing only a pair of black Versace underwear—the thought *Did JD buy those?* flitted through my mind quickly—and as he flexed his leg muscles, I couldn't help but marvel at the definition. His body and muscle development was breathtaking. I shook my head.

He's not much younger than Taylor, I chided myself and fast-forwarded to the end. Below the frame was a place where the poster could write a description of their video. There was nothing there but a link. He'd used a URL shortener, so I just touched it. The screen went gray, and then his iPad's browser opened.

And it took me right back to Just4Fans.

The boxes for username and password were already filled in.

Username: Sxxydancer

Password: ************

I hit enter.

The browser signed me into Brody's account and took me straight to his user page. Since I was signed into Brody's account and it was his page, I didn't have to subscribe—*only $5.99 per month!*—to see any of his content. I started scrolling through pages of content. It looked like he'd been posting videos for his fans for quite some time. The little red bubble on the messages icon read *127*, and it looked like he had about 223 subscribers. I did the math in my head.

A little over thirteen hundred dollars per month based on subscribers alone.

It beat flipping burgers at the mall.

I found the first entry. The date was well over a year ago. Brody had proudly told us he was turning eighteen, so how had he been posting self-porn on this site to make money for over a year? I checked the terms of service for an age limit, and yes, the site was age-restricted to eighteen and up, including the models. So, either they didn't check, or he'd used the same fake ID he used to dance at the Brass Rail. I checked the account's financials, and all the money paid through the site was funneled to a PayPal account with the same username. I clicked on that link and it took me to the PayPal app, also conveniently signed in. The PayPal account was linked to a Hancock Whitney checking account, and the day Brody met with us—the same day he disappeared—he'd transferred over four thousand dollars from his Just4Fans account through PayPal to his bank account. I went back to the Just4fans website and scrolled through his activities. Someone—username Sugardaddy1969—had paid him that same amount of cash through the site the day before he disappeared. I tried to backtrack to find if there was something—a private cam show or something—that would have warranted that kind of payout, but I couldn't find anything.

That same user had sent him thousands of dollars since he opened the page.

Coincidence? Highly unlikely.

Sugardaddy1969's user profile page was locked, even for Brody.

I started taking screenshots of everything: the bank account, the PayPal histories, and the Just4Fans page. I hesitated for just a moment before clicking on the messages icon. Did I really want to know what kind of messages his followers sent him? I started scrolling through them. Most of them were requests for poses or for things for him to wear—everything from certain brands of underwear to thongs to singlets to jocks, brands and colors and styles, you name it. Some were compliments about his cam shows, about how beautiful his dick was, how amazing his muscles were, how sexy and fuckable he was—in much more graphic terms. Apparently, there wasn't anything Brody wasn't willing to do for his fans—there were comments about his money shots—again, not worded quite that delicately—or how beautiful his ass was, especially when the cheeks were spread and—

Yeah.

I started feeling dirty at around the second one, and by the time I was down to the bottom of the first page I felt like I needed a Silkwood shower.

Gay men were really rutting pigs.

In fairness, these men all thought Brody was legal.

But would they have cared if they did know?

I felt a little sick, but I kept scrolling. If there was something here that could help us find him, I could handle the drooling sycophancy of Brody's fans.

But when I reached the second page of unread messages, the top one was from Sugardaddy1969.

Sugardaddy1969: *B, don't forget.*

There was an entire conversation below that first note. I kept scrolling down through the lengthy history. Whoever Sugardaddy1969 was, and my money was on JD, he and Brody had been talking a lot through this website, going all the way back to last summer.

When Brody claimed to have met JD while working at the food court.

The very first message from Sugardaddy1969 was dated last June:

Beats working in food and smelling like grease, doesn't it?

So, had Brody lied to us about how he'd met JD? Assuming Sugardaddy1969 was JD, of course.

I maneuvered over into his Whitney bank app, and of course was able to sign right in with his saved username and password. Taylor's right, I thought as I clicked on his checking account, saving passwords in my browser might save me some time and frustration, but if I ever lose my phone and they figure out my passcode, I'm totally screwed. I made a note to disable autofill passwords on my phone. Most of my passwords were some variation of SEXYFRANK—I always used the same letters—and a variation of numbers and symbols. I was prone to using 69 as the number and an exclamation point as the symbol because I have the mental maturity of a twelve-year-old.

I clicked on deposits and gave a date range going back to last June. The iPad thought for a minute, and then a list of deposits popped up. Since last September, the deposits were all PayPal transfers, in varying amounts, but there was always at least one for four thousand dollars monthly. Last summer, every other week there was an automatic deposit of somewhere in the one fifty–two hundred dollar range, which I assumed had to be his paycheck.

So, why was he working at the mall if he had a moderately successful Just4Fans account?

Because he was a teenager living with his mother, and he had to explain where the money came from.

Wendy hadn't struck me as a naive woman, but working the overnight shift at the hospital left her son's nights free for all kinds of trouble.

I thought he'd seemed more mature for his age than Frank and Colin did. Was it possible he'd known who JD was all along, and been blackmailing him? Those monthly cash transfers had to be for something other than a private cam show. Looking over his lengthy list of video thumbnails was ample evidence that Brody not only had no body image issues but was perfectly willing to put everything on display—there was a column specifically labeled *cum shots*, which I was more than happy to take at its word without looking—but something was rotten here.

Either he'd lied to us, or this was all a lot more complicated than he'd let on.

Brody came to David originally because he got that text message, along with a picture he'd sent JD. But why would he bother with that if JD could just pay a nominal fee every month and have access to everything Brody was willing to show? Brody said he didn't want a scandal following him around for the rest of his dance career—I didn't think Juilliard or any of the major dance companies would approve of him making money this way, but I could be wrong. Things that would have sunk a career ten or twenty years ago were just taken in stride these days, and nobody seemed shocked by anything anymore. Hell, the scandal might even put Brody in more demand. The Naked Ballerino. The Porno Ballerino. I could think of any number of tabloid-like nicknames for him.

But even if the world had become more open-minded about some things, I'd be willing to put money on dance companies not embracing scandal. Their donors tended to be older rich people, who skewed conservative. I doubted his sexuality would be a problem—so many professional dancers were gay it was almost a cliché—but the nudity? Beat-off videos? And who knew what other stuff was on this page that I didn't want to go looking for?

Brody had lied to us. What else had he lied to us about?

I sighed and put the iPad back down on the table. I reached for the joint. I had just taken a hit when Colin said from the hallway, "What are you doing up?"

"I couldn't sleep," I replied as he walked around the couch and plopped down. He was wearing only a pair of black Calvin Klein square cuts that made his legs look enormous. "So, I thought I'd play around on Brody's iPad a bit more, see what I could find."

He took the joint from me. "Any luck?"

As he inhaled and held the smoke, I quickly filled him in on everything I'd found, from the Just4Fans page to the PayPal app to his bank accounts. Colin frowned as he blew the smoke out and pinched the joint out. He reached for the iPad. The screen hadn't locked, and his Just4Fans page was still up on the screen. When he picked it up, he accidentally touched the video queued up as the main image. I watched as Brody winked at the camera and slowly pulled down his underwear while reaching down to grab his erection.

"Oh." Colin quickly tapped the video again, freezing it on a frame with Brody not visible from the waist down, but with his eyes half-closed and his mouth open in what, if this was a porn video, I would have assumed was an orgasm face. He closed the screen quickly and put the iPad down like it had burned his fingers.

"Brody lied to us," I said, leaning back into his body. He wrapped his big arms around me and lay back, so we were lying prone on the couch, him behind me, his thickly muscled arms around my chest. I put my head back against his chest and listened to him breathe, listened to his heartbeat. "Maybe he did meet JD when he was working at the mall, but I'd be willing to bet this Sugardaddy dude on Just4Fans is JD. But why wouldn't they just communicate through that website instead of texting? The website had to be safer."

"Do you want me to see if his text history is on the clone of his phone?" Colin said into the back of my neck as he pressed his lips against it. "Or I can check that in the morning, go back into his phone history. Maybe I can find out who Sugardaddy is."

"You can do that?"

His right index finger started tracing circles around my navel. It tickled a little, so I grabbed hold of his wrist to stop him, pressing back harder against him. "I can do all sorts of things," he whispered.

"And the four grand every month—he didn't tell us about

that." I shifted to get more comfortable against him on the couch. "What else didn't he tell us? But why go to David in the first place?"

"He was spooked," Colin replied without hesitation. "You said yourself you thought Brody was remarkably self-possessed and mature for his age. Maybe he knew who JD was that first time they met. Maybe JD found him through Just4Fans and then saw him working at the mall. And the four grand?" He whistled. "It's enough money to make a substantial difference in a teenager's life, but not enough money, even on a monthly basis—forty-eight thousand per year, which is a decent annual salary—to throw up any red flags anywhere with the IRS or the banks involved."

"I'd think the IRS would want their share."

"The IRS doesn't care about nickel-and-dime shit like this." Colin yawned. "They do, but it's not going to be a priority for them." He nuzzled against my neck again, and much as I didn't want it to happen, I was starting to get aroused.

"I'm really curious who those men were who tried to stop us," I said.

He stopped tracing my navel and grazing the back of my neck. I felt his entire body stiffen for a moment before relaxing again, so briefly I might not have noticed had his body not been pressed up against mine. "Scotty, they had no connection to any of my work with Blackledge."

"You can't know that."

He pushed me forward enough so that he could sit up, and I twisted myself around awkwardly until I was sitting next to him. He put his arm around my shoulders and pulled me into a tight hug. "Because, Scotty," he breathed into my ear, "the kind of people who work against Blackledge? We wouldn't have escaped. They could have capped us both between the eyes at that close range if they were enemy agents. They missed. Every shot. All they got was the windshield and made some holes in the car. Those weren't professional killers." He exhaled. "I would have made both shots. I wouldn't have left witnesses. And we got away from them far too easily." He tweaked my nipple. "And you know, I'm not the only one in this house with enemies. Frank must have made many when he was a Fed. And you've made a few in the time since I've known you. Remember the skinheads?"

"I'd rather not," I replied, shivering at the memory. He wasn't wrong, of course. But it seemed like every time mysterious gunmen appeared out of nowhere trying to kill us, it was much more likely tied to his job than anything else.

I stood up and gave him my hand. "Come on, let's go back to bed."

But as I curled up inside his arms with my back pressed up against Frank's in the bed, I couldn't help but wonder if Colin wasn't lying to us.

Again.

CHAPTER FOURTEEN
SIX OF CUPS, REVERSED
Outworn friendships should be discarded

I woke up to an empty bed and the smell of bacon coming from the kitchen. I sat up in bed. Scooter scowled at me, stretched, and closed his eyes again. It was almost ten. I swore under my breath. Why had they let me sleep? Sunnymeade was about an hour's drive away. We'd not get there until the afternoon now, at the earliest.

I pulled on my sweatpants and went into the bathroom. I washed my face and brushed my teeth. I blearily looked at myself in the mirror. I needed a shave, and I needed a haircut. I'd started trimming it down close to the scalp when my hairline started receding a few years ago—I'd always kept it short because it was too curly to deal with when grown out.

I walked down the hall. Frank was in the kitchen, flipping bacon in my cast-iron skillet. A pile of toasted bagels rested on a serving plate, with butter and jam and cream cheese set out beside it. Pancake batter was bubbling on the griddle. I got a cup of coffee and reached up to kiss his cheek. "Why did you let me sleep in so late?" I asked, scratching between his shoulder blades. "At this rate we won't get out there before afternoon."

"You got up in the middle of the night, so I figured you could use the sleep," he replied as I stirred creamer into my coffee.

"I'm sorry if I woke you up," I replied. "I was having trouble falling asleep, so I decided to get up and be useful."

"Did you sleep better when you came back to bed?" He started moving pancakes to an empty plate. He was wearing an apron over no shirt and gray sweatpants whose waistband was losing its elasticity, hanging a bit low on his hips. "Actually, I woke up when *Colin* got out of bed, and before I fell back asleep, I could hear the two of you talking," he replied. "I fell back asleep before you both came back to bed. Insomnia again?"

"No, I just woke up and couldn't sleep. Probably too keyed up from those guys chasing us on the way home," I said, finishing the coffee and getting another cup. "I stayed in bed for a while, staring at the ceiling and hoping I'd fall back asleep, but when I didn't…might as well do something instead of staring at the ceiling. I was checking through Brody's iPad, trying to see if I could find anything."

"That's what Colin and Taylor are doing right now." Frank started pouring more batter onto the griddle, after brushing it with melted butter again first. "You made a good start."

"Thanks." I kissed the back of his neck and walked into the living room. Both Colin and Taylor were sitting at the dining table. Colin was typing away at his laptop. Taylor was lost in concentration, staring down at the iPad screen with a frown on his face and one eyebrow slightly quirked upward. "Find anything good?"

Taylor looked up and gave me a weak smile. "I actually know Brody," he said, screen-capping something on the iPad. His face flushed. "Not know-know, I mean I know who he is—I've seen him before. In the bars, I mean. He was dancing at the Rail last Friday night—he won the New Meat Contest."

I caught my breath.

The Brass Rail was a disreputable gay bar in the upper Quarter, a significant walk from the Fruit Loop through the straight-infested streets of the central Quarter. In some ways, the Brass Rail felt like a throwback to the olden days before Supreme Court rulings gave us felony-free sex lives. The windows were all blacked out, so no one could see in or out. Like most of the gay bars, it was open twenty-four seven but made most of its money late at night and on weekends. I always had fun there but usually never stayed very long. It was small, just two rooms with a rectangular bar in the front room and a pool table in the back. Video poker machines were shoved into every available corner. The primary draw of the place was cheap drinks and boys dancing in their underwear on the bar. Management there wasn't discriminating—anyone who could come up with the thirty-dollar locker deposit was more than welcome to climb up on the bar and shake their ass or bounce their dicks at the men crowded into the small space. Some of the dancers were young hustlers there to meet potential paying clients, others with drug problems were there to make money to support their habits. Some of the dancers were young straight boys who didn't object to being touched or sucked off for money. They were always young and beautiful, with tragic stories—nineteen with a wife and baby, twenty-one with a girlfriend and two kids, that sort of thing. They always laughed it off as a lark, a clever way to make some extra cash by letting desperate old gay men touch them and fawn over them in ways women never would.

I always wondered about them.

On Friday nights, the Rail had its long-running amateur dance-off, called New Meat Night, originally intended for new guys to get their feet wet and make some money and see if they were comfortable enough to dance there. Dancing for dollars isn't for everyone. The winner won a hundred dollars in cash. At some point after Katrina, though, that changed. You no longer had to be new to dick dancing to compete for the money. But the old name stuck. There was kind of a dive feel to the place that I liked, and the drinks were cheap. The bartenders were long-timers and friendly. They always remembered the locals and what they drank, which was nice.

It was the bar where Eric Brewer drugged Taylor back before Christmas. While it made me happy Taylor'd reached a place where he could go back without being emotionally triggered by what happened to him, the papa bear in me didn't like the idea of Taylor hanging out there.

He's twenty-one years old, I reminded myself sternly. And when you were twenty-one, you were doing a lot worse than hanging out at the Brass Rail.

I couldn't compare Taylor to myself at that age. My parents were dramatically different from his. He'd been raised in a homophobic church and spent most of his life being told he was going to hell for something he had no control over, no say in.

He wasn't groomed as a teenager either.

I pushed that thought out of my head. I wasn't a victim.

"Did you talk to him?" Colin asked without looking up from his laptop screen.

"I even tipped him a couple of bucks," Taylor said, giving me a wink. "I've been taught that you always tip the dancers."

I grinned back at him. As someone who used to dance for dollar bills, I take umbrage with people who look but don't tip. *Always tip service personnel.* "How did he seem to you?" I asked in reply. "Friendly? Like he was having fun?"

"He was nice, and I think—well, he seemed like he was having a good time to me." Taylor leaned back in his chair, scratching his head with his enormous left hand. "He tried to thank everyone who was tipping him—I mean, he came up to me and I talked to him a little, and the whole time he was talking to me"—Taylor blushed deeper—"guys were shoving money into his underwear."

Taylor's blush told me everything I needed to know about their conversation. Taylor had been sitting on a stool, no doubt, while Brody danced seductively in between his legs to draw dollars from Taylor's wallet.

That repressive evangelical upbringing was hard to throw off completely.

"Anyway, he told me he was training for ballet, which explained the body—that body!" He fanned himself a little with his left hand. "I mean, his body was amazing. Solid, too, and I've never seen definition like that before. I bet bullets would bounce off his ass." He swallowed. "And he was the only dancer working there who knew how to, you know, dance."

I never had the best body of all the dancers in whatever club I was working. I'd danced alongside professional dancers and porn stars and models and personal trainers—gay bar go-go boys can come from just about anywhere. There were nights when everyone else shaking their ass in a jock or thong for money was much hotter and prettier than me.

But my ability to keep a beat and move to the music always got me more tips than the others. I used to get annoyed by go-go dancers in gay bars who were terrible dancers. You need to have more than just a hot body that looks great in a Speedo or underwear. There's nothing worse than a go-go boy with an amazing body and handsome face who has no rhythm at all and can't dance. For me, it's a turnoff. I mean, how bad a lay must you be if you have no sense of rhythm?

I took it seriously. If I was going to be a go-go boy, damn it, I was going to be one of the best ones in the entire troupe.

I still dance like a go-go boy.

"Well, he was definitely flirty with me," Taylor went on, "but how seriously do you take the flirting? He's trying to get my money, right? So was he really flirting or was he just doing his job? He seemed to spend more time and play up more to older guys than he did with me—but older guys tend to have more money. I did get the impression he liked older guys more than guys his own age, if that makes sense?"

Frank carried a serving tray into the room and set it down in the center of the table. I helped myself to pancakes and bacon, smearing more butter on the pancakes before drowning them in strawberry syrup.

"Being into older guys puts him at even greater risk," Frank said, sitting down across the table from me. He'd left the apron in the kitchen. When he was wrestling, he shaved his torso. Since taking a leave he was letting it grow in. I liked him better with chest hair. There were some white hairs scattered across his big chest, mixed in with the darker gold ones.

I gave Frank a warning look. Taylor didn't know about Coach Phelps, and for now I wanted to keep it that way. Maybe once I was finished processing the reality that I'd been groomed.

Just thinking about it made me feel sick.

Were they right? Was I a victim and just didn't want to admit it to myself?

I didn't want Taylor judging me.

Frank nodded slightly. Message received. I turned to Taylor, "You find anything in his iPad?"

Taylor flushed again, turning so red it was almost purple. "Besides some really explicit videos on his Just4Fans?" You can take someone out of evangelism, but getting the evangelism out of them doesn't happen overnight. I still thought it was cute that talking about sex embarrassed him, but I hoped he'd eventually accept that sexuality was nothing to be ashamed of or embarrassed about.

Someday.

"I did get some names from his email inbox, and of course a list of people from his social media accounts. His Facebook is dormant, mostly—it's probably a burner account that he lets his mom and relatives see, while he probably has another one under a different name that he actually uses."

I nodded. "Did you try his middle name?"

"Well, his middle name is Stephen, and I couldn't find anything under that name. None of the accounts that came up were him. If he has another account, it isn't linked to his public one." He cleared his throat. "I think I should go with Colin to NOCCA today."

Frank and I exchanged a glance before turning to look at Colin, who shrugged. "It's not a bad idea. He's closer to them in age. Kids are more likely to talk to another kid than to an adult. There's only so much David can do as a teacher to get them to talk, you know."

"Next week are finals anyway, so my classes this week are pointless," Taylor insisted. "I want to help."

Frank looked at me again, and I shrugged. When I was the only one home, I didn't mind being the authority figure. But when Frank was home, I deferred to him as Taylor's blood relative. "Okay," Frank said, "but just this once, and it's not going to become a habit."

Taylor grinned around a mouthful of pancakes and gave us a thumbs-up.

"Were you able to track down Beau?" I asked Colin.

He nodded. "You were right—Beau lives in Houston with a wife and kids now, and unless he can control the space-time continuum, there was no way he could have killed JD. He was at a fundraiser for a cancer organization his wife chairs. Even if he had a private plane and there was a place for it to land in Verdun, I don't think he could have gotten here fast enough to have killed JD and taken Brody."

"I don't believe for a second he ran away," Taylor said. "I think someone took him."

"Someone had to have since he doesn't have a car and he wouldn't get far on foot," I replied. "The question is why." I looked over at Colin. "With the phone clone, can you find what cell towers his phone connected to before it was turned off?"

"I tried," Colin replied. "His phone was turned off around eight o'clock, and the last tower was in the Bywater. So he either turned his phone off, the battery died, or someone turned it off."

I picked up the last bit of pancake on my plate with a fork. "And no calls or texts?"

Colin shook his head. "No."

I closed my eyes. "Maybe you should stop by the coffee shop where he usually went to study," I said. "Maybe they have camera footage of the night he went missing."

"If he made it to the coffee shop at all," Frank observed. "By the way, Paige sent a lengthy email about the hit-and-run, and she even has the crime scene photos and the autopsy report." He frowned at me. "There's no way it was a hit-and-run."

"You're sure?"

"The only injury mentioned in the autopsy report was a blow to the head." Frank frowned at me. "When you're hit by a car, well, it's not possible unless the car hit him headfirst. And the body was flat on its back in the center of the road. Hit by a car? You don't lie down perfectly flat on your back. And the head injury was to the side." He swallowed. "Blunt force trauma. I'm not a doctor or a forensics expert or anything, but it looked like a baseball bat. Someone hit him with a baseball bat. And then staged the body."

"And the parish sheriff took over jurisdiction from the highway patrol even though it happened on a state highway outside of any city limits," Taylor said. "And the investigation was closed once the coroner ruled it a hit-and-run." He scowled. "Someone murdered that kid. And the cops covered it up."

"Which begs the question, why?" Frank replied. "Why would they cover this up?"

"It has to do with the Havers," I replied. "It's the only explanation that makes sense."

"I'm also trying to disentangle the mess behind the casino boat." Colin frowned at his computer screen. "The history of that casino is something. I may have to get someone more experienced in forensic accounting to help me with it." He shook his head. "They went to a lot of trouble to hide the identities of everyone involved with the original company, the companies that formed out of the bankruptcies, and the new one they formed after Isadora to take over. And it's all been handled by the Haver law firm—so I'm sure a lot of this is shady."

Ultimately, we decided that Frank and I would head back out to St. Jeanne to keep looking around and investigating JD's murder, while Taylor and Colin would spend the day at NOCCA, trying to get information out of Brody's friends.

"I want to focus on getting names out of Karen at first," I said as Frank and I hurtled past Metairie on I-10 about an hour later. "If *anyone* knows the dirt, it's Karen." I looked out the window. The problem would be getting it out of her. Karen wasn't a fool—Mom had said at Karen's wedding to JD, "Thank God he married a smart one, so there's some brains in the family now." It wouldn't surprise me in the least if Karen was the brains behind the entire family empire, or JD wasn't as incompetent at managing his businesses as the rest of the family thought. I was searching through my phone, trying to find out when exactly Beau and his family had left Louisiana for Houston. It seemed weird. The Havers' power base was centered in St. Jeanne d'Arc Parish, where they were royalty. I knew both JD and Beau had law degrees from LSU, and I'd always been surprised that Beau hadn't joined Haver & Haver.

Maybe he'd had a falling out with his brother?

Beau had moved to Houston straight out of law school. He'd passed the Texas bar and had hung out a shingle there in Houston. Again, weird. Why start a practice in a big city where you have no professional contacts? There must have been residual bad feeling in the parish from the drunk driving accident. Why else would he leave the duchy his family had ruled since the Civil War? Hell, he wouldn't be able to get out of a parking ticket in Houston. Their home address was in River Oaks, which used to be the neighborhood where all the rich society folk lived, the Houston equivalent of the Garden District. Some more research showed that Beau's wife Lesley, whom I'd never met, was originally from Houston and from a politically active family.

I snickered to myself. It sounded like an arranged marriage, the kind of thing his father would have initiated to increase his power base.

"You've been pretty quiet this morning," Frank said, glancing over at the passenger seat, where I was scrolling through my phone aimlessly. "You doing okay?"

"Just confused." I'd been so busy digging for dirt on Cousin Beau and his move to Houston I'd not been paying attention. We'd crossed the river at the Sheehan Bridge and were almost to the road where we'd turn left to go to Sunnymeade. "Frank, those men with guns last night—I can't stop thinking about that."

"Colin swears it has nothing to do with him, and I believe him," Frank replied.

"Well, that would be the easy explanation, but if they weren't after Colin, who were they and who were they after?" I pinched the bridge of my nose. "I mean, you and I were followed yesterday out here all the way back into the city."

"You think it's the same people?" Frank made a face as he pulled up to the stop sign at Bayou Road.

"We thought it was an unmarked police car," I went on. "So, let's say it was following us, and take it even farther and say it was an unmarked car." I closed my eyes. "So, cops would have access to car registrations and DMV records—"

"And you're listed on the registration for the Jaguar." It had been necessary for us to be able to insure the car, since Colin wasn't technically a resident of Louisiana. Colin had also said it was smarter in case anything ever happened to him, or if something needed to be done about the Jaguar while he wasn't around.

"They might not be able to know where we park the cars—"

"Unless they did follow us all the way back to New Orleans," Frank admitted. "We lost sight of them in the traffic mess around Causeway Boulevard, but that didn't mean they also lost us. And if they saw where we parked—"

"And then checked the car registration—"

"They would have known it was our Jag," Frank finished. "But why block the road and pull guns on you and Colin?"

"Should I spin the wheel and pick a letter?"

The gates at Sunnymeade were open, and I involuntarily winced again when I got another look at the house. I'd have it torn down and rebuilt if it was my inheritance. It's not like it was considered a historic home of old Louisiana, after all. Frank pulled the car into a parking spot in the lot to the left of the house, and we climbed the side gallery stairs, then walked around to the front. All the shutters on the windows were closed. But when we rounded the corner to the front of the house, Coach—*Dan*—Phelps was waiting for us at the front door.

"Karen's in the drawing room," he said, holding up a perspiring bottle of water to the side of his face. "Mr. Sobieski, do you mind if I borrow your partner for a moment?"

Frank made a face, but he said, "Sure—see you both inside," and the front door shut.

Coach Phelps stared at my face. "It—it *is* you, isn't it?" He blinked. "Scotty Bradley. I thought you looked familiar when I saw you yesterday, but when you said your name—" He shook his head. "I've thought about you—"

"Please don't." I held up my hands and was mortified to see

they were shaking. My stomach felt upset, the bacon and pancakes and coffee mixing into something toxic that didn't want to stay down. "It was a long time ago."

He took a deep breath. "I'm sorry, Scotty, I'm sorry about everything. I can't—I don't even know what I was thinking." He either had the decency to look ashamed, or he was an incredible actor. "It was a huge mistake."

"You didn't even say good-bye." I could hear my heart beating, and my eyes—my vision was going gray around the edges. I could hear a roaring in my ears. How many nights had I cried myself to sleep? How much guilt had I carried for so long that I wasn't even aware of it? "I thought it was all my fault." I staggered on wobbly legs over to one of the gallery chairs and sat down, hard. "You were my coach," I whispered.

But I couldn't make myself say the words: *It was abuse*.

Somehow, I pulled myself together. I took a deep breath and looked at him. "Was I the only one?"

He didn't answer, but he looked away.

"Is that how you met JD?" I said, my voice unpleasant. "Some online we-like-to-fuck-teenage-boys chatroom?" The words, meant to be biting and sarcastic, sounded true.

"I got a job out here at Valmont High after I quit Jesuit," he said miserably. "My wife left me—I haven't seen my kids in almost thirty years—and I've stayed to the straight and narrow. No kids, no boys, no women. Nothing."

"That's what priests say."

"JD and I worked together on fundraising for the new gym at the high school, and we hit it off. When his old chief of staff retired, he offered me the job. I was sick of teaching, and I wanted to do some good, so I took it." He folded his arms. "I wish I could go back and change things, Scotty, I do. I never should have touched you. I never should have allowed myself to have feelings for you." He laughed bitterly. "I was jealous when I saw you with your partner yesterday. After all this time. But those feelings aren't real. They aren't there anymore." He clasped his hands together. "Please don't say anything to anyone about our past. It won't change anything but could—"

"Ruin you?" I replied coldly. "No, I won't ruin you, *Coach*"—adding as much contempt to the word as I could muster—"but did you help JD with his boys?"

"I don't know what you're talking about."

I didn't believe him. "So, you don't know who Brody Shepherd is, or where he might be?"

He hesitated long enough for me not to believe him. "No."

I reached for the door handle. "Then you should have nothing to worry about."

Chapter Fifteen
The Empress, Reversed
A selfish and untruthful woman

He was lying. I was sure of it.

I felt an overwhelming sense of shame, followed by a rapid-fire kaleidoscope of emotions as images from our past flashed through my brain.

I'd been wrong about him from day one.

I hadn't been his first or last, let alone the only.

Much as I wanted to believe him, I couldn't.

I hadn't been exceptional. I was in my midteens, hormones raging out of control, worrying about acne outbreaks and passing history tests and writing papers. I was just like every other boy at Jesuit High School other than my deep dark secret. What had made me stand out to Coach? My sparkling wit? My appreciation of foreign language films, my knowledge of fine wines?

No, what drew him to me was my innocence.

My youth.

My inexperience.

My *virginity*.

Frank was right. Coach Phelps was nothing more than a predator, and I'd been his victim.

Whoa.

Victim.

I never ever wanted to think of myself as a victim. Even when I'd been kidnapped or held hostage for whatever reason, I'd never seen myself as their victim. As long as I was alive and my brain was functioning, there was a chance, right?

But I'd been Coach's victim just as much as Taylor had been Eric Brewer's.

I felt sick.

I put my hand on the gallery railing to help keep my balance because I felt shaky.

It didn't change anything. I was still me, Scotty Bradley. I still had a loving family and two great partners who loved me. I'd felt guilty about what happened to Coach. I'd blamed myself for ruining his life. Whenever I thought about him since then, the guilt was overpowering. I'd never forget the moment the bedroom door had slammed open, and his wife stood there, her face white and her lips compressed with barely contained fury and disgust. I hadn't heard anything she screamed at him over the roaring in my ears as I'd fumbled out of their bed, covering myself with my hands while I scrabbled for my clothes on the floor. I'd stumbled out of their house carrying my shirt and my shoes. I'd been crying as I hurried down their driveway, pausing at the mailbox to pull on my shirt and put on my shoes. I'd stumbled down the street and wandered around their subdivision until I managed to find a convenience store. I remember pulling a quarter out of my jeans pocket with shaking hands, wondering who I could call. Storm and Rain were in college, and I definitely didn't want to call a dorm phone. I didn't want Mom and Dad to know, I couldn't imagine telling them, and had finally called Velma. She didn't ask any questions and just drove me home. I'd somehow remembered to grab my gym bag on my way out of the house. I think maybe I told her I'd ridden with someone, we'd gotten into an argument, and they'd kicked me out of the car.

It was a long time ago. But she'd dropped me off at home and I'd fled to my bedroom, locking the door behind me. The next day they told us Coach had left and wouldn't be coming back.

I shoved my hands into my pockets so no one could see they were shaking as I walked into the drawing room. The shutters had been opened and the big room was flooded with light. "Scotty." Karen crossed the room and took my hands in hers. "So glad to see you both."

"How are you doing?" I asked, my voice gentle. She looked much better. The purple smears she'd had beneath her eyes weren't there this morning. Her brown eyes were still a bit reddened and swollen—she'd probably cried on and off a lot over the last twenty-four hours—but she'd put some effort into looking the part of Parish Queen this morning. She was wearing makeup—not much, just enough to bring out her lips and cheekbones. Her smooth forehead was probably courtesy of Botox, and I think she'd had some fillers put into her cheeks. She was still beautiful, and she wasn't the type to keep having work done until it was obvious. She'd taken the time to braid her long hair, coiling it on the crown of her head. Diamonds and rubies glittered at her ears. She smelled of soap and lavender. She was wearing a black knit sweater over black slim-fit jeans, with black ballet flats. I doubted she could still fit in her one-piece Golden Girl uniform, but it wouldn't have to be let out much.

"Dr. Moreau gave me something to help me sleep," she said with a sad smile. "I still have trouble believing any of this is real. I keep thinking he's going to walk through the door and I'll wake up from this nightmare. Help yourselves to coffee." She gestured to the sideboard, where a generous coffee service was set up. I looked over at Frank where he was sitting in a wingback chair drinking coffee from a delicate looking china cup, a small plate holding a croissant balanced on his right leg. "The kids are on their way down from Baton Rouge this morning." She shook her head as I walked over to the antique sideboard and helped myself to a cup of coffee.

Like I needed more coffee.

"Were you talking to Dan?" Karen asked as I stirred a sugar substitute packet into my coffee. She looked back at the doorway for him, but he hadn't followed me into the room. She sounded confused. As far as she knew, we'd just met yesterday.

Feeling no need to enlighten her, I said instead, "How long has Mr. Phelps been working for JD?" I sat down in the chair next to Frank's.

Frank gave me a glance as she answered, "Oh, it's been well over twenty years," she replied, wrinkling her brow. "Dan was already working for Haver & Haver when JD and I were married," she said, tilting her head to one side. "Is it important?"

I smiled. "Just curious." Had he really come out here after leaving Jesuit?

It doesn't matter, I reminded myself.

"Haver & Haver?" Frank asked, picking up his croissant.

"Yes, the family firm, of course." She shook her head with a smile. "Dan works for both the firm and for the parish," she replied with a slight *You know how these things work* shrug.

"Is he married?" I hoped it sounded more casual than I felt. I took a bite from a croissant.

I ignored the very sharp look from Frank and kept my focus on Karen.

"No, he isn't," she replied. "I've always had the impression he had a marriage that ended badly, and he just preferred being single. I don't like to pry. He's been a huge help to both JD and me. JD used to call him his right hand." She smiled faintly, then wiped at her eyes as emotion overwhelmed her again. "Sorry," she said brokenly, holding up a hand.

"Karen, I have something to ask you, but you need to have a seat," I said carefully, getting yet another side-eye glance from Frank.

"Oh dear, that doesn't sound good." She let out an exasperated sigh. "What kind of mess has—*had*—JD gotten himself into?"

"You remember yesterday we mentioned we had a client and that's what brought us out here?" I said carefully. I put my coffee cup on the side table. "Well, there was a reason we came to Sunnymeade, and it wasn't because we'd heard that JD had been murdered. We'd already planned on coming out here."

Her jaw set, and her lips narrowed to a red slash. "Go on." She leaned back in her chair, her eyes focused on me.

I took a deep breath. "I'm sorry to have to tell you this, Karen," I said with a quick look over at Frank. "Tuesday night we were hired by someone who was"—I fumbled for the right words—"involved with JD. A teenage boy, a high school student." Her face didn't move. "Apparently he and JD developed a…a friendship of sorts."

Through tight lips she spat out, "What do you mean by *sorts*?"

"The boy said that he and JD had never been physical." Frank took up the story, to my relief. "But JD used to buy him dinner, and presents—underwear, that sort of thing—and would want the kid to send JD pictures of him modeling the stuff."

"Someone else had gotten hold of the pictures," I said, "and texted him. He and JD had already stopped communicating several months ago, but the kid was worried that someone was trying to make trouble for JD." And that JD might be involved in killing another teenager.

No need to tell her that now.

"So that's why we came out here yesterday," Frank said. "Only when we got back to New Orleans last night, we found out the boy is missing now. Tuesday night he left home to go to a study group and never came home."

"And now the boy is missing, and JD is dead," she said when

I finished. "Terrific. Do you think the kid could have killed JD?" She got up and walked over to the big windows fronting the side gallery. She made a fist with her right hand and slammed it against the window frame without much force. Once, twice, a third time. After the third time, she turned slowly to face us. "You asked about Dan. Is he involved in this...this mess?"

I shook my head. It wasn't a lie. And my past with Coach had nothing to do with this. "No, I was just curious about him and how close he was to JD. If they worked together every day—"

"If anyone knows where the bodies are buried in this parish, it's Dan." Her voice was tight and grim.

"If you're serious about our investigating JD's murder, we need to know everything," Frank said softly.

She barked out a harsh laugh. "Well, that's fair." She walked back over to the coffee service, picked up a croissant, and started shredding it with her hands as she spoke. "There are any number of people in this parish who hated JD. JD liked to believe he was loved, that everyone looked up to us, but that's not the case. There are plenty of people in this parish who would love to see the Havers collapse and burn." She tossed the croissant into a trash can. "JD has been up to something he didn't want me to know about—he also liked to believe he was smarter than I am, which was absurd on its face." She sat back down on the couch with a roll of her eyes. "I'm sure you know about the Isadora insurance lawsuit?"

Frank pulled out a notepad from his shirt pocket. "We've heard about it and read some of the coverage on it, but if you could..."

"Well, since he's dead, I suppose there's no harm in telling you both." She laughed. "I told JD he'd never get away with it, but he never listened to me." She blew out an exasperated breath. "The *River Princess* being wrecked by the hurricane was what started it all, you know. Oh, sure, there're things going back decades—old grudges, hatreds, that sort of thing—but we were all doing fine until Hurricane Isadora." She shook her head. "I *told* him moving the boat into Bayou Maron was a mistake, but does he ever listen? No, of course not. What could I possibly know? I was just a woman, even if I am—was—a thousand times smarter than him." She sighed. "So, of course, the boat was a ruin. It's still afloat, but badly damaged and needs a lot of repair work. The original investment group decided to take the insurance payout and shut everything down." She looked at us. "There aren't many jobs in this parish, you know. If you don't get on at the petrochemical plant or the casino or work offshore, all there is is some low wage job no one can live on. The *River Princess* employed about four hundred people, give or take. In a parish this size that's a substantial voting block, and it was also a tax base the parish couldn't afford to lose. JD decided to put together another investment group to buy out the original group—they only wanted a token payment, really—but we were still a couple million short of what we needed. JD decided to put up the money himself."

"He took out a loan?"

"Every bank turned him down." She laughed at the memory. "The Havers have always had a lot of power here in the parish, but the one thing they've never been able to do is control the banks."

"That's why JD took the Isadora insurance settlements," I said. "He needed the money for the *River Princess*."

She nodded. "He thought he'd take the money, put it into the boat, and be able to move other money around to replace it so no one would ever know. But one of the claimants found out from their insurance company that JD had settled the claim and gotten a check—and never told them." She shook her head again. "When I asked him what he'd planned to do if something like this happened, he said he thought he'd be able to cover it—he figured one or two people might find out, might cause a stink, and he had enough cash on hand to pay out some of the claims. What he wasn't expecting was a class action suit to be filed. And that scared off some of the investors once that hit the papers. And I don't think some of them were exactly reputable in the first place."

"Do you have a list of the investors?" Frank asked.

"Yes, I can get that for you."

"Who was JD meeting out at the boat the night he was killed?"

"One of the investors and someone from the firm he'd hired to renovate the boat," she said. "The investor is Len Gargaro, and the guy from the firm was Rafe Cooper."

I inhaled sharply. Rafe Cooper was Cooper Construction, the firm we were going to hire to redo the house.

Len Gargaro, on the other hand, was connected to the Carocari crime family in New Orleans. The Carocaris allegedly were involved in all kinds of criminal activity in Louisiana, everything from prostitution to drugs to human trafficking. Gargaro's name was familiar to me because he'd been tried three times—once for

murder, once for extortion, and a third time for a different murder—
and always managed to get a *not guilty* verdict somehow.

But how on earth did they ever get Len Gargaro past the state
board?

"Len Gargaro?" I echoed.

She nodded. "Nice man, I really like him and his wife Felicia.
They've had dinner at Sunnymeade several times."

"Are you telling me you don't know who he is?" I stared at
her in disbelief. Outside of the questionable choice of marrying JD,
Karen Haver wasn't a stupid woman and never had been.

"I know what he's been accused of," she replied. "But he's never
been convicted of anything. And his money spends the same way as
everyone else's. Money is money."

"I'm just surprised the state licensing board approved him
being one of the investors."

She gave me an *are you kidding me* face and held up her right
hand, rubbing her fingertips against her thumb. "Money is all that
matters in Louisiana, Scotty, you should know that by now. JD took
care of the state board." She held up her hands. "Did I think it was
smart getting involved with someone with alleged ties to organized
crime in New Orleans? No. But JD never listened to me, ever. He
kept telling me he could handle it." She rolled her eyes. "If the
Carocaris weren't using Len as a front—which they may not have
been, let's be fair here—it still isn't a good look for a casino to have
someone connected as an investor. The IRS and the FBI will be
watching us like hawks from now on."

"What would have happened had JD not been able to get the
money?"

"Since the lawsuit was filed, he'd been acting differently. More
secretive." She buried her face in her hands. "Maybe I should have
been paying more attention. I don't know. I just figured things would
work themselves out, you know?" She rubbed her eyes. "We've been
having cash flow issues since the boat was wrecked."

Frank was taking everything down carefully in his precise
writing.

"Why hasn't Beau ever come back from Houston?"

"It's just as well. Beau is…well, you know him," she snapped.
"When Quint—my oldest son—had his trouble last summer before
the hurricane, it stirred up a lot of bad memories for people in the
parish of that time Beau killed that girl."

"Your son was having problems?"

"Oh God." She got up and walked over to the windows again. "You hadn't heard? I figured it might have made the papers there."

"Not that I noticed," I replied, not bothering to say *I never cared about things happening out here.* "What happened?"

"Someone reported a body lying in the road out near the Bayou Bridge." She breathed. "That's the bridge where Beau had his wreck when he was in high school—and don't give me any of that *alleged* stuff. Beau was driving that truck drunk, and my father-in-law paid off all the other kids and the girl's family. But when that queer kid was found down by the bridge, well, people started talking about the wreck again." She paused. "Beau and JD had been talking about Beau moving back here, taking on some of JD's responsibilities at the firm, but after people started talking about the wreck again, Beau and his family decided to stay in Houston. Typical Beau, he always flees when things get tough."

"A queer kid was killed?"

"It was a hit-and-run. Everyone was talking about it, but the coroner ruled it was a car accident and that was the end of it." Her face darkened. "But because that kid had a couple of run-ins with Quint over at the high school, people started saying maybe Quint had something to do with it. The family kept insisting he was murdered."

"His name was…?"

"The boy's name was Paris Soniat. I didn't know him well, but it wasn't like he tried to fit in or anything." She rolled her eyes in a way that made me want to slap her. "You know the type, dyed his hair blue, tattoos all over the arms, piercings on the face. He and Quint had a couple of run-ins around the high school."

"Do you know where his family lives?"

"No, I don't." She sighed. "But his mother works at that cheap hair salon downtown, Curl Up and Dye? You can probably catch her there." She shook her head. "I understand—I can't imagine what it would be like to lose your child that way—but her insistence that Quint was involved, and Sheriff Perkins was covering it all up? My sympathy only goes so far."

"Do you know if Len Gargaro is staying out here, or did he drive up from New Orleans to meet with JD the other night?"

She laughed. "Gargaro has a house out on Blind Lake. I don't know if he still has a place in New Orleans or not."

The front door slammed, and a young male voice called out, "Mom?"

"Oh, that's my son." She looked alarmed and walked back over to the windows on the side gallery. She pushed one up and gestured for us to go through it. "I don't want to explain to the kids what you're doing here. Do you mind?"

Frank and I escaped out the side window. We walked around the house to where we'd parked the car. "I don't think this was a mob hit," Frank said quietly as we headed down the driveway. When we reached the gates, he added, "Interesting that a Haver came up when Paris Soniat was killed."

"I've never met Quint as an adult," I replied. "And we already know Paris *was* involved with JD. That was how Brody met him."

"Let's not forget Coach Phelps." Frank kept his eyes on the road. "What did he want to talk to you about?"

I wrapped my arms around myself as goose bumps came up on my arm. "He did recognize me yesterday," I said, my voice low. "He didn't react because he said he didn't know how he was supposed to, and he was all full of apologies and how he'd overstepped and *I worried about you* and his wife left him, and he came out here and got a job at the high school and then went to work for JD—"

"I also don't think that's a coincidence, either. I know you don't think—"

"You were right. I wasn't his first, and I don't think I was the last." I felt exhausted, like all I wanted to do was curl up in a ball and go to sleep in a dark, locked room and not talk to anyone ever again for the rest of my life. "I guess…I guess I never wanted to face it before. I just don't like thinking of myself as a victim."

"It doesn't mean you're weak, Scotty." Frank turned right and headed back toward Verdun. "A predator targeted you and groomed you to the point where you were willing to do just about anything for him. You never told your parents, did you?"

"How—how did you know?"

"For one thing, I've lived with you for almost twenty years now." Frank reached over and patted my leg. "I know how you work— and I also know your mother. If she knew one of your teachers had seduced you, no matter how cool she was about your sexuality and open-minded about your sex life, that body would have never been found, so there's no way you ever told your parents. Why did you tell me?"

"I don't know." I remembered the night vividly. It was one of his first nights living in New Orleans. I'd flown up to DC to help him pack and ride in the moving van with him for company. Colin was off in Europe at the time. We'd spent the night somewhere in Georgia on the way home. It hadn't been easy getting used to having someone else around all the time. I'd lived alone ever since moving out of Mom and Dad's. The house wasn't finished being rebuilt from burning down over Southern Decadence, so Frank had moved in with me in the other half of David's double. We'd been drinking wine and smoking pot and watching movies on one of the pay cable channels, and *Summer of '42* had come on. I don't think that movie could be made today—it was a silly and sweet tale of the main character remembering being a teenager and falling in love with a beautiful woman in her twenties whose husband is off fighting the war. The night she finds out her husband was killed, she sleeps with the teenager and leaves a note for him before disappearing the next day. The whole movie is told as a flashback, with the main character still longing for the woman he'd loved as a teenager.

Frank said it was abuse.

I disagreed and told him the Coach Phelps story. He hadn't disagreed with me at the time, but he also didn't judge me or tell me he thought I'd been abused.

Which was why it was such a slap in the face all these years later.

"I'm glad you did," Frank glanced over at me, and then in the rearview mirror again. "And right on cue, there's the car that was following us last time."

Chapter Sixteen
Two of Pentacles, Reversed
Too many irons in the fire

"Great. The pickup truck or the Buick?" I asked.

"Buick."

I craned around in my seat to get a look. Right behind us was a purple Kia, following too closely. Behind it the white Buick—or one like it—was about a car length behind the Kia. Hadn't I read somewhere that cop cars were always Buicks? And the unmarked ones were always white?

My stomach clenched. But why would Sheriff Perkins have put a tail on us? He knew I was kin to the Havers, he'd asked us to help, and he had to know by now Karen had hired us.

But it could be part of some parish political power play.

I turned back around. "I don't like this at all," I said.

"It could be coincidence—"

My phone started blaring Lady Gaga's "Bad Romance," cutting him off midsentence. The ringtone clued me in it was Colin calling. I clicked to accept the call, switching it to Bluetooth speaker and cutting off the Carpenters right in the middle of "Hurting Each Other."

"I put you on speaker," I said. "How'd things go at NOCCA?"

"Hey guys," Colin said. "Taylor and I just got back home. We've talked to some of Brody's friends at NOCCA—Taylor is really good at putting people at ease—"

"Thanks!" Taylor called out in the background.

"And we did find out some more information—nothing that will help us track Brody down, I'm afraid, but…" He hesitated. "Brody wasn't honest with us. You were right, Scotty, and it may even be worse than we originally thought."

"What do you mean?" Frank asked, glancing up into the

rearview mirror and nodding slightly at me, letting me know we were still being followed.

"None of the kids we spoke to knew anything about him being on Just4Fans or dancing at the Rail," Colin went on. "They were kind of surprised, and while they are NOCCA students, I don't think any of them were acting since they would have had to have coordinated beforehand so their stories would match, blah blah blah, so I think they were being honest with us. One of them"—I could hear pages flipping in his notebook. I loved that both Frank and Colin were still old-school when it came to taking case notes. Taylor kept insisting that it was just easier to record everything on my phone and use a dictation app to turn it into text, and he was right. But I still wasn't there yet, and neither was Frank. Apparently, neither was Colin— "one of the kids we talked to, Kayden Dreyer, was the one who got him the job at the food court last summer. Kayden's a boy and he's also a dance major, so he probably knew Brody better than anyone. Nice kid. He said he knew JD as someone who used to come to the food court and hang around and talk to Paris."

"So, this Kayden also knew Paris?" I glanced over at Frank.

Colin barked out a humorless laugh. "Kayden didn't think we were there to talk about Brody, actually. He assumed we were there because we're looking into the death of Paris Soniat. He said he was surprised it had taken so long." Colin cleared his throat. "I didn't tell him we weren't, but I didn't confirm that we were, either. Paris and Brody were close, according to Kayden, and Brody was really upset when Paris was killed."

"What did he say about Paris?" Frank asked.

"Not much. He was a nice guy, very flamboyant, would flirt with male customers and, well, he thought Paris and Brody were seeing each other. It really shook up Brody when Paris was killed. Kayden said JD kept coming around, but mostly to talk to Brody. He quit shortly after that, so he doesn't know anything more than that—Brody and he were friends, but not the kind who confide in each other." Colin sighed. "Brody didn't seem to have any close friends at school."

I remember that feeling, I thought but didn't say out loud.

"So, Kayden knew about JD?" I said slowly, closing my eyes. Something was tickling the back of my brain. Something wasn't right, but I couldn't put my finger on it. Every time my brain got close, it skittered away again out of reach.

"He said Paris told him JD was just a harmless old guy who liked chicken, and he bought Paris presents all the time."

"Why did he think Brody and Paris were involved?"

"Well, it was an impression," Colin replied. "It's not like either of them told him anything. But he said they were close. Sometimes acted like they were a couple, flirting and teasing each other..."

If Brody and Paris had been a couple...

I almost had it but it was gone again.

"...and how Brody reacted when they found out Paris had been killed. It was like he lost a boyfriend, not a friend."

If Brody and Paris had been a couple...

Almost there.

"And it makes more sense to me—Brody and Paris, I mean."

"But why wouldn't he have just told us that?" Frank glanced up in the rearview mirror. Instinctively I checked the side mirror. The Kia was gone, and now the white Buick was a couple of car lengths behind us. The traffic on Bayou Road was much lighter than it had been yesterday.

"Maybe..." Colin hesitated. "Maybe Brody and Paris *were* a couple, and this rich older man took an interest in *them both*. Because they're teenagers we don't want to think in those terms, but it's possible they were both working JD for whatever they could get out of him. And Brody didn't want to tell us everything because, well, it doesn't exactly make *him* look good, does it? And maybe the videos we found aren't the only ones. Maybe they were making videos *together* for JD."

I could see Frank's face starting to color, and the muscle in his jaw was twitching—sure signs he was starting to get angry.

"Karen brought up Paris this afternoon," I said quickly, trying to head off Frank's anger while wondering where it was coming from.

Why did it bother him so much to even consider that Brody and Paris hadn't been innocents?

"She did?" This was Taylor, so Colin must have us on speaker, too. "What did she say?"

"We were going over people who might have motives to kill JD, and his name came up." I tried to remember exactly what she'd said. "She was actually talking about Beau and his drunk driving wreck when he was a teenager, where the girl was killed? Anyway, she mentioned that Beau had been considering moving back from

Texas but after that queer kid's body was found near the bridge, people started talking about it again and Beau decided not to return." I pinched my nose. "Apparently there'd been some issues between Paris and her oldest, Quint."

"Quint?"

"JD's son, Jefferson Davis Haver the Fifth, hence *Quint*." I didn't have to see his eyes roll. I could feel it through the phone line.

"You want Taylor to call him and ask Kayden if Paris or Brody ever mentioned Quint Haver?" Colin asked. "Taylor's got his phone number—they seemed to really hit it off—"

"Fuck you, Colin." Taylor's faint voice sounded amused and pleased rather than upset.

"—and I'm sure he wouldn't mind calling him. Make sure he's legal, though, Taylor." Taylor swore at him again. "Anyway, Kayden was really surprised to find out we were looking for Brody. No one at the school knew he'd disappeared. None of his friends knew anything, none of them had seen him since rehearsal the other day before David brought him over, and he pretty much didn't share a lot of personal stuff with any of his friends. He was more of a loner, and they all hung around together mainly because of proximity—the same dance classes, the same shows, you know how that all works. They all liked him—Kayden thought he was a bit arrogant but was probably his closest friend, if he could be said to have one—and Kayden admitted that he used to cover for Brody with Mrs. Shepherd. Brody used to tell her he was going over to Kayden's when he was doing something else he didn't want her to know about. Kayden swears he didn't know what Brody was doing on those nights, but it was a friend thing to do."

"Were there a lot of those nights?" I casually worked the side view mirror on my door so I could see the cars behind us as we passed the *Welcome to Verdun* sign. The Buick had dropped two cars back now, behind a pickup truck and a green Subaru.

"At least once or twice a week since last summer."

"Have Taylor follow up with Kayden," Frank said, signaling and pulling over into a Starbucks parking lot. I turned back and watched the white Buick keep going into town. "Ask more questions about Paris Soniat—how well did he know Paris, did Paris talk about anything in St. Jeanne d'Arc Parish—you know what to do."

"You think this kid's death might have something to do with Brody's disappearance and JD's murder?"

"We don't know those two things are connected," I replied. "But it's hard to believe they aren't. Paris is the connection between Brody and JD. If Brody thought Paris was murdered..." I gnawed on a fingernail. It was so close. What was I missing?

"I'll text him to set up a coffee date later," Taylor said, raising his voice to be heard clearly. "Text me if you think of anything I should ask him. I'm going to spend some time with Brody's iPad, see what else we can find on it."

"And I'm going to look into those investment groups for the casino," Colin added.

"Len Gargaro is one of them." We'd reached the order menu for the Starbucks drive-through. Frank ordered us each a latte. "He's connected, or at least he used to be, to the Carocari crime family. See what you can find out about him—maybe reach out to Paige, too."

"Will do." He disconnected the call.

Once we were through the line and had our scalding hot drinks resting in the car's cupholders, we pulled back out onto Bayou Road. I typed *Curl Up and Dye* into my map app. "It's past the parish building on the other side of town," I said, "on my side of the street." As we went past a pawnshop, the white Buick pulled back out behind us again. "Who do you think that is?" I asked as we approached the stoplight at Verdun's main intersection, where Bayou Road crossed the state highway. "And how did he know how to find us again?"

"And is he connected to the guys that tried to take you and Colin last night in the Marigny?" Frank looked up into the rearview mirror again. The white Buick was now right behind us, about half a car length away from our back bumper.

"I don't know, Frank, it makes me nervous. Colin swears they had nothing to do with him or Blackledge, but—"

"He's lied to us before." The light turned green. We went through the intersection, picking up speed as we passed an AutoZone, a couple of gas stations, a Domino's Pizza, a Raising Cane's, and a McDonald's. The parish building's lot was half-empty as we went past. The Buick stayed with us.

This part of Verdun was even more depressing than the rest. Storm damage from Isadora was even more apparent on this poorer side of town—houses with blue tarps still covering their roofs, windows boarded up, other buildings abandoned without roofs or an outside wall missing, billboards that were just skeletal frames.

The parking lots for businesses looked more derelict, less kept up, and the houses were the same. Lawns were scabby, unkempt, with weeds and car parts and toys scattered around. I looked down at my app. "Take the next right—it should be Alsace Street."

"Alsace?"

"This whole area was originally settled by Germans back when Louisiana was still French," I explained. "This whole part of the river was called the German Coast. Germans settled here back in the 1730s. It was the site of one of the biggest rebellions in North America. I don't remember when it was, but the enslaved people revolted, killed white people, and put plantations to the torch. They marched on New Orleans, but the city called out the Guard and that was the end of that. The Germans called it St. Jeanne d'Arc Parish to thank the French administration in New Orleans for letting them settle here. But that's why German names are so prevalent out here and why, I would guess, there's an Alsace Street in Verdun."

Frank slowed and turned. Curl Up and Dye was another block toward the river. The houses on the block we passed all looked derelict. The yards were choked with weeds, children's toys, abandoned car tires, and rusting swing sets. Stray cats and dogs raised their heads to look at us as we drove by, going back to sleep once they realized we weren't worth their notice. Curl Up and Dye took up half a rectangular cinder block building set back on a cracked and crumbling parking lot. The other half was Verdun CBD, which specialized in legal cannabis products. A couple of battered cars sat in the parking lot, and Frank pulled up into a parking spot on the Curl Up and Dye side of the building. The white Buick sailed past while I was getting out of the car.

I was slapped in the face with the strong smell of hair chemicals when I opened the door. There was a counter to my right, where a woman somewhere between her late twenties and early forties was reading a dogeared *People* magazine with Chris Evans on the cover smiling seductively at me. The woman was sitting on a stool and smelled slightly of bath water and cigarettes. Her hair was dyed that deep shoe-polish black that doesn't occur in nature, and she was wearing far too much makeup. Her head was shaved on one side, and the thick black hair was brushed to the other side so I could see that her ear had at least ten piercings, as did her lip, her nose, and her left eyebrow. Riotously colored tattoos ran up both arms. She was wearing a pink T-shirt with *Curl Up and Dye* written across the front in gold glitter. She smiled at us, a gold incisor winking at us. "Can I help y'all? We generally don't do men, but for two good-lookers like you, we'd be happy to make an exception."

Frank flashed his private eye badge at her. "Thank you, ma'am. We're looking for a Mrs. Soniat?" He faltered. "Paris Soniat's mother."

A woman stood in the door to the office. She was short and the years had been hard on her. She was carrying some extra weight, and her face was lined and wrinkled and worn. Her yellow cotton dress had seen better days. Her hair was shoulder-length and multihued, blue and orange and red and yellow and purple. It had a jarring effect. "I'm Heather Soniat. What are you looking for?" She didn't sound friendly. She stepped aside and beckoned us to enter the office. "Come in."

The office was small, with a massive computer that was probably about ten years out of date. A multiline phone sat next to a day planner like a relic from a long-forgotten past. Posters from beauty product companies were taped to the cheaply paneled walls. The linoleum was yellowed, scarred, and starting to come up in places. The two chairs on the other side of the desk from her were plain old kitchen chairs, the vinyl cracked and torn in places.

"Who are you and what do you want to know about my son?" she asked, crossed her arms in front of her and scowling at us suspiciously. "And why should I talk to you? What do you care about my son?"

I decided to let Frank take lead. He had the aura of authority I lacked. "Mrs. Soniat—"

"Heather."

"Heather, I'm Frank Sobieski, and my partner Scott and I are private detectives from New Orleans." We both held up the badges, offering them to her, but she waved them away like an annoying swarm of gnats. "We were hired the other day by a young man to handle a problem for him." He flashed her his most winning smile, the one that made wrestling audiences cheer. I could see her melt a little.

He really is handsome.

"That case brought us out here to St. Jeanne d'Arc Parish. We just heard this morning about the tragic accident your son Paris was involved—"

"It wasn't an accident," she interrupted. She opened a drawer and pulled out a pack of Marlboro Reds and a battered metal ashtray that had seen better days. She flicked a lighter and inhaled. "I hope you don't mind," she said in a tone that left no doubt she didn't care one way or the other if we did, "but my son's death wasn't an accident. I don't care what any fucking coroner bought and paid for by JD Haver says. None of it makes sense." She tapped her cigarette on the lip of the ashtray. "Paris runs out of gas and just leaves his car there on the side of the road? And he was walking the wrong way. Gas stations and home were in the other direction. So why the hell would he walk a half mile the wrong way? Why did he leave his phone in the car instead of calling me or his sister to come get him?" Her smile was ugly. "And if he ran out of gas, why did his car start when I picked it up the next day? There was more than enough gas to get him to a station. So why did my son pull over on the side of Bayou Road in the middle of the goddamned night, not call anyone, and then walk in the *wrong* direction, where he gets hit by a car?" She was panting with anger by the time she'd finished, her face flushed and her voice rising with every word.

"We agree with you," I said softly. "The coroner's report was a joke."

She gave me a strange look. She hadn't been expecting that.

"It doesn't sound right to us, either, Mrs.—*Heather*," Frank said.

She plopped down into the desk chair, cigarette ash falling to the floor. "Well, praise be to the Baby Jesus, finally some people with some fucking sense." She took a long puff. "Fuck Perkins, fuck the coroner, and fuck the Havers," she snapped. "Paris wasn't a fool. He was a lot of things, but he was definitely not a fool, nor did he take risks. If he ran out of gas outside of town, he wouldn't have went walking back to town to get gas when he had his damned phone with him. He'd have called someone, not walked by himself along a lonely country road." She flicked ash angrily into the ashtray. "Paris was an out gay boy in a parish that don't exactly like gay people, you know? He wasn't *stupid*."

"Did Paris say anything to you about anything that, I don't know, made you think he was afraid of someone?"

"Paris wasn't afraid of anyone," she said flatly. "He was always different, we knew that when he was a boy, you know. He didn't like playing with guns or balls or boy stuff. He liked dolls, he liked games, he liked Disney Princesses. He was sweet and kind and funny and never pretended to be anything he wasn't. He came out when he was in junior high. Sure, kids picked on him some, but he always had something smart and funny to say back, so they started leaving him alone. He was something, all right." She shook her head with a sad smile. "I didn't think it was smart of him to take that job at the mall in town, but he loved it. He couldn't wait to graduate and move to New Orleans, *get out of this hick place*, he used to say." She smiled sadly.

"Did he ever mention a kid named Brody Shepherd?"

"Doesn't sound familiar."

"Do you think Quint Haver had something to do with his death?"

She ground the cigarette out like she was putting it into Quint's eye. "If y'all aren't from here, you don't know what it's like," she said softly. "The Havers are above the law here. Just like his shit-ass uncle Beau killed that girl twenty, thirty years ago, Quint Haver murdered my son." She leaned back in her chair. "You want to tell me how my son was hit by a car and killed, but the only injury was to his head? No scrapes, or cuts, or bruising, or broken bones? His clothes weren't even torn up, Mr. Sobieski. Someone murdered my son and left his body out in the middle of the road. There ain't no way a car hit him. But for the coroner and the sheriff to close down the investigation and call it a hit-and-run? That means someone powerful killed my son. The only people in this parish powerful enough to pull those kinds of strings are the Havers. Sheriff Perkins and that chickenshit coroner Dr. Landry would only do that for a Haver."

"So, your only basis for believing that your son was murdered by Quint Haver is because they ruled it a hit-and-run?"

She stared at Frank unblinking for a moment, then opened her bottom desk drawer and tossed a file onto the desk. "You look at that coroner's report and tell me what you think," she hissed. "Quint Haver and my son had a run-in about a week before he was killed. He told people he was going to teach that faggot a lesson, a lot of people. And a week later my son is dead. The investigation was closed when the coroner's report came back. And Quint stopped talking about Paris."

"Do you think they could have been involved?" Frank was scanning the contents of the file into his phone. "Was something maybe romantic going on between the two boys? Something that

Quint wouldn't have wanted people to know?" He closed the file and pushed it gently back toward her.

She shook her head. "I don't know." She sighed. "I think part of the reason he wanted to work in the city was so he could, you know, hook up with other people, you know what I mean? He didn't want to be with anyone from out here, so he got a job in the city." Her eyes filled with tears. "If there's anything I can do to help—"

"Where precisely is Bayou Bridge from here?" I asked. "It may not do any good, but it would help for us to get a look at the scene of the crime, get a sense of the layout."

"When you go back to Bayou Street from here, turn right," she said. "You can't miss it. It's right before the land gets swampy again." She handed me a business card. "My cell number is on this. If you need anything, or have any other questions, you call me, okay? Anytime."

The air was damp and heavy as we went back outside, and the sky was filling with dark clouds racing quickly across the sky from the south. Frank clicked the car unlocked, and I was reaching for the door handle when I felt something cold and hard press against my back.

"Don't move or I kill you," a voice said in a thick foreign accent.

Then everything went black.

CHAPTER SEVENTEEN
SEVEN OF PENTACLES, REVERSED
Anxiety about a business deal

I was floating through the warm, soft air through the darkness.
Everything was black, but on the edges of my vision I could see shades of gray fading outward from the pitch-dark where I floated. The air was warm and thick, soft, like a woolen blanket wrapped around me.
The first time the Goddess had called me into this in-between dimension, this alternative place between time and space and worlds and realities, I had been frightened yet remained calm. There was some kind of tranquility here, something like a kind of Xanax in the air that I breathed in and thus felt the calm, the peace. I missed this place during those years when She was angry with me and wouldn't speak to me. The peace, the calm, the clarity I could experience here was always carried back with me when I returned to the mortal realm.
Time had no meaning here. It sometimes felt like I was here communing with Her for hours, even days, only to return to find only a few minutes had passed. This is a dimension beyond time, just as the Goddess is eternal and time is as nothing to Her.
I could sense that I was floating and drifting downward. I turned my head and could only see darkness on every side of me. I tried to control the drift, but I never was able to go faster or slower—I moved at the speed with which the Goddess wanted me.
I turned to face the direction I thought I was moving so I was face downward, squinting and straining to see where She was taking me, what She wanted me to see. There was always a reason She brought me here. I might not completely understand that when I returned to my own realm, but later I'd be able to comprehend and see everything She wanted me to see. I had no control, no say, over any of this, just as I didn't with my Gift. I think the Gift came from Her, somehow, but I don't know why She chose me. All I know is that She did.

I summoned Coach Phelps's face to see if that would disturb this odd peace I was feeling, that I always felt when here. But his face was barred to me, like all memory of his face had been erased from my brain. All I could feel was peace, though, the same feeling I always felt when She called me into this strange space. The older I got, the less She came to me, talked to me, communicated with me. She was a fierce but loving Goddess—one who wouldn't be questioned, especially by the likes of me, for who was I as a mere mortal to question She who exists outside of time, of space, and doesn't answer to descendants of Her original creations? As I drifted farther and farther down, I became aware of other noises— rushing water, the engine of a boat or a car, voices mumbling too quietly for me to pick out words or even try to understand anything being said.

And the darkness began to lighten around the edges, like the sun was rising in the east, bringing gradual light and awareness to the strange blackness, like a fog or a mist rising from the river. I could hear more noise—car engines, a lawn mower, a speedboat, discordant music not in tune or on key, more voices chattering, growing louder.

As the darkness gave way to the strange gray light, I became aware that I was drifting down from the sky to the top of a levee, with a freighter heading upstream in the direction of Baton Rouge. To my left I could see the Warren Sheehan Bridge, so I knew the levee was in St. Jeanne d'Arc Parish; on the other side of the river beyond the levee I could see the marsh that used to drain the river into Lake Pontchartrain and the Manchac Swamp. Cars were passing over the bridge in both directions, and then I saw Her.

She was standing on the east bank levee, looking across the river to the West Bank, in the direction of Verdun and Sunnymeade.

I could never make out Her face whenever She granted me one of Her audiences—the legends and myths all said that no human could ever look on the face of a God and not go mad from the intense inhuman beauty of their faces. This time She seemed to be choosing to appear to me in her guise of Isis, queen of the Egyptian pantheon of gods—golden wings and a white linen dress, Her feet bare and Her long black hair tied back with golden bands, golden bands sparkling with lapis lazuli and diamonds and rubies encircling Her otherwise bare arms. I was looking at Her in profile, or what would be profile if I could see Her face, which was shadowed and blurry. Her linen tunic gathered beneath Her full, bare breasts, almost as though She was a painting on an Egyptian tomb or temple wall.

My body righted itself in the air so that soon my feet drifted down to stand on the cool damp grass running along the top of the levee.

"It's been a while," I said, standing a few yards away from Her.

"Time means nothing to one such as I," She said with a slight twitch of her bare shoulders. "The past, the present, the future—all are as one to me." Her voice was flat, passionless, merely stating matters of fact. "Time as you understand it has no value to an Immortal."

"I thought you might be angry with me."

She turned her head, but while I couldn't make out the features of Her face clearly, there were little things I could make out—the Egyptian eyeliner leading out from her eyes to the side of her face, the dangling earrings with the Eye of Horus, the double crown of the ancient lands on Her head. "I am past such emotions, which belong to those who have yet to evolve into their finer selves," she said, her voice devoid of inflection or emotion. "You are my chosen one, and you will be that until you leave that plane of existence," she went on. "You are in danger."

"From who?"

"That is not for me to disclose," She replied. "I am forbidden from interfering with events in the mortal realm. All I can do is give warnings and hope that will change the future. You are in danger, but if you chose the right path, all will be right and well, and things will work out for everyone. But there are many forks in the path you must follow, and you must always keep your mind focused on choosing the right direction to go. You are being distracted by many things, things from your past—lies and deceptions that divert you from clear thinking, from doing that which is needed from you to save those who cannot save themselves. The past is past, and it cannot be changed, Scotty. Learn from the lessons of the past and always remember that the past is the past...the only thing that can be changed is the future."

The past is the past.

Her words echoed as everything went hazy again...

I opened my eyes and moaned. My head hurt. I tried to reach up to check for bumps and lumps but couldn't. Confused, I pulled harder to no avail. Wherever I was, it was dim and dark. I could barely make out shapes in the gloom. Not only were my hands tied behind my back, but my legs were tied to a chair. Another movement and there was also a rope around my waist, tying me even tighter to the chair. I strained, trying to move my hands again. If I wasn't mistaken, my hands were tied together *and* were tied to the chair, too.

I was sitting up in a dimly lit room, silvery moonlight coming through a round window on the other side of the room from where I was bound. I also realized that the room wasn't level. The porthole window was higher than I was, and as my eyes adjusted to the gloom, I saw the floor sloping upward. My chair was resting against an interior wall.

I was also gagged, and not in a good way.

"Frank?" I said out loud, but it came out *aaaaaahhhhnnnnnk*. It wasn't very loud, either.

I winced. The gag cutting into the corners of my mouth hurt. How long had I been out?

I heard the roar of a motor being started somewhere nearby. It revved for a moment and then gradually grew more quiet as the sound disappeared into the distance. My head hurt, I was getting a crick in my neck, and the gag had completely dried out my mouth. I need some water, I thought as I pulled with my arms again, but whoever had tied my hands had done a very good job. I looked down to get an idea of what kind of chair it was.

My eyes were adjusting more by the second. I was tied to a cheap metal dining room chair. The legs were metal, and the seat and back were covered by red vinyl cushions. I tried to move the chair but only succeeded in moving a few inches to one side. But I could move if I needed to—that was a good thing. The porthole was too far away from me to see anything outside other than the stars twinkling in the midnight-blue sky. I couldn't feel my wallet in my back pocket or my phone in the front pocket of my jeans. I could hear birds and other wilderness noises—tree frogs, cicadas, crickets humming, an occasional splash, the hooting of an owl, and the screech of seagulls.

Splash.

Unlevel room.

A porthole.

The *River Princess*. I had to be on board the *River Princess*, and night had fallen. How long had I been unconscious? My hands were tied behind me, so I couldn't see my watch.

I tried to remember. It had been almost twelve when we left New Orleans. We couldn't have gotten out here before one thirty, tops. I wasn't paying any attention to the time, but it couldn't have been much later than three when we got to Curl Up and Dye—and almost right on cue, my stomach growled. I hadn't eaten since breakfast and could add *hunger* to my ravenous thirst now. If it was dark outside, that meant it had to be…after eight? I tried to remember what time it was getting dark lately without any luck. I never paid attention to what time it got dark because it hadn't mattered before.

Don't think about food.

I did a quick assessment. My hands were tingling because the ropes were cutting off my circulation. I wasn't uncomfortable but would be sore tomorrow—if I got out of this predicament. My head felt kind of woolly. Maybe they'd drugged me? There was a kind of chemical aftertaste in my mouth.

The last thing I remembered was having a gun pressed into my back.

They took us from a parking lot in broad daylight.

That took nerve. Anyone could have seen it happening and called the police—unless it was the police who took us.

I shivered. The cops in this parish were corrupt. I didn't trust Sheriff Perkins as far as I could throw him—and with JD dead, there was a power vacuum in the parish.

Perkins had asked for our help with JD's murder.

But what better way to keep track of the private eyes from New Orleans if you had something to hide?

That had never set right with me. Years of dealing with Venus and Blaine on the NOPD had taught me that cops don't welcome help from civilians. Even when we help them catch a crook, they still don't like it.

Yet Perkins had offered to work with us.

Another moan from somewhere else in the room interrupted my thoughts.

"*Faaaank?*" I asked again, cursing the goddamned gag again.

"*Cah-eee?*" This came from the same direction as the moans. There was some rustling, which I assumed was Frank realizing he was bound and gagged, too. I didn't have to hear what he said next— he was clearly swearing as he tried to figure out how to get freed from his bonds.

I turned my head and peered through the gloom in the same direction the sounds had come from and spotted him—there he was. I could barely make him out, but he was about two or three yards away from me. The moonlight coming through the porthole stopped just to his right.

The rest of the room appeared to be empty—no boxes, no furniture, no lamp, no nothing.

I took a deep breath and strained. Pushing off with my feet, I tried to move the chair in Frank's direction. It worked, but I'd only moved a few more inches closer. The jouncing also sent spikes of pain through my head. I hoped I didn't have a concussion.

I was about to try to move again when there was a loud crash from Frank's direction. He'd tipped over onto his side and now was trying to right himself again. I took a deep breath and launched myself again, moving almost an entire half foot this time. I would be exhausted, but maybe if I could get my chair close enough to Frank's hands, he could untie the knots and—

I moved again, shooting daggers of pain through my head. Frank rolled over to his knees. He launched himself violently to the side again. I winced because that had to have hurt when he crashed into the floor again. He groaned. I couldn't figure out what he was doing. I braced myself again, took a deep breath, and pushed with my feet again. This time I lost my balance, going up on the right two chair legs, and went over onto my side, hard.

There was a flash of pain, and then everything went dark.

When I opened my eyes again, I could feel Frank tugging at the ropes on my hands. My vision was a little blurred, and my head really ached. It took me a moment to understand he was behind me. I couldn't turn and look at him, but he was pulling at the knot with his teeth. I felt his breath against the skin on my arms—it tickled a little bit—and then he was pulling with his teeth again. I tried pushing my wrists apart. I felt pain in my shoulders and stopped— but there was more give to the rope than there had been.

I heard Frank take a deep breath and attack the ropes again with his teeth. He yanked with his head, and the ropes gave, falling away from my wrists. I moved my arms, little needles of pain in my hands as blood started flowing again through the muscles. I reached up and yanked off the gag before reaching down and untying the knots around my ankles. I pushed myself up to my feet and almost lost my balance when blood rushed to my head. More pain darted through my skull like someone had just drilled a spike through it. I felt in my pockets for my phone and my wallet. I was right—both were gone. Just as well—if we were deep in the swamp, there was probably no cell service either. I knelt down, wincing as both knees cracked, and felt around until I found Frank. I removed the gag before going to work on his wrists. "Are you okay?" I rasped. My throat hurt, and the dry mouth was horrible—I couldn't gather any spit at all.

"My head is killing me," Frank said in a muffled voice. "Where are we?"

"I think we're on the *River Princess*—you can hear the water lapping against the side of the boat. What happened?" The knot loosened at last, and I pulled the rope free, feeling my way down his legs to the rope looped around his ankle. "The last thing I remember is we were leaving Curl Up and Dye. We were going to go look around where they found Paris's body, but before I could get into the car someone put a gun in my back and everything went dark. I didn't even see them."

"I didn't get a look," Frank said grimly, "but they ordered me to not make any moves before they knocked me out, and they had Russian accents."

Don't move or I'll kill you, I heard again my head.

"It *might* have been Russian," I amended. "It also could have been Eastern European."

Russian accents would mean this had something to do with Colin.

What the actual fuck, Colin? I get you can't talk about cases with us but if our lives are going to be at risk—

"*Maybe* Russian," I added.

"I'd rather not think this has anything to do with Colin or Blackledge," Frank said as he stood up, cracking his back and shaking out his arms, "but it would be a bit of a coincidence if Russians turned up and it wasn't Colin related."

"Every time there's been Russians involved, it had something to do with Colin," I said. I started trying to climb the slope to the porthole. "But I'm trying to keep an open mind. We're always so quick to think—"

"Because it usually does," Frank interrupted.

"We can deal with that later. But for now, we need to get the fuck out of here before whoever put us here comes back."

My hamstrings and calves burning, but I made it to the porthole. I grabbed hold of the little ledge beneath to take some of the pressure off my calves. I looked out through the glass and saw a vast expanse of flat, black water. Cypress trees and live oaks, all dripping with Spanish moss, broke the still surface here and there.

This had to be Blind Lake, I realized, and if this was Blind Lake, we were definitely on board the *River Princess*. The moon reflected in the still black water. I could see the opening into Bayou Maron on the other side of the lake.

We were going to need a boat, and I had no idea where we were going to find one out here.

But the *River Princess* had gone out onto the water and cruised the river.

That meant there had to be lifeboats somewhere, or it would have never been allowed to leave the dock.

Once we found a boat, we could take Bayou Maron straight back to Sunnymeade.

I wondered if our car was still at Curl Up and Dye.

I tried remembering my geography of St. Jeanne parish. The swamp reached the back end of Sunnymeade, and Bayou Maron drained into the wetlands.

The North Star. Blind Lake was south of Sunnymeade, so we just need to head toward the star to get to land.

I wished I had my phone—the flashlight app would really come in handy. Of course if I had it, the ability to call for help would have been more useful than the flashlight app.

"Where's the door?"

"Over here," Frank said. I turned, barely making his figure out against the frame of a door in the shadows. "Door's locked, but—" He stepped back and kicked at where the door latched onto the frame. He kicked a second time, and on the third there was a crashing sound of splintering wood, and the door swung open out into the hallway. "This way."

I followed Frank through the door into a dark interior hallway, but at the far end we could see a staircase. The wood beneath our feet was soft and rotting, giving here and there with a slight cracking sound, and the smell! The smell of rot and death was everywhere. We were probably breathing in toxic black mold, which the ship had to be riddled with—it had been sitting here for nearly a year, rotting in the swamp and the damp. There'd been storm damage to the boat, too, which was why the ship was tilting to one side. The hull was probably breached, and the ship had settled down into the water, listing toward the damaged side.

The stairs led up to a mezzanine, which was missing part of its roof and thus open to the sky. In the gloomy spare moonlight,

I could see mold and mildew all over the walls of the mezzanine. On the other side of the mezzanine from us was an open doorway leading out to the gallery on one of the upper decks. Frank and I carefully made our way across to the doorway and stepped out into the fresh air and cool breezes of the swamp. I gulped in air, wishing I had something to drink, when Frank grabbed my arm.

"Look." He pointed down to where a pirogue was tied to the side of the *River Princess*, just below us. Without another word, he swung his left leg over the side of the railing and climbed down, his legs swinging a bit before his feet found purchase on the railing below, and then he repeated the climb down before dropping gently down a few feet into the pirogue. He waved at me. "Come on!"

I've never been a fan of heights, and climbing down the side of a rotting riverboat wasn't my idea of a good time. But there was naught for it—*pray for a brave heart*—but to climb, so I took a deep breath and swung my leg over the railing, getting a death grip on the railing before shakily sliding down until I was supporting my weight with the lower rail while my legs dangled, my feet trying to find the railing—

And I lost my grip and fell.

I fell in slow motion, my eyes staring up at the cloudy gray sky, the railing disappearing and getting smaller in the distance as I fell, and then all the air was knocked out of me as my back hit the water hard. For a brief second, I was suspended there on the water's surface. Then I sank beneath the surface into the slimy murky depths. The shock of the cold water and the lack of air in my lungs had me scissoring my legs frantically, flipping over and opening my eyes. I could see the surface just above, and the bottom of the pirogue and—

There are alligators in this swamp.

I broke the surface in time to hear Frank shout, "Scotty, look out!"

I saw the eyes gliding along the top of the water.

I started swimming frantically, closing the three or four feet to the pirogue. Frank grabbed me, yanking me so hard out of the water he almost pulled my left arm out of the socket. I sprawled in the bottom of the pirogue, gasping. Frank swung the oar like a baseball bat. "Get the fuck out of here!" he shouted, and there was a cracking sound. "Go on, now! *Get out of here!*" He plopped down into one of the seats, breathing hard, still clutching the oar.

I was breathing hard in the bottom of the pirogue while Frank untied us and pushed us away from the *River Princess*.

"Let's get out of here," Frank said, using the oar to push off from the side.

As we floated away in the dark, Frank poling us through the water with the oar he'd hit the gator with, I looked back at the *River Princess*.

How, I wondered, was it worth it to try to fix that wreck?

CHAPTER EIGHTEEN
NINE OF WANDS
More fighting must be done to achieve victory

"You know," I said, as Frank paddled us away across Blind Lake, "the last time I was in a swamp at night was that first weekend we met." We'd covered a lot of distance in a short period of time. We were almost all the way across the lake and heading for the opening between the cypresses on the far side. I suspected that was the entrance to Bayou Maron. Looking up and locating the North Star, I was confident I was right.

That last time I was in a swamp at night had not been a good time. I'd been kidnapped by some neo-Nazis, and they'd brought me out to their headquarters, deep in the Atchafalaya Swamp Basin. Different swamp, of course—southern Louisiana is a patchwork of swamps and wetlands. An owl hooted and I shivered. The night sounds of the swamp were almost comforting in a way. I could understand why the original settlers here came up with so many legends and myths about strange creatures in the swamps—the swamps were big and mysterious and filled with creatures most of them had never seen before.

The pirogue was still gliding forward on its own momentum as Frank brought the oar out of the water and rested it across the sides of the boat. There was no wind. Everything was still, other than the night sounds of the swamp—the occasional splash as something jumped into the water, the cicadas, the crickets, the occasional hoot of an owl, the tree frogs keeping the bass line going. I looked back over my shoulder at the *River Princess*. The great boat rested there in the water, leaning toward the shore, and I could see that one of its smokestacks was missing. For a moment I saw it in its prime: all lit up, the sounds of calliope music and clanging of slot machines, the shouts and groans of those gathered around the craps table, the paddle wheel turning lazily in the dirty brown river water, plumes of white smoke rising from the twinned smokestacks.

And then it was just a wreck in a swamp, listing to one side and looking haunted.

"Not all memories are good ones," Frank replied. He stared up at the cloud cover. "We're south of Sunnymeade and Verdun, aren't we?"

I nodded. "I'm pretty sure this opening we're heading for in the trees is Bayou Maron." I looked up to find the North Star again and was startled to see the sky was filling with clouds. The ones behind us were dark, and I saw lightning flash back there, deeper into the wetlands. "And if we don't get there before that storm catches us—"

"Bayou Maron empties into Blind Lake, right?" Frank frowned. "So we couldn't go the wrong way on the bayou because there's only one way?"

"That's right." My wrists ached. I had rope burns on both. "Even if we were to somehow miss Sunnymeade, the bayou runs alongside Bayou Road, so we'd eventually get out of here." My head was still throbbing, and my wrists and ankles still ached from being tied so tightly. "I wonder why they didn't just kill us?"

"What?" Frank stared at me. "Aren't you glad they didn't?"

"Obviously," I replied. "I'd rather be alive than dead, of course, but I'm looking at it from *their* perspective." If only my head didn't hurt so much! "They took us for a reason, but what was the reason?"

"Maybe they didn't want to add murder to whatever other laws they're breaking?"

"Then the people who took us aren't the same people who killed JD," I pointed out, "because they've already killed someone. I'm willing to believe that different criminals killed JD, but who are they?" I held up my hand and started ticking off my fingers. "So, last summer Brody got a job at the Lakeside Mall food court, where he met Paris Soniat. Paris was involved with JD somehow— although his mother thinks it was Quint, JD's son. Anyway, Paris was murdered, and the sheriff covered it up as a hit-and-run, which it obviously wasn't. Sheriff Perkins wouldn't do that for just anyone, so it had to be a favor for the Havers."

"And then JD started messing with Brody, Brody's mom found out, and he broke it off." Frank picked up the story. "Then he gets a message from a burner phone. The message includes one of the pictures Brody took for JD and said *Paris was murdered*. That's what brought him to us."

"And that same night, Brody disappears and someone kills JD," I finished. "We come out here and start poking around Paris Soniat's mother, and we get kidnapped at gunpoint and dumped in the swamp. Why didn't they just kill us and be done with it?" I shook my head. "Someone would eventually find us—workers, or investors, someone out fishing—so why not just shoot us both and throw our bodies out into the water as a midnight snack for the gators?"

"Good point." He frowned, tapping his index finger against his scarred cheek. "So why did they leave us alive?"

"We can't identify the guys who took us—at least I can't," I replied. "All I remember is having the gun shoved in my back and hearing a Russian—*Eastern European*—accent before everything went black. I came to tied up."

"They don't have to worry about us identifying them, sure," Frank mused. "I didn't get a good look at the guy with the gun on you. I only had maybe a couple of seconds after the guy came up behind me before he knocked me out." He tapped his forefinger more rapidly. "They also took us in broad daylight from a public parking lot. They had to knock us out to get us out of there. And nobody saw?"

"There wasn't much traffic on that street," I remembered. "And there weren't many people around. All the store windows for Curl Up and Dye and the CBD joint next door were completely covered with signs and posters and things." I closed my eyes, tried to ignore the regular throb, and pictured the cinder block building again. "I don't think anyone inside could see out."

"It was a risk," Frank agreed, "but it paid off. No one noticed it happening—and if any alarms were raised, we've got no way of knowing anyway. But why wouldn't they just kill us, if they've already killed JD? It doesn't make sense."

"Maybe the people who took us aren't the same people who killed JD." I thought out loud. "And maybe what's going on with the casino boat has nothing to do with JD's murder." A breeze came up, and my teeth started chattering. I was still soaking wet from my fall into the water, and the breeze was cold. I felt along the bottom of the boat for a blanket or anything I could wrap around myself to protect my wet skin from the wind.

Frank moved quickly from his seat to mine, rocking the pirogue so hard that one side almost went below the surface. He put his right arm around me and pulled me into his warm body, while using his other arm to rub my chest to create friction warmth for me.

"It makes sense if we start looking at everything as separate," I went on somehow as my teeth keep chattering. "The connection between everything is JD—the casino, his murder, Brody, and Paris. I think the casino issues and the murder are different cases. But why did Mrs. Soniat think it was Quint, not JD, her son was involved with?"

"Put yourself in Paris's place. You didn't tell your parents about your wrestling coach." Frank started rubbing my shoulders. "I wish there was something in this boat to wrap you up in."

"I'll be okay," I said. It was cozy there in his arms, feeling his body heat against my wet skin. "And Paris *was* murdered. Mrs. Soniat was right about that. You saw that coroner's report."

"The coroner's report was a joke," Frank agreed. "The only injury was to his head from a cylindrical blunt object, like a baseball bat. And there's no way that injury was from a car. His clothes would have been fucked up, he would have scrapes and cuts all over his hands and legs—even if the car hadn't sent him flying away, he would have gone over the car. And you can't go over a car—or bounce along pavement—without more injuries."

"The coroner's report was a lie," I went on. "And who has the kind of power you'd need to convince the coroner to rule the way you wanted them to? The boss of the parish certainly does. And why would JD want it ruled as an accident unless he—or someone he cared about—was involved in the murder?"

"But *why* kill Paris?" Frank asked. "I mean, you heard his mother. Everyone in the parish knew Paris Soniat was a queer kid—it's not like it was a secret. It made him a target for every homophobe out here who might get drunk and think it fun to go queer bashing." He shuddered. "Remember that gang of kids who went on a rampage that summer before Katrina?"

That last summer before the world changed, several gay men had been attacked in the early hours of the morning. The attacks were spread out over several different weekends between Memorial Day and the Fourth of July. One had lost an eye, another had all his fingers broken and smashed, and another had been in a coma for nearly a week. The only thing all three attacks had in common was they were gay men walking alone after four in the morning in the lower Quarter or within the first few blocks of the Marigny. The only description anyone had for the attackers was they were five white teenagers in a white unmarked van. The story wasn't covered much in the paper or on the local news, but word got around the gays the way things always get around the community. There were talks of self-defense classes, the need for an increased police presence in the Quarter late at night, or possibly getting volunteers who could escort men by themselves to their cars or homes late at night. There was a lot of talk, but nothing was ever done. The attackers were finally caught when they targeted a man walking across the street from La Peniche in the Marigny. Unfortunately for them, two patrol officers were at La Peniche having breakfast and saw the entire thing go down. The officers came out of La Peniche with guns drawn and made the arrests. They were just some punks from St. Bernard Parish, losers with nothing better to do than cause trouble, who thought it was great fun to go out gay-bashing on the weekends.

They all got five-to-seven in Angola, which was far too lenient, in my opinion.

If there were gay bashers like that in St. Bernard Parish, there surely were quite a few in St. Jeanne d'Arc Parish.

Paris had been out here, unafraid and in-your-face, as his mother said. His piercings and hair alone would have made him a target for guys insecure in their own masculinity.

"Why didn't he call someone for help?" I said into the silence. "Why did he start walking?"

It's easy to forget sometimes there are people out there who'd just as soon kill a queer as look at one. No matter how many rights we gain, those won't save us from people who don't think we're human.

I was constantly reminding Taylor to be careful on his way home late at night.

Which brought me full circle to being deep in a swamp after dark and no one knowing where we were. Like that other time I'd been kidnapped by skinhead white supremacist homophobes who were trying to create a mass-death incident of gay men in the Quarter.

Homophobes and swamps. Like peanut butter and jelly, from my experience.

"The story was he'd run out of gas," Frank mused. "Or maybe he had car trouble of some kind, who knows? Maybe it just overheated and it had cooled off by the time his mom tried to start the car."

"Maybe he was supposed to meet someone at the bridge that night," I said. My head was starting to really ache. "There's no place to park near there, and that's why he was walking away from town."

"You think JD lured him out there to kill him?"

"Someone did, I'm sure of it," I said to Frank. The cuddling and rubbing was warming me up despite my clothes being soaked through and clinging to my skin like murky, mossy water. I probably needed a tetanus shot at the least, I thought, wondering how much pollution from the petrochemical plant along the river got into Bayou Maron, before deciding that I'd rather not know.

Frank carefully moved back over to the other seat, trying not to rock the boat. The pirogue didn't rock nearly as much as it had the first time. I missed his warm body almost immediately but gritted my teeth to keep them from chattering. Using his oar, Frank started paddling back across the waveless flat expanse of black water. Frank was a good rower. Soon he had the boat skimming across the surface of the water, the *River Princess* growing smaller in the distance as he paddled. We skimmed past the opening in the trees, and I relaxed. This was definitely the bayou—in some places there was a barely visible bank on either side.

I sighed in relief. I couldn't wait to get out of these wet clothes and get cleaned up. Surely someone at Sunnymeade would have clothes that would fit me. I didn't want to ride all the way back to New Orleans in wet clothes. I hoped the car was still at Curl Up and Dye. I wondered what time it was. Colin and Taylor would be raising holy hell if they couldn't get hold of us—and if our attackers took my phone, they'd probably taken Frank's, too.

No one would think to come looking for us out here in the swamp.

"If the only way to get to the *River Princess* is by water…" I hesitated. "Frank, they went to a lot of trouble to get us out of the way. Why? Why didn't they just kill us? That would have made a lot more sense—"

The world exploded.

It was so sudden, fast, and shocking we weren't prepared for it.

One moment we were paddling up Bayou Maron, getting away from Blind Lake and the swamplands in the dark. The next minute the entire night lit up like broad daylight, blinding me suddenly. A few seconds later the roar of the explosion and the shock wave reached us. My ears were ringing, my head was aching, and I couldn't see anything other than that horrible reddish-yellow reflection on my corneas from the brightness of the explosion. I was still blinking, tears running out of my eyes from the pain in my ears, which made me completely forget about the headache, when the first wave the explosion had sent from the lake coming down the bayou lifted us into the air. The wave passed and we hung there in midair for what seemed like an eternity before the pirogue dropped. The pirogue smashed down hard into the water and both sides went under the surface, water flooding over the sides as another massive wave swamped us yet again. The smelly, muddy, dirty water went up my nose and into my mouth as the pirogue tipped over and I fell again into the water. I barely had time to take a deep breath before my head went under the surface for the second time in less than an hour.

I kept my eyes closed while I floundered around in the water, aware more, smaller waves were passing by now. I waved my hands through the water, striking plants and other kelpy slimy feeling things that wanted to grab my arms and encircle them, tying me up and leaving me at the mercy of the water and whatever was in it. A litany was running through my brain—*Please spare us, Goddess, please don't let us die out here in this swamp please*—as I sank into the water, frantically trying to get my bearings, trying to head back to the surface. My feet grazed the muddy, slimy bottom, and I bent at the knees, pushing against the soupy floor and springing through the water, breaking the surface and gasping for air, waiting to go back under—

When I realized I could stand up. The water was only up to my chest.

I shook my head. My ears were still ringing from the blast, and my eyes, finally adjusting after the sudden bright flash, started to clear. I could make out shapes, forms and finally realized that the night sky was bright. And I smelled smoke.

The *River Princess* was burning so brightly it might as well have been noon. The entire boat was aflame, the angry yellowish-red flames reaching higher to the sky, sparks flying into the air and then blinking out. Burning wood was dropping out of the sky. I couldn't hear the splashes over the ringing in my ears.

Frank was holding the pirogue out of the water, pouring out the filthy water the waves had splashed into it. He grinned at me, and his mouth was moving but I couldn't hear him. I shook my head and pointed at my ears. He nodded, putting the pirogue back into the bayou water. He waded over and grabbed the oar where it had floated up against the base of a massive live oak. I waded through the water, covered in muck and ooze and feeling slimy. I carefully climbed back over the side, back into the pirogue. Frank did the same and, once we were both settled, started paddling again.

I turned around to look back at the blaze. It was so bright and the flames were shooting so high, it could probably be seen in New Orleans.

And I realized with a gulp, that was why they left us there, tied up below deck. So we'd be killed when the boat blew up.

They did, in fact, care about leaving us alive.

Since I couldn't hear, I sat there as Frank paddled us up the bayou back to Valmont, my mind racing.

Everyone would have assumed we'd been exploring, looking for clues or something and had been caught when the boat blew.

I looked back at the burning boat. It couldn't have been a bomb—a bomb would have made it murder. So they'd rigged something—maybe the engine—to blow. They'd tied us up, put us in that room, and sped away—that was the motor I'd heard when I'd woken up.

The men who tried to kill us had Russian accents.

Russian accents.

Every single time we got involved with bad guys with Russian accents, Colin and Blackledge were involved. I didn't want to consider Colin was lying to us again. Russians didn't mean he was involved…and the accent could have been Eastern European.

Give him the benefit of the doubt for once.

It was so easy to think he hadn't turned up out of the blue because he'd quit Blackledge and wanted to be with us full-time from now on.

He'd come back on assignment—an assignment he once again couldn't be honest with us about. Like the other times he'd lied to us.

How can we be in a relationship with someone we can't trust?

"You have to trust him," I muttered to myself.

It was still possible that whatever had happened out here

tonight with the *River Princess* was completely unconnected to JD's murder and Brody's disappearance.

Brody and Paris.

I wished I had my phone. Yes, I wanted to call Colin and Taylor and let them know we were okay, but it would be great to have them check Brody's iPad for anything having to do with Paris Soniat.

This whole business started because Brody got a job at the food court and met Paris.

My head hurt.

We'd just accepted Brody's word for everything, but he hadn't been honest with us, either. I'd never once gotten a gay vibe from JD, ever. I hadn't been looking for one because JD was one of those horrible straight boys, the ones people mean when they say *locker room talk*. JD's room at Sunnymeade had always been filled with *Playboy* and *Penthouse* and other girlie magazines. JD had to know that I'd come out—Mom had told everyone in the family.

So why had he never talked to me about it?

Maybe...

Maybe the person identifying himself as JD...wasn't JD?

Brody had seemed reluctant about coming to us for help. Hadn't really wanted us to get involved and basically just wanted us to let JD know there might be a blackmailer gunning for him—and of course the thing about Paris being murdered.

And then he'd disappeared without a trace the next day.

That was the part I didn't get. He hadn't had to go to David. He could have said no when David suggested he speak with us.

He was seeing someone in the city, I recalled Mrs. Soniat saying, *and so he said if he was going to have to drive into the city to see his boyfriend, might as well get a job there too to pay for the gas.*

Brody and Paris, Paris and Brody.

Brody would have known the Havers owned this parish and the sheriff's office was basically their enforcers. When Paris was killed, Brody might have had questions, too. Had Paris been involved with JD before he met Brody? Had they met *before* they got the jobs at the mall?

Maybe Brody had been trying to get justice for Paris?

So why hadn't he been honest with us from the first?

The only person with the answer to those questions was Brody.

If he was still alive.

If we could find him before it was too late.

My ears were still ringing, but I could hear sirens above the tinnitus.

I didn't know how firetrucks were going to get out to the burning boat, and based on what I'd seen, there was no saving it. Just as well. Karen certainly seemed to have no stomach for running it.

We moved out of the swamp into a clearly defined channel between two levees. That meant we were out of the swamp and moving closer to Sunnymeade.

We came around a corner and were almost swamped by two speedboats roaring past, throwing up a huge wake that rocked the pirogue back and forth.

Then I saw it, on a rise in the distance. The ugly house was ablaze with light.

The dock was just ahead of us.

We were almost home free.

CHAPTER NINETEEN
THE EMPEROR, REVERSED
A weak character, potential loss or injury

I didn't have to point the dock out to Frank since he was clearly heading for it.

There was a speedboat tied up to one side of the dock, so Frank maneuvered us around to the other side, where the boathouse was. The doors to the boathouse were closed as Frank pulled up to the ladder on that side of the dock. Shivering, I climbed up the rungs and collapsed with relief on the worn, warped gray wood of the dock. A few moments later Frank plopped down beside me. "I didn't tie up the boat," he said, panting. His forehead was covered with drops of sweat, and his shirt was damp with sweat, clinging to his perfectly formed torso. "How's your hearing?"

"Fuck the boat," I said. "I can hear better, but my ears are still ringing, and I have a horrible headache."

"We need to get you to the emergency room," he said, getting to his feet and holding out his big hands to help me to mine.

"Do you still have the car keys?" I asked.

He patted his pockets, but he didn't need to for me to know the answer. They'd taken our phones, so of course they took the keys. That meant the car might not be at Curl Up and Dye; there was no telling where the car might be. But in the distance, across gardens and a rice paddy and past the outer buildings and the rolling lawn, I could see the lights of Sunnymeade. The entire house was lit up—probably because of the explosion—and maybe someone, anyone there might have clothes I could borrow so I could get out of these filthy wet ones. I shivered again. I really felt slimy and gross. A hot shower was just the ticket I needed to feel better, to feel like myself again. I needed some aspirin or something—sure, sure, I'd get an

MRI or whatever else was called for to make sure I didn't have a brain injury or something, but I wanted to be able to think clearly, and that just wasn't possible with it hurting the way it was.

The answer to everything was right in front of my face, but I couldn't get to it because I couldn't *think*.

The ringing in my ears wasn't helping, either.

"Come on, let's get up to the house," Frank said grimly. "Someone's in for a big shock."

We trudged slowly past the rice paddy and then past a couple of the guesthouses. Sunnymeade may have been the ugliest mansion in Louisiana, but they had some of the most beautiful gardens. We made our way up the path through the rose garden on the left and a topiary of animals on the right, up the lush perfectly kept lawn and past the swimming pool to the back steps to the first floor gallery. We climbed up, but the back door was locked. I rolled my eyes and started walking along the gallery around to the front of the house. The shutters to the drawing room were open, and the room was ablaze with light.

I reached a window and pushed it upward. It wasn't latched and slid up with a practiced ease so smooth it was soundless.

"Scotty!"

Before I could register who said it or what was happening, I was smothered in a massive embrace. It was Taylor, and I pushed him back away from me. "Careful, babe, I'm wet."

"What on earth happened to you both?" I heard Karen's voice above the ringing.

"We've had quite an adventure," Frank said from behind me. "We were on board the *River Princess* right before she blew up. I think the idea was for us to go up with it."

A hush fell over the room. As I stepped away from Taylor, I was aware I was dripping filthy bayou water on Karen's polished floors...and didn't care. I glanced around the room. Karen was standing over by the bar. Sheriff Perkins was standing by her, Colin was seated on the couch, and Coach—*Dan*—Phelps was sitting in a wingback chair blinking at us.

The pieces in my head began rearranging themselves.

I was still missing something important.

"Karen, I hate to bother you, but I really need to get out of these wet clothes and maybe take a hot shower, if it's not too much trouble?"

"You both need one," Karen said, clapping her hands. "Come on, let's get you upstairs and into the shower. We can finish talking once you're back downstairs."

"Sorry about the mess," I said as Frank and I followed her up the grand winding staircase to the second floor.

"Don't, that's what we hire people for," she said with a wave of her hand as she walked us down the hallway and opened the door to a bedroom. "This is one of the guest rooms—I'll get you some of JD's clothes, if you'll give me a second." She disappeared down the hallway and around a corner.

I peeled off my shirt and tossed it into the bathroom sink. It was all done in white and gold, very austere and expensive looking but cold. I opened a cabinet door and found towels, big and fluffy and smelling like fabric softener. Through the open door I saw Karen placing sweatpants, sweatshirts, underwear, and socks on the bed, heard Frank say thank you, and the hallway door closed. I turned on the hot water spigot and pulled up the gear to get the shower going. I peeled off my pants, underwear, and socks and placed them in the sink as well. Frank appeared in the doorway naked, holding his dripping clothes, and placed them on top of mine in the sink. We showered together, luxuriating in the hot water and the lavender-scented lather from the bar of soap. We cleaned each other off as best as we could—ignoring the distraction that our close bodily proximity and the hot water were trying to cause for us—and finally rinsed off all the soap and climbed out into the steamy air of the bathroom. The mirror was all fogged over. I handed Frank a towel and started toweling him dry—he did the same for me. We could easily have spent at least another fifteen minutes there in the bathroom, but now was not the time to consummate our love and passion for each other. That could wait until we got back home.

By the time we finished dressing, my ears weren't ringing as bad anymore. I could still feel pressure in my eardrums from the concussive blast, but I could hear, even if my own voice sounded funny to me. "Frank, I think I have this all figured out except for a couple of things," I said, sitting on the edge of the bed so I could put socks on my feet. "But I can't prove anything, and I don't know where Brody is or what happened to him," I went on. "That's the thing that doesn't make any sense to me. I'm worried—"

"That he might be dead?" Frank sighed. "I'm afraid that may be the case."

I blinked away surprising tears and shook my head. "But it doesn't fit," I replied. "Even JD's murder. I think we have two different cases going on, and JD is the only thing that connects them. I don't think the lawsuits or anything having to do with the *River Princess* have anything to do with Brody and JD. I believe JD was up to something with the boat all right—I don't know exactly what—but since the boat was blown up, I bet it has something to do with Len Gargaro and some serious insurance fraud."

"Okay."

"JD is the only common link. And we can't make sense of everything because we've been thinking all along this is all the same thing. Come on, let's go downstairs and see if we can get to the bottom of everything."

But I still don't know where Brody is.

"I made coffee," Karen said when we walked back into the living room, "to help you warm up. Now what on earth happened to you both?"

I made my cup the way I liked it—some cream and sweetener—and sat down in a wingback chair, smiling at both Colin and Taylor, ignoring Dan Phelps and Sheriff Perkins. I crossed my legs. I felt so much better. The shower felt like it had sluiced worry and care and fear off my body along with a layer of dirty bayou water. My head still hurt slightly, but it was getting better. I'd still need to get checked for concussion, though.

"Paris Soniat," I said, after taking a sip of coffee. It was hot and strong and felt like life as it coursed down my throat. "The key to everything was Paris Soniat."

It was deadly silent in the drawing room other than the grandfather clock's gears moving. I didn't look at Sheriff Perkins or Karen as I kept talking. "Paris Soniat was murdered last summer, and his body was found on Bayou Road." I glanced over at Sheriff Perkins, who had the decency to start flushing red in the face. "The coroner ruled it a hit-and-run accident, but looking at the report and the crime scene photos, there's no way Paris Soniat was killed by a car. No reasonable person—you don't have to be trained in forensic science to look and see that he was killed by being hit in the head with a baseball bat–like object. But the coroner ruled and the case was closed, right, Sheriff?"

"I didn't—um, I didn't see any reason to not go along with

the coroner's findings." Sheriff Perkins couldn't even look any of us in the eye. He was staring down at his hands, which were twisting inside of each other.

"Who told you to close that case, Sheriff?" I asked gently. "It was JD, wasn't it?"

He cleared his throat. "JD did make, um, some suggestions about how the case should be handled."

"But why—" Karen started, but cut herself off. She refilled her cut-glass tumbler with whiskey, neat.

"JD would have asked for that case to be closed only if it was in his interest for that to happen," I went on. "So, JD knew something about Paris Soniat's death. He might not have been the one to kill him, but he knew who did kill him, and he wanted it swept under the rug and forgotten." My voice took on a bitter edge. "And Paris was just some backwater fag, right, whose family was nothing but trash anyway, right, and who would miss him? What did he have to offer the world? It meant nothing to Sheriff Perkins, hell, it made his job a lot easier. Case closed, file sealed, dismiss the mother as hysterical, and it's all wrapped up nice and neat with a big bow on the top. But what neither of you expected was that Paris actually had a boyfriend in New Orleans. That was why he wanted to work at the food court, so they could go hang out together after work and he had spending money. Paris's boyfriend knew all about Paris, knew all about St. Jeanne d'Arc Parish and how it operated—*because Paris told him.* Paris also told him about the older man he used to be involved with back home, back here—and Paris's ex even came to visit him at the food court, trying to get Paris back. But that meant he also met Paris's new boyfriend. And he took a liking to the new boyfriend."

They were all staring at me. Frank smiled and took up the narrative from me. "We may never know why Paris's ex decided he needed to get rid of Paris. Maybe Paris wanted money to keep his mouth shut. Paris had big dreams, according to his mother—he wanted to move to New Orleans, he wanted to go to school there, he wanted to build a life with his new boyfriend away from St. Jeanne. And who could blame him? I can only imagine what Paris's life was like out here, growing up and going to school here, trying to stay alive out here while not being like other boys."

"Yes, I can't prove what happened, but it's easy enough to figure out." I smiled at Sheriff Perkins. "Paris became a problem, so Paris had to go. When you own the sheriff, it's easy enough."

"Wait." Karen's hand trembled, making waves in the whiskey in her tumbler. "Are you saying *JD* was who Paris was seeing?"

"Brody hired us to come out here and warn JD someone had gotten a hold of their private messages and pictures they'd shared with each other and was now texting them to Brody," I said. "That's what brought us out here in the first place. And of course, JD was already dead by the time we got here. Brody disappeared the same night JD was murdered. Coincidence? Unlikely."

"Wait—are you saying JD, my husband…" Karen took another big swig of whiskey. "JD wasn't gay, Scotty. That's the hole in this entire case you're building. JD liked to fool around some—hookers, usually, because they were discreet—but there's no way JD could have been messing with men, let alone boys, without me knowing."

"The wife's always the last to know," Sheriff Perkins muttered. He held up his hands. "The hell with it." He took his badge off and slammed it down on the coffee table. "I'm retiring, effective immediately. I am sick and tired of cleaning up Haver messes, no disrespect intended, ma'am," he said, inclining his head to Karen, who rolled her eyes in acknowledgment. "JD told me he'd consider it a big favor if we closed the investigation in Paris Soniat's death and ruled it a hit-and-run." He swallowed. "I knew it wasn't, but I wasn't going to go against JD."

"And no one can blame you for that, Sheriff." Colin took up the narrative now. "What good would it have done you? He would have just replaced you—or made you disappear."

Karen's face had drained of all color. She finished off her whiskey and poured more into the glass. "I don't believe any of this."

"I think Brody played up to JD because *he* didn't believe the coroner's report, either," I went on. "Brody knew damned well there would never be any justice for Paris here, so I think he kept playing up to JD, stringing him along, trying to find out the truth about Paris's death." I sighed. "He didn't have enough to go to the cops or the Feds—because that's what it would have taken out here—so I think he played Nancy Drew, trying to get information out of JD, trying to get him to confess or admit to something. When he started getting the text messages showing someone else had access to their private conversations, it freaked him out. He talked to one of his teachers, who brought him to us. He didn't tell us everything because he wasn't sure he could trust us. He wasn't sure who he could trust. I can't imagine how scared he must have been." What I sensed as arrogance and self-confidence had been him overcompensating to hide how afraid he was. Now that I knew more about what was going on with him, I could see it.

No, a voice whispered in my head, *you took an instant dislike to the kid, and so you weren't paying as close attention as you should have been. He reminded you of yourself at that age, and you knew on some level that your affair with Coach Phelps had been abuse and not romance, so you reacted the way you did.*

And now that you know Dan Phelps groomed and molested you, you can finally see it clearly for the first time in your life.

"And you had us followed from the moment we left your office, didn't you, Sheriff." I turned to Sheriff Perkins, who very determinedly was looking down at the floor. "Only you didn't have any of your deputies do it—you had some Russians available."

"Russians?" Karen gasped out the word.

"That's who took us from the parking lot at Curl Up and Dye, tied us up, planted a bomb on the *River Princess*, and left us out there to die." My eyes met Colin's, and mentally I promised to make it up to him later. "Len Gargaro is part of the new investment group. Let me guess—the *River Princess* is insured to the hilt, right? My guess is the explosion was rigged to look like some kind of accident—a fuel leak and a spark, something like that. And if Frank and I were blown to bits, so much the better."

"Joe Perkins, what do you have to say for yourself?" Karen demanded in a very shaky voice.

"I say you can't prove any of this in court." Sheriff Perkins met my eyes, and a smug smile appeared on his face. "And without proof, no one around here will care."

"But I care, Sheriff." Karen's voice dripped acid. "And I'm head of the family now."

He sneered at her. "Do your worst, lady." He folded his arms. "If you don't think I have enough dirt on your family to sink you all, think again." He winked at her. "I mean, Quint's still on probation for that drunk driving incident over Christmas—"

"You wouldn't dare!"

"I think you'll be surprised what all your sheriff is capable of, Mrs. Haver," Colin said smoothly from the couch. "But if Len Gargaro is acting as a front for the Russian mob, and your sheriff knew about it—the Feds will be *very* interested in talking to him."

"But what happened to Brody?" Taylor interrupted. "Where is he?"

"I'm right here," a voice said with a quiver from the window.

CHAPTER TWENTY
SEVEN OF WANDS
Victory over one's adversaries

All eyes in the room turned to the window.

Dead silence. I glanced around at the tableau in front of me. Sheriff Perkins looked angry but surprised, Karen's face was an expressionless mask, Coach Phelps looked super nervous.

As well you should, I thought, turning back to Brody.

Now I could see that what I'd taken for arrogant self-confidence was just natural shyness, part of a wall constructed to keep out the rest of the world and protect him. He was wearing a black T-shirt with *Saints* written across the front in gold lettering. His snugly fitting jeans were dirty and stained. He looked like hadn't shaved in a couple of days, so his cheeks and chin looked bluish-black from the stubble—almost like his olive skin had bruised. His curls were messy-looking and unkempt. His eyes kept moving around the room…

But he never looked at Coach.

I fought the roiling in my stomach. I felt nauseous and set my coffee cup back down. I felt like I was going to throw up.

How could I have been so wrong?

"Your mother is worried sick," Frank said into the silence. "Not cool, disappearing on her like that, son. Maybe shoot her a text, let her know you're not lying in a ditch somewhere."

Brody flushed. "Yeah, yeah, I get it, I know I'm a bad son." He folded his arms, the roadmap of thick veins popping out on his forearms. "But I didn't have much of a choice." He raised his chin defiantly.

"And just who are you, young man, and what are you doing in my house?" Karen asked. Her tone was pleasant enough, but her neck was drawn taut, and she was clutching that tumbler of whiskey hard enough to shatter it.

"Karen, may I introduce you to Brody Shepherd," I replied. "This is our client—the one who hired us to come out here to clear some things up with JD." The catalyst who kick-started this entire mess into gear. "Brody, where have you been?"

He had the decency to blush even darker. "I'm sorry, I know I should have said something to Mom, or let you guys know what was going on and where I was, but I didn't…" He winced. "I didn't know how to explain everything, and I was scared." His voice broke on the last words. "I've been hiding out in one of the guesthouses here at Sunnymeade. I'm sorry, Mrs. Haver, but I've been trying to figure out what to do." He pulled his phone out of his pocket. "My phone died, and I didn't have a charger." He grinned ruefully. "I've been sneaking in and out of this place looking for a charger, but after I almost got caught the last time, I decided that tomorrow morning I was going to head for town, see if I could call Mom. I'm sorry, I didn't mean for anyone to be worried." He collapsed into a chair and wiped at his eyes. "The last couple of days have been horrible."

"I can't imagine," Colin said gently. "Just start at the beginning, Brody, and tell us everything."

"You weren't completely honest with us, were you?" I said gently. Out of the corner of my eye I saw Dan Phelps creeping toward the double doors to the hallway. "Where do you think you're going?" I said, whirling around.

Coach's face drained of color as we all turned to look at him. "Well, I was…" He cleared his throat. "I don't think you need me here for—"

"Why wouldn't we need you here, JD?" Brody's voice cut like a knife through the tension in the room. Someone gasped.

"JD?" Karen whispered.

And everything clicked into place in my head, the very last piece I'd been missing all along. "That isn't JD Haver, Brody, but I think you already knew that, didn't you?"

"I only found out a few days ago." Brody's voice was bitter. "Everything you told me was a lie, wasn't it?"

"You didn't leave me a choice," Coach Phelps replied, pulling a gun out of his jacket pocket. He aimed it directly at Karen, whose face turned even paler.

"*You* were the one who was involved with Paris Soniat," I said, feeling a bit of a chill as now the muzzle of the gun swung around to point at me. "JD was never involved with any boys, was he? That's always been *your* thing, right, *Coach* Phelps?" I emphasized the word *coach*. "Teenage boys, preferably innocent and virginal, right, Coach? Like I was?"

It was the first time I'd said it out loud, the first time I'd admitted it to myself. There were some gasps and shocked faces, but…I felt *good*, like a load had been lifted off my shoulders that had been weighing me down for decades.

The truth shall set you free, the Goddess's voice echoed in my head.

He hadn't loved me. He'd never loved me. He saw a lonely, vulnerable young gay child on his wrestling team—with talent—and decided to make me his next conquest. Mom and Dad had accepted me, my siblings were fine with me being gay, but that hadn't made me any less lonely. I hadn't had any real friends at Jesuit.

He'd not seen me as a person. He'd seen me as *prey*.

It didn't change anything. I was still me, I still knew who I was. So I'd spent the last thirty years thinking he'd been in love with me and I'd ruined his life. I'd carried that guilt all these years—his marriage, his career, his family.

And now I was free from that.

It felt *amazing*.

"That was different," Coach Phelps replied, his voice shaking almost as much as the gun he was holding. "I loved you, Scotty."

"Sure, you did." My voice dripped with contempt. "I'm sure you loved Paris, too, didn't you? And all the others before and after me? You loved them all, didn't you, Coach? It's all just a wild coincidence that you only fall for teenagers, right?"

"Shut up!" He was backing toward the doors. "All of you, *shut up!*" Spittle flew from his lips as he screamed out the last.

"JD didn't know, did he?" I said, keeping my voice calm and conversational. I didn't look at either Frank or Colin. I could see in my peripheral vision that they were shifting, getting ready to do something. Better keep him distracted, keep his attention on me, I thought, hoping they weren't planning on rushing a man with a gun. He was already shaky, his mental state crumbling before our very eyes. He'd already killed Paris and JD. If we weren't careful, someone in the room could get hurt. "JD had no idea you murdered Paris Soniat, did he? He had no idea that you were grooming boys, did he?"

"*Shut up!*"

"I met Paris at the community center a year ago," Brody explained. "I was just starting to come out—"

"*I said, shut up!*" He'd backed up almost to the doorframe now, the gun shakily swinging from person to person.

"Just put the gun down, Dan," Sheriff Perkins said calmly. "We can talk this all out, and no one needs to get hurt."

"Oh sure, do I look like an idiot?" Dan shouted. "I killed someone. How are we going to talk our way out of that?"

"Coach, you don't want to make this worse than it already is," I purred, trying to keep him looking at me. "Just put the gun down. You're never going to get away. You'd have to kill us all." As the words left my lips, I thought, don't be giving him any bright ideas! "You're not a killer, Coach. I'm sure Paris and JD weren't deliberate." I tossed him a lifeline, keeping my eyes locked on his.

"You need help," Karen added from over by the desk. She leaned back against it, keeping her eyes on her husband's chief of staff the entire time. "You're obviously not in your right mind, Dan. All those years of repressing your sexuality, it had to have done some damage to you emotionally and mentally. I'm sure you didn't mean to kill Paris."

I didn't believe that for a minute, but hey—when you're trying to talk down someone unstable with a gun, all bets are off.

"He was going to blame me for *everything*," Dan stated bitterly. "Once he knew about Paris, he was going to set me up to take the fall for everything. And you would have stood by his side the entire time, Karen, so don't give me that act like you give two shits about anyone besides yourself. I know you were the one who brought Gargaro on board—and you knew all about the plan to blow up the *River Princess* for the insurance money. JD figured there would be enough for the investors and more than enough for him to pay off those insurance settlements he embezzled to buy the *River Princess* back from the original investors. Oh yes, that's what happened to that money—and don't believe for a minute Karen wasn't in it up to her own swanlike neck."

"And you weren't going to let that happen, were you?" Frank said quietly. He stood up from his chair, keeping his hands up where

Coach could see then. "Why should you go down for the Havers' criminality?"

"You didn't have to kill Paris," Brody said softly.

"*He wanted money!*" Coach screamed back at him. We all flinched and braced for the gunshot, but it never came. "He wanted money." His voice broke.

And that was when Colin launched himself at him over the back of the couch. It all happened so fast that it seemed like a blur to me. One moment Dan started to cry in the doorway, then Colin was flying over the back of the couch. Dan recoiled from him and fired the gun three times. Glass shattered as people dove for the floor all around the room. I tackled Brody and brought him down, shielding his body with mine. My ears ringing again from the gunshots, I raised my head to look around. The mirror over the mantle had shattered, hit by a bullet. I didn't see anyone else who looked injured—

But Colin and Coach were gone.

Fuck.

I pushed myself up to my feet and ran for the doorway. I looked to my left just in time to see Colin go out the open back door at the end of the hallway. I ran after him, every step sending shooting pain through my head—I really needed to get my head scanned—and my ears still ringing from the gunshots and the earlier explosion. The pressure in my eardrums was painful. I reached the back door in time to see Colin launch a flying tackle at Coach that took them both into the pool and under the surface. I stopped running. By the time I reached the concrete area around the pool, Sheriff Perkins caught up to me, panting, his gun out and pointing at the pool. I could see them struggling together under the surface, and then they both came up gasping. Colin had the gun in one hand and swung it, connecting with Coach's forehead with what must have been a satisfying crack. I just couldn't hear it. Coach slumped in the water. Colin dragged him to the side of the pool and hoisted him out with one hand. I always forget how fucking strong he is. Sheriff Perkins quickly handcuffed Coach's hands behind his back.

Coach rolled over, opened his eyes, and moaned. Sheriff Perkins and Colin dragged him up to his feet. Sheriff Perkins started reading him his rights as they shuffled back up to the house. Perkins didn't bring him inside, instead perp-walking him around the gallery to the front, and I heard a car door slam. An engine started up, there was the sound of tires on pavement, and then the siren split the night. I winced and covered my ears.

They'd stopped ringing by the time we got back to the drawing room.

Well, okay, they were still ringing, but not so loud that I couldn't hear above it.

"Sheriff Perkins has him," Colin announced as we walked back into the drawing room.

Karen was handing a glass of whiskey to Frank and she looked up. "He was lying about the *River Princess*," she said quickly. "I didn't know anything about the plans—"

"Don't worry about it, Karen." I sank wearily down onto the couch again. "I don't care. All I cared about was making sure Brody was okay. You are okay, aren't you, Brody? Does anyone have a cell phone he can use?"

Taylor tossed him his. "Call your mom, let her know you're okay," he said softly.

Brody nodded and went back out onto the gallery.

"Will someone please explain to me what is going on?" Karen asked, refilling her own glass shakily, spilling some whiskey drops onto the sideboard.

"At some point over the past couple of years, Dan Phelps and Paris became involved," I said, accepting a bottle of water from Karen. I gulped some down. The adrenaline was wearing off, and I was feeling incredibly tired. "We'll never know how it happened or for how long it happened, but it's a pattern with Dan Phelps." I waved my hand. "Just take my word for it." I was in no mood to explain my own past with my former wrestling coach. It was going to take some getting used to—the idea that we weren't involved in some tragic doomed Shakespearean romance, the way I had always believed, but were rather groomer and victim. "But Paris had dreams, and he didn't want to stay out here in St. Jeanne. He wanted to move to New Orleans, go to school there, live his big gay life there. So he started driving into the city to go to the youth group meetings at the LGBT Center, which is where he met Brody."

"She's relieved," Brody said as he walked back in through the window. He handed Taylor his phone with a shy smile that Taylor reacted to by blushing almost purple. *Uh-oh, does Taylor have a crush on Brody?*

Brody took up the story. "Scotty's right—Paris and I met at the youth group." He blushed. "You have to understand, most of us at the group were still closeted, still trying to come to terms with, you know." He blushed even further. "Paris was different from all of us. Paris had already been through it all—coming to terms with it, accepting it, coming out to everyone—and he had so much self-confidence. And he was so funny and kind and sweet. How could I not fall for him? But he was seeing someone, he told me, but he needed to break it off because it wasn't going anywhere, and it had to be a secret, and he was tired of hiding everything." He smiled faintly. "And he loved me, I know he did. And then we got the jobs at the food court. Paris was already in the process of breaking it off with his older man, but the man started showing up at the food court every weekend, trying to talk to Paris, trying to get Paris back. I asked Paris what his name was, and he told me JD."

Karen inhaled sharply.

Brody shook his head and looked at her with a sad smile. "But it wasn't really JD. I'll never know why Paris told me that—he probably thought it was funny, he did have a weird sense of humor. And then...he was killed." His jaw set. "And when I talked to his mom, she made it clear to me that he'd been murdered, and the parish government was covering it up. JD was still coming to the food court—he'd started flirting with me, and buying me gifts, and things. And he gave me his phone number—"

"Which you stored as JD," Frank interjected.

He nodded. "I was pretty sure JD had something to do with Paris's murder, but who would believe me? So I decided to keep stringing JD along, see what I could find out. And yeah, I was crazy. What was I thinking, investigating a murder? If JD had killed Paris, he was dangerous, and there was no reason he wouldn't kill me if he ever figured out what I was really doing. So I decided to let it go." He gave me a broken look. "Life isn't fair, after all, and people get away with murder all the time. Plus, I got my audition at Juilliard, and I decided to break it off with JD and move on with my life. He didn't take it well, but he finally got the message. So when I started getting those text messages from an unknown account, I freaked. Someone had the pictures I'd sent JD, someone had screenshots of our messages. I wanted nothing to do with any of this anymore, so that's why I spoke to Mr. Andrews, and he brought me to you."

He nodded at me, Frank, and Colin. "But when I got back home that night, I thought about it some more. I knew JD Haver was the president of the parish—I'd seen his name in stories about the wrecked casino boat—and so I called his office. He wasn't there, but the lady who answered the phone transferred me to his cell phone."

"And it wasn't JD, or the man you knew as JD, was it?" I asked.

He bit his lip and shook his head. "He was very confused, and then he got angry. He asked me to forward him the messages I'd gotten, so I did. He told me he was going to come to Orleans Parish and pick me up, and we were going to come back to St. Jeanne and get this settled once and for all. I told my mother I had a study date and went to a coffee shop, where JD picked me up about an hour later. And it was not the man I knew as JD." He barked out a sad laugh. "I made him show me his ID, and then he showed me some things from the paper out here, his picture with the captions—and of course, the man I knew as JD was actually Dan Phelps." He swallowed. "JD hid me in one of the guest cottages here and then went out to meet Dan, privately, to confront him. I'd turned off my phone because I didn't want anyone to know where I was. And then JD—the real JD—never came back. I snuck up to the main house the next morning, and that was when I found out JD had been murdered." He exhaled. "And I've been hiding out there ever since, trying to figure out what to do and how to get back to New Orleans so I could tell the police everything." He took another deep breath. "But I didn't trust the police out here. I didn't know what to do."

"You should have called us," Frank said gently, getting up and enveloping him in a big hug. "We would have listened."

"I know." He held on to Frank for dear life before letting go. "If I had just been honest with everyone from the start—"

"It's a lot to handle," Taylor cut him off. "And it's not like you can just google this stuff or anything."

Brody smiled at him shyly. Was it my imagination, or were sparks flying between the two of them? They both could certainly do worse—and have. "Thanks. I don't think we've met?"

"Taylor." He got up and shook hands with Brody, looking deep into his eyes. "The old bald one is my uncle."

"Hey!" Frank said. "Not cool, nephew!"

We all started laughing, and I leaned back against Colin, who'd sat next to me on the couch. He leaned in and whispered, "I bet when you heard the Russian accents, you thought it had something to do with me, didn't you?"

I looked into his beautiful eyes and smiled back at him. "Didn't even cross my mind once," I lied.

Sometimes, telling a lie is the right thing to do.

EPILOGUE

About a month later, I was wrapping dishes in newspaper and packing them into a moving box. We were moving into the Dower House on Papa Diderot's property while Cooper Construction turned our building into the perfect home for us. The Vieux Carré Commission granted us permission to put a roof over the third floor balcony, and we were turning the first floor into our own personal health spa. Taylor claimed he was still going to go to the New Orleans Athletic Club, but I liked the idea of having a gym on the first floor. We'd hired movers, but I preferred that we pack everything up. It was being moved into a storage facility for the duration of the construction work. It was estimated to take a month...but it's New Orleans. We probably wouldn't be moving back in before Southern Decadence.

I put the last dish in the box and taped it shut, writing *Kitchen Eating Ware* on the outside with a black Magic Marker. I sparked the joint resting on the kitchen counter and inhaled deeply.

It was going to be weird for a while, living in the Garden District. Other than the reconstruction after the fire all those years ago, I'd been living in this building since I was twenty-five.

The state police *and* the Feds had descended on St. Jeanne d'Arc Parish along with the IRS and forensic accountants. The Havers were broke and had been for quite some time. JD had been borrowing from Peter to pay Paul. He'd gotten away with it for years—trying to follow all the labyrinthine paths from account to account made my head ache. I hadn't had a concussion, after all, and after a few days my hearing had gone back to normal. Everything had been taken over by a court trustee. It looked like over a century of Haver domination had finally ended out in St. Jeanne d'Arc

Parish. Sheriff Perkins himself was under investigation pending indictment for obstruction of justice in the Paris Soniat case, and the forensic accountants were digging through his accounts and the sheriff's department records as well.

It was all a mess, and I was glad to not have anything else to do with it all.

Heather Soniat had thanked us for finding justice for her son. Coach Phelps had taken a plea bargain—concurrent sentences for second-degree murder. He was going to prison for a long time.

As for Brody, well, we've seen a lot of him since that fateful night at Sunnymeade. My instincts had been right. Taylor and Brody were dating now, and Brody was over a lot. He was upstairs helping Taylor pack up. They were a cute couple, but I wasn't sure what would happen if Brody got into Juilliard. I'd been completely wrong about him. He was a sweet kid. He'd taken down his YouTube channel and his Just4Fans page—"It seems wrong, now that I'm seeing Brody"—and he wasn't dancing at the Rail on Fridays anymore, either.

I just hoped we weren't a bad influence on him.

It's great having Frank and Colin home with me all the time, too.

I took another hit and stubbed the joint out.

All's well that ends well, right?

But somehow, I just don't think I'm cut out for a quiet life.

Life doesn't hand you anything you can't handle.

It's how you handle it that matters.

And so, until the next adventure, adieu.

About the Author

Greg Herren is a New Orleans–based author and editor. He is a co-founder of the Saints and Sinners Literary Festival, which takes place in New Orleans every spring. He is the author of thirty-three novels, including the Lambda Literary Award–winning *Murder in the Rue Chartres*, called by the *New Orleans Times-Picayune* "the most honest depiction of life in post-Katrina New Orleans published thus far." He co-edited *Love, Bourbon Street: Reflections on New Orleans*, which also won the Lambda Literary Award. His young adult novel *Sleeping Angel* won the Moonbeam Gold Medal for Excellence in Young Adult Mystery/Horror, and *Lake Thirteen* won the silver. He co-edited *Night Shadows: Queer Horror*, which was shortlisted for the Shirley Jackson Award. He also won the Anthony Award for his anthology *Blood on the Bayou*.

He has published over fifty short stories in markets as varied as *Ellery Queen's Mystery Magazine* to the critically acclaimed anthology *New Orleans Noir* to various websites, literary magazines, and anthologies. His erotica anthology *FRATSEX* is the all-time best selling title for Insightout Books. He has worked as an editor for Bella Books, Harrington Park Press, and now Bold Strokes Books.

A longtime resident of New Orleans, Greg was a fitness columnist and book reviewer for Window Media for over four years, publishing in the LGBT newspapers *IMPACT News*, *Southern Voice*, and *Houston Voice*. He served a term on the Board of Directors for the National Stonewall Democrats and served on the founding committee of the Louisiana Stonewall Democrats. He is currently employed as a public health researcher for the NO/AIDS Task Force and served four years on the board of directors for the Mystery Writers of America.

Books Available From Bold Strokes Books

Mississippi River Mischief by Greg Herren. When a politician turns up dead and Scotty's client is the most obvious suspect, Scotty and his friends set out to prove his client's innocence. (978-1-63679-353-5)

Murder at the Oasis by David S. Pederson. Palm trees, sunshine, and murder await Mason Adler and his friend Walter as they travel from Phoenix to Palm Springs for what was supposed to be a relaxing vacation but ends up being a trip of mystery and intrigue. (978-1-63679-416-7)

The Speed of Slow Changes by Sander Santiago. As Al and Lucas navigate the ups and downs of their polyamorous relationship, only one thing is certain: romance has never been so crowded. (978-1-63679-329-0)

Felix Navidad by Nathan Burgoine. After the wedding of a good friend, instead of Felix's Hawaii Christmas treat to himself, ice rain strands him in Ontario with fellow wedding guest—and handsome ex of said friend—Kevin in a small cabin for the holiday Felix definitely didn't plan on. (978-1-63679-411-2)

Manny Porter and The Yuletide Murder by D.C. Robeline. Manny only has the holiday season to discover who killed prominent research scientist Phillip Nikolaidis before the judicial system condemns an innocent man to lethal injection. (978-1-63679-313-9)

Corpus Calvin by David Swatling. Cloverkist Inn may be haunted, but a ghost materializes from Jason Dekker's past and Calvin's canine instinct kicks in to protect a young boy from mortal danger. (978-1-62639-428-5)

Murder at Union Station by David S. Pederson. Private Detective Mason Adler struggles to determine who killed a woman found in a trunk without getting himself killed in the process. (978-1-63679-269-9)

A Champion for Tinker Creek by D.C. Robeline. Lyle James has rescued his dad's auto repair business, but when city hall condemns his neighborhood, Lyle learns only trusting will save his life and help him find love. (978-1-63679-213-2)

Heckin' Lewd: Trans and Nonbinary Erotica, edited by Mx. Nillin Lore. If you want smutty, fearless, gender diverse erotica written by affirming own-voices folks who get it, then this is the book you've been looking for! (978-1-63679-240-8)

Inherit the Lightning by Bud Gundy. Darcy O'Brien and his sisters learn they are about to inherit an immense fortune, but a family mystery about to unravel after seventy years threatens to destroy everything. (978-1-63679-199-9)

Pursued: Lillian's Story by Felice Picano. Fleeing a disastrous marriage to the Lord Exchequer of England, Lillian of Ravenglass reveals an incident-filled, often bizarre, tale of great wealth and power, perfidy, and betrayal. (978-1-63679-197-5)

Murder on Monte Vista by David S. Pederson. Private Detective Mason Adler's angst at turning fifty is forgotten when his "birthday present," the handsome, young Henry Bowtrickle, turns up dead, and it's up to Mason to figure out who did it, and why. (978-1-63679-124-1)

Three Left Turns to Nowhere by Jeffrey Ricker, J. Marshall Freeman & 'Nathan Burgoine. Three strangers heading to a convention in Toronto are stranded in rural Ontario, where a small town with a subtle kind of magic leads each to discover what he's been searching for. (978-1-63679-050-3)

One Verse Multi by Sander Santiago. Life was good: promotion, friends, falling in love, discovering that the multi-verse is on a fast track to collision—wait, what? Good thing Martin King works for a company that can fix the problem, right…um…right? (978-1-63679-069-5)

Fresh Grave in Grand Canyon by Lee Patton. The age-old Grand Canyon becomes more and more ominous as a group of volunteers fight to survive alone in nature and uncover a murderer among them. (978-1-63679-047-3)

Loyalty, Love & Vermouth by Eric Peterson. A comic valentine to a gay man's family of choice, including the ones with cold noses and four paws. (978-1-63555-997-2)

A Different Man by Andrew L. Huerta. This diverse collection of stories chronicling the challenges of gay life at various ages shines a light on the progress made and the progress still to come. (978-1-63555-977-4)

Bury Me in Shadows by Greg Herren. College student Jake Chapman is forced to spend the summer at his dying grandmother's home and soon finds danger from long-buried family secrets. (978-1-63555-993-4)

Best of the Wrong Reasons by Sander Santiago. For Fin Ness and Orion Starr, it takes a funeral to remind them that love is worth living for. (978-1-63555-867-8)

Death's Prelude by David S. Pederson. In this prequel to the Detective Heath Barrington Mystery series, Heath discovers that first love changes you forever and drives you to become the person you're destined to be. (978-1-63555-786-2)

Death Overdue by David S. Pederson. Did Heath turn to murder in an alcohol-induced haze to solve the problem of his blackmailer, or was it someone else who brought about a death overdue? (978-1-63555-711-4)

Death Takes a Bow by David S. Pederson. Alan Keys takes part in a local stage production, but when the leading man is murdered, his partner Detective Heath Barrington is thrust into the limelight to find the killer. (978-1-63555-472-4)

Death Checks In by David S. Pederson. Despite Heath's promises to Alan to not get involved, Heath can't resist investigating a shopkeeper's murder in Chicago, which dashes their plans for a romantic weekend getaway. (978-1-163555-329-1)

Death Goes Overboard by David S. Pederson. Heath Barrington and Alan Keyes are two sides of a steamy love triangle as they encounter gangsters, con men, murder, and more aboard an old lake steamer. (978-1-62639-907-5)

Death Comes Darkly by David S. Pederson. Can dashing detective Heath Barrington solve the murder of an eccentric millionaire and find love with policeman Alan Keyes, who, despite his lust, harbors feelings of guilt and shame? (978-1-62639-625-8)